DEAD RUN

AN AMOS CARVER MYSTERY THRILLER

JOHN CORWIN

OVERWORLD PUBLISHING

—— ◆ ——

CHASING DEATH

The cartel has Paola in their sights.

They know where she is and they're coming for her.

Carver has no idea where she is. He's tried contacting her and she's not answering. She might already be captured. She might already be dead.

He gets a lead on her last location and it's the last place he expected her to go. It's also the last place he ever wants to visit again, but he has no choice.

He soon finds out that there's a dangerous bounty hunter on Paola's tail. A man with powerful connections. A man who's hunting down not just Paola, but all the women who were sex trafficked by Jasper Whittaker.

Carver soon finds out that federal agencies and the shadow organization, Enigma, are involved. And they're willing to throw everything they can at him.

And that's fine. Just fine.

Carver never let the possibility of dying scare him off before and he never will. He's a bull charging at a dead run after one of the few people he cares about in this life.

And anyone who gets in the way is going to find that out the hard way.

BOOKS BY JOHN CORWIN

Books by John Corwin
Want more? Never miss an update by joining my email list and following me on social media!
Join my Facebook group at https://www.facebook.com/groups/overworldconclave
Join my email list: www.johncorwin.net
Fan page: https://www.facebook.com/johncorwinauthor

PSYCHOLOGICAL THRILLERS
The Family Business
AMOS CARVER THRILLERS
Dead Before Dawn
Dead List
Dead and Buried
Dead Man Walking
Dead By The Dozen
Dead Run
Dead Weather Days
Dead to Rights
Dead but not Forgotten
CHRONICLES OF CAIN
To Kill a Unicorn
Enter Oblivion
Throne of Lies
At The Forest of Madness
The Dead Never Die
Shadow of Cthulhu
Cabal of Chaos
Monster Squad

PROLOGUE

Lucas's plans for the night hadn't included dying.

He was on his way to see his girlfriend. It was supposed to be their fifth date. Things were going great even though she was the reserved and untrusting sort. That was to be expected after everything she'd been through.

Getting to know her had been a slow and steady endeavor. She didn't like to talk about her past. She didn't trust men. Lucas had done everything he could to earn her trust. He'd started by becoming her friend.

After she felt comfortable with him, he asked her on a date. Told her he wanted more if she was okay with that. She hadn't been certain at first but eventually agreed to give things a try.

She liked simple dates. Coffee and conversation. Walks on the beach. Going to the movies. Ordering dinner to go and taking it to his place so they could watch television. After a month of this, she finally became intimate with him.

It had been an amazing night. He'd been with other women, and none had been as challenging as this one. She didn't trust easily. She didn't take a man to bed easily. Nothing about this had been easy.

But it was going to be rewarding. Very rewarding.

All he needed was for her to whisper those three little words: *I love you*. Once that happened, he would unlock all her mysteries. She would finally tell him everything. And then he could finally get what he so desperately wanted.

Vengeance.

It was enough to put a skip in his step. Finally, after all this time he would make them pay. He would burn their empire to the ground and pour their blood on the ashes.

Lucas grinned as he stepped off the elevator. Rather than exit through the front door, he turned toward the side door. The one that led into the alley. He always went that way to avoid the multiple cameras in the main lobby and in front of the apartment building.

He walked down the long hallway to the end. One door led into the parking deck. He went past it and to the end of the hall. He pushed on the metal latch and stepped outside into the alley.

Strong hands grabbed Lucas by the arm. A rag went over his mouth. He nearly sucked in a surprised breath. It would have been his undoing. He fought against instinct. Stopped himself from breathing in.

He planted his feet. Raised his right arm and drove his elbow straight back. It slammed into a midriff.

There was a loud grunt. An exhalation of air. The grip loosened. The hand holding the rag jerked away from his face.

Lucas slammed his head back. Heard a loud crack. Felt soft cartilage bend. Felt bone crunch. Someone's nose had just broken. But there was a problem. A big one. There was more than one attacker.

Another pair of hands gripped his left arm. The first attacker renewed his grip on Lucas's right arm. Lucas crouched and sprang up, flinging his legs up and over his head. He flipped backward, twisting in their grips. The men holding him lost their grasp momentarily.

That was all he needed.

Lucas kicked sideways with his right foot. Struck one assailant in the side of the knee. There was a cry of pain. He shifted weight to his right foot and lashed out with his left. The other man dodged nimbly.

Lucas drove his elbow up and back, smashing the first man in the bridge of the nose. He went down hard. The second man swept Lucas's legs. At least, he tried to. Lucas jumped and dodged the blow.

Before he could come back down and regain his balance, the second man drove a fist into his chest. The air burst from Lucas's lungs. He fell backward. The other man released his arm and let him fall.

Lucas twisted sideways and landed on his shoulder instead of his back. He rolled and jumped to his feet. He ran out of the alley and into the street. Collins Park was right across the road.

The other man was right behind him, apparently unconcerned about people witnessing the chase.

It was nighttime. A concert in the park was in full swing. Live music filled the air. People danced and drank. He saw his date standing on the sidewalk waiting for him.

Her black hair hung well past her shoulders. She wore a form-fitting red dress that perfectly complemented her long, tanned legs. Other men were looking at her as they walked past. Some alone, others with significant others. All of them with lust in their eyes.

She saw him coming and smiled. Her smile just as suddenly vanished when she saw that he was running. When she saw the fear on his face. Her eyes darted to something behind him. Probably to the second assailant right behind him.

He couldn't run to her. That would put her in danger. He needed to keep her out of this and alive. Because if something happened to her then all his planning over the last few months would be for nothing.

Lucas dodged sharply left and ran down the sidewalk. He ducked into the crowd. After a few seconds of running, he looked back. His pursuer was no longer there. Had he given up? Had he decided it was too risky trying to kidnap someone right in front of a crowd?

Probably.

He looked around. His date was standing in the same place as before. She stared at him, questions in her dark eyes. But she didn't come after him. She knew better than to run toward danger because she'd experienced plenty of it firsthand.

She'd never told Lucas about the real danger she'd experienced. She hadn't told him a lot of things. She hadn't had to tell him because Lucas already knew everything about her before they even met. She was the entire reason he was here.

Because Paola had a deep, dark secret.

Her secret was the key to his vengeance. The one who would help him deliver blow after bloody blow to the Herrada Cartel. With her help, he could finally kill Pedro Herrada, the man who'd ordered the murder of his parents.

Now his dreams of revenge were turning to smoke. He hadn't gotten the drop on the cartel. They'd gotten the drop on him. And everything was in jeopardy. Including the woman he'd tried to use.

The cartel wanted her just as much as they wanted him. They might want her even more, due to who she was and what they'd done to her. His actions had put her in grave danger. She might die because of his obsession. All he could do now was to make sure they came after him and not her.

The public bathrooms were in the middle of the park. Lucas ran into the men's side. The urinals were crowded. He went into a stall at the end. Closed the door and locked it. He took out his phone. Unlocked the screen.

Lucas tapped out a message detailing what he'd done and why he'd done it. He told her how he wanted to use her to lure her former lover to Miami. How he wanted to use her to find and systematically destroy cartel operations.

How he planned to eventually lure Pedro into the United States, so he was vulnerable. How he would murder him with his own hands. He explained that he was working for a federal agency and using their resources but that his goals, unbeknownst to his bosses, were purely personal.

There was so much more that he wanted to say but none of it mattered. The most important thing he told her was this:

Run!

Lucas scheduled the text to be sent in four hours. The toilet paper holder was the kind with two receptacles. When one was empty, the bottom door slid sideways to close the empty receptacle and open the full one.

He slid aside the door covering the empty receptacle. He wedged the phone inside. He slid the door back into place. That would prevent anyone from finding it for the time being.

If he survived, he'd return to stop the text from being sent. If he didn't survive, the message would be sent to his girlfriend and one other person he trusted completely.

He chuckled ruefully. She wasn't his girlfriend. She was his pawn. He'd been so blinded by hatred. So obsessed with killing the people who'd killed his parents. What had he become? What kind of man put a woman in mortal danger so he could destroy his enemies?

His mind turned to other questions. How had the cartel found him? Had someone within his own agency betrayed him?

Normally, the DEA would deal with drug cartels, but the Herrada Cartel was another beast altogether. They sold drugs, sure, but that was just a small part of their endeavors. They had access to military hardware inside the United States. They owned politicians and people in power.

Their human trafficking operation was nationwide and nothing like anything he'd seen before. Lucas had been tracking their operations for years. His investigations had led to the arrest of some cartel members. As revenge, they'd murdered his parents.

That had turned him from a dispassionate investigator into someone who would stop at nothing to destroy the cartel.

Then he'd discovered the location of Paola Barros. A woman with intimate knowledge of cartel operations. A woman Pedro Herrada wanted found and delivered to him.

When a facial recognition scan found her in Miami, Lucas knew she was the perfect person to help him enact his revenge. But he'd have to approach her very cautiously if it was going to work.

He'd come up with a rational sounding reason for him to start a field operation involving her. He'd convinced his boss that this was something the DEA couldn't handle. This was something his agency, the NSA, had to do.

His boss had looked at his plan. Agreed that it was a matter of national security. Agreed that using Paola was an excellent way to lure important cartel members into the light.

He gave Lucas the greenlight and assigned him resources. Everything had been going according to plan.

At least until tonight.

Lucas's cover hadn't been blown. Someone had betrayed him. Someone with access to privileged information. Someone within the NSA. There was no other possible explanation.

Now that he'd left his message in a bottle, his next task was simple. Survive. He'd known a day like this could come, so he'd planned accordingly. His exit strategy was two blocks north. He'd stashed weapons in a car in a parking garage.

He just had to get there.

Lucas exited the bathroom. He leaned around the corner of the exit. Scanned the crowd outside. He looked where his date had been. She was gone. Probably long gone at this point. Even if he survived the night, it would be nearly impossible to find her again.

Finding her the first time hadn't been luck. The NSA's computer systems were second to none when it came to eavesdropping via security cameras, social media, cell phones, and all forms of digital communications.

Online chatter among cartel members about Paola Barros suggested that someone with inside information had given them her approximate location. They'd also given information about the locations of other women who'd been victims of sex trafficking in Morganville, Georgia.

That was how Lucas had known to start looking in Miami. He'd narrowed it down to areas with higher Brazilian populations. With the vast resources at his disposal, it hadn't taken long for him to get a hit. From that moment on, it had been a race against time to find her before the cartel did.

After that it had been a matter of getting her on his side by any means possible and doing so before the cartel found her. The timing had almost worked. Almost. Now everything had gone to hell.

All he could do now was escape Miami and hope he could find her again. The next time he'd tell her the truth. Beg her to help him get his revenge. First, he had to survive tonight.

Lucas hurried from the bathroom. Walked across the park. Kept a sharp eye out for anything suspicious. Everyone around him was dancing. Talking. Laughing. Having a great time. No one seemed to notice as he slipped through the throng of revelers.

The crowd thinned as he approached the edge of the park. The moment he left the cover of dancing bodies, he'd be visible. He lingered at the edge of the crowd and looked for any suspicious people. He noticed a man standing on a park bench scanning the area intently.

There was another man on a bench a hundred feet from the first. Lucas wondered just how many people the cartel had sent to search for him. At least five or six if he had to guess. That was nowhere near enough to sift through this many people.

Lucas watched the men and timed his escape when they were looking in opposite directions. He sprinted out of the park and into the neighboring parking lot. He bent as low as he could while still running and made it to the other side.

He ran two blocks and reached the parking deck. He ran downstairs to the lower level. The car was parked at the dead end right next to the concrete wall. The best plan was to hide out here and wait a few hours. Then he could return to the park and retrieve his cell phone.

Maybe he could salvage what little was left of his brilliant plan. It was highly doubtful but worth a try.

Lucas reached his car. He pulled a magnetic case from inside the wheel well. Took out the key. Unlocked the trunk. He hadn't brought any weapons on his date because there was no way to hide a gun from someone you were hugging and kissing.

Paola would have eventually touched the hard object and known it wasn't because he was happy to see her. She would have become instantly suspicious.

Lucas had plenty of weapons in his trunk. He popped it open. The light came on. He reached for the hard case with the rifle inside. It wasn't there. Neither was the smaller case with a handgun and ammunition. The trunk was empty.

Tires screeched behind him. He turned and saw a black van coming down the ramp. How had they known he was here? What had happened to his stash? The answer was obvious.

The stash had been placed here using agency resources. There was no telling how many eyes had seen the order to set up an exit stash at this location. One of those sets of eyes belonged to the person who'd betrayed him.

They'd probably set up a tripwire or a camera that activated when he came here to access the stash. And now the ending to his story was obvious.

He wasn't getting out of this alive.

Lucas pulled up the cover over the spare tire well. He lifted the spare tire and found his Plan B beneath it. It was a little something extra he packed in case he found a hub of cartel operations with a lot of targets inside. Plan B was a noisy but convenient way to kill them all at once.

He'd put this in the trunk himself. Whoever had given him up to the cartel hadn't known about it. That was good. Real good. They were in for a surprise.

Lucas grabbed Plan B and ducked behind the car. Six men exited the van. Three of them approached, guns drawn. They held the guns low to their sides, obviously expecting him to be unarmed since his trunk was empty.

The other three men remained behind at the van. That wasn't optimal. He needed them to be grouped together for Plan B to work. He resigned himself to the fact that it wasn't going to work. At least not the way he wanted.

"Come out, little rabbit," one of the men said in Portuguese.

Lucas clenched his teeth. Rage burned through him. Images of his dead parents flashed through his head. Images sent to him by Pedro after having them brutally murdered and strung up by their ankles.

He could still clearly see that gloating smile on Pedro's face in the selfie he'd taken with the corpses. That was how brazen the man was. How powerful he was. The law would never take him down. Only another killer could stop him.

Unfortunately, he would not be that killer. There was no escape. All he could do was go to his fate knowing he'd failed.

The man spoke again. "Come on, Lucas. Pedro wants to have quality time with you. He wants to help you join your parents."

The other men laughed.

Another man spoke. "Hey, Lucas, don't you want to go see your parents? They reserved a nice spot in hell for you."

Lucas trembled with rage. He didn't care about dying anymore. He'd tried his best and he'd failed. There was only one thing left to do. He set the timer. Tucked Plan B into the front of his pants at the crotch. It was the one area they probably wouldn't check. He began counting down the seconds in his head.

Lucas emerged from behind the car with his hands up.

"Good boy!" The man who'd chased him earlier walked up to him. Slapped Lucas lightly on the cheeks. "Poor, poor Lucas. You keep trying and you keep failing. Today you failed for the last time."

Lucas just stared at him, hate naked in his eyes. *Just let them think they have you.*

The man punched Lucas in the stomach. He doubled over, gasping. The men laughed and laughed as if they hadn't seen something like this a thousand times before.

He frisked Lucas from head to toe, feeling the inside of Lucas's thighs but not reaching the crotch.

"Not a single weapon?" The man tutted. "You're too stupid to be a threat."

Lucas stared blankly ahead.

The man grabbed Lucas's arm. "Let's go now. Don't resist. Pedro wants you back in one piece."

Lucas didn't resist. He walked, counting down in his head. The man shoved Lucas into the high-topped Sprinter van. He pushed him onto the bench seat on the other side. Two men sat on either side of him.

The man who'd punched him sat across from him next to the other guy who'd tried to grab him outside his apartment. That guy's nose was bloody and crooked. He'd stuffed gauze into his nostrils.

Lucas smirked at him. "Did you fall down the stairs?"

The other man reached over and backhanded Lucas hard enough to split his lip. "Keep talking and I'll cut out your tongue."

Warm blood trickled down Lucas's chin. He bared his teeth in a grin and spat.

Blood spattered. The other man roared in anger and tried to hit Lucas again, but the first guy grabbed his arm and pulled him back down. "Come now, Marco. Take it easy on our little friend. He has a long journey ahead of him."

Marco bared his teeth in a grin. "He's lucky I can't do more. Pedro doesn't want his prize coming back too damaged."

The van turned around, tires wailing on the polished parking deck concrete. The men took turns taunting Lucas. Gloating over his capture.

Marco leaned over. "You know where Paola is, eh? Just tell us and save yourself some pain. We'd love to give Pedro two presents at once."

Lucas didn't answer.

"He has special plans for your torture. He's going to take your balls." The other man leaned across and slapped Lucas's crotch. His hand hit something unexpected.

Lucas kept counting down in his head. Just a few more seconds left.

The other man tapped his crotch again. "What's that?"

Lucas laughed. "This is almost worth dying for." He smirked. "Almost."

"What?" The other man fumbled with Lucas's belt. Pulled on his pants button. He yanked down the zipper.

"Hey, I didn't know you rolled that way. Are you going to get me off before you hand me to Pedro?"

"Shut up!" The man pulled down the front of Lucas's underwear and saw the digital timer counting down the last four seconds on the C4 charge.

Lucas bared his teeth. "Die, you filthy animals."

Men shouted in alarm.

"Stop the van! Stop!" One man screamed.

Marco tried to open the sliding door. He probably thought he could jump out while the van was in motion. But it was too late.

Lucas thought one last thing as the timer reached zero.

Goodbye, Paola.

The detonator trigger. The C4 unleashed its fury. The explosion burst outward from Lucas's crotch, caving in Marco's face. It spread through the van, the concussive wave turning bodies into mangled masses of meat.

The windows on the van burst next. Tempered glass sprayed in all directions followed shortly by sheet metal, plastic, and body parts. The full tank of gas ignited. Raw meat sizzled like steaks.

The men in the front seats were somehow still alive, but not for long. Their bones were broken. Their skin was shredded. They couldn't move. Couldn't save themselves. All they could do was scream in agony as intense heat charbroiled their flesh.

The coroner would later say in his report that their final seconds of life were like burning in the fires of Hell. And he would also note that the man with the explosive near his crotch had died with a strange expression on his face. An expression that still remained on his blackened flesh.

He'd died smiling.

CHAPTER 1

Blood trickled from the wound in the woman's shoulder.

A crimson line ran down her bare arm and onto her hand. From there, it dripped slowly onto the seat of the wooden chair she was tied to and formed a small puddle between her legs.

She was crying. Screaming uselessly into the bloody rag stuffed in her mouth. Struggling against the bonds that held her. The chair rocked back and forth but the feet were too wide for her to tip it over.

Her husband's muffled screams echoed hers. He fought the nylon straps holding him into his chair. It looked like he might be strong enough to tip it over. He could struggle all he wanted. It wouldn't save him.

The man who'd tied the married couple to the chairs sat in another chair directly across from them. He held up the picture again. Made sure they both got a good look at it. He spoke in Portuguese. "I know you've seen her. Someone else told me she was in your hair salon last week."

The woman nodded. Her eyes were pleading. She was ready to talk. When he'd approached her at her salon, she'd told him that she didn't know anything. She'd told him to go away. But he'd already confirmed that his prey had been there.

So, he'd followed her to this rundown apartment. He'd waited until her husband came home. Checked to see if they had young children. They didn't, unfortunately. Children were excellent leverage in any interrogation.

He sighed. "I wish you would have talked at the salon. I wish we could have avoided this unpleasantness."

The woman made muffled sounds. She was trying to talk. He reached for the gag. "Don't scream, or I'll cut your husband's throat. Okay?"

She nodded fervently.

His phone rang. He held up a finger. "One moment." He answered in English. "Hey, baby, what's up?"

"Where are you? It's late."

"I'm sorry, baby. I got tied up with work." He looked at the bound woman and her husband. "I'm almost done here."

"I'm all cooped up at the hotel. You promised we'd go out."

"Don't worry, Angie. We'll go out. I'll take you to that steakhouse you wanted to try out, okay?"

"Really? You'll be done soon?"

"Yeah, I'm just tying things up right now."

She made a kissing sound. "I can't wait!"

"Me either, baby. I'll call you soon." Decker ended the call. His smile faded. His expression turned stony once more. He leaned over and removed the bloody rag from the woman's mouth. Spoke in Portuguese. "Tell me."

"Yes. That woman came to our salon once when her regular stylist wasn't available at another salon." She shook with fear and leaned her head toward her injured shoulder. "I think she goes to the place on Powers Ferry."

He leaned closer. Put the blade of his knife on her leg. "Be more specific. I want a name."

"It's a small shopping center. Only Brazilian stores there. I know the name of the butcher store."

"Give it to me."

She gave him a name. He looked it up on his maps app. Found the address. It wasn't far from his current location. Her husband watched silently, fear in his eyes. Sweat trickled down his forehead and dripped off his nose.

"You serviced her when she came in?"

The woman nodded.

"How often does she go to the salon?"

"Weekly, I think."

Decker nodded. "Typical Brazilian woman. They like to take care of themselves."

"Yes." The woman nodded fervently, as if she detected a friendly tone in his voice. A flicker of hope shone in her eyes.

Decker traced a finger down her cheek. "What's your name, sweetheart?"

The hope in her eyes died. "Nilva."

"Pretty name." Decker pocketed his phone. He shook his head. "You two gave me a lot of trouble. Why is it so hard to cooperate?"

Nilva's chin quivered. "Please, I just thought you were a stalker."

Decker smiled. Looked her up and down. "Lucky for you, I don't want to make a mess here." He observed the dripping blood. "A bigger mess, at least. I'm willing to let this go. It'll save me time not having to dispose of two bodies."

"Please let us go." She whimpered. "Please. We won't tell anyone. We are just trying to survive."

"I know." Decker shivered with pleasure. This was his favorite part. He turned to the husband. "I know how you can make it up to me." He explained the situation.

The husband sobbed. The wife sobbed. But they agreed.

Decker undid the nylon straps. He took Nilva to the sofa and turned the husband's chair so he could see everything.

He told Nilva to undress for him. To make it sexy. She did her best, considering the injured shoulder. He made her service him with her mouth. Then he had her lean on her husband while he had his way with her. He was so excited it only took him a few minutes to finish.

When he was done, he told Nilva to sit on the couch. He got her a glass of water. Patted her head. "You did good. Now, I'm going home to take my girl out for a nice night on the town. You two go clean up. Keep quiet. If I get even a hint that you said something about tonight, I'll torture you both to death. Okay?"

"We understand." Nilva huddled against her husband, sobbing. "We will say nothing."

The husband had a dead look in his eyes, but he nodded all the same.

Decker sighed. Thought it over long and hard. Killing was sometimes necessary. But it complicated things. Cleanup was a nightmare. He was just a one-man crew. A freelancer. He could stage a scene, but it was more of a risk than just scaring people into silence.

The wife and husband sensed that he was mulling it over. Nilva dropped to her knees and begged. The husband was biting his ball gag so hard, it looked like he might actually chew through it.

"Good night." Decker tipped his wide-brimmed hat at them and left the apartment. He closed the door behind him. The lights were out in the breezeway corridor. He'd broken them earlier. He'd also checked for doorbell cameras and other surveillance devices.

He'd found nothing. This was a place where illegal immigrants lived. They were just barely getting by. Survivors. Just like his mom. She'd come to the U.S. from Brazil. Cleaned houses for two years.

She'd met an American. Pumped out baby Decker a year later. He had dark hair. Blue eyes. He could pass for American or Brazilian which made it easy for him to slip unnoticed into places like this.

Well, maybe not unnoticed. He was tall like his dad. Lean and muscular. He stopped to check himself in the reflection of a window. He took off his cowboy hat. Ran a hand through his thick black hair.

He looked good. The cowboy hat, dirty jeans, and t-shirt toned down his good looks, so he didn't stick out too much. He almost fit right in. He put the hat back on. Pulled the brim low. He still looked damned good. Nilva was a lucky girl. He'd given her a good time and let her live.

Decker whistled as he walked down the wooden staircase and out of the breezeway. He stood on the sidewalk. Looked at the parking lot. There were rundown pickups. Brand new pickups with lift kits.

Minivans by the dozens. More Japanese compact cars than he could count. This apartment complex was probably ninety percent Brazilian. Almost all of them illegals. The people who did all the dirty work.

Decker texted his employer. *Got a strong lead. Following up tomorrow.*

He drove to the address Nilva had given him. Found the salon. It was one of those places that did hair and nails. Facials. All the necessities for a self-respecting Brazilian woman. They liked to look good for their men.

As it should be.

Decker studied the other buildings. It was a one-stop strip mall for Brazilians. A butcher, a bakery, a restaurant, a salon, a grocery store. His mark probably came here at least once a week. If not to go to the salon, to get food or eat at the restaurant.

Marietta was the city of choice for Brazilians in the Atlanta area. The population wasn't huge, but it was big enough to give Brazilians a taste of home. But that wasn't why his mark was here.

She was here to lie low and survive.

His employers had almost caught her in Miami thanks to inside information. But someone else almost nabbed her first. She'd fled town and been off the radar for two months.

That was when they'd put out an open contract. They wanted her alive. Decker had seen the price on her head and immediately started the job. He'd done work for the cartel before. Good work.

They were happy to have him onboard. Happy to help him however they could even though he had vast resources at his disposal. He'd used those vast resources to see where she'd been and to predict where she might be going.

He'd also discovered there was a list of women they wanted found. Women who were linked to his primary target. Decker had a feeling if he found her, he would find some of the others. Even better, she could tell him where to find the rest.

The target's path had taken her to Morganville. A chain of events caused her to flee from there. Facial recognition had picked her up again here in Marietta. Now he just had to pinpoint her location.

It seemed she felt most comfortable being close to the Brazilian community. That was almost certainly why she'd come here. But it might also be possible she'd come here looking for the other people on his list.

She thought she could hide here, but no one could hide from Decker. The Brazilian community here was much smaller than in Miami. There were far fewer Brazilian-owned businesses. Far fewer salons.

With his skills and acumen, the odds were in his favor.

Decker knew she wouldn't be able to resist getting her hair done. He knew she wouldn't patronize an American or Asian owned salon. Brazilian women were picky. They felt more comfortable with their own people.

That wasn't unique to Brazilians. Not by a long shot. Put anyone into a foreign country and they'd seek out familiar places and things. They'd want a touch of their own culture to feel grounded.

Decker slid into an old Honda CRV he'd purchased to remain incognito. It was black and blended into its environs seamlessly. No one ever looked twice at an old Honda. No one ever expected danger to come from a family car.

He drove toward downtown. Parked the car at a parking deck a few blocks down from his hotel. He ditched the cowboy hat inside.

Decker walked the rest of the way to the W Hotel in downtown Atlanta. He got a few strange looks from the people in the lobby. He didn't look homeless, but he looked like someone who didn't belong.

A security officer approached him. "Can I help you?"

"I'm going to my room."

"I'll need to see your ID and a keycard, sir."

Decker bristled. He didn't like being told what to do. But he also didn't want to make a scene. He smiled politely. "Of course." He pulled out his wallet. Showed him the fake ID for a Walter White. Showed him his keycard.

A woman hurried over from the concierge desk. She waved off the security guard. "I'm so sorry, Mr. White." She turned to the guard. "Mr. White is a penthouse level guest, Brad."

Brad paled. "I'm very sorry. I just—"

"Don't judge people based on their looks, Brad." She scowled at him. "It's racist!"

Brad backed off. "No, I just saw—"

"His clothing?" She took Decker by the arm. "I am so sorry. Can we comp a meal for you?"

Decker gave her his thousand-watt smile. "It's not necessary, really."

"No, I insist." She hurried to the counter and wrote something down. Brought back a voucher. "This is to any restaurant downtown."

He took it and glanced at her nametag. "Thank you so much, Joanna."

"You're welcome." She seemed to melt a little in his gaze.

"How did you know who I was?"

She looked down as if ashamed. "You're hard to miss, Mr. White."

He took her hand. Smiled. "So are you." He could take her to his room right now if he wanted to. But there was no challenge in that.

Joanna managed to look at him again and smiled. "Thank you."

Decker left her and went to the elevator. Took it to the top floor. Freelancing hadn't made him wealthy, but it let him enjoy the best life had to offer.

Angie called out from the bathroom. "Mike, is that you?"

He went into the bathroom and hugged his girlfriend from behind. Her hair was wet, but she was already dressed and ready for a night out. "Remember, it's Walter."

She pretended to gag. "Why do you choose such horrible aliases?"

"Because I like names like that."

She laughed. "You're so American sometimes."

"I know." He bit her neck.

Angie shivered. Turned and kissed him hard. Bit his lower lip. Her nostrils flared. "You stink. What has work got you doing now?"

"Nothing I can talk about, baby." He shed his clothes. Examined his abs in the mirror. They were starting to fade. He'd been enjoying the good things too much lately.

Angie ran a hand up his stomach. "You look good enough to eat."

He winked. "I know." He walked into the big shower. Turned on the water and soaped down.

Angie kept talking about her day. She'd gone shopping. Walked around downtown. Watched TV. Talked to her friend, Monique, about a girl's trip to Cancun.

Decker kept thinking about what he'd do tomorrow. How he might get lucky and find the mark on the first day. It wasn't likely, but it might happen. He thought about what he might do to her when he found her.

His employers wanted her alive. They wanted the money she'd taken. And they wanted information about the people who'd helped her. She and her accomplices had made off with millions in cartel cash.

Decker could deliver her damaged but alive. They wouldn't complain about that. They never did. Then they'd pay him his finder's fee and a percentage of any money recovered. They'd give him a bonus if he found the people who'd helped her.

Pedro Herrada was especially eager to meet one of them in particular. The man who seemed to be at the center of everything in Morganville. A man by the name of Carver. They had no pictures of the man. No file.

He was a ghost.

Decker made a living finding ghosts. He made a living letting his employers turn them into real ghosts.

He got out of the shower and dried off. Went to the closet and put on nice slacks and a button-up shirt. He checked his burner phone. No new messages. He checked his company phone.

One of the techs had messaged him. They had a hit on Carver. Over in California. That was a long way away. He'd planned on using his mark as bait. It seemed Carver didn't care about her. There was only one way to find out.

Maybe Paola Barros and Carver had simply been business partners. Nothing more. Carver had used her to help him steal cartel money. He'd split it with her and left. Paola was nothing more than a means to an end for him.

If that was the case, Decker understood completely. But there might be something more. Something he could exploit. It was certainly worth a try. Why catch one fish when you could catch two?

He read another message from his section chief. *Why are you tasking resources to look for Carver? We buried the Morganville cases for a reason. Call me first thing in the morning.*

"Typical bureaucratic bullshit." Decker stuck the company phone back in his briefcase. Right next to his work ID. It had his picture on it. His name, Mike Decker. It was a very American name.

It was the perfect name for the job. A perfect name for a special agent of the FBI.

CHAPTER 2

Carver stared at the message.

It was a text to Paola. A text he'd sent two days ago. She hadn't replied. He'd emailed her using the secure account he'd set up after the time he'd had his phone stolen in San Francisco. She hadn't replied to that either.

It wasn't unusual. Sometimes she didn't respond. She might not even carry her burner phone with her all the time. Maybe she decided she didn't want to hear from Carver anymore. He was just a reminder of bad luck and trouble.

His message to her was simple. *911 Go to cover. Send me your location.*

Paola knew the drill. Carver had explained it to her several times. She'd asked him why he cared what happened to her. She was just a burden to him.

He knew why. He didn't want to think about it or admit it. He had a connection to her. Why he had a connection, he didn't know. But it was there, and he had to deal with it. It gave him peace knowing she was okay.

Now she might not be okay. That might be why she wasn't answering. And Carver didn't know where to start looking for her. He hadn't asked her where she was. Where she'd been. Where she was going.

It was safer not knowing. Just in case he was compromised. Leon didn't know where she was either. He'd found information tucked away in a laptop. The laptop had been taken from the cartel leader's sister. A sister who was now deceased after several savage blows to the head.

The laptop had a message from a freelancer. It said he had a possible location for Paola Barros. That he would confirm and follow up. The message had been forwarded to the laptop from Pedro Herrada, the cartel leader.

By now, Pedro would know his sister was missing. Probably dead. He wouldn't know that her remains had been cremated and her ashes and ground bones scattered across a wildlife preserve.

El Fuerte had been purged of cartel influence. Gang members, cops, the mayor, city council members, and more had been eliminated, cremated, and their ashes scattered to the winds or dumped in the ocean.

Pedro would almost certainly send enforcers into town to find out what happened. Finding out what happened to his sister would consume him for a while. But that wouldn't stop his search for the money and drugs stolen from Morganville. It wouldn't stop him from hunting down Paola.

Carver had left El Fuerte. He'd driven northeast to Denver, Colorado. He figured it was a good central area to start from once Paola told him where she was. He couldn't fly commercial. It was too risky.

He didn't know if any federal agencies were looking for him. He figured there was a fifty-fifty chance they had a flag on his fake ID. They might not even know who he was. They might just know his last name.

Leon hadn't been able to investigate. He had problems of his own. He'd promised to get Carver a new fake ID but that hadn't happened yet. He had given Carver access to a bank account with enough money to charter a flight or buy his own fake ID if he wanted to.

In the meantime, Carver was staying at a motel that didn't care about an ID. It was a place that had been set up as a shelter for the homeless. Denver was overrun with tent cities and the local government was using motels like this to ease the pressure on their sidewalks.

Carver looked up from his phone and watched a man drop his pants and defecate in the parking lot. There were almost no cars parked there. No one who lived here had one. Carver's nondescript Toyota Camry was parked in the far corner, well away from the people.

The defecating man toppled over in slow motion. Right into his own mess. He'd probably just taken a hit of fentanyl. It was by far the most popular drug in these parts. Maybe even nationwide. According to the records on the laptop taken from Jessica Herrada, the cartel had shifted away from cocaine and toward the synthetic opioid.

Carver studied the information Leon had sent him. There was nothing in it that hinted at Paola's location. Leon had tried to have someone trace the last locations of Paola's burner phone but had no luck.

Carver had known people who might be able to help him, but he didn't have their contact information. They were people he'd encountered and left in the past. Now he was starting to think that had been a mistake.

It didn't matter in the here and now. He'd made choices. Those choices led him here. Staring at his phone screen wasn't going to make Paola reply any faster. Maybe it would be better if he didn't worry about it.

Maybe he should find another beach. Maybe he should find a nice mountain cabin and get away from people for a while. Both options sounded nice. But Carver knew that when he closed his eyes at night, he'd see Paola's dark eyes looking back at him.

He turned off the burner phone. Took out the SIM and looked at the carrier details. All the national carriers offered pay as you go options. Some were cheaper than others. He didn't know which carrier Paola was using, but there was an easy way to find out.

Carver called her burner's number. It went straight to voicemail. The phone was off or in do-not-disturb mode. The automated answer told him what he wanted. "This Mint Mobile customer has not set up a voice mail. Please call again."

He ended the call. Checked the map app. Found a local store. It was maybe a mile from the motel. He picked up his duffel bag and backpack from the room. Carried them to the car and put them in the trunk.

It wasn't safe to leave anything in the room or in the car. He'd learned that the hard way in San Francisco. He noticed several people watching him closely as he loaded his car. They were eyeing his bags. Looking for an opportune moment to snatch them when he wasn't looking.

Carver drove to an ATM and got cash. He drove to the Mint Mobile store. It wasn't busy inside, but the woman at the front asked him to sign in anyway.

"Someone will be with you shortly," she said.

Carver saw four employees. One was helping someone. The others were near a door in the back talking to each other. The store had a twenty-foot ceiling. Modern minimalist design. Five cameras.

The door in the back likely led to the security room. The footage was probably recorded and stored on a server in the cloud. It probably wasn't actively monitored. The four people he saw were probably the only ones here.

A young man came over. He had a tablet in his hand. A patchy beard. Glasses. "Hi, I'm Paul." He looked at the tablet. "I see you want to be a new customer, Mr. Reynolds. Do you currently have service with anyone else?"

"I had a pay as you go phone. Unfortunately, someone stole it." Carver sighed. "I had so much stuff on that phone and now it's gone forever. Pictures of my daughter, my wife."

"I'm very sorry to hear that, sir. There are ways to save your personal data by installing our cloud app. We also have a phone tracker app that can help you find lost devices."

Carver knew for a fact that a tracker app wouldn't have been installed on Paola's phone. "What kind of phone do you use, Paul?"

"Oh, I have an iPhone." Paul pulled a phone from his back pocket. There was a picture of him and a husky on the lock screen.

Carver gasped. "Oh, wow. Your dog looks just like my Charlie. He died two years ago."

"Oh, really? I'm so sorry for your loss." Paul looked genuinely sad. "What happened?"

"Old age and cancer."

"I am truly sorry, Mr. Reynolds."

"And all the pictures I had of him were on that phone." Carver squeezed his eyes shut and clenched a fist. "God, I feel so stupid right now."

"That's awful!" Paul set the tablet on the nearby table. "Are you sure you didn't have the find my phone app on your device?"

"I didn't. Someone told me I should talk to the phone company because they could see the last cell tower it connected to, but I wouldn't even know how to go about that."

Paul snapped his fingers. "That's true. We can do that." He winced. "But we'd need to know for sure it's your phone. Those pay as you go phones don't really have a way to prove ownership."

Carver looked down. "You're right." He wiped his eyes. Blew out a breath. "Charlie saved my daughter one time. Knocked her out of the way of a speeding car. The car hit him, and I thought he was going to die, but he amazingly pulled through."

"Seriously? That's an amazing story." Paul bit his lower lip. Looked back at the others in the store. "I don't have access to anything, but our manager, Linda might be able to help. She has a husky herself."

"Does she really?" Caver nodded. "I would be so grateful just to have some idea where the phone is."

"Now, this won't pinpoint the location, but it will give a general idea. A lot of times, these phones are stolen and sold at the illegal night markets that pop up all over town."

"I appreciate anything you can do for me." Carver blew out a breath. "Sorry. I don't usually get emotional, but Charlie—" He feigned a pained look.

"I totally understand. I'll be right back." Paul walked over to a middle-aged white woman. Talked to her. Her mouth dropped open and her eyes went wide.

Carver felt almost certain she'd help just judging from her body language. She disappeared into the back room.

Paul returned to him, grinning. "She put in an order. It might take a few hours before it goes through. Do you have another phone we can text?"

"No, that's actually why I'm here. I wanted to get a new phone."

"Do you want pay as you go again?"

Carver nodded. "I don't use my phone much, so it makes sense for me."

"I understand." Paul led him to a display with cheap phones and prepaid SIM cards. "Which one would you like?"

Carver bought a cheap smartphone that came with a prepaid SIM. Paul took down the number and said that he'd text him the moment they had a geolocation on the stolen phone.

"Thank you, Paul. This means the world to me." Carver looked at the picture on Paul's lockscreen. "What's your dog's name?"

"Jerky." Paul offered an empathetic smile. "I really hope we can help you recover your phone."

"Thank you." Carver left. He wondered what they would think when they found that the phone wasn't even in Colorado. Maybe that wouldn't bother them. Or maybe they'd think he was trying to stalk an ex-girlfriend.

If that was the case, he'd have to resort to other methods. Less pleasant methods. It seemed best to be ready for that possibility, so Carver went to a restaurant in the same shopping center and sat outside so he could keep an eye on the mobile phone store.

He noticed a silver Altima driving back and forth along the rows. It stopped and started several times. Not because the driver was looking for parking. They were looking for suitcases in cars.

Carver spotted the snatcher looking in car windows. He was wearing a black hoodie and a mask to conceal his identity. The snatcher used a small sharp tool to easily break car windows. Then he'd unlock the door, snatch anything of value inside, and toss it into the Altima.

This kind of thing was so normal in these parts that Carver had moved his car close to the restaurant so he could safeguard his belongings. When the snatcher reached the row with his car in it, Carver strolled out and stood next to his car.

The thief was so focused on looking in the windows that he didn't see Carver until the last minute. He was a short, skinny guy. He shouted in surprise when he came around the minivan next to Carver's car.

Carver gripped the thief's wrist and yanked him between the cars. He took him in front of the minivan. There were trucks parked in the adjacent slots, concealing them from sight. He pinned the guy to the grill of the van and yanked down his mask.

"Hi." Carver gave him a long, steady look. "This is MS Thirteen territory now. If we catch you stealing here again, we'll gut you and hang your body from a streetlamp. Got it?"

The man's eyes widened. "What the hell is MS Thirteen?"

"It's a gang, you idiot." Carver gripped his neck and pinned him to the minivan. "This is all our territory now. I'm helping put out the word. Keep stealing and end up dead. Got it?"

"Yeah, man, I got it!" The thief struggled. "Let me go. I swear we won't steal no more."

"Good." Carver yanked him off the van. Shoved him. "Get out of here."

The man ran to the Altima where it was sitting one row over. The car squealed out of the parking lot and left.

Carver went back to his seat. Got his coffee refilled. Watched the cell phone store. Paul exited the store about an hour later and climbed into a blue compact car. He drove away. He wasn't the person to follow.

Linda walked out of the store thirty minutes after Paul. She climbed into a large, black SUV. Carver got in his car and pulled out of the parking spot. He got behind Linda as she waited at a traffic light.

She drove straight across the road to another shopping center and parked in front of a gym. She got out. Pulled a small bag from the back seat. Went inside. Carver resigned himself to waiting. He parked in front of the building.

The front windows were glass, giving him a clear view inside. He leaned back in his seat and watched. He'd been there an hour when his new phone buzzed. It was a text from Paul.

Good news! We found the last three locations of the phone!

The last three locations were nowhere near Colorado. Apparently, he needn't have worried about Paul being suspicious. Maybe Paul thought the thief had shipped it out of state already. Maybe the person who found the information was just too busy to ask questions.

Carver looked at the last three cell phone towers the phone had pinged, and he couldn't believe what he saw.

CHAPTER 3

Carver didn't like where Paola's phone had been.

The last three locations were all in one state. A state far, far away from Colorado. A state he didn't want to visit if he could help it.

It seemed the person who looked up the cell phone records had selected three locations from a list. Not the last three times the phone pinged a cell tower. The phone had probably pinged dozens of towers as it moved from south to north.

The phone was in Georgia. It had been in Macon, Atlanta, and ended up in Morganville. The date stamps next to the locations were just hours apart. That meant Paola had been driving through these areas.

The phone had probably pinged several more cell towers along the way. Whoever collected the information summarized it to show a travel path going from south to north. The final location was the important part.

Why in the hell had Paola gone to Morganville? And where had she come from? The phone had pinged the cell tower in Morganville over three weeks ago. Why hadn't her phone moved since then?

Had something happened or was she hiding out in Morganville?

Carver didn't like having partial information. He wanted the whole picture. He wanted to see the entire journey the phone had taken. There were ways to get that information, but it might get messy.

The most concerning part was that the phone hadn't been online for a little over three weeks. Had something happened once Paola reached Morganville? Why in the hell had she gone back to that place?

The FBI had covered up most of what happened in Morganville. It was possible they'd done it to protect the shadow organization, Enigma. It was possible they'd done it to protect themselves or politicians.

It didn't really matter. What mattered was that the cartel had probably sent people to the town to look into matters for them. They wanted to find out who really took their drugs and money.

Carver had hoped the cartel would think Paola was dead. He'd asked Leon to give her a new identity. She should have been able to remain off their radar indefinitely. Going to Morganville would have risked putting her right back on the radar.

So, why would she have done it? Even if the cartel didn't have their people constantly watching the town, they almost certainly had informants who would tip them off. People who would be in a position to notice when wanted individuals made an appearance.

They probably didn't have a picture of Carver, but they almost certainly had images of Paola. They might have seen her there. Notified the cartel. The cartel would have sent one of their people to investigate.

There was too much Carver didn't know. Had she been in Morganville an entire week? Had she just passed through? He needed more details. It irked him that the phone company employee who looked up the records hadn't simply sent over a complete list of cell phone towers.

It looked like he'd have to go to Georgia to find out for sure if Paola was okay.

Carver drove to the gas station. Fueled up. Got some coffee for the road. He could charter a flight, but it would take a chunk out of his bank account, and it might take just as long to find a company as it would to drive.

It was twenty hours and some change to Morganville. He hit the road, taking Interstate 70 across the Midwest. It went through Kansas City and over to St. Louis where he switched to Interstate 64.

Traffic was bad near the cities but there wasn't much he could do to avoid it. St. Louis traffic was the worst. By the time he made it to the other side, he was almost an hour off target.

He was about fifteen hours into the drive when he started to feel the fatigue set in. He pulled into a rest stop about an hour north of Nashville. Leaned the seat back and got some shuteye. He woke up four hours later at zero three hundred and got back on the road.

Traffic was light at that hour. He picked up the pace, hoping there weren't any zealous traffic cops waiting for speeders in the wee hours of the morning. He cut some time off the drive only to lose it again when he hit rush hour traffic in Chattanooga, Tennessee.

He'd given a lot of thought about what he'd do when he reached Morganville. It was a tiny town. Almost a ghost town. He had contacts there. People Paola might have spoken with when she reached town.

If her phone had been off for three weeks, it was reasonable to assume she wouldn't be turning it back on anytime soon. She hadn't returned his text and maybe she never would. She might already be dead.

Leon had sent Carver a message. He opened the encrypted messaging app and glanced at it as he waited for the logjam of cars in front of him to move.

I'm using one of my contacts to see everywhere Paola's phone has been. I'll update you the moment I find out.

Carver checked the map. There was a wreck ahead. The maps app didn't have a good detour. All the side streets were jammed. He pulled into the emergency lane and drove up the ramp to the next exit.

He pulled into a Waffle House. Sat at the bar and ordered coffee and breakfast. He polished off a waffle, eggs, and bacon. Downed a few cups of coffee. He took a bathroom break, got a cup of coffee to go and went back to the car.

The map app showed that traffic was clearing. The wreck was off the road and the interstate on the other side of it was green. He navigated back to the interstate and got past the emergency vehicles fifteen minutes later.

Carver couldn't stop wondering why Paola had chosen to return to Morganville. There were far better places to hide. Which meant she'd gone there for a reason. If that was the case, she almost certainly would have contacted the locals.

Holly Robinson was the most likely person she'd spoken to, but Abe Ritter was a close second. Maybe Paola had run out of cartel cash and had returned to get more from Ritter. There was still plenty that they'd hidden away, safe from the feds.

That seemed like a good reason to go back. She knew she was in danger and needed money to stay alive. So, she returned to Morganville. Maybe she'd trashed her phone while she was there.

She should have bought a new phone and transferred the encrypted messaging app to it. Maybe she'd done that. Maybe she hadn't been able to respond to Carver's message on her old phone before the app deleted it.

If that was the case, why hadn't she contacted him to let him know she had a new phone? There had to be a good reason. A damned good reason. Maybe Holly or Ritter would know the answer. He couldn't just barge into town and go to the police station to ask them.

People would see him. They'd recognize him. Phone calls would be made. Interested parties would be notified. Carver would be back on the chessboard.

Then again, it felt like he'd only been off the chessboard for a short while before being found again. He'd unknowingly dealt with the same Brazilian cartel during his time in El Fuerte. So maybe showing his face in Morganville wouldn't affect anything.

Maybe it would send a warning to the people chasing Paola that he was chasing them too. If she wasn't dead, maybe they would divert their resources to getting him first. Or maybe it was better to stay under the radar. Take them by surprise.

Both approaches had their pros and cons. It wasn't a decision he could make until he knew the situation better. It wasn't the first time or even the second time he'd been through something like this.

During his time with Scion, Rhodes made liberal use of local assets. If an asset was exposed, she'd help them disappear. Sometimes, they didn't disappear well enough. If the asset was valuable enough, Carver's unit would be tasked with protecting them or getting them out of the country.

Rhodes had successfully saved three assets. Two times, the assets had already been killed before the team could respond. In the first three cases, they'd known where the assets were located.

The way it worked was simple. His unit would trigger an emergency protocol. The asset would go to a safehouse and await extraction. It usually went like clockwork. This was nothing like those situations, mainly because Paola wasn't following the protocol Carver and Leon had outlined for her.

The northern outskirts of Morganville appeared. Carver slowed as he passed the location of the motel where he'd killed a squad of men trying to kill him while he slept. The motel was no longer there. Just a concrete slab and burnt timbers.

He kept going. Stopped at a local diner he'd visited a few times when he'd been here. It was lunchtime but the place didn't look too busy. He'd hoped to spot a patrol car out front. Maybe find Holly eating breakfast there.

There were no patrol cars. Just a couple of pickup trucks. He went inside. Ordered breakfast. Considered what to do next. He knew from Elena Diaz, a reporter who'd covered the aftermath of Carver's brief time here, that some of the sex slaves rescued from the cartel were still living at the Whittaker mansion.

He finished breakfast. Drove to the mansion. He turned onto the long private road. It wound through thick woods. The bushes were so overgrown they were hanging over the sides of the driveway.

He reached the iron gate leading to the circular drive. The gate was bent inward like something had rammed it. He drove around the circular drive. The grass was long and full of weeds. The shrubs were unkempt.

The house came into view, or what was left of it. Bits and pieces of wood and masonry were scattered around the foundation. Some of the house was still intact, but most of it looked like it had exploded and then caught fire.

It had to have been a big explosion to cause such damage to a house that size. Carver took out his phone and used an app to scan for wireless signals. More specifically for signals used by wireless trail cameras.

The app detected nothing. Carver just wanted to make sure he wasn't being watched. Some might think he was paranoid, but he'd learned long ago there was no such thing. He tucked away the phone and approached the house.

The iron door frame was rusted but intact. The wooden door was gone. He walked through the doorway. The foyer was in the open air. The office where he'd talked to Holly and Paola was nothing but blackened walls.

Carver walked carefully through the ruins. Judging from two massive holes in the floor, it looked like the gas lines had ruptured and exploded upward. That had been enough to cave in the ceiling and bring parts of the second floor down.

The dry antique wood had burned like kindling. The house had almost been consumed by the fire, but it looked like the flames had been put out before that happened.

It was no coincidence that this place and the motel had been burned down. It pointed to the cartel. It was likely they discovered their former sex slaves were living in the mansion and wanted them dead.

Carver couldn't understand why anyone would have lived in the very mansion the cartel once owned. They should have used their cartel money to vanish. Instead, they'd made themselves easy targets.

It didn't make sense. Sometimes people just didn't consider the possibilities, no matter how obvious they were.

He tested the stairs, but they looked too unstable to use. Most of the second floor was gone, anyway. And if someone had died in the bedrooms, there wouldn't be anything left by now. The investigators would have everything.

Was this why Paola returned? Had she discovered the women here were in danger? Had she heard they were killed? Maybe that was why she'd come back to a town that had once been a living hell for her.

Carver went outside and walked a circuit around the house. He didn't see anything else of note. It was still cold outside. Gray clouds covered the sky. It would probably rain soon. He went back to the car.

He sat inside and considered his next steps. He didn't have Holly's number so he couldn't just text her and ask to meet. He could call the police station, but if the cartel had eyes and ears there, he might raise suspicions.

Carver drove back to the highway. Kept to the northern side. He circled down to the paint factory and drove down the road toward it. There were cars parked in the front. A hint of steam coming from a smokestack. It looked like the place was still in business.

He turned around and went into town. Drove past the pink house where Rhodes had lived before being murdered in cold blood. He kept going and stopped down the street from the police station.

The building looked just as rundown as it had the last time he'd been here. There were two patrol pickups parked in front. The chain link fence around the motor pool didn't conceal much.

There was an old police van parked in the back. Several old patrol cars that looked as if they hadn't been in service for decades. A few civilian cars that probably belonged to the people who worked in the building.

He wondered if Maberly still worked there. He'd been the eyes and ears for the mayor and the cartel. Once Ritter took over as chief, he should have fired him. Not just because Maberly was a mole, but because he was useless.

Carver parked down the road. He cracked a window to let the cool air in and leaned his seat back a little. A man in the beige Morganville PD uniform stepped outside. He lit a cigarette. Walked toward a patrol pickup.

He looked young. Probably mid-thirties. Lean and in decent shape. He climbed into a pickup. Started it, backed out, wheeled onto the road. Disappeared around the bend.

Carver kept waiting.

A little while later, a fat man with a balding head stepped outside. His uniform was dusted with something orange. Probably fake cheese dust. He lumbered to a bench and sat down. Took out a phone. Made a call.

It was Maberly. For some reason, Ritter had kept him around. It wasn't like Maberly had actively done anything illegal. He'd been phoning information to the mayor. The mayor had been in league with the cartel.

That didn't make the man any less guilty of other things. He was a mole, plain and simple. But it wasn't Carver's place to do anything about it. Ritter had kept the man around for a reason.

Carver took out his monocular and zoomed in on Maberly. He tried to read his lips. Only a few words were clear. One of them was "biscuits". It looked like he was ordering food even though it was too late for breakfast and too early for lunch.

Another police officer emerged from the building. His lip curled up when he walked behind Maberly. Like he couldn't stand the sight of the guy. Maybe it was the odor, judging from his flaring nostrils.

It made sense. The armpits of Maberly's uniform were stained with sweat. He wasn't obese, but he wasn't in marathon condition either. The only finish line he was going to cross was death by heart attack or diabetes.

The second officer hurried to a pickup and drove away without saying a word to Maberly. That was odd. Real odd. Not because he hadn't spoken to Maberly but because the last time Carver had been here, there had only been a couple of patrol officers and two detectives.

Maybe Ritter had promoted Holly to detective. She'd wanted to follow in her father's footsteps. It made sense that Ritter would want to see that through after everything they'd experienced.

Then something else caught Carver's eye. Maberly's name badge. He hadn't bothered looking at it before because he knew the man on sight. He hadn't seen something important that he was only seeing now.

And it made his blood run cold.

CHAPTER 4

Carver zoomed in on Maberly's name badge.

He wanted to be certain he was seeing right. And he was. Right above Maberly's last name was a title. *Police Chief*. How in the hell had Maberly become the chief? Even if Ritter had retired, he sure as hell wouldn't have promoted Maberly.

Holly Robinson would have been his pick for chief. Literally anyone else with a pulse would have been Ritter's pick over Maberly. Something was wrong. Horribly wrong. The roadside motel and Whittaker mansion weren't the only casualties in this town.

The entire local system had burned to the ground.

Carver didn't see much choice except to call the police station. There were no public phone booths in town that he knew of and no easy access to a local directory. He didn't want to call 911 just to reach the police department, so he'd have to find the phone number elsewhere.

Carver searched for the police department online. There was no official website. No social media presence. But there was a main number to the station. He called it.

A woman answered. "Morganville Police Department, Chief Maberly presiding. How may I help you?"

"Hello, my name is Carl Reynolds. I had some camping equipment stolen when I was visiting town and spoke to Officer Robinson about it. It's been a while and I just wanted to see if progress had been made on my case."

"Oh, I'm sorry. Officer Robinson is no longer here. I can direct you to one of our detectives."

"I think a detective Ritter was working on it."

"I'm sorry, he's no longer here. I can find out if either of them was working the case."

Carver almost hung up but remembered another name. "I remember a Detective Davis. Is he still there?"

"No, I'm afraid not." Her voice took on another tone. "You seem very familiar with those names. When were you in town?"

"It's been over a year ago."

"And you said your name was?"

"Carl Reynolds."

"Perhaps you can come into the police station and one of our detectives can talk to you about it."

There was something strange about the tone of her voice. Like she was suspicious.

"I live about an hour outside of town," Carver said. "But I can make the drive."

"Perhaps you can send us some more information in advance. Send me a picture of your driver's license so they'll know which records to look up."

"I'd be happy to. I can fax it over?"

"I'll text you a number that can accept pictures, but your number appears to be blocked from caller ID."

"Oh, yeah. I always block my number. It keeps the telemarketers away." Carver chuckled. "Here let me—" he ended the call.

More specifically, he ended it at twenty-nine seconds. It seemed like the woman was stalling for time. Like she was trying to trace the call. He didn't know why he had that impression, but his gut told him something was off.

Maberly had finished his phone call and was staring at the phone screen. He frowned and lifted the phone to his ear. His face grew strained as he stood faster than a man his size should be standing.

A woman came outside. She was young. Dressed in street clothes. She said something to Maberly, and he nodded. Hurried inside after her. Carver felt certain she was the person he'd spoken to.

He felt more certain about his suspicions now. Something was up. This place was somehow just as rotten as before. Maybe worse. It was almost certain he'd find out if that was true before he left this town.

Morganville had tried to kill him once. Now he was giving it a second chance.

The woman who'd come outside looked Latina. Her accent was American but not southern. Probably Californian if he had to guess. That didn't necessarily mean anything, but it couldn't easily be discounted.

Carver started the car and drove through town. The hotel and restaurant were the only two places open, just like last time. There weren't as many cars parked at the hotel, probably because it wasn't prime hiking season.

Going inside seemed risky. Someone might recognize him. He searched for Holly's information online. Didn't find anything. Like most people she probably only had a mobile phone. No landline.

He decided to risk it. The hotel saw a lot of tourists. They'd be more likely to have a local directory. Carver parked next to a truck. He got out and went inside the lobby. A group of young adults were checking in.

The single attendant was busy with the group. Carver looked around for a phone book. He didn't see one. He walked into the neighboring room. It looked like a waiting area. There was a couch, some chairs, and a gas fireplace.

There was a pushbutton phone on a table at one end of the couch and a thin directory beneath it. Carver lifted the phone and opened the directory. He looked through it and found Holly's address.

He went a few pages further and found Ritter's address. He plugged them into his maps app. Ritter was thirty minutes east of the Whittaker mansion. Holly was listed on the south side of town, maybe five minutes away.

Carver put the directory back. He went outside. Climbed into his car. Drove to Holly's. The town was dead and so were most of the neighborhoods. Holly's house was next to two derelict houses.

Her overgrown lawn gave him a sense of foreboding. Something wasn't right. He checked for wireless signals using a cell phone app and found several. The house across the street had multiple cameras and Wi-Fi.

He didn't find anything else. It wasn't likely the cameras across the street were angled to watch Holly's place, but he couldn't be certain. The garage was closed. He couldn't tell if a car was parked inside.

The safest bet would be to wait until night and approach from the back. But it was early in the day. There were still six hours of daylight left. Every hour wasted was another hour separating him from Paola.

He couldn't afford to wait. He couldn't afford to be as cautious as he normally would be. He'd have to maintain due diligence but at an unrelenting pace. Rhodes had a name for missions like this.

Dead runs.

Other members of Scion called them suicide runs. She'd countered by saying a dead run just meant you were flat-out running the entire time. Adjusting your tactics on the fly. Giving the enemy no time to react.

Dead runs weren't ideal, but sometimes you had no choice. Sometimes you were on a time limit. If the timer hit zero, that was it. Game over.

It might already be game over for Paola, but Carver wasn't going to stop running until he knew for sure. And that meant he wasn't going to wait until nightfall to enter Holly's house and search it from top to bottom.

He'd done plenty of dead runs, so it didn't take him long to come up with a suitable alternative. Driving one street over and coming in from the back yard would work just fine. He could do that and stay out of sight of the cameras on the neighbor's house.

Carver drove a street over and parked on the side of the road. He called the number listed for Holly in the phone book. As far as he knew, mobile phone numbers weren't listed in phone books. This was a landline phone.

It rang once. There was a click, and it rang again. The second ring had a different tone to it. Like the call had been redirected to another system. A woman answered. "Hello?"

The voice sounded familiar, but it wasn't Holly's. The woman who answered didn't have a southern accent. It sounded like the same woman who'd answered the phone at the police station.

The woman spoke again. "Hello?" This time she was faking a southern accent. It was a bad attempt.

He ended the call.

This didn't look good. Not for Holly. Not for Ritter. He needed to know if they were dead or not. To be dead certain. Not because he felt he owed them anything but because if Paola had been here, she might have stumbled over a tripwire.

She might have tried to find Holly and attracted the attention of the cartel. Maberly was almost certainly working for them. Now that the heat had died down, it was back to business as usual in Morganville.

It wasn't because the FBI was incompetent. It was because Enigma was pulling strings. Manipulating events. The paint factory was probably distributing drugs again. It was probably full of Brazilians with guns. But that didn't matter.

It could be manufacturing nuclear weapons for all Carver cared.

He had no interest in looking into them again. He needed to find Paola. To make sure she was okay. It didn't seem likely that Holly or Ritter were okay. They might be dead, or they might have skipped town once things went south again.

There was a wooded lot behind Holly's house. Most of this street was vacant. There were boarded up houses further down, but most of the area looked undeveloped. That was hardly surprising since Morganville was nearly a ghost town.

The wooded lot gave Carver an ideal approach to Holly's backyard. He got out of the car. Pulled the hoodie over his head. Pulled the facemask over his mouth and nose. He hadn't detected any wireless signals on the back side of the house, but it was better to conceal his face just in case.

He pushed through the bushes. Stopped at the edge of the yard. The backyard had patchy grass. Lots of pinecones and pine straw. Carver didn't know much about lawn maintenance, but this looked like several weeks' worth of growth.

It was possible she hadn't been gone that long. That the changes in this town had been recent. Maybe the changes coincided with Paola's visit here. Maybe they didn't. It was hard to say.

Carver surveyed the nearby trees. Looked for wired trail cams. Clever people would hardwire cameras, so their wireless signals didn't betray them. It was harder to do, of course. Luckily for Carver there were more lazy people than clever ones in espionage these days.

He saw no signs of wires or cameras mounted in any of the trees. He hadn't expected to find them, but it was best to be certain.

Carver turned his attention to the house. The windows were dirty. There was a light on inside the kitchen. He crouched low and kept behind a pine tree to stay out of sight of the window. The tree was just big enough to conceal him if he turned sideways.

Carver ducked lower the last few feet and pressed himself against the wooden siding just below the window. He rose slightly and peeked inside. The kitchen ceiling light was on. There was another light on in the next room.

The kitchen looked tidy. There were clean dishes on a towel next to the sink. The kitchen table had a stack of paper on it that looked like bills. There was a large glass bowl with bananas and apples in it. The bananas were black. The apples were covered in dark spots.

It looked like everything had been fine one minute and gone to hell the next. Something had happened to Holly, or she'd left town in a hurry. That would explain the clean kitchen with the rotting fruit.

The back door was nothing fancy. Just a cheap steel door with a foam core. Carver knew the type. Not because he was a home renovation expert, but because he'd kicked open doors like this a lot over the years.

The door type didn't even matter all that much. What really mattered was the door jamb. Unless it was reinforced with metal, a solid kick with the bottom of his foot would usually splinter a wooden jamb and open the door right up.

Carver had read a novel once where the guy described how to kick down a door. The description was three pages long. It was like the writer copied instructions from a breaching manual.

Carver wasn't ready to kick the door down just yet. For all he knew, Holly was just on vacation. She might not be happy if Carver broke her door down. But he doubted she was just on vacation. He doubted that a lot.

Carver went to the other windows. They were old-school wooden windows. Single-paned glass. He looked through them. The rooms on the other side were dark. He tested each window. The one on the end wasn't locked.

He checked the inside of the window. He was looking for an alarm sensor. There wasn't one. Carver pushed up on the window. It resisted. He took out his survival knife and used it to pry the window open. It finally screeched up on thin metal rails. He got his fingers underneath it and pushed it all the way open.

Carver half expected to smell decay inside the room. The odor of rotting flesh. But that wasn't what greeted his nose. Something stank but it was a good kind of stink. By the time he climbed through the window, he knew what the source of the smell was.

There were two scented candles on a table next to a bed. They weren't burning but they still had a strong odor. One was apple cinnamon. The other was pumpkin spice. Together, they smelled like a suburban woman's fever dream.

The bed was neatly made. The room was clean. There was a small walk-in closet with women's clothing inside. Several police officer uniforms hung from a rack.

There were two pairs of black shoes that went with the uniform. Several pairs of tennis shoes and well-worn flip flops. There was an open dresser. It looked like it had been rummaged through.

Panties, socks, and bras were scattered on the floor. There was a large, open suitcase. There was a pile of clothing inside. Like everything had been thrown inside in a hurry. That rang alarm bells in Carver's head.

Had Holly tried to pack up and leave only to be interrupted by intruders? Or had someone arrived after she'd left then searched her room?

One thing gave him hope. There were several empty hangars on the floor and on the closet rods. Most of the area for hanging clothes was empty. The big suitcase was still half empty, meaning some of the clothing was missing.

Holly might have packed a smaller suitcase first. She might have wanted to take everything else in the large suitcase and decided it would take too much time. She'd left town with only the essentials.

That was a smart move.

There was a gun safe in the back corner of the closet. It was open and empty. She'd gone for the essentials first. Another good move on her part.

The bathroom was in a similar state. There were open drawers. Missing items. Nothing else looked touched. It didn't look like the place had been tossed.

There was an alarm panel on the floor in the hallway. It had been yanked off the wall and the wires had been cut. Carver hadn't seen any motion sensors in the house. There were no magnetic sensors on the windows either. It looked like only the front and back doors were covered.

All things considered, it was a crappy system even if it was operational. Holly should have upgraded it to cover every window and room in the house, especially after giving away cartel drug money to sex trafficking victims.

Carver went into the den and saw the first evidence that someone else had been here. There was dirt on the floor. A muddy footprint left on the hardwood floor. It was a men's size twelve. Just a little smaller than Carver's boots.

It wasn't Ritter's footprint. He was of medium build. Size ten shoes max. It belonged to someone else. Judging from the pattern, it looked like they'd walked around, leaving dirt on the area rug in the living room and den.

The front door was cheap steel like the back door. The deadbolt wasn't locked. Neither was the bottom lock. Holly probably left in a hurry. Slammed the door shut behind her but didn't stop to lock it.

Whoever entered after her departure was able to just walk in. Maybe they'd thought about kicking in the door too. Maybe it took them three mental pages to decide how to do it. Then they reached out and turned the doorknob. Found out it was open.

Carver had almost tried to open the back door, but he hadn't known if there was an alarm system. Even if the door was unlocked, that didn't mean the alarm wasn't armed. The window had been the safer choice. He could see if there were alarm sensors on the frame.

Carver studied the other footprints. He found a faint one, this one from a smooth-soled shoe, not a boot. It was size eleven. There had been at least two people. He followed the prints. The rugs in the other rooms had absorbed the rest of the dirt so it was hard to tell where they'd been.

He found a landline phone in the den. It looked like the only one. There were 99 missed calls. That was probably the maximum it kept track of. The dates went back years. It looked like Holly didn't use the phone much. She'd probably kept it around in case of emergency.

The most recent missed call was from Carver. There was a slip of paper next to the phone. It said *72 Enter forwarding number. There was a phone number after it. The unknown visitors had set the call forwarding on the phone.

Carver took a picture of the forwarding number. With that done, there didn't seem to be another reason to hang around. He went to the kitchen. The back door was unlocked. Morganville wasn't the kind of small town where you could leave your doors unlocked.

Had Holly fled through the back door? Did she not lock her doors? Knowing what she knew about this town, it seemed unlikely she'd leave her doors unlocked even if she'd thought the cartel and other criminals were gone.

There might be another reason. The people who'd come in and left the footprints might have left the doors unlocked. He examined the door frame and found the reason a moment later. There was a small switch attached to the door casing.

When the door was opened, it pushed in the switch. A thin wire ran down the wooden casing and onto the baseboard. The wire ran along the toe kick board beneath the cabinet and up to the countertop at the far end.

It connected to a black box on the countertop. The box was plugged into the electrical wall outlet. He knew what it was. It was a cellular device. When triggered, it would call a preprogrammed number.

Carver went into the den and found another one attached to the front door. He opened the plastic cover and looked inside. There was a small touchscreen. He tapped it. It turned on.

There was a gear icon for settings. He touched it. It asked for a PIN. Someone had thoughtfully left a piece of paper with the PIN inside the box. He entered the code. The settings screen appeared. The number the phone called was the same one Holly's landline forwarded to.

Carver examined the box. It was a simple affair. He could turn on a keypad screen to manually dial a number. It was basically a simplified mobile phone. It had a battery and could probably run in sleep mode for several days without being plugged in.

The device didn't have any normal apps. It didn't seem to have a GPS built into it. It was just made for one simple purpose. To call a number when it was triggered. The ones Carver had used during his time in Scion were much smaller and more elegant.

This looked like something used by home security companies. It was probably the same module used in their panels when a landline wasn't available to make outgoing calls for triggered alarms.

He unplugged the device. Pulled the USB cable out of the tiny staples holding it to the toe kick and baseboard. He removed the trigger mechanism from the door. It was held on by a stronger staple so it wouldn't move when the door opened.

His knife pried it up easily. Carver opened kitchen drawers and tossed the items. He went to the bedroom and did the same. He wanted it to look like someone had been here looking for something. He was wearing gloves so he wouldn't leave fingerprints.

Ideally, he would have left the alarm trigger on the door frame. But there was another possibility he couldn't discount. This place might be rigged to blow like the mansion. Even though the phone called the same number the landline forwarded to, that didn't mean whoever answered the phone couldn't press another button to detonate a bomb.

Carver walked through the backyard to the car. He got in the car and drove it back to Holly's street. He parked on the curb at the far end right behind a pickup truck.

Then he pushed in the trigger.

CHAPTER 5

Decker waited for the target.

This was day two of waiting in the shopping center. He sat down outside the bakery with a cup of coffee. From there he had a good view of the other stores and the salon. Women came and went from the salon all day.

They vanished inside for hours, emerging later with a new hairdo or freshly painted nails. Then they'd go to the other stores and come out with enough food to feed an army. They'd haul it to their cars and leave, probably to spend the next few hours cooking.

That was how it was with Brazilian families. He'd been to countless cookouts and family parties. The women would congregate and talk while the children ran around and played. The men would stand around the grill drinking and talking.

It was a good time. His father had said Americans used to be that way, but those traditions were gone and fading fast. Decker enjoyed those times. He liked traditional women. Mainly because they were far more satisfying to conquer than modern women.

This shopping center was a small slice of Brazil. It wasn't much, but it was decent. It had just about everything a Brazilian could want. Far more than the shopping center with Nilva's salon in it.

Angie had texted Decker a dozen times. She was bored. He'd given her money. Told her to enjoy herself while he worked. She didn't like being alone. She wanted him there. He was beginning to wish he hadn't brought her along on the trip.

She used to be more traditional. She used to cook for him. Do whatever he wanted. But he'd spoiled her with too much time and money. Now she was just needy. Always wanting more and more.

Taking her on business trips used to be fun. Not anymore. She'd be excited for the first couple of days but quickly become bored after that. He told her he was doing FBI work and couldn't just drop everything to keep her entertained.

There were also missed messages from his day job. His boss, Dennis, had questioned him about tasking department resources to look for Carver. Decker had called him. Told him the orders came from higher up.

Decker had already reported the texts to his real bosses at the department. They'd obviously spoken to Dennis because he'd apologized for the confusion. The funny thing was, Decker didn't even know who those real bosses were.

He knew they were connected to FBI Director Alonzo Vasquez, but he didn't know how. He didn't ask how. He didn't ask any questions about it. All he knew was that they seemed to know what he was doing no matter how secretive he tried to keep it.

They knew he freelanced for various criminal organizations. That his fee was high but that he always came through. They made it crystal clear that they knew all about him and his nefarious dealings.

They also made it clear that they didn't see a conflict of interest. That there was no reason he couldn't keep doing what he was doing as long as it fit within their framework. And if it didn't, they would let him know.

Decker was happy to comply. Happy to keep doing what he was doing. Happy to follow their rules. His work for the cartel aligned with what they wanted. They'd been interested in Paola and Carver for a while.

Morganville was still a sore spot for the cartel and his mysterious handlers at the FBI. The cartel promised Decker a big bonus if he delivered Carver and Paola alive. The other women on the list were preferred dead. He just needed to bring pictures and thumbs for verification.

They also promised a percentage of any recovered cash. The potential bounty would be enough to set him up for life. He didn't know if they'd let him retire, but it would be nice to have the option.

An old man at a neighboring table spoke to him in Portuguese. "Are you new around here?"

Decker nodded. "I just moved nearby."

"It's a good area. I think you'll like it."

"Thanks." Decker put his phone away and kept watching the area while he conversed with the old man to keep up appearances. Noontime came and went. The old man left after lunch. Other people came and went.

He knew it would look strange if he sat outside drinking coffee all day, so he got up and walked around the shopping center. He was itching to show Paola's picture to people. To see if anyone else had seen her.

It was risky showing a picture and asking questions. Especially if a man was asking about a woman. He couldn't flash his FBI credentials, either. This was a community of illegal immigrants. They wouldn't talk to the feds.

When he arrived in town, he hadn't had much of a choice except to show the picture. He'd told people he'd just arrived from Brazil and was looking for his sister who hadn't contacted the family in months.

He was worried about her. Her family was worried about her. It had worked with an older woman. She'd seen Paola and remembered her. It hadn't worked so well with the hair stylist. She'd immediately become suspicious. She'd probably planned to tell Paola about it the next time she saw her.

That was smart. That way if it was a family member Paola didn't want to see, she'd know that someone was looking for her. Some people were just too trusting. They'd believe anything and anyone.

It helped that he was handsome. That he had remarkable blue eyes and an athletic physique. Women were more likely to talk to good looking men than ugly ones. They were just as visual as men when it came to that.

It went along with the old joke that it wasn't sexual harassment if the man was handsome enough. And Decker had good looks in spades. But illegals weren't your typical trusting people. Most of them had been taken advantage of already.

Some had been charged their entire life savings just for a coyote to get them across the border. Some had been abused during the journey to the border. Some had lost family members along the way.

Some had been raped, beaten, robbed, and barely crossed the border alive. Others were controlled by cartels. Turned into human slaves. He'd seen Mexicans at the border spank immigrants on their bare asses until they were bloody and bruised because they didn't have any money left to give them.

That was why most immigrants didn't blindly trust people who were looking for someone. Nilva had done the right thing even though it pissed him off. He'd had to put her in her place for that. Teaching a lesson was infinitely better than killing her.

He caught a glimpse of a woman entering the bakery. She resembled his target. He strolled back down to the bakery. Walked inside.

The woman behind the counter smiled at him and spoke in Portuguese. "Back again?"

Decker smiled back. "I'm waiting on my cousin. He's always late."

"What do you mean?" She laughed. "Brazilians are never late. We always arrive when we get there."

He faked a long, loud laugh. "So true!" He glanced at the woman who'd caught his attention. She was at the other counter ordering. Decker walked up to stand next to her. She looked like Paola. Light skin. Full lips. Dark eyes. Long black hair.

She also looked like several other Brazilian women he'd seen. There was an identifying mark that would tell him for sure. A scar on the inside of her wrist. But she was wearing a coat. The long sleeves covered her arms.

She finished ordering. Decker ordered coxinha with corn and chicken. He went to the counter to pay. The woman was already there paying in cash.

The cashier engaged her in small talk. "Everything is good?"

"Yes, thank you," the woman replied. "I'm so hungry. I didn't have lunch today."

"Sometimes I'm too busy to eat." The cashier gave her change. "It looks like I'll have lunch late again today."

"You should snack," the other woman said. "I'm sure a coxinha here and there won't be missed."

The cashier laughed. "I don't know. The owner has a very sharp eye.

They shared a laugh and then the woman took a seat at a table to wait on her order.

Decker paid the cashier. The cashier tried to talk to him because she was clearly attracted to him. He smiled. Pretended to enjoy talking to her, but she was short, fat, and ugly.

He turned and got a straight on view of the woman's face. He took out his phone and looked at the picture. Compared it to the woman. Something was off. The nose was slightly different. The woman's lips weren't quite as full.

Decker's excitement faded quickly. He'd felt certain the prey was right in front of him. But now he knew it wasn't Paola. It was just some random woman.

She saw him looking at her and looked down at the table. She took out her phone and started scrolling. Her cheeks flushed slightly.

Decker knew the sort. She was traditional. Demure. Probably married. He sat at the table next to hers. "It's very cold today."

She blinked. Looked over at him. "Yes, very cold." She looked back at her phone.

"I'm new in town. Is this the best bakery in these parts?"

"It's very good. They have the best coxinha, I think." She offered a small smile, but it had no warmth to it. She was uncomfortable.

Decker felt a stirring in his groin. He liked this woman. Fit and attractive. Playing hard to get. He wished he had more time to seduce her. Traditional woman like her didn't go to bed easily, but they could be convinced.

They were always surprised to find that even though Decker was uncommonly handsome, he was also extremely smart. He could talk about anything. Most importantly, he could make women laugh.

Even an ugly man could attract a woman if he made her laugh. He'd learned that long ago and never forgotten it. And he was tempted to shirk his duties and bed this tempting little vixen.

The gravity of duty pulled him back to earth. The burning in his loins was still there, but he could deal with that later. By force if he had to. Angie was gorgeous and fit, but she didn't quench his thirst like a new conquest did.

"I'm sorry for bothering you." He flashed a grin. "My cousin is late, but he's on Brazilian time."

She didn't laugh. If anything, she looked a little confused. Decker figured she wasn't very smart. That was the problem with his humor. It required intelligence. The women who didn't laugh were usually hot but stupid.

That was okay by him, but he felt a little insulted that she didn't even smile at the joke. He felt tempted to try again with something even an idiot could understand. But he needed to get back outside and make sure his quarry wasn't at this very moment getting her nails done.

He left without waiting for his order to be ready. He wasn't hungry. He was angry. He couldn't stop thinking about that bitch in the bakery. She should have been all over him. Decker took deep breaths.

It took a few seconds to calm the rage inside. She hadn't rejected him. He just hadn't softened her up enough. Decker was working. He was distracted. If he brought his full A-game to bear on her, she'd eventually be his.

He wasn't angry at her. He was angry at himself for trying to rush things. For trying to take the easy route. Traditional Brazilian women took more work to break. All that religious and family programming was like a shield.

Decker walked down the sidewalk to the salon. He looked inside. The place was full as usual. There were five women in the chairs, all of them in various stages of getting their hair done. On the other side were the manicure and pedicure chairs, also full.

He walked inside. Looked in the mirrors on the right side of the room where the hair stylists were. Studied the faces of the women in the chairs. He looked left at the mani-pedi chairs. Didn't see his quarry in any of them.

A woman gave him a questioning look.

"I thought my wife came in here." He looked apologetic. "She said she had an appointment."

"What is her name?" the woman asked.

"Paola." He pretended to look for her picture on his phone. "We're new here." He found it. Showed it to her.

The woman looked at it. "Oh, her appointment is in one hour." She laughed. "You should try texting her next time."

Decker laughed. "She never answers me."

The woman in the salon chair laughed. "You have to be patient with us women. Even a handsome man like you sometimes has to wait."

The other women cackled in amusement like a roost full of clucking hens. Decker laughed along with them. He could see the looks in their faces. They were into him. They thought he was funny. He could have any one of them he wanted, married or not.

But he was also laughing because he was in a much better mood now. Paola was coming to him. She would be here in an hour. He would be here waiting. He might even try to take her before she went inside.

It could take hours for a woman to get her hair done. On the other hand, it would be better to wait until she went home. He could follow her there. Come up behind her after she unlocked the door and force his way inside.

Then he could have some fun. Find the stolen money. Maybe use her as bait to lure Carver into a trap. Then he'd have everything the cartel wanted tied up in a neat little package. Today would be the best day of his life.

Decker left the salon. He saw the other woman leaving the bakery and going to her car. Flush with confidence and excitement, he made a split-second decision to kill some time by following her home.

Once he was done with Paola, he could pay this bitch a visit. It would be fun making her cry and scream for help.

He kept his face averted so she wouldn't see him and went to his car. He waited for her to pull out of the parking lot. She immediately stopped at a traffic light. He waited a few seconds until the light changed, then pulled out of his parking spot.

Her car was already moving forward as the cars ahead accelerated. Decker pulled into traffic a few cars back. She didn't go far, turning into an apartment complex two miles down the road. He watched her remove several packages from the front of her car and go into the breezeway.

Decker got out and walked toward the breezeway. He listened. Didn't hear her climbing stairs. He looked around the corner. Saw the woman opening the door at the far end. He made a note of the apartment number.

Then he went back to his car. Drove back to the shopping center. He remembered he'd ordered coxinha from the bakery and went inside to retrieve it. The girl behind the counter looked confused as to why it took him so long to come get it.

He flirted with her a little to make her stop thinking about it, then went to the chair outside with a fresh cup of coffee. He snacked on coxinha while he waited. At about fifteen minutes before the hour, a silver Honda pulled into the parking lot.

It parked. A woman got out. She wore a heavy coat. The hood covered her head and concealed her face. She turned toward the bakery for an instant and Decker got a good look at her.

It was Paola.

Decker couldn't stop the grin from spreading across his face. This was going to be the biggest score of his life. He leaned back and watched her go into the salon. She was inside for two hours. He killed the time by reading a newspaper and drinking coffee.

When she came out, she hurried to the bakery. She went inside and ordered something. Decker watched her the entire time. He shivered with excitement. She had no idea how close she was to the most dangerous man in the city.

Paola lowered her hood. She sat inside and ate tapioca. Most people stared at their phones while they ate. She didn't. She picked up a local newspaper and read it.

She was even more beautiful in person. A picture didn't do her justice. The other woman Decker had mistaken her for wasn't even a pale imitation of the real thing.

Decker was definitely going to enjoy ravishing her. She was going to enjoy it too even if she didn't want to. He could hardly wait to pin her down and have his way with her.

Paola stood. She tossed her bag in the trash and came outside. She went to the silver Honda and got in. Started the car.

Decker had to shove down the urge to hurry after her. This was it. He couldn't afford to lose her. But he had to be patient. Make sure he didn't do anything to trigger suspicion. After everything Paola had been through, she would be skittish as a rabbit.

Stealing from the cartel was not something for the faint of heart. She would be looking over her shoulder for the rest of her life. A life that was about to get considerably shorter. Her car pulled out of the parking lot.

Decker left his coffee on the table. He went to his car. Got in. Waited for her to clear the same traffic light the other woman had been stuck at. Then he drove after her.

Paola was his.

CHAPTER 6

Carver pulled the trigger.

The device inside the black box called the preprogrammed phone number. Someone answered but said nothing. The device beeped three times and the call ended. Nothing else happened.

He felt a little surprised the house didn't explode. After seeing the ruins of the mansion, he'd suspected an explosive device might have been placed under the house. Tactically, it didn't make any sense to do that, but people did dumb stuff all the time.

It made more sense to trigger an alarm and send a squad that could find the intruder and bring them in for questioning. That was far more valuable than a scorched body.

Since the house hadn't exploded, Carver drove to the street behind Holly's house. He tossed the black box into the woods. Then he drove back to the end of the street. Went to an abandoned house he'd picked out earlier.

He drove around the back. Parked out of sight. The back door wasn't boarded over. The entrance was open to the elements. He went inside. The place smelled musty. There was black mold growing on the ceiling.

There were spiderwebs all over the place. Weeds growing through the floorboards. Animal droppings. The skeletons of rodents that had been eaten by something bigger. Probably a house cat.

A raccoon scurried from a bedroom and stared at him. It was a big one, but it didn't look rabid. It was probably wondering why a human was intruding in its home. Carver let it be and went into the den.

The windows were boarded over, but the wood was old and there were holes in it. Broken glass lay on the floor around the window. He used a piece of broken lumber to clear out the jagged pieces around the edges. Then he took out his monocular and put it through one of the larger holes.

Carver wondered what kind of response the alarm would trigger. Would they send the local cops? A kill squad? Something in between?

The bodies had been piled hip deep when he left this town. The cartel and Breakstone had lost a lot of people, not to mention the locals who were part of it. Jasper Whittaker, Mayor Morgan, his son, and one of the local cops were among the casualties.

The feds had arrived, and the roaches had scattered under the light. Everything had been covered up and swept under the rug. The feds left, and the roaches came back out of hiding. The feds truly had to be looking the other way if the cartel was back in business here.

Carver checked the time. Five minutes had passed. Maybe no one was coming. Maybe the unexpected alarm caught the watchers flat-footed. Maybe they didn't have a response plan in place.

A black high-roofed Sprinter van turned onto Holly's street. The driver gunned the engine. Another van turned onto the street behind the house. Men in gray and black urban camouflage piled out of the vans. The first group approached from the front.

The second group hurried through the woods and came up behind the house. In seconds, they had the place surrounded. The two teams stacked up on either side of the house. Standard military CQC formation.

Police and SWAT units used a similar close-quarters-combat formation, but there was a precision to these guys that spoke volumes. They were almost certainly military. Probably special operators.

They didn't need to break down the doors because they were already unlocked. They filed inside. Carver couldn't see what was happening, but he imagined they quickly cleared the house room by room.

They saw the mess he'd left. They would hopefully assume someone had tossed the house. That someone was looking for something. He wished he still had specialized surveillance gear. It would have been interesting to listen to the conversations inside.

Carver looked at the map on his phone. Both Sprinter vans came from the direction of town. There were no plates on the front, and he couldn't see the back. The vans were windowless. Their tires were all-terrain and wider than the ones on most civilian vehicles.

Almost certainly federal government issue.

A third Sprinter van turned onto the road. It pulled up in front of the house. Three figures in white Tyvek suits stepped out. The operators left the house and formed a perimeter. The CSI folks went inside. It seemed like overkill.

What were they looking for? Carver had been careful not to leave prints or DNA behind. Whoever had been in the house before him hadn't been careful at all. They'd left behind mud and footprints.

Carver zoomed in on the uniforms. There were no insignias. Nothing identifiable. They could be cartel mercenaries, but it seemed unlikely. They could be special units with a federal agency like FBI HRT, but that also seemed unlikely.

They way they moved pointed to special forces. Military special forces. Except the military wasn't supposed to operate domestically. That included special forces. The NSA could act domestically, but they didn't have their own combat teams.

At least, not as far as Carver knew.

Had Paola come here looking for Holly? Had she been nabbed by these people? Was that why her phone had gone offline in Morganville?

There were a lot of things that could have happened, none of them good. Carver reviewed the evidence. The burned down motel. The destroyed Whittaker mansion. Holly's and Ritter's disappearances. A military-style special forces team raiding Holly's empty home.

It seemed highly likely that Holly was dead. Paola too. Ritter might still be alive but even that seemed doubtful. Carver's fists clenched. They'd better hope Paola was alive and well. Otherwise, he was looking at a lot of dead men.

He needed answers before he took action. He needed to find someone who could provide him with those answers. Maberly might be a safe bet, but he wasn't exactly the brightest bulb in the light factory.

The woman who answered the phones seemed to be a far better candidate. It seemed obvious that calls to the police station and to Holly's house had been redirected to her cell phone. She was the central clearing house for this operation. The person who coordinated everything.

She was his first target.

A pair of operators hustled through the woods. One of them was holding a device. Carver couldn't get a clear look through the trees, but they seemed to be tracking the whereabouts of the black box.

One of them bent over and picked it up. They walked around Holly's house. Went to the Sprinter van. Set it inside.

A black pickup arrived. It was sporty. A Ford Raptor. A woman hopped out of the driver's side. The same woman who'd spoken to Maberly at the police station. Almost certainly the same woman who answered the phones.

Her skin was tanned but not dark. She looked Latino. Given the cartel's history in this town, she was probably Brazilian and probably here on their orders. She was five feet, seven inches, give or take. Long black hair tied up in a ponytail. Dark eyes.

She went to the van. Spoke with the two operators who'd recovered the black box. She unclipped a radio from her belt and spoke into it. A lab tech hurried out of the house a moment later. She pointed to the van. The tech picked up the evidence bag with the black box in it. Nodded. Listened to her speak. Nodded again.

The woman was probably telling him to dust it for prints. To examine it thoroughly. She pointed to the house across the street. At the cameras there. She probably wanted the footage from them.

It wouldn't do much good. Carver had noted that the cameras were angled down to watch the front door and the driveway. They weren't facing out at the street. He might have missed a camera. If that was the case, they'd have a description of his car.

The car belonged to a deceased security guard for the deceased mayor of El Fuerte, California. They wouldn't be able to trace it to Carver. But they could put out an APB on the car and find him that way.

Carver didn't think it would be a problem. He felt confident there were no street-facing cameras and that they'd come up empty. They would have nothing on him. He would, conversely, have something on them.

That woman was important. Maberly might be police chief, but this woman was really in charge. The big question was who was she working for? Was she with the cartel? The government? All of the above?

He took a couple of pictures through the hole in the plywood. The burner phone camera wasn't great, but it did the job. He sent the image to Leon using the encrypted messaging app. He texted him. *Can you ID this woman?*

Carver continued watching through the monocular. He lowered it after a while and paced around because he was getting stiff from standing so long. The raccoon sat on the dusty kitchen table, watching him.

He stared back at it. Wondered if maybe it was a mother raccoon with a litter of babies somewhere. Maybe that was why it hadn't run away when he came into the house. Then again, it was wintertime. Didn't animals usually give birth in the spring?

Carver turned back to the window. The operators were piling back into their vans. The one in front of Holly's drove past the Sprinter van and did a U-turn. The license plate didn't have government markings on it.

That didn't mean anything. It could be a government car with regular plates to hide that. It even had upgraded rims instead of the usual, black-painted steel rims that were usually dead giveaways for government vehicles.

One of the techs returned from the house across the street. He talked to the woman. Shook his head. Probably telling her the cameras didn't see anything. She looked frustrated. Pointed at Holly's house. Gestured angrily.

Probably asking him why there were no cameras watching the house. He shook his head. Shrugged. It was a legitimate question. Why didn't they have cameras? And why had they set up such a strange alarm system?

The woman gave the tech an earful, judging from the look on her face. Then she stalked back to her pickup. Climbed in. Pulled onto the street. She didn't make a U-turn. She drove straight toward Carver's hideout.

She stopped at the stop sign right across the road from him. She sat there for a moment, staring straight ahead. Staring at nothing. Like she was deep in thought. She shook out of her thoughts and took a left.

Carver turned his monocular back to Holly's house. There were no techs outside. He walked toward the kitchen. The raccoon was gone. That was good because he hadn't felt like battling a wild animal just to leave the house.

He hurried around the side of the house. Watched the Ford take the next left. It was probably headed back to the police station. Probably. Carver wanted to be sure of that. He wanted to follow her.

He climbed into his car. Drove through the backyard and the neighboring backyard. That should keep him out of sight of the techs if one happened to be outside. He turned left around the house. Pulled onto the street.

Carver drove to the intersection and nosed forward past the house at the corner. He saw the pickup already several streets away. It kept going straight. Right back to the police station. He turned onto the road and went the same way.

At the intersection before the police station, Carver turned left down a side street. He parked. Got out and walked toward the station. He stood at the corner building and looked around it.

The Raptor was parked on the side of the police station. The woman wasn't in it. She'd probably already gone inside. It was almost noon. Unless she left for lunch, she wasn't going anywhere anytime soon.

Carver hoofed it over to the restaurant next to the hotel. Rose's Café was crowded with the tourist lunch crowd. All the deaths, investigations, and more hadn't done anything to dampen tourism in these parts. If anything, it looked busier than ever.

That was good. It gave Carver a crowd to hide in. It gave him a plausible reason for being here. Unless that woman had a picture of him, he could probably walk freely in these parts without standing out too much.

He got a couple of sandwiches to go since there was no place to sit inside. He went back to the car. Parked it in a lot across from the police station so he could keep an eye on the woman's pickup.

He ate. Leaned his seat back. Watched the police station. Maberly came outside again. His shirt was even dirtier than the last time. He stared at his phone screen and stuffed his face with potato chips.

About once an hour, Maberly would return, each time with a different snack. Carver didn't know why he kept coming outside. He could simply eat inside his office. Maybe that woman didn't allow him to eat inside.

Leon replied to Carver's earlier text. He didn't have an easy way to identify her. He'd sent the image to a couple of his contacts anyway in case they knew. That was fine. Carver figured he might be able to identify her up close and personal later.

The woman left the building at a little after four. She climbed in her pickup. Backed it up and wheeled out of the parking lot. She went left. Carver gave her a head start before following her.

He saw the pickup turn left a few streets ahead. When he reached the street, he didn't see the pickup anywhere. He turned down the same route. Continued after her, looking both ways down each side street.

The black pickup was parked in a driveway on the third road down. This was a nicer section of town. The houses here were older. Larger. Better maintained. There was a mix of Victorian and Tudor styles.

The pickup was parked outside the garage. It looked too tall to fit inside. There were thick hedges under the house windows. There were trees and bushes separating one house from the next. The backyards were large and wooded.

Carver drove through the neighborhood. Most of the homes looked occupied. The exteriors looked well maintained. The lawns were recently cut. There were cars parked in driveways and kids playing outside one house.

He drove to the next intersection. Took a right. Drove down the road behind the woman's neighborhood. The homes here were about the same. Most looked occupied. The one directly behind her house had an old Buick Century parked out front.

The car was at least twenty years old because that model hadn't been made since 2005. It was the choice of the older generation. Odds were the owner of the house was an older person. Probably in their eighties if Carver had to make a wild guess.

The yards on this street were similar in size to the ones on the mystery woman's street. There were no fences in the front or back. They didn't need them because there were strips of trees and bushes separating the lots.

Approaching the woman's house from the back was the best tactic. That meant going through this yard. It shouldn't be too hard if an elderly person owned the house. So long as they weren't the nosey neighbor type.

Carver parked on the curb in front of the house. He leaned back in his seat and waited. Ten minutes passed and the front door opened. A middle-aged man in a bathrobe and flipflops came outside.

He walked to Carver's car. Rapped his knuckles on the window. Carver lowered the window. "Can I help you?"

The man frowned. "You've been parked in front of my house for twenty minutes. Do you need something?"

Carver knew it had barely been ten minutes. "I'm parked on a public road."

"In front of my house."

"I'm in front of a lot of houses." Carver pointed to the other nearby houses. "That one, that one, that one. Take your pick."

"You're directly in front of mine."

Carver was curious. "You drive a Buick Century?"

The man flinched. "Yeah, why?"

"I thought mostly old people drove that kind of car."

"It was my dad's. He left it to me."

"Left you the house too?" Carver asked.

"That's none of your business."

Carver knew all he needed to know about the guy. Crossing through his yard would be risky. He was the nosey neighbor type. He looked middle-aged but at heart he was an old man. The kind to tell kids to get off his lawn. It looked like a frontal approach would be better.

A side approach would work too.

"Did you hear me?" The man was still talking.

"I heard you." Carver put the car in drive and pulled away. The man was probably going to write down his license plate. Might even file a report. He was probably the kind of person who did that a lot. The cops probably ignored him.

Carver drove to the end of the street and hooked back around to the woman's road. He drove past slowly, using the wireless app to search for cameras. It detected weak signals. He also noted a doorbell camera and a camera over the garage door.

He reached the end of the road and went left to the next road over. He drove to the house behind the house that was directly across the road from the woman's residence. This house was for sale.

He parked in the driveway. Looked in the front windows. If anyone asked, he was just looking around. He went to the back yard. There was a thick patch of trees between this lot and the next one over. A thick patch of trees and bushes between houses too.

Carver went through the wooded area. He pushed through bushes and found a spot with a good view of the woman's front yard. The bushes here were thick enough that the houses on either side wouldn't know he was there.

Once the sun went down, he was going in.

CHAPTER 7

Decker followed the target.

Paola didn't seem to be in any hurry. She stopped at a grocery store a mile down the road from the salon. He followed her inside. She picked up a carton of eggs, a half-gallon of milk, and a few other odds and ends.

He was yawning from boredom by the time she went to the checkout. There was a long line, so he went outside and got in his car to wait for her. She appeared a few minutes later, pushing a shopping cart.

Decker watched her load the plastic bags into the backseat of her car. He watched her push the shopping cart into a cart corral. He yawned again and watched her climb into her car. She started the engine and sat there staring blankly out of the window.

There were several notifications on Decker's phone, so he took a moment to look them over. One text caught his attention.

Alarm triggered at Holly Robinson's house.

He replied to the sender with several questions. The reverse lights blinked on Paola's car. It backed out of the parking spot. Decker waited for her to turn out of the parking lot before he went after her.

A few miles later, she turned into a gated community. The houses looked dated. They were probably built in the eighties or nineties. A tall brick wall surrounded the complex. It was one of those places built to give people a false sense of security.

He watched the gate slide open. Counted the seconds it took for the barrier arm to go up and come back down. Following a car through wouldn't be a problem. He pulled into the dedicated turning lane for the subdivision and put on his hazard lights.

The target's car disappeared around a curve. He looked at the map app. The subdivision was small. Just one main street and two cross streets that both ended in cul-de-sacs. The houses had garages. If she parked inside, it would be harder for him to identify the right house.

He waited for another car to enter the gate, but none came. He considered climbing the wall, but it was probably too late. She would have already parked her car by now.

These homes weren't something any old illegal immigrant could afford. They were pricey. Had she purchased a house here, or was she just renting? Decker opened a real estate app. Two houses had recently been sold inside the subdivision.

One went for nearly seven hundred grand. Another had gone for considerably less. The listing showed it needed major repairs and renovation. If she'd recently purchased a house, it would be one of those two.

Then again, just because Paola had a lot of cash didn't mean she'd purchased a house. She couldn't just plop down a wad of cash and get one. He was no real estate expert, but he felt reasonably certain it didn't work that way.

Not only that but using large sums of cash would get you noticed by the wrong government agencies. The IRS would certainly investigate it. Local law enforcement might also want to find out where that cash came from.

She would want to stay off the radar. Renting or staying with a friend seemed more likely. He checked the real estate app for rental properties. Three homes in the subdivision were for rent or lease. They were all occupied.

Decker marked them as possibilities.

A car drove past him. The driver pulled into the dedicated turn lane and went to the gate. He waved a keycard in front of a card reader and the gate slid open. Decker pulled up behind him. The man pulled forward after the gate arm lifted.

Decker pretended to wave a keycard over the reader, then gunned the engine to follow the other guy through before the arm came back down. He was a fraction too late. The gate arm came down and struck the roof of the car.

That triggered a safety feature and the arm rose again. Decker pulled through and waited for the other car to drive around the corner. Then he advanced, looking at the driveways. Most of the driveways were empty.

He turned left down the first crossroad. Drove to the cul-de-sac. Saw Paola's car parked behind a blue Toyota in the driveway. The garage door was open. There was a minivan parked inside. The rest of the space was taken up by junk.

This wasn't one of the houses that had recently sold or was being rented. It had sold almost a year prior, according to the real estate app. He called a tech at his division office. A guy who would do what he was told and not ask questions.

The tech answered on the second ring. "This is Paul."

"It's Decker. I need to know who owns a house and how it was bought."

"Address?"

Decker gave him the info.

"Just a minute." Paul went silent for a moment. "The owner is Aliyah Butler. Purchased it five years ago. She's unmarried and works for Davis, Davis, and Smith, an accounting firm."

"That's all I need, thanks." Decker ended the call and grinned. "Two birds with one stone." Aliyah Butler was one of Jasper Whittaker's former playthings. One of the sex slaves the cartel procured to keep him happy.

She was also one of the people who'd made off with cartel money. One of the people on his list. Paola had led him right to her. He was going to have double the fun tonight and hopefully recover some of the cartel's money.

The house didn't look like Butler had spent much money on it. Not unless she'd renovated the inside. It didn't look like she'd spent it on a fancy car either.

There had been nearly twenty million in unlaundered cash at the paint factory. According to the records kept by the factory, there had been twenty-one women held captive at the factory. Two had been found dead when the FBI raided it. Dead by drug overdose. That left nineteen.

Local law enforcement had confiscated the cash and drugs before the feds were involved. They'd distributed it among the trafficking victims. Helped the victims remain anonymous so they could melt back into the population.

They hadn't even shared the women's identities with the FBI. They probably suspected the cartel had moles in the organization. They were right to be suspicious.

The cartel was worth billions. Twenty million was a drop in the bucket. They could have let it go and not missed a beat. But that wasn't how cartels worked. You couldn't just let people steal from you. It sent the wrong message.

They wanted to make sure the right message got out. Steal even a penny from the cartel and they'd hunt you to the ends of the Earth. There was no safe place for you to hide.

The cartel invested money into finding out who these women were. They'd hired people to live in Morganville and keep their ears close to the ground. Then they'd waited for the feds to conclude their investigations so they could resume business as usual.

All that time and money had paid off.

Now here Decker was, right outside Paola's door. He drove around the cul-de-sac and down the street a short distance. He turned around and parked on the curb. That was probably frowned upon in this neighborhood, but he was willing to take the chance.

This location gave him a clear view of the house. He leaned his seat back so he wasn't as visible but could also still see over the steering wheel. He angled the rearview mirror so he could see out of the back.

He didn't see any external cameras. The doorbell was just a regular button. A woman emerged from a neighboring house thirty minutes later and walked her dog around the front yard. It did its business, and she took it back inside.

Decker saw movement in the rear-view mirror. Someone was jogging down the street away from his car. Moments later, a car pulled onto the road and turned into a driveway several houses back.

He kept waiting and watching until it was dark. The streetlamp in the cul-de-sac was out, making it easier to stay concealed. There were lights on inside the house, but no outside lights. They were almost making this too easy.

There was a wooden fence around the back yard. It was identical to the fences in most of the backyards here. He unlatched the gate and slipped through it. He peered into a window, but the curtain was drawn, and he couldn't see inside.

Decker worked his way around the house, pausing to look inside each window. The kitchen window didn't have a curtain. He saw the kitchen sink on the other side. An oven. Cabinets. A stainless-steel refrigerator.

He edged further to the side until he saw the doorway between the kitchen and the next room. He saw Paola sitting on a couch. She was staring at an iPad. Mindlessly scrolling. No one else was visible in the slice of den he could see.

There were three cars in the driveway. That didn't mean there were three people in the house. The minivan threw him off. Butler was unmarried and had no kids. So, why did she have a minivan?

People without kids bought SUVs all the time. People without kids didn't usually buy minivans. At least not as far as he knew. He needed to make sure there were no surprises lurking inside.

This was a capture mission. He needed Paola alive. The other woman didn't matter except as leverage. Paola might be willing to spill her guts to protect someone else. If there were other pressure points, namely kids, inside, he wanted to know before he planned his infiltration.

He went to the front of the house. The curtains were open on the first window. A dining room was visible through it. An open doorway connected it to the den. He could clearly see Paola and another woman on the couch.

The other woman was dark skinned. She wore her hair in a fluffy afro. He knew from the description that was Butler. She was watching television. It looked like she was watching a murder documentary. The irony was delicious.

The upstairs windows in the front and the back were dark. Unless there were kids sleeping upstairs, there was no one else in the house. It was hardly seven in the evening. Too early for even kids to be sleeping.

He couldn't really be certain without going inside and clearing the rooms. That probably wasn't necessary. He could go inside and hold his pistol on both women. Secure them. If anyone else was in the house, he would find out quickly.

Decker put his ear to the window. The television volume wasn't blaring, but it was loud enough to be heard through double-paned glass. It was probably loud enough to cover him jimmying open a door.

He went to the front door. Tested the handle. It was locked. He went into the garage. He had to use a flashlight to see his way through the junk. There was a path to a door. He tested the handle. It was unlocked.

Decker rolled his eyes. These women were idiots. That was good for him. Bad for them. He should be able to ease open the door without them hearing anything. The kitchen was on the other side of the door. It was adjacent to the den.

He closed his eyes and envisioned the interior layout. The garage door opened into the kitchen. The kitchen was small with two doors. One door went into a dining room. The other door went into the den.

If he went through the latter, he would be facing the couch, and the women would be facing him. That was no good. He needed to go through the dining room door first then exit the other side and into the foyer if he wanted to sneak up behind the women.

It didn't matter if he came at them from the front or the back. With his pistol in hand, it would already be game over. Sneaking up would be more fun though. The looks of surprise on their faces would be worth the extra effort.

Then he could secure them with plastic restraints. Make sure the house was clear of other occupants.

If it was, he could toy with them at his leisure. Butler meant nothing to him. She was trash. Disgusting leftovers from Jasper Whittaker. Paola, on the other hand, was one of the grand prizes. He could use Butler as leverage. Force Paola to tell him where to find the other women.

She would also help him find the other grand prize. The big man who'd helped her and the others in Morganville. The man the cartel so dearly wanted to have a word with. With any luck, he'd have things tied up within days.

And Amos Carver's bounty would be in his bank account.

CHAPTER 8

Carver was ready to go in.

It was dark. The woman was still inside the house. He had to find a way inside. To make sure she was alone in there.

A man on the other side of the street wheeled a large black garbage can to the curb. Carver had watched several people roll their cans to the curb while he'd waited in the woods. He wanted to make sure no one was doing that when he finally broke cover.

Carver looked both ways. He studied the street with his monocular. Didn't see anyone outside. Didn't see any cars coming. He low-crawled out of the trees. He crossed the street and hurried into the trees next to the target's house.

He waited for a moment to make sure he was in the clear. He surveyed the street. Listened. Ten minutes passed. All remained quiet. It looked like he was good to go.

The target's house was two stories tall. Lights were on upstairs in the front and side windows. Light shone from the front windows on the first floor. Carver was able to see through the windows from his position in the trees.

He saw a large open kitchen and den. The television was on, but he didn't see anyone watching it. He left the trees. Pressed himself against the house and moved along the perimeter, keeping an eye out for cameras.

There were no cameras on the side of the house. The woods were too close and would hinder visibility. That was good for him. There were floodlamps on the back of the house. He slipped under the sensors so they wouldn't turn on.

There was a large, screened porch jutting from the back of the house. He didn't see any cameras on the soffits, but he still didn't have much freedom of movement thanks to the floodlamps.

He edged along the back of the house to the windows. They gave him a clear view of the first floor. The house had been renovated. The kitchen, den, and dining room were all connected. He appreciated this modern style when it came to reconnoitering. It made his job a lot easier.

Carver reached the porch door. It was one of those lightweight glass doors. It was locked. That was no problem because the screen next to the door was easy enough to cut if he wanted to. He wasn't ready to do that just yet.

The rear upstairs windows were dark. That most likely meant the upstairs hallway lights were off. Since he didn't see the woman downstairs, it meant she was probably in the upstairs room on the front of the house.

He kept working his way around the perimeter. Kept looking through the windows. Before long, he was almost at the front of the house. He couldn't go in that way due to the doorbell camera and the camera over the garage.

It looked like the porch might be the answer, but the back door leading into the house would almost certainly be locked. Then he'd have to pick or jimmy it. He'd have to get a good look at it to know for sure.

Another option occurred to him. A smarter option. All he had to do was wait. He returned to the back window. Saw the woman walking downstairs. She'd been wearing slacks and a blue button-up shirt earlier. Now she wore shorts and an oversized sweater.

She opened the refrigerator. Pulled out a frozen dinner. Read the back of it. She pursed her lips and worked them back and forth. Like she was making a momentous decision. She put the dinner into the microwave, punched the buttons, and started cooking it.

The woman stared blankly at the refrigerator for a moment. She bit her lower lip and pulled a bottle of red wine from inside. The cork was already halfway out of the bottle since it had been previously opened.

She plucked a clear plastic cup from a cabinet and filled it halfway with wine. Set her phone on the countertop and stared at it while sipping her drink. The microwave dinged moments later. She pulled the steaming meal from inside and peeled the plastic film off the top.

Carver hunkered down and got comfortable while she ate fettuccini alfredo with broccoli and drank her red wine. She never moved from the counter. She just stood there staring at her phone.

When she finished, she dropped the fork in the paper tray. Kept sipping wine and looking at her phone. Carver figured she was looking at social media or a video site. She had that same mesmerized gaze people got when they were mindlessly entertained.

He took the time to get a better look at her. Her legs were toned and athletic. She was young. Probably mid-twenties. Long black hair tied in a ponytail. Dark eyes. Light skin on the face. Slightly darker on the legs and arms.

She wasn't wearing makeup. At least none that Carver could see. Not even lipstick. She hadn't been wearing any when he saw her earlier either. He'd noticed but he hadn't made a point of noting it. Now he did.

It went hand-in-hand with how she'd acted around Maberly earlier. She might be one of those all-business types. Someone who didn't care about dressing up. She was all about her career.

Her English was perfect, but she had a faint Brazilian accent. She might have been born in the U.S. but raised speaking Portuguese as a child. English was her second language, but she'd grown up with it, almost erasing the Brazilian accent.

That happened with second-generation Americans. They grew up with the culture and language their parents brought with them. Then they went to school around age five or six and were assimilated into the dominant culture and language.

If she was Brazilian, there was a good bet she was working for the cartel. There was also the faint possibility that it was just coincidence, and she was working for a federal agency or the shadow organization, Enigma.

Only time would tell.

After another good twenty minutes, the woman blinked out of her phone-induced stupor. She dumped the paper tray into the garbage. Stared at the garbage can for a moment. She sighed and went upstairs. Came back down with a small plastic trash bag.

She dumped that into the kitchen garbage. Lifted the bag from that can and went to the door leading into the garage. Carver heard a hum and creaking as the garage door began to lift. This was the moment he'd been waiting for.

As he'd noticed earlier, the other neighbors had put their garbage at the curb. The woman hadn't. Her can was still sitting on the side of the house, half full and stinking to high heaven. Maybe it had only been sitting there for a week, but he doubted it.

The odor told him it might have been there two weeks. It smelled like a lot of lonely nights with microwave dinners. She'd probably forgotten to take it out last week. If she was living alone, it probably took her two weeks to fill the outdoor trashcan even halfway.

Now her garbage was going to give him an easy way inside the house. He waited at the back corner of the house. Watched from the darkness as she lifted the lid on the large garbage can and hefted the kitchen bag inside.

She gripped the handle on the back of the can. Turned it toward the street. Pulled it behind her down the driveway. Carver hurried around the corner. Between it and her big truck. Went into the garage. Past another car, a midsized sedan.

He went through the door and into the kitchen. He made sure to wipe his feet quickly before entering so he didn't track dirt inside.

He saw a gun in a holster on the counter. He hadn't seen it from the window because of the angle. It was the same Glock she'd had on her hip at Holly's house. He didn't have much time before she returned inside, and the open floor design didn't give him many places to hide.

Carver wanted to take the gun, but she'd notice it was gone and immediately go on guard. Removing the bullets from the magazine and chamber would be better, but he didn't have time.

He made a split-second decision and left the gun where it was. If she left it down here it meant she wasn't particularly concerned about her safety. It meant she felt secure. She might also have another handgun upstairs in her bedroom.

He didn't have time for anything except finding a hiding place. Once she put the garbage can at the curb, all she had to do was turn around and she'd see him plain as day through the windows since there were no walls to conceal him.

Carver hurried through the den. He made it to the stairs and out of sight of the front windows. He went upstairs and looked both ways down the hallway. There were three upstairs bedrooms. One had a light on. The hallway light was off.

The upstairs was carpeted. He walked slowly. Even though the carpet masked his footsteps, it was possible there was creaky plywood subflooring underneath. He was a heavy guy. The kind who had trouble treading lightly.

The flooring was apparently built to a high standard because the subflooring didn't creak once. He went into the lit room. The clothing strewn on the floor and the unmade bed told him it was the woman's bedroom.

He took a quick look around. There was a snub-nosed revolver in a small leather holster on her nightstand. He slid it out. Checked the chambers. They were loaded. It was a nice little Ruger. Hammerless design. This one used nine-millimeter rounds.

Carver put the revolver back into place. He went into the bathroom. There wasn't much in there. A couple of towels on the floor. Hand soap. The woman didn't have the usual ensemble of hair care and body products women liked. That jibed with her lack of makeup.

Carver took a quick peek inside her walk-in closet. It was big and mostly empty. There were multiple pairs of business slacks, mostly beige, navy, and black. Multiple button-up shirts in the same colors.

There were a couple of summer dresses. A few body-conforming long dresses. Black dress shoes. Three pairs of high heels. Most notably, there were two long black cases on the ground. They weren't suitcases. They were rifle cases.

He heard the hum of the garage door closing. The woman was coming back inside, and he needed to decide how to handle this. Reasoning with her didn't seem like the play. Taking her prisoner at gunpoint seemed the smartest move. Then he could figure out where she stood on the danger meter.

Carver didn't know what to make of this woman if he was being honest. He'd pegged her as an office worker earlier. Then as a cartel agent. Now he was starting to think she was something entirely different.

One thing was certain. She wasn't a neat freak. Her room was a mess. The bathroom was a mess. That didn't mean she couldn't handle a gun or protect herself.

Carver left the bedroom. Went to the top of the stairs. The hallway was dark, so he felt safe peeking around the corner and looking down. The woman was back in the kitchen. Drinking her red wine and staring at her phone again.

Carver used his monocular for a closer look, but he didn't have a good angle on the phone screen. He wasn't going to learn anything this way.

Her phone rang. She answered it. Grunted a few times. Nodded. Said, "Okay. Uh-huh. Yep. Keep me posted." Ended the call.

Spying on her obviously wasn't going to reveal very much. Not if every phone call she had went like that. It would be simpler to tie her up and interrogate her. Maybe. He noticed other details about her.

There was a jagged scar on her right hand. Several fine scars on her right leg. A thin scar behind her right ear. Had that all happened at the same time? Or from other instances?

She set down her wine glass. Drummed her fingers on the countertop. Like she was impatient about something. She turned so her back was to him. Stared at her phone again. It was a good opportunity to strike.

The stairs didn't creak. The carpet would mask his footfalls. He could walk downstairs and take her at gunpoint right now. He'd noticed a basement door in the kitchen. He could take her down there and interrogate her.

She would almost certainly know what happened to Holly. She might know why Paola had been in Morganville. She could tell him who in the hell all those people were at Holly's. Most importantly, she could tell him who he had to kill to ensure Paola's safety.

He considered waiting a while longer. She might have a visitor, or she might make a phone call and reveal information through conversation. Information that interrogation wouldn't pry out of her.

Judging from what he'd seen so far, that wasn't going to happen.

Just as he was readying himself to sneak downstairs, he noticed two things. First, there was a window at the other end of the kitchen counter. It faced the stairs. Since the lights were on inside and it was dark outside, it might show him in the reflection when he came downstairs.

Second, something was missing from the kitchen counter. Carver zoomed in the monocular and saw that the missing item wasn't missing. It had been moved. He could see it in the window reflection.

That missing item was the Glock. It was now in front of the woman, hidden by her body. She was pretending to look at her phone, but she was actually looking at the window at the other end of the counter from her.

She was waiting, the handgun right at her fingertips. Somehow, she knew someone was in her house. She wasn't panicking. Wasn't calling emergency services. She didn't even look worried, at least not from what Carver could make out in the weak window reflection.

That didn't mean she hadn't texted someone. That she wasn't waiting for the cavalry to show up. Either way, it was bad news. And Carver had trapped himself on the second floor.

Well, trapped was a strong word.

He could drop from a second story window right into the thick shrubs. The problem was, falling into bushes didn't really cushion your fall. Not if you hit them the wrong way. Bushes had branches. Branches were hard and sometimes sharp.

Hitting them just right might soften a fall. Hitting one the wrong way could mean a branch stabbed you in the gut or the back or the leg. Carver wasn't going out the window. Not if he could help it.

There was only one way to handle this. She was ready for him. The moment he started walking downstairs, she was going to turn around and point the handgun at him. Take him by surprise.

It might have worked. Even if he hadn't noticed she was ready, he still would have had his gun out and pointed at her. Being cocky and overconfident was a sure way to end up dead. It had nearly happened to him when he was a rookie. He'd seen it happen to others.

He was at the edge of darkness. The reflection in the window wouldn't catch him until he was halfway down the stairs. The woman obviously didn't think he was here to kill her if she was just standing there waiting for him to show himself.

She could be waiting for backup to arrive. Carver didn't have much time to act if that was true. So, he did the one thing she might not have expected. He slid his Glock from the shoulder holster. Attached the suppressor.

He aimed. Fired. The silencer coughed. The wine glass next to her hand shattered. She flinched. Didn't shriek. Didn't shout. She put her hands up. They were empty, but that could change in a heartbeat.

Carver spoke. "Don't make me put the next bullet through your head. Keep your hands up. Back away from the counter five steps. Slowly turn and face the stairs, then take four more steps."

She did what he said. Kept her hands up. Backed up five slow steps. Turned and faced the stairs. Took four more steps. Carver reached the bottom of the stairs by the time she finished.

Her lips were pressed into a thin line. Her face was slightly red. Like she was angry. Not with Carver, but with herself. He knew that feeling all too well.

"How did you know?" she asked.

"It doesn't matter." Carver kept the gun trained on her. Circled around her, out of reach in case she lunged. He picked up her phone. Brought it to her. "Unlock it."

She unlocked it with her thumb.

He took it quickly, wary of any sudden moves. After his encounter with an assassin in Miami, he knew there was no such thing as being too careful. No such thing as overestimating someone's capabilities.

He looked at the texts. Looked at the open apps. There was no evidence she'd requested backup.

Which meant she was all his.

CHAPTER 9

Decker turned the handle on the door in the garage.

He eased it open in case it squeaked. The sound from the television might cover any sounds he made, but he didn't want to risk startling the prey. Not when he was so close to capturing it.

The door hinges were apparently lubricated because they didn't make a sound. There was a mudroom on the other side. Tile floor. A bench on one side with multiple pairs of shoes beneath it.

There were shelves and coat hooks on the other wall. The kitchen was just a few feet away. A long wall with cabinets blocked the line of sight into the den. He left the garage door open a crack. Then he crept through the kitchen.

He could hear the television more clearly now. It was a reality show. A woman was complaining about a man. She didn't like that he was obsessed with cleanliness or that his apartment was immaculate. She bitched and moaned about things that should be viewed as positives.

Typical woman, he thought.

Decker passed the back door leading to the porch. He stopped next to the kitchen sink. It was in front of the window he'd looked in earlier. Right across from it was the doorway leading into the dining area.

He looked through the door. Saw the women still on the couch. The stairs to the second floor were near the front door. The ceiling in the den was vaulted. There was a balcony at the top of the stairs.

There were doorways on both ends of the balcony. They probably led to bathrooms and bedrooms. It was a decent sized house so it might even have a game room up there. He didn't see light coming from either doorway.

It seemed almost certain these women were the only two people here. The silver Honda was Paola's. The minivan and SUV probably belonged to Butler. Why she hadn't treated herself to a nicer car was something Decker couldn't understand.

You could buy a nice car with cash without worrying too much about the IRS. Hell, you could even get a Lamborghini as long as you didn't flaunt it in front of jealous neighbors who might report you.

He noticed another door at the end of the kitchen. He knew it didn't go to the pantry because he'd already passed that door. This door might lead to a basement. If so, that would be a good place to set up shop for interrogation.

That was something he could decide once the women were secured. He already knew how he was going to do that. His favorite method was a hogtie. Facedown. Wrists bound. Ankles bound. Wrists and ankles bindings tethered so they could hardly move.

It was humiliating. It left the prisoner vulnerable not just physically, but emotionally. It let him do anything he wanted to do to them without much resistance. It also broke men faster than it did women.

Decker had the essentials in his back pocket. Strong nylon straps. A plastic bag with a chloroform-soaked rag inside. He probably wouldn't need it because his primary tool, a gun, would get them submissive in a hurry.

He drew his handgun. Clicked off the safety. Crept through the dining room. Around the corner and into the foyer. The back of the couch was in front of him. The women were facing away.

This was it.

There was a loud banging on the front door. Decker froze. He stepped backward into the dining room. Backed into the kitchen. Crouched next to the counter.

Butler jumped up off the couch. Paola was on her feet in an instant. The women stared at the door.

"You were expecting someone?" Paola said.

Butler shook her head. She reached to the side of the couch and picked up a handgun. Aimed it at the door. "Who is it?"

"It's Fani. Open the door please!"

Butler grimaced. Put the gun down.

Paola frowned. "Who is Fani?"

"The HOA president." Butler stormed to the front door. Opened it. A short, chubby woman stood on the other side.

"How many times do I have to warn you about leaving that garage door open and about having too many cars parked in the driveway?" Fani gave her a disbelieving look and shook her head. "It is also against HOA rules to have a garage so full of trash that it can't accommodate two cars."

"Well, you're more than welcome to clean it out yourself," Butler said. "This is my home. You don't dictate to me what I do with my property."

"You agreed to the HOA rules when you bought this house."

"You changed those rules two months after I moved in." Butler shook her head. "You can bother me all you want about it, but I ain't bowing to a petty little HOA dictator."

Fani gasped. "I'm calling the police."

"About what?"

"About your disregard for HOA rules!" The other woman took out her phone and dialed.

Decker fantasized about putting a bullet through the woman's head. He'd dealt with an HOA before. It was worse than the mob. It had only ended when the HOA president and several board members met with a series of terrible accidents that things had changed for the better.

They'd messed with the wrong man and paid for it. A bullet to the forehead would be so very nice right now. But it wasn't the best course of action.

Killing Fani here and now wasn't going to work out. She might have someone at home. Someone who'd come looking for her if she was gone too long. Decker wanted to use Butler's house to question the women and he didn't want any interruptions.

The HOA president needed to leave so he could finish his business. He tried to unlock the back door, but the deadbolt required a key for both sides.

Butler scoffed. "You really think the cops are going to come for something that stupid?"

Fani ignored her and spoke on her phone. "Yes, I'd like to report a domestic disturbance."

"Domestic disturbance? You came banging on my door about my garage!"

Decker gritted his teeth. Butler's shouting was almost certain to trigger a police response. His perfect plan wasn't going to work. Not tonight. He definitely didn't want to be here if the cops came. And judging from the shouting match between Butler and this Fani woman, things weren't going to cool off anytime soon.

He quietly exited via the door to the garage. He crept between the boxes of junk. Hooked a right so he could enter the darkness between this house and the next one. It was dark thanks to the broken streetlamp. Wandering too close to the neighboring house might trigger a floodlamp.

He walked to the asphalt and hugged the outer curve of the cul-de-sac. The women were shouting even louder. What Decker wouldn't give to put a bullet through Fani's head right now.

Fani walked into Butler's garage and started pushing over boxes. Butler shoved the other woman out of her garage. She went into the garage and pressed the button to close the garage door.

Decker grew even angrier. That was his only way inside unless he kicked in a door or broke a window. He went to his car. The dome light was off, so it didn't come on when he opened the door.

He was about to get inside when he saw a parking ticket under the windshield. The writing on it said he'd parked illegally on the curb. The fine was $200 payable to the HOA. He snatched the ticket. Got into the car.

He gripped the steering wheel and stared at the woman. Butler had long since gone inside and closed the door. Fani was still standing there waiting next to a BMW SUV. She probably drove around the neighborhood looking for fineable offenses.

Fifteen minutes later, a police car rolled past Decker. It stopped at the end of the cul-de-sac. Two officers got out. They spoke to Fani. They knocked on the door. Butler answered. She spoke to one of the officers while the other cop stayed next to Fani.

This wasn't going to be over anytime soon. Decker didn't want to risk them coming to his car and noticing it either. He turned the headlights off so they wouldn't come on automatically. He started the car. Backed up slowly.

No one noticed. He kept backing up until he reached the crossroad. He turned around and headed for the gate. Then he thought of something else. Fani had probably taken down his license plate information.

She had a record of his car being there. That wasn't good. The ticket was written by hand. It looked like the kind that made a carbon copy when you wrote on the pad. It meant Fani had that copy on her.

"That dumb bitch." Decker ground his teeth together. It looked like he was coming back tonight.

Decker left the subdivision. Drove across the road to a shopping center. He parked there. He got his duffel bag from the back seat. Pulled out his black hoodie and mask. Put them on. Grabbed a few more supplies.

He got out and crossed the road. Turned left on the sidewalk. Followed the subdivision's brick wall. It turned right after a couple of hundred yards. The weeds and bushes had been trimmed away from the back of the wall, leaving a trail.

He followed the trail along the back of the wall. The wall was about eight feet tall. Too tall to see over, so he estimated when he was close to Butler's back yard. Most people wouldn't have a chance at scaling such a height, but he was tall and athletic.

Decker jumped. Gripped the edge. Muscled himself to the top. The wall was wide enough for him to sit there so he could orient himself.

He'd almost nailed the location perfectly. He was just one house down from Butler's. He walked along the top of the wall until he reached her backyard. He sat down and listened to the loud conversations on the other side of the house.

It sounded like Fani was still arguing. Trying to get Butler arrested for shoving her out of the garage. The police officers weren't talking loudly enough for him to hear. They were probably trying to deescalate the confrontation.

Decker hopped down off the wall and walked behind the house. He went to the fence where it intersected the side of the house. He was able to hear Butler and Fani arguing. It went on for another twenty minutes, mostly because of Fani.

Finally, Fani agreed to leave. The cops asked for her address. She gave it to them. They told her to get in her car. They told her they would follow to make sure she went home. Butler thanked them. The front door slammed shut.

The fence was too tall to see over, so Decker cracked open the back gate and watched Fani veer her BMW around and roar down the road. The police car followed her. She turned left at the intersection.

Decker didn't need to follow her. He knew her address, thanks to the cops. He would take care of her later once he secured his primary targets. Unfortunately, he'd have to find another way in because Butler didn't reopen the garage door.

If he'd been thinking straight, he would have unlocked a window once he realized the back door deadbolt couldn't be unlocked without a key. But he'd been in too much of a hurry to get out before the cops arrived.

He pondered the situation. Wondered if maybe it would be better to wait until the next day. Butler would probably open the garage door again and leave it open. But what if she didn't? He'd end up having to break in another way.

Decker still didn't know what he was going to do. There was another possibility. One that might be easy to pull off since the cops had just been here. All he had to do was go to the front door and knock.

The women would think the cops had returned, probably to ask some questions and file a report. They wouldn't suspect anything at all. One of them would come to the door. Decker would put a gun in their face. Walk them inside. The other woman would comply with whatever he asked.

He would make Butler give him the handgun she'd brandished earlier. There might be other weapons around the house, but he wasn't too concerned about them. Once the women were secured, they'd be helpless.

First, he tested the windows on the back. He wanted to be sure he wasn't overlooking something. The windows were all locked. It looked like he'd have to go with his second option.

He went to the gate. Opened it. Headlights turned onto the road at the intersection. They kept coming straight. Decker waited behind the gate. Waited for the vehicle to turn into another driveway.

It didn't. It drove onto Butler's driveway. Parked. The headlights turned off. It was an SUV, but Decker couldn't make out the details since it was dark. Both doors opened and two figures stepped out.

The front porch light was still on so he could see they were men. They were carrying bags of groceries. Were they delivery men? The question was answered a moment later when the men went inside without knocking.

Decker walked to the kitchen window and looked through. Butler met one of the men with a kiss on the lips. Both men were black. Definitely not Brazilian. They went into the kitchen. Decker backed up and retreated next to the back wall.

The kitchen light came on. The men started putting groceries away. It was obvious the one was Butler's boyfriend. The other one bore some resemblance to Butler. He might be a brother. He might be Paola's love interest.

Either way, it didn't matter. He wasn't getting in tonight. Not with this many people. It would be too hard to control all the variables. It was good he hadn't acted impulsively. By being patient, he'd discovered the two men apparently staying at the house.

He would need to wait and watch. Learn their patterns. Find a good time to strike. In the meantime, he had other business to attend to thanks to the HOA president.

Decker left the backyard through the gate. He skirted around the dark cul-de-sac. Walked to the end of the street. Took a left. Queens Court Lane was the last street in the subdivision. Fani's address was at the end of the cul-de-sac on the right.

There were no cars in the driveways here. No kids' toys in the yards. No open garage doors. All the mailboxes were identical black metal with the same style numbering. The houses were traditional red brick.

There was a sameness to all the residences here. Probably because these people had the misfortune to live next door to the HOA president. Then again, maybe they enjoyed it. Maybe they were on the HOA board. Maybe they enjoyed being mini dictators.

Decker had dealt with their kind in all walks of life. Whether it was at the department of motor vehicles or in the military. Give someone a tiny bit of power and they would abuse it to the max.

Fani's mailbox wasn't black metal. It was painted gold. There was a fancy wooden sign that said *Fani Wilson, President*. The sign and her gold mailbox probably were against HOA rules. As usual for people in power, the rules probably didn't apply to her.

The house was three stories tall. There was a long flight of brick stairs leading up to the front door. The garage was on the lower level. It was probably connected to a basement.

Her outside lights were off. Lights were on downstairs. The upstairs was dark. There were two streetlamps, one on either side of the cul-de-sac. Decker kept to the dark front yards of the houses on the left side.

He worked his way to Fani's front yard. Studied the house for cameras and sensor activated floodlamps. There was a camera doorbell, but no other outside cameras he could see. The sensors on the flood lamps were pointed straight toward the yard.

The one on the corner wasn't angled properly, so he skirted outside of its range and reached the side of the house. There was a wooden fence identical to all the other ones in the neighborhood.

The gate was latched, but not locked. He opened it and studied the side and back of the house. There were floodlamps, but not the sensor variety. Probably because she didn't think anyone would scale the tall brick wall in the back yard.

Decker didn't make any assumptions. Just because there were no sensors on the floodlamps didn't mean there weren't any cameras in the back. He stayed low and crept around the hedges that surrounded the house.

There was a back deck. It rose about ten feet off the ground. There was a concrete patio beneath it. A steel door with no windows. There were no windows on this lower level. Probably because the garage and basement were on the other side.

He tested the door handle. Locked. He could probably jimmy open the door but then he'd only be inside the garage. If she locked the door leading into the house, he'd have to jimmy it open as well.

He tested the wooden deck stairs. They creaked under his weight. He couldn't see them in the dark, but they felt dangerously unsteady. He took out his small tactical flashlight and shielded it with his hand. Shined it on the stairs.

The wood was moldy and rotted in areas. It looked like it hadn't been maintained at all. Even the pressure treated lumber was succumbing to the elements. He carefully made his way up the stairs, avoiding places where the rot looked the worst.

There was a hole in one of the stairs. It looked as if someone's foot had gone through it. He stepped over it. Climbed the last few stairs and reached the top. There was a rusting grill and moldy furniture on the deck.

A picture window looked into the kitchen. The plantation shutters were open, giving him a clear view inside. French doors led into the living room. There was another picture window on the other side of the doors.

The kitchen looked renovated. A half wall separated it from the living room. It wasn't quite an open floorplan, but it was close enough. Decker could see Fani pacing back and forth in the den. She was shouting at her cell phone. Probably complaining that the police hadn't done what she'd wanted.

She stared at the phone in disbelief. Probably because the person on the other end hung up on her. She stormed to the fridge. Dragged out a box of wine. Poured the pink liquid into a regular cup. She consumed half of it in one gulp.

Fani stared at the far wall in the living room. Decker angled his position so he could see what she was looking at. There was a gas log fireplace. Above the mantle was a portrait of her. He wasn't surprised.

Classic narcissist.

He surveyed the area. Saw a purse on the kitchen counter. Next to it was a notepad. No, not a notepad. It was the ticket pad she'd used to give him the parking ticket. He'd wait until she went to bed then break in and take it.

As much as he wanted to torture her, it would be better to get in and out undetected. He didn't want the cops crawling all over this subdivision. That would put his prey on alert and make it that much harder to carry out his mission.

He needed to be laser focused. Paola and Butler were within reach. All he had to do was time things right and they would be his for the taking.

CHAPTER 10

Carver trained his Glock on the mystery woman.

He checked her phone. There were no texts or calls within the last hour. It didn't look like backup was coming, but appearances could be deceiving.

She might have used a police radio. It didn't look like she had one on her, but she could have used one in her car. If she'd known he was here it would have been foolish of her not to call for backup.

She stared at him. Her jaw was tight. Her eyes were narrowed. She was angry, but she was also surprised. She'd really thought she would get the drop on him. That she could take him alone.

It wasn't surprising. Carver had seen plenty of overconfident people in his time. People who wanted to prove themselves. People who thought they were better than anyone else. People whose overconfidence backfired in the worst way possible.

Maybe that was the case here. Maybe this woman was young and overconfident. But the opposite might also be true. She seemed to be the one running things for the cartel. If that was the case, then she might be far more capable than he knew.

There was only one good way to find out. Asking questions and getting answers. But first he wanted to make sure that she couldn't catch him off guard like the assassin in Miami had almost done.

"Come over here." Carver motioned with his free hand. He pointed to the floor in front of the couch. "Sit cross-legged on the floor."

Her fists clenched. Her jaw worked back and forth. She shook her head. "I'm not moving."

"I can shoot your leg and make you sit."

"Then do it."

Carver sighed. "Okay." He aimed at her shin. Called her bluff.

"Wait!" The anger in her eyes turned to fear. "Fine. I'll sit."

"Thank you." Carver backed up.

She walked in front of the couch. Lowered herself to the floor and sat down like he wanted. "Criss cross applesauce. Are you happy?"

Carver glanced out of the front window. He didn't see anything, but that didn't mean she hadn't used a radio to call for backup. He knew asking if she'd done that would be a waste of time.

She'd been confident enough to think she could catch him off guard when he revealed himself. She'd been confident enough to rely on the reflection in the window to give her time to turn around and point her gun at him.

If she thought she could have captured him single-handedly, then she wouldn't have told her backup to use stealth. They'd come roaring into the driveway and rush inside. If that was the case, he'd see them coming.

Hopefully.

Carver watched her carefully. "I'd like to start with some simple questions."

"You're Carver, aren't you?"

"I'll ask the questions."

"Or what?"

He fired a shot into the couch just inches from her head. She flinched. Something flickered in her eyes for just an instant. Carver had seen that look before. It was the same look a prisoner gave him when they realized no one was coming to save them.

Carver walked to the kitchen counter, keeping the gun trained on her. Her purse was there. He unsnapped the top. Turned it upside down and emptied it. A wallet and two full magazines of nine-millimeter fell out.

He opened the wallet with one hand. Studied the ID. "Maggie Jones from Indianapolis?" He slid the ID from the holder while keeping his eye on her. It looked legitimate. It even had a holographic marker on it.

There was a single credit card inside. It had the same name on it. He still didn't buy it. "What's your real name?"

"Maggie Jones."

"What are your parents' names?"

"Melinda and Jason Jones."

"What do they do for work?"

"My father is a programmer, and my mother is a nurse at Indianapolis General."

"Where did your parents meet?"

"On a blind date."

"Who set up the blind date?"

She shook her head. "I don't know."

"Do your parents have siblings?"

She shook her head. "No."

"What's the name of your paternal grandmother?"

"Alice."

"Your great grandmother?"

She missed a beat. "Michelle."

Carver was certain she'd just made up the name. Most undercover people had a pre-pared background, but it only went so deep. Most of the time they adapted their real experiences to the cover story.

Carver switched it up. "What happened to Holly Robinson?"

She blinked. "She quit and moved."

"Looks like she moved in a hurry." Carver kept emptying the wallet. "It looks like someone was after her."

"You sound crazy."

"I saw you and your crew arrive at her house. Now that was crazy."

"You're the one who tripped the alarm?"

He wasn't going to answer her questions. "What happened to Holly Robinson?"

"Nothing."

"What happened to Chief Ritter?"

"He retired."

Carver didn't detect any overt signs that she was lying, but something didn't add up. Holly's house hadn't been tossed. Only her closet had been a mess. It was obvious she'd packed and left in a hurry—or tried to.

Questioning her like this wasn't getting anywhere. He needed to move her to another location and make things less comfortable. A lot less comfortable. That was the only way to force compliance.

Her eyes flared ever so slightly. Like she saw the change in his demeanor even though he didn't think he'd shown his hand. It was too late for her to answer now.

He pulled zip cuffs from his back pocket. "Lay flat on your stomach and put your hands behind your back."

She uncrossed her legs. Rather than go to her knees she planted her feet and lunged. Carver checked her with his elbow. Right on the bridge of her nose. She folded like a wet noodle and slumped on the floor.

He rolled her over. Secured her wrists behind her back. Secured her ankles. He bent her legs toward her hands and finished hogtying her. He turned her head to the side. Checked her pulse. It was strong and she wasn't bleeding.

Carver went to the garage and looked through the car. It was a regular civilian sedan. No police radio or computer. There was another Glock in the glove box and a small survival knife between the seat and the armrest.

Several tins of mints were inside the center armrest. One tin was open and half empty. It looked like she had an addiction. Or maybe she'd replaced one addiction with another. She might have quit smoking.

He looked under the seats, in the trunk, and under the hood. Didn't find anything else. The garage was mostly empty. No shelves, no boxes, nothing.

The truck in the driveway was as empty as the car aside from mints and another survival knife. He couldn't fault her for not being prepared.

Carver moved the search inside. The kitchen cabinets were nearly empty, aside from plastic cups and dinnerware. He looked inside them and ran his hand around the inside edges to make sure nothing was hidden in any of the nooks.

The refrigerator contained a half gallon of milk. The freezer was packed with frozen dinners. They weren't the cheap kind of frozen dinners. These were from a company that specialized in healthy meals for people who didn't want to cook. At least, that was what it said on the package.

He found the box they'd come in. Found the order slip. The plan covered three meals a day, seven days a week for a couple hundred bucks. That explained the empty cupboard. It explained the disposable dinnerware.

Maggie, or whatever her name was, had a nice kitchen with an expensive-looking gas stove, hood, and all the fixings, but she wasn't the kind of person who wanted to cook. Maybe she was the kind of person who never stayed in one place too long. Buying premade meals was just easier.

The invoice had her name and address on it. The credit card number matched the one he'd found in her wallet. It was possible that Maggie Jones was a real person whose identity had been stolen.

Carver knelt and checked her pulse again. She was moaning lightly. Probably getting ready to wake up any minute now. He made sure there was nothing near her that she could use to cut her bonds then used her thumbprint to unlock her phone again.

The phone had pictures of Holly's house. It had pictures of other random places in town. A few selfies of her and other police officers. Almost like she'd done it for show. There were no pictures of family or anything sentimental.

The phone was registered in her name. There was a work email account but no personal email account. She had a handful of contacts, all of them tagged as working with the police department.

He looked through the apps. She might have an encrypted messaging app like his that was disguised with a fake icon. He tapped on a poker game app. It asked for a passcode. That was almost certainly it. Maybe he could wring the information from her when she woke up.

Carver pocketed the phone and continued to search the rest of the ground floor. Like the kitchen, there wasn't much to find.

There was toilet paper in the half-bath off the den, hand soap and a roll of paper towels. The other rooms were empty. He checked all the vent covers. The screws didn't show signs of being tampered with and the covers were secure.

He went upstairs. Repeated the process with the vents. Checked the closets for any hidden compartments. The master suite was the only room with furniture, so he moved the search in there.

Carver opened the nightstand. Turned it over. Checked for any hidden compartments. Didn't find any. He lifted the mattress off the bed. Removed the sheets. Checked for zippers or hidden seams. Didn't find any.

The bathroom didn't yield any secrets either. He moved to the closet. Checked all the clothing. Didn't feel any unusual bumps or bulges. The only anomaly was a small coat hook with a threaded end. It looked like it had fallen off the coat rack when he'd removed the clothes from it.

Maybe she didn't have anything hidden here. Maybe she traveled light and didn't risk bringing along her real ID. The cartel had probably given her a top-notch fake ID. He felt certain it was fake because she only had one credit card.

Most people accumulated several credit cards over their life unless they preferred a cash economy like Carver. Maggie also didn't have any pictures in her wallet. Didn't have insurance cards, business cards, or the other useless items that accumulated in most people's wallets.

Her purse hadn't been full of makeup, old receipts, or anything else that typically filled a woman's purse. He was no expert on purses, but even women who changed purses frequently still collected junk in them.

Maggie might be all business. She might hate purses. She might be a tomboy. There were plenty of explanations, but in this context, it seemed most likely that she was undercover for the cartel or possibly even the shadow organization, Enigma.

Carver knelt in the closet and examined the baseboards. The toe kick for the shelf had a small hole in the center of it. He pushed it but it didn't move. He pressed the edges to see if it wiggled, but it was firmly in place.

He stood and went to the coat rack. Found the coat hook that had fallen off. He knelt and pushed it into the hole. It was a perfect fit. He threaded it until it was tight. Pulled. The toe kick board popped loose.

It didn't scrape the sides or leave marks. Otherwise, he would have noticed it. The reason it didn't was because it had been held on by magnets and had a thin layer of felt on the sides. It was simple, but effective.

There was a thin briefcase behind the board. Carver pulled it out. It was protected by a combination lock. He used his flashlight and looked at the toe kick on the neighboring shelf. It didn't have a hole in it.

He unscrewed the hook from the toe kick he'd removed and pressed it against the other toe kick. He threaded it into the wood and pulled on it. It didn't budge. Carver hadn't expected to find another hidden nook, but it was best to be certain.

There was nothing else in the nook the briefcase had been hidden in, so he took the briefcase downstairs. Maggie was awake and lying on her side. Her hands were working at the zip cuffs, but she wasn't making any progress.

She saw Carver and stopped. Watched him apprehensively as he walked toward her with the briefcase. She was trying not to let anything show, but there was a hint of worry in her eyes.

The briefcase was nothing special. It wasn't fortified like the one he'd encountered in San Francisco. He could probably pry it open.

Carver stood over the woman. "What's the combination?"

She stared at him silently, her face stony.

He sighed. Knelt next to her. "You have information I need. It would be much easier for both of us if you told me what I need to know. I don't want to go through the trouble of breaking you, and you probably don't want to deal with the pain that will cause."

She said nothing.

He'd expected as much. Mainly because he hadn't done anything to pry answers out of her yet. That was going to change in a few minutes. He pushed her back onto her stomach. Stood, and walked into the kitchen.

She wriggled, trying to turn so she could see him. The couch blocked her line of sight.

Carver used the survival knife he'd found in the car to pry at the sides of the briefcase. There were no latches on the side. He worked it around toward the middle. Pushed hard against the side of the latch.

The briefcase flexed just enough to jog the latch loose. He pulled it open. Inside were small stacks of cash and a bundle of passports secured with a thick rubber band. He removed the rubber band around the passports.

He spread them out on the countertop. Counted five of them, all U.S. passports. He opened the first. A California driver's license was inside with a picture of the woman on it, but she had blond hair and blue eyes. The passport had a similar picture. There was a credit card from the same bank as the one in her wallet.

The name on the driver's license was Megan Johnson. The only information that seemed true was the height and weight. He opened the other passports. Found more aliases, more fake addresses, more fake hair and eye colors.

Two of the IDs were closer to the truth. Brown hair, brown eyes, ethnicity Hispanic or Latino. He had to admit that she looked good with just about any hair and eye color combination. She was one of those people who could blend in anywhere.

He pulled the cash out of the briefcase. The stacks were all twenties. He estimated it was about twenty-five or thirty grand. This was her emergency escape stash. She could become someone else and vanish anytime she wanted.

The passports and driver's licenses were top-notch quality. Carver was no expert on forging IDs, but these looked legitimate. In fact, he was almost certain they were authentic IDs made by various state governments.

There were ways to get authentic IDs with false information on them. Official ways and illegal ways. Federal and state government agencies could get real IDs with aliases. Criminals had various means at their disposal as well. One of the easiest ways was to steal the identity of a real person or steal an ID and insert a new picture.

These IDs didn't look as if anyone had tampered with them. The edges looked perfect. No signs someone had removed the original pictures and replaced them. He'd seen a lot of amazing forgeries over the years, but these didn't show any of the usual tell-tale signs.

The holograms were supposed to be the hardest parts to fake. A forger told him they were the easiest part for him. He hadn't explained why, so Carver still had his doubts. Looking at forged holograms sideways was a fast way to see if they were the real deal or not.

There were other signs to look for as well. Peeling laminate, scuffed edges, or bits of glue. Carver had put that knowledge to good use during his short time as a bouncer at a Miami nightclub.

These IDs looked official. None of the telltale signs of forgeries were present on any of them. Carver had seen the cartel giving out real IDs to illegal immigrants in El Fuerte. They had friends in high places. Friends who could provide them with official fakes like these.

"What are you doing?" Maggie wormed her way to the end of the couch, but she couldn't see what Carver was doing.

Carver picked up the empty briefcase and tilted it back and forth. He heard something sliding around. Something beneath the vinyl lining. He tested the edges and found a loose section. He lifted the lining and tilted the case towards that side.

A blue booklet fell out. No, not a booklet. A passport. He flipped it over. It was another U.S. passport. He opened it and found two IDs inside. One was a driver's license. The other belonged to a federal agency.

And it wasn't one he would have expected.

CHAPTER 11

Decker was growing restless.

Fani was still awake.

It was past midnight and he was getting frustrated and angry. It was a weekday. Most working people were in bed and snoring by now. Not this woman. Her bedroom light was still on and from his spot in the backyard, he could see the television was on too.

He paced around and decided he was going in. She probably wouldn't hear him anyway, not with the television on. Some people needed light and noise to fall asleep. Maybe she was already dozing.

Unfortunately, he couldn't see her from down here. Unless he found a way to climb up to her bedroom window, he wouldn't know if she was awake or asleep. At this point, he didn't care. If she came downstairs and found him, she was going to regret it. He'd make damned sure of that.

He put on a ski mask. Crept cautiously up the deck's rotting staircase. The French doors at the top had a protective wooden strip over the middle to protect the jamb. It was supposed to keep it safe from slim jims.

It was an effective deterrent for anyone who didn't want to leave marks. But this back deck was so poorly maintained that the strip was moldy, and half rotted already. He could probably pull the strip off without much effort.

Decker didn't need to. He wasn't going in through the door. Even though he could jimmy the latch, the deadbolt was probably engaged and that was something he couldn't force open. At least not without kicking in the door.

He tested the door first, just in case. It was locked.

He pulled out a very thin, flexible strip of metal. It was his own twist on a slim jim. A little wider across with notches used to catch the inside of window latches. He slid it between the panes of the vinyl window.

The window was old, but it had a dual-latch system. It would take a little longer but was still no problem. The notch caught the rounded side of the first latch. He braced both hands on the side of the slim jim and pushed.

The latch budged a few fractions of an inch. Just enough for the edge to present itself. He backed up the jimmy and pushed the notch on the edge of the latch. This time it opened completely.

He repeated the process with the second latch. Then he pushed up the window. It resisted at first, probably because it hadn't been opened in years. The resistance abruptly gave way and the window shot up faster than expected.

It made a thump when it hit the top.

Decker grimaced. He pushed the window closed and waited. He gave it a full five minutes. Fani didn't come downstairs. Either the television drowned out the noise or she was asleep. He gave it another two minutes to make sure.

He backed up to the edge of the deck, careful not to lean on the wobbly railing. Looked up at Fani's bedroom window. Nothing had changed. The television was still flashing inside. The overhead light was still on.

He went back to the window. Pushed it up, careful not to use too much force. The rails were free of muck and crud this time, so it opened silently. He slipped through the window. Crouched and crept to the counter.

The ticket pad was on top. He took it. Thumbed through the pages. It looked like multiple pages had been torn from inside. A carbon copy of his ticket was on top. He gently tore out the pink page. Mission accomplished.

He noticed a thick piece of carboard behind it to prevent the pressure of the pen from scoring the next layer of carbon. He flipped past the cardboard. Found a white page behind it. The ticket on his car had been on yellow paper. He flipped past the white page and found a black sheet of carbon. Behind that he found the yellow sheet.

There was another carbon page behind the yellow sheet and a pink page behind that one. This pad made copies in triplicate. So, where in the hell was the white copy?

He looked on the kitchen counter. It wasn't there but Fani's purse was. He opened the purse and looked inside. It wasn't there. Her keys were next to her purse. He took them and went to the door leading to the garage. He unlocked the door and went through. Closed the door quietly behind him.

He walked down the stairs and into the two-car garage. Only Fani's car was parked there. There was another door that probably led into the basement. The door leading outside was on the back wall.

He pressed the button on the fob. The car beeped and the locks clicked. The bedroom was on the opposite side of the house from the garage and on the second floor. Fani most likely couldn't hear any noises he made down here. Not unless she had super hearing.

Decker opened the driver's side door. The car was pristine inside. A perfumed deodorizer hung from the rearview mirror. There were no papers on the front or back seats. Nothing in the center console. Nothing in the glove box.

The ticket wasn't in the car. Maybe she had an office in the house. Maybe she put the tickets there. He clenched his fists and pounded the steering wheel. His face grew hot. She'd better pray he found it before he had to ask her in person, because he was getting pissed.

He closed the car. Went back upstairs. Quietly opened the door. He stepped into the kitchen. There was a scream. Something flew past his head and bounced off the wall. The smell of wine hit his nose.

Decker saw Fani scrambling toward the stairs. He ran after her. Grabbed the hem of her robe. She tripped on the bottom stair. Fell. Grabbed at the railing. He gripped her wrist. Squeezed it until she cried out in pain and released the railing.

He grabbed her ankle. Dragged her into the living room. Rolled her onto her back and straddled her. He clamped a hand over her mouth. She tried to bite him. He slapped her just hard enough to daze her.

"Try that again and I'll choke you." He spoke in a cockney British accent to disguise his true voice. Just in case he decided to leave her alive.

But now he had a problem. He couldn't just ask for the ticket. It would link him to the car. If he went that route, she'd have to die. And to ensure he didn't startle his true prey he'd have to make sure it looked like an accident or that the body wasn't discovered for a couple of days.

Two ideas quickly came to mind. His above-average intellect rarely let him down. It was a benefit of being something of a genius.

His body flushed with pleasure as hopelessness filled Fani's eyes. *That's right*, he thought. *I have complete power over you. I own you.* There was nothing more satisfying than seeing that look in the eyes of his prey.

Fani hadn't realized she'd made a new enemy tonight. A very dangerous enemy. Now her life was in his hands. Would he be merciful or wrathful? Her fate partly rested in her hands.

"You will follow my commands without question." He gripped her hair and pulled it. "Tell me where your valuables are. I will take them and be on my way. If you resist, it will be very unpleasant for you."

"Please don't hurt me. I'll do whatever you say."

He released her hair. Stood. Held out a hand. She took it. He pulled her clumsily to her feet. "Where are your valuables?"

"I have a jewelry box upstairs in my bedroom closet. That's everything."

"I know that's not everything." Decker had a feeling she wasn't an honest HOA president. She was power hungry. Controlling. He wouldn't be surprised if she embezzled money from the association.

He put that theory to the test. "I know you're stealing from the HOA. Where do you keep the money?"

Her eyes flashed wide with surprise.

"No lies now, dear Fani." His fake cockney accent almost broke because he wanted to laugh at the look on her face.

She gasped. Shivered violently. "Who are you? How did you—"

He backhanded her hard enough to send her stumbling sideways. "Fani, my dear, you're not following the rules." He loved the sound of his British accent especially when chiding people.

Sobbing, she pointed upstairs. "I have a safe in my office. That's where I keep my valuables."

Decker gripped her long hair close to the roots. He pointed her at the stairs and pushed her ahead of him. She stumbled forward, her house slippers falling off. He felt invincible. Flushed with arousal even though she certainly wasn't up to his standards.

He wanted to take her right then and there. But he also didn't want to leave a trail of DNA. As much as he wanted to ravish her, his logical side overcame his primal instincts. He had to remain disciplined.

He stopped at the top of the stairs. "Where is the office?"

She whimpered. "At the end of the hallway."

The bedroom was through the first door. The television was on but the show on the screen was paused. She'd thrown a wine glass at him. That meant she'd gone downstairs for more wine, not because she heard him.

He could ask her if that was accurate, but it really wasn't important. Decker pushed her down the hall and into the office. He turned on the light. It was a decently sized room.

There was a filing cabinet on the wall next to the window. A desk with a computer monitor on top. Under the desk was a computer tower. There was a shelf with some odds and ends on it and a couple of books about taxes.

There was one thing he didn't see. "Where's the safe?"

"In the closet."

He shoved her toward the closet door. "Open it." He drew his compact Glock. Aimed it at her. "Don't do anything idiotic."

Fani recoiled away from the gun. Tears dripped down her cheeks. "I won't!"

She opened the closet door with trembling hands. Inside was a large gray safe with a keypad. She punched in a combination. It beeped and clicked. She opened it. Inside was a plastic box filled with stacks of cash.

The bills were all Benjamins. Hundred-dollar notes. Next to the box was a wooden jewelry box. "Take out the cash box and the jewelry box."

Fani took them out one at a time and set them on the desk. She was shaking with fear. Crying. "How did you know about the money?"

"Your computer records." It was a wild guess, but it stood a good chance of being correct.

"Y-you hacked my computer?"

"I've been watching you for a while, Fani. I have copies of all the records." Decker saw a way to get what he wanted without penalty. He saw from the look in her eyes that it would work.

She shook with sobs. "That's everything, I swear. Please take it and go."

"I almost sent the information to the police. Instead, I decided to take the spoils for myself."

Fani looked confused. Like she wanted to ask a question but knew better. She wanted to know if he lived in the neighborhood, probably. The British accent was also confusing her. She looked down and noticed his arousal. She gasped.

He couldn't blame her. He was well above average size. Well above average intellect and physical prowess.

"I'll tell you what, Fani." He put a hand around her throat. "You can keep doing what you're doing, and I won't tell anyone. The police don't need to find out and neither do the other neighbors." He worded it to make her think he lived there.

Her eyes widened. She seemed to believe him, but she was worried. "Why?"

"There's something you can do for me."

She trembled because she already knew what it was.

Decker looked at the cash. At the jewelry. He had no interest in the latter because it was too much trouble to fence. Then he saw what he really wanted sitting in an inbox on top of the desk. His ticket. He made a show of looking through the papers.

There were six more tickets under his. "You're worse than the city government, do you know that?"

She said nothing.

"Have you entered all of this into the computer yet?"

She shook her head. "No. I wait until they pay."

"Then you falsify the payments in the accounting software."

She nodded. "Yes."

He crumpled the tickets. "I'm going to give these poor people a reprieve." He stuffed the crumpled paper into the cash box. Then he pointed to the door. "Now, let's go pay off your debt to society."

She walked to the door. Turned toward the bedroom. She was shivering violently. He was throbbing so hard he could hardly bear it. He hadn't brought any protection with him, but he couldn't control it anymore.

Fani entered the bedroom. She took off her robe and undergarments without being told to. She lay face down on the bed. He shivered in anticipation. Pulled his pants down to his ankles. Set the gun on the dresser. Took what was his.

When he was done, he had a talk with Fani. Told her she could never talk about what happened, or he would send her files to the police and everyone in the neighborhood. She would be ruined. Considering how she'd submitted to him and how horrified she looked at the thought of being found out, he knew she would never talk.

He took the box of cash and the crumpled tickets. Fun money was always nice. He could get his girl something nice. Something unexpected.

Most importantly, he had the ticket with his license plate on it. There would be no record of his rental car having been here. The scene would be clean once he finished with his primary objective.

CHAPTER 12

Carver stared at the woman's ID.

He'd seen countless variations of it. This one had a picture, a hologram, and a chip. It had a magnetic strip on the back and a mailing address at the bottom in case the ID was lost and found.

The picture on the front matched the face of the hogtied woman on the floor. Her hair was black, eyes dark brown. Height and weight were nearly identical to the fake IDs. Five feet, seven inches, a hundred and forty-five pounds.

The name was Liana Cardoso. That was her real name. And this ID was issued by the Department of Defense. It was a special section DoD card. It correlated with the other ID behind it. The one issued by the National Security Agency.

Carver whistled. "Why did the high and mighty NSA decide to send an agent to Morganville?" He wasn't expecting an answer, but he could make a pretty good guess about the answer.

Liana glowered at him from the floor.

"I clearly underestimated who you are," Carver said. "You probably knew I was outside. Hidden cameras or gut instinct?"

"I heard something and turned around when I was taking out the trash. I saw you sneaking inside." She laughed sarcastically. "If lumbering around like a giant could be considered sneaking."

Carver didn't remember making a sound, but he'd been visible in the garage for several seconds when sneaking inside. She might have glanced back and seen him. At this point, it wasn't important.

He put the IDs on the counter. He walked to Liana. Gripped her wrists and ankles and picked her up. She grunted in pain but held it in better than most people would. That told him something about her. She was trained to resist physical pain.

Knowing who she worked for answered other questions. Told him more about who she was and what kind of training she'd taken to have this career. But it didn't tell him anything about what he really needed to know.

He set her back down. She bucked and wriggled, trying to break the segment holding her wrists and ankles together. Carver let her have at it. She finally stopped and lay gasping on the floor like a fish out of water.

"Liana, a friend of mine came through town a few weeks ago."

"Who is your friend?"

"I think you know who she is. I think her coming to town has something to do with Holly Robinson and Ritter no longer being at the police station."

Liana craned her neck, trying to give him a shrewd look, but it was hard to do from her position. "I would be willing to share information, provided you do the same."

"I could just torture it out of you."

"You can try, but I think you'll find I have a very high pain tolerance."

Carver studied her face. Her eyes were hard. Not because she was angry. Because she was determined. Driven. What was driving her? Her career? Ideology? "Let's test your pain tolerance."

She bared her teeth. "Go for it, big guy."

He heard something in her voice. It wasn't desperation. It was determination. Maybe a bit of resignation too. She didn't give off the same kind of psycho killer vibes that the assassin from Miami had.

That didn't mean she wasn't dangerous. It didn't mean she wasn't crooked and acting hand-in-hand with Enigma or some other corrupt government operation.

Carver had dealt with countless people from the three-letter agencies. The CIA, mostly. An inflated ego usually came with a federal badge. Those who wielded them thought they were above local law enforcement.

They thought they were smarter than the average bear. Invincible and infallible. They were typically far more politically motivated than cops.

He sensed that in Liana, but there was something else. Something more human and pleading in her gaze even though she was trying to cover it up.

Carver drew his survival knife. He put the tip to her throat. Right against the carotid artery. Liana went still. Sweat beaded on her forehead. She didn't beg for her life. Didn't say anything. Just stared straight ahead.

"I'm going to ask one more time about my friend."

"Go fuck yourself, big boy."

He grinned. Repressed a laugh. Then he got serious and hoped he wasn't about to make a fatal error. He slashed with the knife. She flinched. Gasped.

The knife cut through the cuff holding the ankle and wrist cuffs together. Her legs went flat. She blinked. Turned her head sideways and looked at him. Her eyes narrowed.

Carver rolled her onto her back. He picked her up and placed her in a seated position on the couch, her arms still behind her. He was taking a chance, but he was also keeping the odds in his favor.

A new question popped into his head. A question that hadn't been all that important until he'd seen the way she reacted to his actions. Any sane agent would have called for backup the moment they knew someone was in their house.

She'd already asked him if he was Carver. He hadn't answered, but that was probably an answer in and of itself. She'd clearly seen him entering the house. Probably guessed who he was just from his size.

If that was the case, she would have known that he was high on the most-wanted list. She would have known that he was potentially dangerous. Despite all of that, she hadn't called for backup.

That hinted at one of two things. Either she thought she was good enough to take him or she didn't want anyone else to know he was in town. Considering the special forces squad seemingly at her disposal, that was very strange.

So, why had she done what she'd done? Why had she left herself alone and vulnerable?

Liana stared at him. Some of the hardness was gone, but there was still mistrust in those eyes. Like any good agent, she was holding her cards close to her chest.

Carver found a chair in the corner of the kitchen. He carried it over and set it down in front of the couch. Sat down and faced Liana. "You didn't call for backup. Otherwise, this place would be swarming with agents. You have your own personal agenda."

"Is there a question in there somewhere?"

"What's your agenda?"

She blinked a few times. Like she hadn't expected that question. "You'll share information with me?"

"I will, as long as I think you're telling the truth."

"A high-value target was seen in this area. I was sent to take the target into custody."

"Who is the target?" He already suspected the answer, but he wanted specifics, not ambiguities.

"Paola Barros."

"Why is she a high-value target?"

Liana hesitated. She looked uncertain. "She is only valuable because she could draw out a higher value target."

"She's bait."

Liana nodded. "For you."

Carver thought as much. "Okay, it's your turn to ask a question." He'd learned that letting someone ask questions was another way to learn valuable information. It could tell him what she was looking for and whose orders she was following.

She took a moment as if considering her question. "How did you know Paola was here? And do you know where she went?"

"Why does that matter anymore? I thought my capture was the end goal."

Liana bit her lower lip. "Not for me it isn't."

That look of determination Carver had seen in her eyes made more sense now. She was acting on official orders, but there was a personal element to it as well. "I don't know where she went. Her last known location was here."

"You think she's still here?"

Carver shook his head. "Doubtful. And since you're still looking for her that means she's still free and alive."

Liana looked into Carver's eyes. Like she was trying to see if something was there but couldn't find it.

Carver didn't know what she was looking for. "What's wrong?"

"What do you intend to do with me?"

"Good question. I don't want the NSA hunting me down once I leave."

"They've been hunting for you, and they'll continue no matter what happens to me."

Carver noted that she spoke of her own agency in third person. "Don't you mean 'we'?"

"Yeah, sure." She sighed. "I don't know anymore."

"Why is this personal for you?"

"It's not personal."

"It obviously is." Carver waved a hand around the room. "Otherwise, the cavalry would have arrived by now."

Liana stared so hard at the floor it looked like she was trying to burn a hole through it. She stiffened her shoulders. Seemed to come to some internal decision. "I need to talk to Paola. She has information I need. Information I don't want anyone else to know."

"Because you don't trust your superiors?"

"I don't trust certain elements within the agency."

Carver studied her face. "Tell me about Enigma."

She tried to control her reaction, but her eyes twitched ever so slightly. She seemed to realize she'd failed to hide the emotional response. "How do you know about them?"

"I know that they have infiltrated a great many federal, state, and local governments, agencies, and political positions. But they operate in cells, so I only know bits and pieces."

"You're looking to take them down?"

Carver shook his head. "I'm looking to enjoy time on a beach. But people don't want to leave me and mine alone."

"You consider Paola yours?"

"I consider her someone who deserves to live her life." He shrugged. "I guess it's not that simple."

"It never is." Something softened in her face, her eyes. "It's hard to read you, but I believe you."

Carver found it hard to read her too. He'd nearly lost life and limb because he'd trusted the words of someone he shouldn't have. This woman was an NSA agent. She might be trying to win him over so she could gain his trust and achieve her end objectives.

He would operate under that assumption unless something definitively proved otherwise. In the meantime, he would glean whatever information he could from her. "You're Brazilian?"

"I'm American. Second generation. My parents are from Brazil."

"What's your connection to the Herrada Cartel?"

She looked disgusted. "None. You think just because I'm of Brazilian descent that I'm connected to a cartel?"

"I'm asking because there's evidence the cartel knows or knew Paola's location and is going after her."

Liana looked down at her lap. "I don't have a connection. But I think I know how they found the subject."

"How is that?"

She looked up. Met his gaze. "How did you know they knew?"

Carver decided it was best to be forthright. "An associate of mine downloaded information from a cartel laptop and discovered Paola was on their radar."

"Leon Fry?"

He nodded. "Your turn."

"The subject was living in Miami."

Carver frowned. "Paola was living in Miami?"

"Yes."

Carver tried to process that. Paola never once mentioned living in Miami.

Liana studied him. "You seem surprised."

"I am a little. I can't blame her, though. It's a nice place."

"It has one of the largest Brazilian communities in the States."

Carver hadn't been aware of that, but it made sense. It was nice and warm there. Plenty of beaches. Wanting to be close to the Brazilian community made sense too. But it was also more dangerous for obvious reasons.

The cartel was sure to have connections in all major Brazilian communities. Not just business connections, but family connections. Mothers, fathers, sisters, brothers, aunts, uncles, cousins, children.

Liana took his silence as an indication to resume talking. "She was in a relationship."

Carver wasn't surprised that Paola had found someone. She was an attractive woman with a lot to offer. Carver just hadn't had a lot to offer her. Not in the ways that really mattered.

Liana noticed his demeanor. "She means a lot to you."

"More than most." Carver wasn't sure why. He'd liked other women he'd met as well, but Paola was the one who got stuck in his head. "How do you know this?"

"Because I know her boyfriend."

Carver raised an eyebrow. "How do you know him?"

Liana's gaze went distant. "I'm not sure I should answer that."

"It's no coincidence you know this guy, is it?" Carver mulled it over. "He's one of your people, isn't he?"

"What do you mean by that?"

"NSA."

She hesitated and that told him all he needed to know.

"Is he Brazilian too?"

"He's an American of Brazilian descent."

"How many Americans of Brazilian descent does the NSA have?"

"I don't know."

Carver watched her closely. "Takes a Brazilian to catch a Brazilian?"

"Something like that."

"What happened to make Paola leave Miami?"

Liana tried to move her arms, but her hands were bound behind her back. "My hands are falling asleep."

"I feel safer with you tied up."

Her lips curled up. "You're a big boy. Surely, you can handle little old me."

"Size doesn't matter. I learned that the hard way a few times."

Liana laughed without humor. "A former special forces guy who doesn't overestimate himself. How refreshing."

"I simply don't underestimate my opponents. At least, I try not to."

"Fine, I get it. Can you at least secure my hands in front of me instead? This is extremely uncomfortable."

"You seem capable of handling pain."

"That doesn't mean I enjoy being in pain, you idiot."

Carver stood. Gripped her under the arms. Lifted her into a standing position. He turned her around. Cut off the zip cuffs. Backed away. She massaged her wrists. The ligature marks were deep and set in the skin.

He motioned at the couch. "Have a seat."

Liana raised an eyebrow. Sat down. Held out her wrists.

Carver pulled his seat a little farther away. Sat down.

She worked her jaw back and forth. Lowered her wrists. "Thanks, I guess."

"The NSA is notoriously compartmentalized. Information sharing among operatives isn't exactly their strong suit."

Liana tilted her head slightly. "What are you getting at?"

Carver imagined the setup. Imagined some guy from the NSA pretending to be interested in Paola. Fooling her into a relationship under false pretenses. His fists clenched reflexively. That was a guy he'd like to have a word with.

"You look angry."

"Your acquaintance lured Paola into a fake relationship. Something went wrong. She ran. Came here. I want to know why she ran."

"You're deceptively smart for someone who looks like a giga-Chad."

"I don't know what that means."

She rubbed her wrists again. Stared into the distance for a long time. Took a breath and nodded. "Something did go wrong."

Carver could guess what happened. "Your guy is dead."

"His name is—was—Lucas."

"Keep going."

Liana bit her lower lip. "I received a text in the middle of the night a little over a month ago. It was from Lucas. It was addressed to Paola, but he copied me on it."

"Just you?"

She nodded. "Just me."

"You know each other outside of work. He trusts you."

"Yes." She seemed to be fighting to control her emotions. "He told Paola that he'd gained her trust and affections under false pretenses. That he wanted to gain her trust so he could use her as bait to lure someone close to her."

Carver assumed that someone was him.

Liana paused as if waiting for him to ask. When he didn't, she stated the obvious. "He wanted to lure you in."

Carver just nodded.

"He said if we received that text, it meant he was dead."

"Message in a bottle." Carver nodded. "Good idea."

Liana continued. "Lucas had a deep personal hatred for the cartel. He thought Paola could also help him locate more of their facilities in the U.S. Help him cripple their operations."

"Why did he think Paola would know that?"

She shrugged. "I don't know. I don't have access to his files."

"And he wanted to lure me in for the NSA?"

She nodded.

"Why is the NSA interested in me?"

"I don't know. I just follow orders."

Carver let that hang in the air for a moment. He'd been in her shoes before. Following orders. Being a good soldier. "How did you get assigned to the search for Paola?"

"I volunteered. There aren't many field agents who speak fluent Portuguese. Most agents with Latino roots speak Spanish."

"Portuguese is a whole other animal," Carver said. "Some words look the same, but the pronunciation is different."

Liana nodded. "Brazilians can understand Spanish, but Hispanics can't understand Portuguese."

Carver thought of several questions. He discarded most of them as irrelevant. They were personal questions. Questions that he probably didn't want answered anyway. He needed three things. Lucas's starting place. The timeline from there to here. A trail to follow since then.

He started at the beginning. "How did Lucas find Paola?"

"I don't know. The file said a CI gave it to him."

"A confidential informant?"

She nodded.

"How long ago did he start this operation?"

"He went to Miami about five months ago. Started building the relationship then."

Carver thought about where he was five months ago. It was after he'd left Florida. Right around the time Paola said she was travelling the country. In reality, she was in Miami. Hell, he and Paola were probably both in Miami at the same time.

That was right around the time Carver was working as a bouncer at Club Periclean. Around the time an assassin nearly took his life.

Paola had left him in Clearwater and gone to Miami. He'd followed her there and hadn't even known it. She'd known he was there because he'd texted her. Told her it was nice. She'd told him she was travelling.

It had been for the best, all things considered. If he'd discovered that she was also in Miami, he probably would have left to give her space even though Miami was a big place.

None of that was important now. What mattered was finding her and making sure she kept breathing. He stopped dwelling on the past and got his mind back in the present.

Carver didn't think Liana knew the answer to the next question, but he asked anyway. "Where do you think Paola went from here?"

"I don't know. By the time I was stationed here, I think Paola had already come and gone."

"So, this is a dead end."

Liana nodded.

"If that's the case, why are you still here?"

She stared at him. "Waiting on you, of course."

CHAPTER 13

Carver had taken the bait.

He was right where the NSA wanted him to be. He should be a prisoner in the back of a van right about now. But he wasn't.

"I'm here. Now what?"

Liana shook her head. "I don't know."

"You wanted to take me down by yourself. That tells me a lot."

"Yeah? What does it tell you?"

"You're personally invested. Otherwise, your team would have the house surrounded by now."

"Who's to say they don't?"

Carver had considered that possibility. Maybe Liana wasn't the one being interrogated here. Maybe she was hoping to draw out a bad guy monologue where he told her everything she wanted to know. Maybe the NSA wanted Carver and Paola and he was the key to that plan.

Unfortunately, Carver didn't know squat. Liana already knew he didn't know where Paola was. So, if this was a reverse interrogation, it wouldn't accomplish much. She should have realized that already and given the signal for her people to come get him.

Liana seemed to take his silence as doubt. "Obviously you don't believe that, or I'd be dead already."

"Not necessarily." Carver shrugged. "I might just punch you in the face. Break your nose. No need to kill you."

"That's sweet of you."

"I'm a sweet guy."

She bit her lower lip. "Look, maybe we can help each other. Let's find Paola together."

Carver considered his next steps. Liana didn't know anything. She couldn't help him if she wanted to. For all he knew she was trying to gain his trust like Lucas had with Paola.

She wanted him to think she was useful. That she could help him. When really, she was embedding herself with the enemy. Using him to help her find Paola. Once Paola and Carver were together, the trap would be sprung.

Then Carver and Paola would both be in NSA custody.

One way or the other, Carver needed to make up his mind and leave. "Lucas trusted you enough to send you the same text he sent Paola. He knew you'd have his back."

"What are you getting at?"

"You had the chance to call for backup and you didn't. I want to know why."

Liana looked away from his gaze. She stared at the floor. "I—I don't know if I can trust my own people. I think someone betrayed Lucas. I think they'll do the same to me."

It was exactly what Carver would expect to hear from someone trying to gain his trust. "You think someone in the NSA told the cartel where to find Lucas?"

"It's the only thing that makes sense."

"If she was hanging out in little Brazil then the odds of her being seen by cartel people is much higher than if she was anywhere else."

"I realize that, but as a Brazilian she'd also blend in. There are plenty of women who resemble Paola."

Carver didn't think so, but he kept that opinion to himself. "There's more you're not telling me."

"The Herrada cartel wants to find Paola and the other victims from Morganville. They want their money back. They want to punish anyone and everyone who took their money." She met his gaze again. "Paola is the key to all of that. I don't want that to happen."

"If the cartel has a mole, then you think they'll know what you know." Carver could see it now. "You thought if you captured me single-handedly, that I'd help you find Paola. But what makes you think she has any connections with the sex-trafficking victims from Morganville? Some of them hate her. They view her as complicit in the crimes."

Liana pressed her lips together. "After Lucas gained Paola's trust, she eventually told him about Morganville. She told him that she formed a network with the other women so they could watch each other's backs in case the cartel found any of them."

Carver didn't like that. He didn't like it one bit. Maintaining contact with the other victims made Paola extremely vulnerable. Paola had never mentioned keeping in touch with the women during their time together.

"You don't give away much, but I can tell you don't like what she did."

"I don't."

"There's more," Liana said.

"More what?"

"About the victim network."

"Does it matter?"

She nodded. "Yeah. It matters a lot."

"Explain."

"The Morganville victims were kept anonymous. Their identities were only known to Gavin Ritter and Holly Robinson."

"I think the FBI would have something to say about that."

"I'm sure they did, although I'm not privy to what was said in backroom meetings between federal agents and the local Morganville police."

"Was there anything in Lucas's files?"

She shook her head. "He did say something in the text he sent to me and Paola."

"Is that text on your phone?"

"No. I deleted it immediately."

"You work for the NSA. You know deleting it from your phone doesn't protect you."

"I know. But Lucas sent it from a number I didn't recognize. He probably had a burner phone. So, there's a good chance they won't even know he sent it to me." Liana gave Carver a grim look. "He said the list of women had been leaked. That the cartel had some of their identities. He wasn't sure if their locations were known."

"And that's when you asked to be tasked to this assignment."

Liana nodded. "They put me here with a DEA squad."

Carver raised an eyebrow. "You're talking about the men who showed up to Holly's house after I triggered the alarm?"

"Yes."

"They're not DEA."

"How would you know?"

Carver shrugged. "I just know. Unless the DEA has a squad of former special forces guys, these aren't your average feds."

"You're probably right." Liana sighed. "DEA special operators are usually just glorified cops. These guys were something else."

"What happened to Ritter?" Carver asked.

"He retired the minute we rolled into town. Said he was too old for this shit and turned in his badge."

"And Holly?"

Liana laughed wryly. "I don't know exactly, but I have my suspicions."

"Tell me."

"She didn't show up at the office one day. She usually came to the office every morning to do paperwork."

"I can't imagine there was much work for her to do."

"You're right about that. This place is practically a ghost town."

"Did you find her?"

"I radioed her. She said she needed a personal day." Liana shrugged. "The GPS on her unmarked car showed it was at her house."

Carver just listened.

"That night, the Skylark Motel caught fire. Emergency services responded. Most of the police department showed up there."

"It was a diversion."

"Yep." She pressed her lips together. "The Whittaker mansion went up in flames right about the same time. The gas lines exploded. The victims who were living there were gone."

"No bodies?"

"Two female skeletons." Liana pursed her lips. "The house burned so hot that the DNA in the bones was useless."

"So, you don't know if they belonged to the women or not?"

She shook her head. "We also couldn't find evidence any bodies had gone missing from morgues recently. The skeletons were the same heights as the women. So, they're presumed dead."

"And yet, you stayed in town."

"Yes, because we had nowhere else to go. We put alarms on Robinson's house and surveillance on Ritter's place, but until you rolled into town, we found nothing."

"What's your relationship with that DEA special squad? Are you friendly with them?"

She laughed. "Hardly. I was told to stay put. To pretend I'm a dispatcher at the police station. That's been my life for the last month. I don't know where they're based. I don't know what they do in their spare time. All I know is that the two times I've rung the alarm bell, they came running."

"I assume one of those times was at Holly's."

"Yes. And the other time was when Paola was spotted in Morganville. Supposedly spotted, at least."

"Where?"

"At Spencer's Diner north of town."

"The one near the Whittaker mansion?"

She nodded. "If it was her, I think she was going to check on the women at the mansion."

"Was that before or after it burned down?"

"Just before."

If that had been Paola, it told Carver two things. One, Paola knew the women were in danger. Two, Paola and Holly probably had something to do with the motel burning down and the Whittaker mansion blowing up.

Holly had connections. She could have found two bodies to leave in the mansion and make it look like the women there were dead.

"Why weren't there cameras covering the mansion and Holly's place?"

"We did have cameras watching Robinson's house and the mansion. But they kept getting taken down." Liana laughed to herself. "In retrospect, I think Robinson had a signal detector and kept disabling the cameras, so we stopped replacing them."

"Wired cameras with local storage could have solved that problem."

"I suggested that, but no one saw value in cameras they couldn't watch remotely."

"There's always value." Carver knew many ways to hide wireless signals. The easiest was simply to use a wired camera and a few hundred feet of cable with a wireless access point at the far end. He wasn't about to share that knowledge with her.

"Okay, so now what?" Liana looked up at him. "You got your answers."

"Yep." Carver still didn't know the answer to the most important question. "Where did Paola go after Morganville?"

"I really don't know."

Carver had a strong feeling that was the only reason Paola had come here. The catalyst had been the murder of Lucas. He just needed to confirm that. "How was Lucas killed?"

Liana stiffened. "He killed himself."

"I thought the cartel captured him."

"They did. He had a C4 charge. He blew himself up after they took him. Killed six cartel thugs."

Carver whistled. "Now, that's commitment. What was he doing with a block of C4?"

"He told me he always kept one on hand in case he found a cartel operation he wanted to blow up."

"And the NSA armory just gave it to him?"

"I suppose so. I really don't know how he got it."

"Paola got his message in a bottle and bailed."

Liana nodded. "Yep."

"She came here, coordinated with Holly to fake the deaths of the other women."

"That's my bet."

"Then they took off for parts unknown."

Liana shrugged. "Maybe not to parts unknown. Maybe to parts known. Parts where other women in their network are hiding."

Carver wondered why Paola hadn't simply texted the women in Morganville. Told them to leave town. Maybe it wasn't that simple. He put himself in her shoes. Envisioned what she'd done after receiving Lucas's text message.

Paola probably left Miami immediately. She found a cheap motel several hours down the road. A place that didn't require an ID. She was probably crying. Probably angry with herself that Lucas had fooled her for so long. She probably thought about calling Carver for help.

But she hadn't.

The last three phone locations showed her trail. She'd gone from Miami, through Atlanta, and to Morganville. Maybe she didn't have direct lines of communication with the women in the mansion. Maybe she'd contacted Holly or Ritter in advance. Maybe asked them to warn the women.

Holly probably came up with the idea to fake their deaths. Blowing up a mansion with cadavers in it didn't seem like something Paola would have considered. Maybe it had been Ritter's idea.

Paola arrived in town. They wanted a diversion to keep the firemen from responding to the mansion fire. To make sure the cadavers were burned down to the bone. Someone decided burning down the motel where Carver killed all those men would be a nice touch.

Someone started the motel fire. Once emergency responders were busy with that, Holly or Ritter knocked a gas hose loose in the mansion. They let it build to critical levels and blew the mansion's roof off.

Then Paola, Holly, and the women piled up in a car and went somewhere. Ritter wouldn't have gone with them. He was an older guy. He was married. It was doubtful his wife would want to go on the run at their age.

Carver plotted it out in his mind. Tried to imagine Paola's next steps. Had she gone with the other women? It seemed doubtful. She probably asked Holly to get the victims to safety. Then Paola went to the next closest person on the list.

Carver had a good idea where that would be. He remembered one of the women talking about her hometown. He remembered her saying she loved the Brazilian culture there and thought Paola would like it.

He couldn't recall the woman's name. He remembered she was black and that was about it. He remembered the name of her hometown, though. It was part of metro Atlanta. Just an hour and a half away from Morganville.

The city's name was Marietta. He remembered Paola talking about it during their time together. She said when she was trapped at the factory, she dreamed of being able to go to Marietta and get some real Brazilian food.

"Are you deciding whether to kill me or not?" Liana sounded calm but not resigned. Her hands were free. She knew she had a fighting chance if she got to Carver before he drew a gun or knife.

Something caught Carver's eye. Something outside. The streetlights were out. They'd been on moments earlier. Power was still on in the house. His own reflection against a backdrop of pitch black was what had caught his attention.

How long had they been out? He didn't know. He'd checked his six fewer times than he should have. The last time had been maybe five minutes earlier. Which meant the streetlights had been out for at least that long.

More movement got his attention. Liana lunging for the other end of the couch. Her hands went under the cushion and came back with a compact Ruger 9mm. Carver was already moving. Already drawing his own weapon.

He wasn't moving toward her. He was moving sideways. Toward the light switch.

"Stop!" Liana had her gun on him already. He was so close it would be like hitting the broad side of a barn.

Carver didn't stop. He pressed himself against the wall. Flicked off the light switch. The den went dark, but the kitchen lights were still on. "Get down!"

"Get down for what?" Liana kept the gun trained on him. "I'll shoot you if you don't comply with my orders!"

"Shoot me then." Carver ran to the stairwell and turned off the light. It was dark enough inside to see outside. He pulled the monocular from his back pocket. Turned on night vision. He didn't see anything. No movement.

That meant it was too late. They were already at the house.

Carver did a mental count. Eight men, minimum. The same as the ones who'd come to Holly's place. He couldn't see them yet, but he knew they were there. Preparing to break down a door and enter.

"I thought you didn't call backup," Carver said.

Liana's gaze flicked to the window. Her eyes widened. "The streetlights—"

"Yep."

She rolled off the couch. Onto the floor. Grabbed something from beneath the couch. A knife flashed. Cut her bonds.

Carver had underestimated her. "I should have known you'd have stashed weapons."

"Do I look like the kind of person who stashes weapons?"

"In retrospect, yes."

She low crawled to his position.

"Why are you doing that? Those are your people outside."

"I didn't call them," she hissed. "Something doesn't make sense. What's taking them so long to breach?"

"They want to synchronize with their people in the back."

Something smashed through the window in the den. Another projectile smashed through the rear window and fell behind the couch. Carver covered his eyes and ducked into the bathroom to the right.

Flashbangs exploded. Smoke flooded the room. There was the smashing of wood. Of glass. Carver was already running. He ran into the utility room at the end of the hallway and toward the window there.

The vinyl windows were triple-paned. He could probably dive through one, but the utility room window was about six feet off the ground. He knew because he'd looked at it on his way to the backyard.

He didn't feel like risking a head injury by crashing his skull into the tempered glass. He didn't want to cripple himself or risk a broken neck by diving head-first through the window either.

Carver flicked open the locks. Raised the window. He slipped out feet first. Hung from the sill. Dropped to the ground. He dashed across twenty feet of open ground and ducked into the woods. A shadow moved from behind a tree.

He didn't see it so much as he sensed it. His arm reflexively swung out. His forearm struck the end of a rifle barrel. He couldn't see it, but that was what it felt like. Two suppressed shots coughed a few inches from his head.

He ducked. Lunged forward and upward. Hit the shooter in the midsection. Heard a man grunt. He felt the body armor blunt his blow. It was too dark to make out anything but now he had his hands on the man.

Body armor usually protected the vital organs. Wearing pads on the legs was typically too bulky and unwieldy. Carver gripped the soft, unprotected spot a few inches below the armor. In other words, he grabbed the man by the balls.

He squeezed hard. The man shouted in pain. Carver reached up. Felt night vision goggles on the man's face. He yanked them up and off. Kneed the guy hard in the crotch for good measure. This time, the man doubled over.

Carver sensed the guy was maybe a head shorter than him. He was loaded down with body armor and weapons. He was wearing a helmet. Now he was as blind as Carver. Knocking him out with a blow to the head wasn't realistic.

Even if he wasn't wearing a helmet it wasn't all that easy to knock someone out short of killing them. Carver kneed the guy one more time. Wrapped an arm around his neck. Squeezed hard.

The other man struggled. His gloved hands clawed at Carver's forearms. If he was smart, he had a knife sheathed on one of his thighs. He'd pull it and try to knife Carver in the leg, the abdomen, anywhere he could.

Carver felt the other man tense. He couldn't see what he was doing, but his right arm was moving out and away. That was the hand with the knife. Carver yanked hard. Swung the man around by his neck.

The man gurgled. Went limp. Carver gave it another couple of seconds then released him. He lowered the body to the ground. Checked the pulse. It was still there. The next few minutes would determine if that remained the case.

Carver felt the ground around him. Found the NV goggles. Put them on. They surprisingly weren't the kind designed to swing down from the helmet. These strapped around the helmet.

He saw the guy on the ground. The face matched one of the men he'd seen raiding Holly's house. It stood to reason it was the same team. This guy was watching the outside perimeter. There was probably someone on the other side too.

These guys were special operators. No doubt about it. They definitely weren't regular soldiers. They also weren't aboveboard operators. They were black ops or maybe even further off the books like dark ops.

Carver was just guessing, but he felt reasonably certain that they weren't operating even remotely inside the law.

The rest of the assault team had split in two and breached from the front and the back. Left no avenue for escape. At least, not for most people. Carver wasn't most people, but it had still been a close call.

He studied the downed operator. Picked up the rifle. It looked like an M4 CQBR. Basically, an M4 with a slightly shorter barrel and stock for close quarters combat. Some of that compactness had been compromised with the addition of a suppressor.

It was a good house-clearing rifle. Better than a pistol if you had a lot of targets. Worse than a pistol if you wanted to blind fire around corners or navigate tight spots.

The knife was on the ground next to the operator's hand. Carver had probably just narrowly avoided getting stabbed. He removed the man's helmet. Found an earbud. Put it in his ear.

A man was shouting. "Where is he, you stupid bitch?"

A woman groaned. Tried to talk. She sounded disoriented. Dazed. Probably due to the flashbangs and smoke grenades.

"They told us she couldn't be trusted, man." That was another man's voice. "She's got her own agenda."

"Braggs is right," another man said. "She's not one of us."

"Yeah, but she drew him in. He's got to be here somewhere." Equipment rustled. "There's a basement door. Go check it." He paused. "Janowitz, check in."

"Clear," another man responded.

"Adler, check in."

There was a long silence. Carver realized he must be talking to the unconscious man. He kept his voice to a harsh whisper. "Clear."

"Gotta be the basement," Braggs said.

"Do it by the numbers," the apparent squad leader said.

"What about her?" Braggs said.

"She's outlived her usefulness," the squad leader said. "Carver isn't getting out of here."

Braggs laughed. "We'll just say Carver killed her."

"Sounds good to me," the squad leader replied. "Stack up on the basement door. There's no other way out according to the schematics. That means we will be in a bottleneck. I want two flashers and two smokers in the channel."

Another man spoke. "There's no wall on the right side. We've got an open stretch."

The squad leader shouted, probably down the basement stairs. "Carver, if you're down there, you might as well give up. We've got orders to bring you in alive if possible. I'll give you one chance to comply. If you don't, you're playing a losing hand."

Carver made up his mind. He put a bullet in the unconscious man's head. He circled around the front of the house. The lights were on inside now. He had a clear view of the operators. Two were positioned outside the basement door, flash grenades in hand.

The squad leader was still talking. Carver picked him out of the crowd. Saw the guy who volunteered to kill Liana standing next to him. Saw Liana sprawled on the floor. She looked unconscious or dead. Her head moved slightly. She was studying the operators.

She wasn't as injured as she looked. Probably faking. Playing opossum. The rest of the operators were lining up near the basement door. Carver counted six. Total of eight, including the dead man and the guy on the other side of the house.

Carver rocked out the rifle magazine. Standard .556 rounds. Not armor piercing. Armor piercing rounds could be dangerous in close quarters. They would punch straight through walls, often striking unintended targets.

They were mostly useful against armored targets. A lot less useful against soft targets. Bullets were supposed to make big holes. Bounce around inside the target. Turn their insides to mush. That was the point of hitting them center mass.

Since these guys were armored, armor piercing rounds would be a lot more useful to Carver right now. Shooting them center mass with standard rounds would just knock them back. Then he'd have six angry operators shooting back at him.

He could shoot the operators in the legs. He might cripple a few of them. But that was no guarantee. And they'd still be able to shoot back. Direct confrontation wasn't the best strategy here. He could practically hear Rhodes whispering that into his ears.

He had a better idea and spoke into the earbud. "Motion! Motion!" He whispered loudly to disguise his voice. "Runner headed down the side of the house toward the back."

"How in the hell?" The squad leader made a circling motion above his head. Pointed two fingers toward the back yard. "Everyone out and pursue. Braggs, put the girl down. She's a liability and we don't need her anymore."

Braggs responded. "On it."

The other five members of the squad rushed out of the splintered remains of the back doors. Braggs nudged Liana in the ribs with his boot. His lips started moving but he must have turned off his mic because Carver couldn't hear him over the headset.

Carver sighted Braggs through the aimpoint. Centered the red dot on Braggs' forehead. Braggs turned sideways. The armored helmet was in the way of a clear shot. Braggs booted Liana harder. She burst up from the floor.

Her fist shot toward Braggs' crotch. He jumped back just in time. Aimed his rifle at her. Fired.

CHAPTER 14

Braggs pulled the trigger.

At the same instant, he staggered sideways. His shot went wide. Not because his aim was off but because Carver had shot him in the side. The bullet didn't penetrate the armor, but the force knocked him off balance.

Carver aimed at Braggs' helmet. Fired again. Braggs' head rocked to the side. He stumbled sideways. His head was still in one piece, but the bullet had rung his bell hard. He was dazed and off balance.

Liana lunged for his crotch again. This time it wasn't a punch. This time she had a knife.

The blade slid in right at the top of the leg. Right where the femoral artery was easiest to hit. She twisted and yanked the knife out. The serrated top ripped clothing and flesh during its exit.

Braggs shouted and went down.

Liana stumbled through the wrecked front door. She tripped down the stairs. Rolled to the bottom. Her eyes were red and watering from the smoke and flash grenades.

Chatter exploded on the earbud. "Braggs report in. Braggs?"

Carver made a quick calculation. Something about the enemy of his enemy being a friend. He'd thought this could be a setup. Something to get him to trust Liana. But having seen Braggs try to put a bullet in her head changed things.

She wasn't an enemy. She wasn't a friend. But she was useful. He ran across the lawn, the rifle in one hand. He gripped her under the arm. Jerked her to her feet. She stumbled alongside him, barely standing up.

Carver stooped lower. Put her arm over his shoulder. Wrapped his arm around her waist and half-carried her down the street. He slung the rifle strap over his shoulder and lowered the NV goggles so he could see in the pitch black.

A boxy silhouette appeared down the road. A Sprinter van. A second one was directly behind the first. He made a beeline for them. Liana went limp. She was dead weight in his left arm.

He scooped her off the ground with his right arm and cradled her. She was tall and athletic. Not a lightweight. Not an easy person to carry like this. It was the worst possible carry if Carver needed to use the rifle.

The vans looked empty. There were no dishes or antennae on the outside, so they probably didn't have tactical stations inside. They were just troop transports with extended cargo bays, all-terrain tires, and dually wheel configurations.

He tested the front door on the first one. It was unlocked. The key fob was on top of the center console. The dome light didn't come on when he opened the door. That was standard operating procedure for a nighttime raid.

Carver checked Liana's pulse. It was rapid and felt weak. She had probably been hit by something or cut. He carried her to the passenger side. Hefted her into the seat. Buckled her in.

He saw a dark pool on her shirt right at the shoulder. He cut the shirt with his knife. Found a wound. Braggs' bullet hadn't gone as wide as Carver had thought. She was losing blood but there wasn't much he could do about it now.

Carver ran to the other van. He grabbed the key fob. Tossed it into the trees. Jabbed his knife into the sidewall of the front tire.

He noticed that no one had spoken on the headset for a full minute now. He looked back at Liana's house. Saw men storming out of the front door. They'd probably heard Braggs shout in pain.

They'd come back for their comrade. Found him in a pool of his own blood. Discovered Liana missing. They probably assumed she hadn't escaped on her own. Now they'd fan out and look for her, keeping radio silence.

Carver hopped in the driver's seat of the first van. He pressed the push start button. The engine hummed to life. It was quieter than he'd expected. Probably had extra insulation in the engine compartment to make it stealthier.

He rolled down the window. Wheeled the van around. One of the men pointed at the van. The rest of the squad raced in his direction. Bullets pinged on metal and windows. The passenger window webbed and cracked but there was no penetration.

The van was armored. The operators were firing standard rounds. Carver put the pedal to the metal. The engine growled and the van surged forward. He turned the corner. Felt the van leaning heavily. The armor protected it but weighed it down.

It handled like a full bathtub on wheels. To be fair, it probably wouldn't have handled much better without the armor. It wasn't designed for high-speed chases. It wasn't going to be his escape vehicle anyway.

A van like this was probably chipped with a GPS tracker. He drove it into the yard next to the house where his car was waiting. He parked it. Turned off the engine. Went into the back and turned on the dome light.

The light flared in the NV goggles. He yanked them up and left them on his forehead. There were bench seats in the back. Enough room to seat eight grown men, four to each side. There were hardened cases made of ABS plastic under the seats.

He took the red first-aid kit. It was the size of a carryon suitcase. He opened it. Saw everything he needed inside. He checked the other cases. Found more gear. Night vision goggles. Handguns. Ammunition.

There was a small table with a hardened laptop bolted to it. It was on but required authentication to unlock. It could probably be tracked anyway.

Carver grabbed some equipment from the hard cases. He didn't take the cases themselves. They might be tagged or chipped. He tossed what he could grab into the trunk of his car. NV goggles. A tactical monocular. Flash and smoke grenades.

He took the entire first-aid kit because it was doubtful they'd have a tracking chip in it.

He put Liana in the front seat. Buckled her in. She was still bleeding. Her pulse was faster. Weaker. She probably didn't have much time but neither did he. The operators had probably run to the other van.

The laptop in the other van probably had the GPS locator on it. They probably saw the first van sitting still at the end of the road. They were probably hoofing it toward his location right this moment.

Carver turned on the car. Pulled the NV goggles back down. Drove through the back yards with the lights off. He pulled onto the road three houses down and kept driving. He checked Liana's pulse with his right hand.

She was still among the living for now. He reached the highway. Drove northeast for ten minutes. There was a small country church on the left. He pulled into the gravel parking lot. Drove around the back. Parked.

Carver took off the NV goggles and turned on the dome light. He reclined Liana's seat all the way back. Cut her shirt open with his knife. The wound was nasty. The bullet had smashed through soft flesh.

The slug had mushroomed. Bounced off bone. Exited diagonally down. It was too large of a hole for the blood to coagulate properly. At least not without something to stanch the bleeding. He had basic first aid training, but it wasn't his forte.

He opened the first aid kit. Pulled out the gauze. Pulled out the antiseptic spray. He sprayed the wound. Liana whimpered. Her eyelids fluttered. He stuffed gauze into the wound on both sides.

It was probably the worst patch job in history, but it was all he could do for now. There was a slim chance of finding help. He didn't know anyone out here and the nearest hospital was thirty minutes away, according to the map app.

Taking her to a hospital was risky. They'd have to report a bullet wound. That would just expose her and him. Then again, maybe it wasn't true that he didn't know anyone. He knew Ritter. Ritter had a cabin not too far away, provided he hadn't abandoned it after helping Holly.

Carver only knew about the cabin because of Elena Diaz, a reporter who'd covered the aftermath of his first visit to Morganville. Thanks to Elena, he also knew that Ritter's wife was a retired nurse.

He couldn't tell if Liana was stable or not. She'd lost a lot of blood. There was a blood transfusion kit in the first-aid case. He knew how to use one, but he didn't know her blood type.

Carver had O positive blood. Liana was Latina so she probably had the same blood type. That was just based on what he remembered from basic field training. Something about O positive being the most common blood type in South America.

Maybe he wasn't remembering correctly. He knew if he pumped her full of incompatible blood, it would only make things worse. The best choice was to find Ritter's cabin.

He didn't know the address, but the street name was unusual enough to have stuck in his memory. Horse Church Road was fifteen minutes away. Ritter's cabin was near the end.

Carver started the car. Got back on the road. Gunned it north toward the destination. He got there in ten minutes. The road was paved for the first mile then turned to gravel. He counted three driveways on the paved portion and only three more over the next four miles.

He reached a dead end. There was a gate in front of the last driveway. A sign that said *Private Property No Trespassing!* There was a mailbox to the left of the gate.

Carver got out and opened the mailbox. Found a piece of junk mail inside addressed to Abe Ritter. He unlatched the gate. Swung it open.

Got back in the car and drove it another hundred yards to a two-story house at the end. It didn't look like a cabin. More like a farmhouse. Light leaked out around the curtains on the first floor.

There were floodlights and cameras on the front of the house. Ritter probably already knew someone was here. Carver figured the best way to not get shot was by getting out of the car and making himself visible.

He got out. Walked toward the house, hands up by his sides. The flood lights sensors clicked. The lights came on. He walked slowly toward the front door. It swung open a moment later and Ritter stepped outside.

"Carver?" He sounded confused. "What in the hell are you doing here?"

"Your wife is a retired nurse, right?"

He hesitated. "Yes. Are you injured?"

"No. My passenger is."

Ritter stepped onto the porch. He looked like he had a lot of questions. But he nodded. "Okay. Bring them in."

Carver scooped Liana out of the front seat. Blood had soaked into the fabric. A lot of blood. He hoped that was from before he'd tried to patch her up. She still had a pulse, but her lips looked a little blue.

He brought her inside. Ritter flinched like he'd been hit. "Why in the hell would you bring that woman into my house?"

"I'll explain."

A woman who looked a little younger than Ritter came downstairs. She gasped. "Who's that? What happened to her?"

Carver ran back to the car. Got the first aid kit. Brought it inside. "She's shot. I tried to stop the bleeding, but I'm not sure I did."

She looked it over. Nodded. "You did sloppy work, but it did the trick. Unfortunately, it looks like she lost a lot of blood already."

"I have a transfusion kit. Not sure what her blood type is, though."

She took out the kit. Pulled an envelope from behind the blood bag. Opened it and took out a stack of cards. She took one of the cards. It had four circles on it. There were cotton-tipped plastic pieces inside.

She dabbed the four swabs into Liana's blood. Used one for each of the four circles. She went through a process of spreading the blood in the circles. A few seconds later, the blood in the third circle began to look sticky.

"She's O positive." Ritter's wife nodded. "I thought she might be, but this verifies it. Unfortunately, Abe and I aren't compatible."

Carver held out his arm. "I am."

"Okay. Let's get her properly situated." She turned to Ritter. "Abe, your easy chair is the best."

He winced. "My good chair?"

His wife gave him a sharp look.

Ritter nodded sheepishly. "Okay." He went to his recliner and leaned it back until she told him to stop.

Carver picked up Liana and gently set her in the chair. Then he let Ritter's wife jab him in a vein. Blood pumped through the syringe and into the bag that came with the kit. She let it fill a little above the one-pint line.

"Do you have HIV? Any bloodborne diseases?"

Carver hadn't been expecting that question. "Does it matter at this point?"

She smiled. "No, I suppose it doesn't."

She slid the needle out of his vein. Ritter pulled a high-backed stool over. His wife hung the bag on the back of the stool. She wiped the needle with alcohol and shook her head. "I don't know why I did that. We're about to put your blood in her so it doesn't much matter that the needle was just in your arm."

"Force of habit," Ritter said.

"Old habits die hard." She pushed the needle into a vein on Liana's arm and watched the blood flow down the tube. "This might take a little while." She put a finger on Liana's neck. "Her pulse is stable at least."

Carver sat on the couch. Looked at Ritter. "Liana here told me about recent events. She said you retired."

"I thought things were finally settling down after the feds swept everything under the rug." His face soured. "Then a little over a month ago this new crew rolled into town, and I didn't have the stomach to deal with it anymore. I told Sandra I was calling it quits."

His wife gave him a look. "And about time if you ask me." She turned to Carver. "I think he just hated being home with me all the time."

Ritter cleared his throat uncomfortably. "Now, dear, you know that's not true."

She laughed. "Don't lie to me Abraham. I know you too well."

Ritter stood. "Want a drink, Carver?"

"Sure."

Ritter got three beers from the fridge. Handed them out.

Carver twisted off the lid. Took a sip. "I suppose you want to know how we ended up here."

"I do." Ritter sat on the other end of the couch. "I didn't even know you knew where I lived."

"Elena Diaz told me a long time ago. I only remembered because of the unusual street name."

He grunted. "I remember her. I thought she was going to get us all killed with her questions. Holly was about to run her out of town." Ritter gave him a look. "Now, how about you tell me why this little lady almost bled out in your car?"

Carver summed up the last few hours.

Sandra didn't look the least bit shocked. "After everything that happened when you were here the first time, I'm hardly surprised things went south again."

"Me either," Ritter said. "What that woman told you is more or less how things happened. I thought about moving across the country before someone in the cartel decided to kill me for giving away their money."

"I'm surprised they haven't done anything," Carver said. "Probably not too hard to find you."

"We didn't keep any of their money," Ritter said. "The feds investigated that thoroughly even though I was within my rights to do what I wanted with the confiscated cash."

"The cartel is going after the women." Carver sipped his beer. "Not because they need the money, but because they need to make an example out of them. They'll probably leave you alone because you are or were with law enforcement."

"I hope so." Sandra sighed and shook her head. "We have cameras and guns but there's only so much you can do to defend against people like that."

Ritter leaned forward. "You're looking for Paola?"

Carver nodded. "Did you help Holly with the Whittaker mansion? Did you help her fake their deaths?"

Ritter's mouth dropped open. "How in the hell did you know about that?"

"Liana filled in some blanks. I filled in the rest." Carver sipped his beer. "The way I figure it, Paola called Holly. Holly came up with the idea to fake the deaths."

"Actually, I did," Ritter said. "I told them I knew a professor over at the University of Georgia who could give us some cadavers that matched their sizes and shapes."

Carver nodded in approval. "I didn't know you had it in you."

"He can step up to the plate when it matters." Sandra rubbed Ritter's arm. "He's a good man."

Carver leaned back. "Whose idea was it to burn down the motel as a diversion?"

"Well, I said we'd need a diversion." Ritter chuckled. "Paola asked if burning down another building would work. I said yes. She said she wanted to burn down the motel where you killed all those soldiers."

"Holly went along with all of this?"

He nodded. "She volunteered to take the women somewhere safe afterward. She was real sad about leaving Morganville. She grew up here. Lived here all her life. But even she finally realized this place was too dangerous for her."

"Paola didn't go with them?"

"Nope. She went her own way."

"Did she say where she was going?"

He shook his head. "We all agreed it was best not to tell each other anything. Just in case."

"Smart move." Carver glanced at Liana. She didn't look much better than before, but she was still breathing. "Did Paola have a cell phone with her?"

"She sure did," Ritter said. "She kept staring at it and debating whether to contact you."

"Abe told her she should." Sandra patted his shoulder. "He said you'd be far more capable of handling things. But Paola kept saying it wasn't your problem. She felt like we had things in hand and that she'd save you for an emergency."

Carver sighed. "Most reasonable people would consider everything that happened an emergency."

"I sure as hell did, but I couldn't force the issue." Ritter shrugged. "I did what I could to help her and those women."

"I tracked her cell phone to Morganville. It went offline weeks ago."

"Probably because she accidentally dropped it in the mansion when we were getting ready to blow it up." Ritter put a hand on his chin. "There were a couple of spots in the house with flexible gas hoses. One was the utility room, and the other was the laundry room. Paola had some problems removing the laundry room line. The phone probably fell out around then."

Carver didn't like the sound of that. "Was the phone recovered?"

Ritter shook his head. "That thing probably melted down to nothing."

That at least explained why the phone had gone offline. It meant Paola had no way to contact him unless she used the emergency email backup. Judging from what Ritter had told him, she didn't plan to contact him anytime soon. Not unless things went completely off the rails.

Ritter gave him an uncertain look. "Well, now that you're here, what do you think of our plan?"

"It's good. Real good. They might assume the women and the money burned up in the fire. As long as Holly does a good job hiding those women, they might be okay."

Sandra patted Ritter's shoulder. "I'm proud of him."

Carver nodded. "He did good."

Sandra smiled. "I also know where Paola went."

Ritter flinched. "How do you know that?"

"I overheard her talking to someone on her phone the night before the mansion job. She mentioned Marietta. Said the name Aliyah a couple of times."

That jibed with what Carver thought. "That's very useful. Thanks."

"You can stay here tonight if you want," Sandra said. "I just hope those men didn't track you here."

"Doubtful, but I'll stay alert." Carver finished his beer. "I think you two should seriously consider leaving town. Not in a few days. Not in a week. But tomorrow. After the events of today, they'll be following any lead they can think of."

"You really think they'll come to us?"

"It's possible." Carver stood and stretched. "I'm going to sleep. If you can give me a pillow, I'll sleep down here."

Sandra nodded. "I get you a pillow and blankets."

Ritter looked at Liana. "What are you going to do with her?"

"Good question." Carver had already thought about it. He knew she was capable. She was motivated. She had ulterior motives.

He was bringing her with him.

CHAPTER 15

Decker was ready to pull the trigger.

He had a plan. It wasn't a great plan, but it would work. The two men who'd shown up at Butler's house probably had day jobs. They'd be gone by morning. Butler and Paola probably stayed home.

He would strike in the morning.

It wasn't ideal, but it was better than wasting another twenty-four hours sitting around. The target was in sight. All he had to do was reach out and take her.

After he left Fani's house, he climbed back over the brick wall. Went to his car. Drove to a hotel down the street. He sat in the car and messaged Angie. Told her he wouldn't be coming back to the hotel tonight.

She replied right away. *Baby, you promised to take me out!*

His jaw tightened. *It's work. No choice. I'm on a stakeout.*

Get your ass back here now! I want to go out!

Decker clenched his fists. *I told you it's a stakeout.*

You promised me a fun trip! All you've done is work! Get back here now or I'm leaving!

His face flushed with heat. He had a response typed out, but he deleted it. She wanted him back at the hotel? Fine. She was going to get what she asked for.

Decker gunned it out of the parking lot. Got on the interstate. He crossed three lanes of traffic to reach the HOV lane. It was reserved for cars with two or more passengers, but he was in a hurry. He passed the other cars like they were standing still.

A car in the HOV lane was barely going over the speed limit. He flashed his brights. They didn't move. He honked his horn. They slowed down. Flipped him off.

"You want to play that game?" Decker drew his sidearm. He veered a lane over, narrowly missing another slow-moving vehicle. He pulled up even to the car in the HOV lane. He aimed his handgun at the car.

The other driver's eyes flared wide. He slammed on the brakes. A truck plowed into his rear end. The two cars crashed into the concrete median. Decker roared with laughter. He wished he had time to stop and execute that asshole if he wasn't already dead.

He veered back across traffic and onto an exit. A right turn on the next street took him to the hotel. Decker screeched to a stop at the valet. He tossed the key to the attendant and snatched the ticket from the man's hand. He checked his phone and found several messages from Angie.

What? No response?

Come back now and take me out!

FINE! I'M LEAVING!!!

His hand tightened around the phone. His other hand clenched into a fist. He stepped into the elevator and pounded the button. This was the last time he was bringing this bitch along. Maybe the last time he'd do anything with her.

She was hot but replaceable. He'd remind her of that. He could boot her out on her ass anytime he wanted. There were plenty of gorgeous babes out there for the taking. Plenty of women who'd throw themselves at his feet.

The elevator doors opened. He stormed out. Pressed the keycard to the room door. Walked in and tried to slam the door shut but the hydraulic arm prevented it.

Angie was throwing clothes into a suitcase. She looked up and smiled sarcastically. "That's what I thought. You knew you'd better get your ass back here."

He didn't say a word. Stormed over and gripped her by the neck. Slammed her against the wall. He squeezed. "You really think you're the one in control here?" He bared his teeth in a feral grin. "Really, Angie?"

She wriggled. Tried to pry his hands from her neck. Ragged gasping escaped her throat.

He released her. She fell to her knees, gasping for air. Tears streaked black eyeliner down her cheeks. She cried out and charged toward him. He gripped her wrists and held them above her head.

She tried to knee him in the crotch. He blocked the clumsy strikes with his legs. He threw her back down on the floor. She looked up at him, face red, makeup wrecked by her tears. Decker towered over her. He was hard as a rock.

He grabbed her by the hair. Yanked her off the floor. Threw her on the bed. He pushed her down on her back. Pulled up her dress. Ripped off her panties. He held her down and bared his teeth.

"Who's in control, Angie?"

She shook with sobs. "I'm calling the police!"

"You think they'll help you?" He laughed. "I'll tell them you were resisting arrest."

"Liar! You can't do that!"

"The people I work for control the police." His grin grew wider. "They'll believe whatever I tell them."

"The FBI doesn't control the police!"

"You think I'm here working for the FBI?" He laughed. "You're a moron, but even you have to know that I can't afford everything I own on a government salary."

Her eyes widened. She was already afraid, but now the fear was burning even brighter.

He slapped her. "I can do whatever I want to you and there's nothing you can do about it."

Angie's chin trembled. Her teeth chattered.

Decker smiled. "Who's in control, Angie?"

She whimpered. Tried to shrink back. But there was nowhere to go. "You."

"I can't hear you, Angie. Say it a little louder for those in the back."

"You're in control."

"Damned right I am." And then he showed her that it wasn't just control. He owned her.

When he was finished he left her on the bed. Went and took a shower. She was still lying there when he came back, her dress torn, hair a mess. Still crying.

Decker stood over her. "You know what? You deserve a night out. Get yourself presentable and we'll go somewhere nice."

Angie stared up at him with big eyes. "You're a monster." She said it in a hushed voice. Almost like she was saying it to herself.

Decker nodded. "I am a monster. I do what I want. I take what I want. I make no apologies for being who I am." He sat next to her. Stroked her hair. Smoothed it back off her face. "And you get to be with me. You have my protection as long as you're loyal. What other man can offer you that?"

She shivered. Stared up at him like she couldn't understand what he was saying.

He kissed her forehead. "You got too confident. Thought you had control." He laughed. "Baby, I'm the one in charge."

She kept staring at him.

Decker had about had enough. "Go get ready now, or I'm kicking you out."

Tears pooled in her eyes. She nodded. Pushed up slowly. Limped to the bathroom.

"Don't pretend you're hurt. I can see right through you."

She took off what was left of her dress. Left it on the floor. There was a bruise around her neck. Some bruises on her backside. A bruise on her cheek.

He walked over. Gripped her chin and inspected her. Pushed her in front of the mirror and pointed to her neck and cheek. "Make sure you cover that up with makeup." He pushed her into the bathroom. "Now, get ready and do it fast. I'm tired of waiting."

She went in and turned on the shower. Decker lay on the bed. He was exhausted. It had been a long day. But he deserved a fun night out. He'd tracked down the target and was so close to taking her that he could taste it.

He dozed off. A clicking noise woke him. He instinctively rolled off the bed, ready to fight. He expected to see someone with a gun, but no one was there. No one at all. He stood. Went to the bathroom.

Angie wasn't there. Her suitcase was still on the dresser, but her wallet was gone. He ran out of the room. Didn't see her. He raced around the corner. Saw her punching the elevator door buttons.

There were cameras in the hallway, but he'd disabled them the same day he'd arrived. He didn't like being watched. There was no one else in the hall so he charged Angie. She was in shorts and a t-shirt.

She must have changed clothes while he was sleeping. She must have thought she could get away. She tried to run but he was too fast. He was tempted to level her with a punch but held back. He grabbed her arm. Yanked her alongside him.

"Angie, Angie. Why would you do something so stupid?"

"I just want to go home. Please, Mike. Please!"

He nodded. "You know what? I think that's for the best. Let's get your suitcase."

"R-really?"

"Yeah, baby. I've got a lot of work to do. It's best if I don't have to worry about you."

"Thank you." She shuddered. "I'll go home, and we can talk about this when you get back."

"I would love to sit down and talk all about it." He kissed her cheek. "We can talk about our feelings and make sure this doesn't happen again."

He went into the room. Pointed to her suitcase. "Get your stuff and then I'll get you a taxi to the airport, okay?"

"Okay." She hurriedly gathered her things.

Decker went to his suitcase. He opened his spare toolkit. Inside were all kinds of useful things. Things he used when he needed to pick locks, hotwire cars, or take someone without a struggle. He plucked a small vial from the kit.

He unscrewed the lid. It had a dropper built onto the end. He squeezed the top and drew in a few milliliters of fluid.

Angie was fumbling things into her suitcase. Trying to close it, but she'd just tossed things haphazardly inside and clothing was overflowing from the sides.

Decker came up behind her. "Here, let me help." He gripped her hair. Yanked her head back. Her mouth reflexively opened. He dripped the liquid right under her tongue. It was a well-practiced move, and he was lightning fast with it.

He released her. Smiled. "I gave you something to help you relax."

She blinked in confusion. Realization dawned in her eyes. She was a recreational drug user. She'd taken fentanyl before. But she'd never taken this much. It wasn't enough to kill her, but it would put her in a daze.

Angie tried to spit it out, but it was too late. It had absorbed into the soft tissue beneath the tongue already. "What did you do?" She stumbled toward the door. "What did you do?"

Decker caught her by the arm. He smoothed her hair back from her face. "Nothing, baby. Just gave you something to help you relax for your flight."

"I don't need..." Her words trailed off. Her head lolled. "I don't need anything for flying."

"You'll be happy I did." He closed her suitcase. "Come on, baby. Let's go." He led her out of the door. He took her down the hall and to the stairwell. She was barely able to walk on her own so he half-carried her down a flight of stairs to the next level.

He took a device from his pocket. Turned it on. Held it against the card reader on the first room door he came to. It hummed softly. The reader beeped and a green LED flashed. He slowly opened the door.

There was a suitcase inside. Clothing on the bed. But no one was in the room. Angie was almost limp. He dragged her across the room. Opened the door on the other side. He took her out to the balcony.

"Wow, look at that view, baby."

She whimpered. Spoke in a heavily slurred voice. "Decker...what...doing?"

"Sending you on that flight." He looked at her face. Her body. He sighed. "God, what a waste." Then he threw her over the railing. Sent her flying out into the night sky. She was too stoned to even scream.

Decker tried to watch her fall, but this room had an alley view. There wasn't enough light to see anything. He heard a wet thud when she landed. He closed the balcony door. Exited the room.

He went back to his room. Gathered his things. Found a few things of Angie's that she'd missed. Then he went over the room with a fine-toothed comb. He found spots of blood on the sheets, so he stripped them.

He put on nitrile gloves then used a spray from his kit to wipe down the room. It wasn't really necessary, but he preferred leaving his rooms as sterile as possible just in case. He changed into jeans and a t-shirt and pulled a ballcap on.

Decker rolled the suitcases out of the room and took the elevator down. He left by a side entrance to avoid as many people as possible and went to the valet. A young guy fetched the car. Decker loaded the suitcases in the trunk, hopped in the car, and pulled out of the circle drive.

He drove past the alley where Angie had fallen. It was dark and no one had even noticed yet. He blew her a kiss and drove away, back to the hotel he'd planned to stay in near Butler's house.

It was a good thing he hadn't taken Angie out for a night on the town. He was even more tired than earlier. Probably from lugging Angie downstairs and tossing her over the balcony. Moving a limp human body was harder than it seemed even if the person didn't weigh much.

Unfortunately, he still had a few things to do. He checked into the hotel under the alias Gus Fring. The hotel manager raised his eyebrows when he saw the name. He probably recognized it from the TV show.

Decker unpacked his stuff in the room. He looked longingly at the bed, but duty called. It was for the best that he hadn't taken Angie clubbing. What had he been thinking? There was way too much to do for him to party the night away.

He threw on black cargos and a black t-shirt. He drove a short distance and parked across the road from the subdivision. He put on his backpack. Crossed the road and walked behind the brick wall around the subdivision.

He climbed the wall and perched on it right behind Butler's house. The lights were on downstairs and upstairs. The curtains prevented him from seeing inside. He thought about placing a camera on the wall but didn't think it would be very useful.

If anyone came into the back yard, they wouldn't be going anywhere. He wanted to know when the men left. That was all that mattered. He could eliminate them if he wanted to. He could storm in and headshot them both, but he wasn't getting paid to kill two extra people.

Terminating Butler and taking Paola alive were the mission objectives. He preferred to minimize collateral damage. Plus, the husband and brother, or whatever they were to Butler, would return home and find the mess.

They would learn the valuable lesson that it doesn't matter how well you hide, the cartel will find you and end you if you take their money. A teachable moment wasn't necessarily part of his assignment, but it would be a nice touch.

He lowered himself off the brick wall and into the yard. He crept to the kitchen window. Everyone was in the den watching television. Butler was curled up next to her man. The other guy was sitting next to them, a beer in hand.

Decker could barely see Paola sitting on the sectional couch against the wall. She was staring at her phone. He couldn't understand why people were obsessed with those things when the real world was so much more interesting.

She wouldn't be sitting around staring blankly at a phone for much longer, that was for sure. Life was about to get a lot more interesting.

Butler's man said something. Butler gave him a sad look. She kissed him and said something back. The two men stood. Butler walked them to the front door. Decker didn't have a good angle from the window.

He quietly slipped through the front gate. Crept to the corner of the house. Peered around it. The men climbed into their vehicle. It rumbled to life. Backed out. Turned around in the cul-de-sac and took off.

Decker could hardly believe his luck. Butler's man didn't live with her. Apparently, he'd gone grocery shopping for her and made dinner. Now he was going home without even getting laid? What a sad little beta male.

What was even sadder was that he'd missed his last chance to have some fun with Butler. At least, not unless he was into necrophilia. Because the next time Butler's boyfriend saw her, she was going to be cold and dead.

Decker waited until the vehicle's taillights vanished around the corner, then he hurried to the front door. It was closed already. He'd hoped to force his way in right behind Butler, but she hadn't wasted any time going back inside.

These bitches were really testing his patience.

He tested the doorknob just in case. It turned all the way. He gently pushed inward. The door opened with a faint whisper. Decker grinned.

This was all but over.

CHAPTER 16

Decker eased the front door shut behind him.

The television hummed in the room just ahead and around the corner. He stepped softly into the tiled foyer floor and went to the corner. The women weren't on the couch. They must have gone upstairs.

He stopped and listened. The heater was on. The hum of the blower was loud enough to drown out the sound of anyone walking upstairs. That was okay. There wasn't anything the two women could do to stop him.

Even so, he preferred stealth. He liked taking his prey by surprise. It was so much more satisfying to see the shock on their faces. To watch the shock morph into disbelief and then fear. Most people simply froze in place, unable to act.

These women would be no different. They would be little more than deer in the headlights. The only question was how much fun he wanted to have before he terminated Butler and secured Paola.

He crept up the stairs. Peered around the corner. Lights were on in the rooms to the left. The rooms to the right were dark. He stopped and listened. Didn't hear anything except the running HVAC system.

Decker went to the balcony overlooking the den. He didn't see anyone downstairs. He didn't have a clear view into the kitchen, but he didn't see any shadows or movement.

He went to the first bedroom. There was a messy bed. Clothing strewn on the floor. A dresser with odds and ends on it. No one was inside.

The bathroom across the hall was empty too. The next bedroom looked lived in, but neat. The bed was made and there were no clothes on the floor. He went to the next room. Also, empty.

Where were they?

The answer came quickly. They must have gone to the basement. Why they would have done that, he didn't know. But it was the only place left in the house.

A faint noise caught his attention. He went to the window. Saw the silver Honda backing out of the driveway. It spun around. The tires chirped and it took off down the road.

Decker flew down the stairs. He ran to the front door. Watched the car turn the corner ahead. He was stunned. Confused. Had they known he was here or had they left for some other reason?

He went into the den. Paola's smartphone was on the couch. He picked it up. It wasn't a phone. It was a small tablet. He pressed a button, and the screen came on. It was divided into four sections.

Each section showed a view of the yard outside. The view from the cameras told him where they were. He found the closest one. It was a small pinhole camera attached to the upper corner of the windowsill.

That was why he hadn't seen it. It was hardwired, not wireless. That was why he hadn't detected it with his phone. Paola hadn't been staring at her phone. She'd been watching him the entire time.

He threw the tablet across the room. It smashed into the television. They'd waited for him to come inside and then run like cowards. That wasn't going to save them. Not by a long shot.

The heater turned off and silence returned to the house. He heard a hum. It sounded like a microwave. He heard popping and crackling. Like popcorn popping. He went into the kitchen and a familiar odor hit him.

The microwave door was open but somehow it was still running. Something metallic was inside and it was sparking. He noticed all of that in an instant and realized at the same time what the odor was.

Natural gas was flooding out of the stovetop.

Decker ran. He dove behind the couch. There was a loud whoosh as the sparks ignited the gas. Heat washed over his back. And then it was over. The gas hadn't been running long enough to reach critical mass. The heater had been sucking it in and redistributing it all over the house.

He went into the kitchen. The burners were all lit. The hood and nearby cabinets were slightly blackened from the flash fire. He turned them off. Laughed to himself.

That bitch had tried to kill him. It was a good thing she didn't know the first thing about igniting a natural gas explosion. The burners didn't emit enough gas to flood an entire house. You had to disconnect the hose on the back of the oven.

A half-inch hose with full street pressure would flood the house with enough gas to create an actual explosion in about twenty minutes. Five minutes would be enough to create a burst of heat that would severely burn anyone caught in the blast.

It was almost amusing. Almost. If he'd caught her, he'd be laughing right now. But she'd gotten away and tried to spring a trap on him. The flames could have disfigured him if he wasn't so fast on his feet.

He took out his phone and pulled up a map app. There was a red blip moving north. That red blip represented Paola's car. Decker was good at what he did. Damned good. He knew it was best to give himself a margin for error.

That margin was in the form of a GPS tracker he'd planted on Paola's car earlier just in case. Sometimes, prey was unpredictable. Sometimes, the target would do something unexpected.

This was one of those times. Paola had been more prepared than he'd thought possible. She had known Decker was there but understood it was suicidal to confront him even with the other men present.

"Clever girl," he said to himself. "But not clever enough."

He sighed. It looked like he wouldn't be getting much sleep tonight. But there was an upside to this. She'd already led him to Aliya Butler. Maybe she would lead him to more women on his list.

The most realistic scenario was that she and Butler would go somewhere they thought they couldn't be found. Maybe they were going to stay with Butler's man. Maybe Butler had relatives. The best-case scenario was that they were going to stay with another woman on the list.

He left the house by the back door. Climbed the brick wall. Walked across the street to the hotel. The red blip was on Interstate 75 heading north by northwest. They weren't going anywhere nearby.

Decker took a quick shower. Changed clothes. He put his stuff in the car and headed in the same direction as the targets. Something was nagging at him. Something that should have bothered him earlier, but it hadn't occurred to him until now.

Had Paola only known he was there because of the cameras, or had she been preparing all along for someone to come after her? It made sense for someone in her position to be paranoid. But did a paranoid person think it was okay to keep regular hair appointments at a salon?

Would a person being hunted by a Brazilian cartel think it was okay to live in a Brazilian community without being spotted at some point?

Paola had done it in Miami. Maybe she'd felt safe in Marietta and decided it was okay to get back to her routine despite everything that happened in Miami. She'd put cameras around Butler's house just to be safe.

Putting them there had paid off. At least temporarily. But Decker had her scent and a tracker on her car. Now there was no escape.

His good detective work and excellent instincts had brought him to this moment in time. Decker could connect the dots better than most. That was what made him such a good bounty hunter.

He thought back to that first dot. That first link in the chain of events that put him on Paola's trail. It had been when he heard about Morganville. He'd volunteered to be on the investigative team the moment he heard about the events that rocked the small town.

He'd done work for the cartel before. This sounded like the perfect opportunity to get in on the ground level of a real money-making opportunity.

What he'd found in that little redneck town was a true work of art. The work of a professional. Carnage beyond anything he'd seen on U.S. soil.

The local police chief, Ritter, seemed clueless about what had really happened. In fact, most of the cops there seemed clueless. Only one guy had been forthcoming and that was because he'd been giving information to anyone who paid him.

The cop's name was Maberly. Decker remembered him as an obese desk jockey. The kind of guy with a permanent layer of donut powder and fake cheese dust on his fingers and clothes. The kind of guy who did as little work as possible and sweated even when standing still.

Maberly had mentioned a man named Carver. Described him. Said he was arrested for the murder of the former police chief. He'd told Decker that Carver had to be involved in this somehow, but he had no specific knowledge.

That made perfect sense. It was like being hit by a tornado in the middle of the night. You could hear the sirens. Hear the sound like a train speeding through town. The next morning, you could go outside and see the destructive wake of its passing.

But you had no specific knowledge of the tornado. You hadn't witnessed it destroying anything. But you knew it had. Maberly felt certain Carver was the tornado that had ripped through Morganville.

He sort of knew what Carver looked like. He thought Carver might be the kind of person who could kill a boatload of people and not have a care in the world. But he didn't know for sure.

The best thing Maberly had done was the list. Ritter and his lacky, Holly Robinson, had tried to keep it secret. But Maberly had managed to get a list of names. Only a few of those names had corresponding addresses because they were either undocumented immigrants or people yanked right off the streets.

The cartel thugs hadn't exactly cared about documenting who Jasper's victims were or where they'd come from. They viewed them as disposable commodities. Once Jasper was done with them, they'd be discarded like trash.

Maberly had no clue Decker was working two different angles. One for the FBI and the other for the cartel. Maberly had been proud, practically puffing out his chest when he gave Decker the list. As if it made him a real detective. Decker had stroked his ego. Let him bask in the adoration.

He'd told Maberly not to breathe a word about the list. He'd told him it was vital to keep the women safe and protected from retaliation and that he would know if the list was leaked. Maberly had quickly agreed.

Decker considered killing him just to make sure, but months had passed, and the list hadn't leaked. Decker, meanwhile, had already found two people on the list. A couple of women in the Los Angeles area.

Those two had been the easiest to find. The easiest to kill. They were low-hanging fruit. Finding others, however, had proven difficult if not impossible.

Connecting the names with the people was harder than it sounded. Even unusual names by American standards were hard to track down because there were so many immigrants in the system. Then he'd been contacted by his mysterious benefactors.

They'd offered interagency assistance and told him he could do whatever he wanted with the list. It sounded too good to be true, but they hadn't interfered—only helped. After a while, he'd connected eighty percent of the dots with extreme confidence.

Then he'd made an offer to the cartel. They'd accepted. Offered a bounty for every head. A cash bonus for money recovered. So far, Decker had culled four women on the list. The two in the Los Angeles area had been the starting point.

He'd recovered a little stolen money but not much because the women had already spent most of the cartel cash Ritter had given them. Their bounties were decent, but nothing to brag about.

Then he'd received word that Paola was in Miami. The tip had come from an unexpected source, but he was happy to have the information. It also helped him remove another name from the list.

He'd immediately left for Miami, set up shop, and spent hours watching various cameras around the area. Hoping facial recognition could zero in on her current location.

It hadn't yielded results. At first, he thought maybe she'd moved on. Then he suspected she avoided cameras as much as possible. There were a lot of cameras but most of them didn't have high resolution, making it much harder for facial recognition to find matches.

Facial recognition technology didn't work as depicted on television shows. Hollywood made it seem as if they could find a reflection in a hubcap, zoom in 100x, and identify the person. In reality, the software needed a clear view of identifying features as a starting point.

If someone was being careful, they could avoid detection for a long time.

Then an image had finally been flagged. Decker examined it. Found Paola walking in a crowd. She wore sunglasses and a facemask, but it looked like she'd pulled the facemask down for a moment. Maybe to scratch her face. Maybe because it was too hot.

Decker zoomed in and noticed a V shape. The shape was made by two arms. By two people holding hands. Paola was holding hands with the man next to her. Facial recognition identified the man next to her.

His name was Lucas Duarte. Most of his information was shielded, but his face matched someone on the cartel's most wanted list. Apparently, he was a federal agent of some kind who was obsessed with taking down the cartel.

It took help from his mysterious benefactor to find out who Lucas worked for and what he was doing. Lucas was with the National Security Agency. He was a field agent working on an unsanctioned mission.

It turned out Lucas had been disciplined before for using agency resources to find information about the Herrada Cartel. He'd nearly lost his job once. He'd somehow discovered Paola Barros was in Miami and couldn't help himself.

Lucas had seen an opportunity to use her against the cartel. At least, that was what Decker assumed Lucas had intended. That meant Lucas was living in Miami. It meant he had regular contact with Paola.

His intent was obvious. To lure Paola into a relationship so she'd trust him. So she'd eventually tell him things she wouldn't tell him if he'd simply taken her in for questioning. Little did the man know that it also made Decker's job easier.

Tracking down two people in a city was easier than tracking down one. It practically doubled his odds. Decker had set up facial recognition traps all around the area where Lucas and Paola had been seen.

He'd finally gotten a hit. An image of Lucas entering an apartment building. Decker had gone there and cased the area. Found a good spot to keep watch.

Lucas hadn't emerged until later in the evening. He was dressed up like he was going out on a date. Decker had been ecstatic. It meant he was going to meet Paola. And then disaster struck.

It turned out that other people were waiting on Lucas to emerge from his apartment building. Cartel men. They'd chased him before Decker had a chance to follow. By the time Decker reached ground level, they were long gone.

Not long after that, an explosion rocked a parking deck not far from the park. Decker rushed to the scene and found the remains of a van and body parts strewn all over the street. He later learned Lucas had suicide-bombed himself and six cartel men.

It was a hell of a way to go out. Decker actually kind of respected it. But it also pissed him off, because he hadn't found Paola. And there was no doubt in his mind that she was long gone.

But now he'd finally caught up. Things were finally going his way. Decker looked at the blip on the map. Paola couldn't run. She couldn't hide. It didn't matter where she went or what aliases she used.

Decker could find her.

CHAPTER 17

Carver woke up early.

He'd gotten a good four hours of rest and was ready to get going. Liana was awake too. She didn't look well rested. Her face was pale, but the color had returned to her lips.

Sandra had disinfected and stitched the wound. Put fresh dressing on the injury. She'd given Carver a bottle of antibiotics for Liana to take and warned him that any injuries that exposed the bone required her to take the pills or risk major infection.

Carver knew most of that already. Severe injuries and gunshot wounds were problems he'd faced plenty during his time in Scion. But they'd had a dedicated medic most of the time and paid off local doctors when they needed something more.

Liana pushed herself into a sitting position and winced. She stared at him. Didn't say anything. Just kept looking at him with a dead expression on her face.

Carver fixed himself a cup of coffee. "Want some?"

She shook her head. "I need food."

"Toast? Cereal?"

"I don't care." She shivered. "I just need something in my stomach."

Carver looked around the kitchen. He looked out the back window. There was a nice deck there. A lake. A small dock with a small fishing boat tethered to it. Ritter probably spent a lot of time fishing instead of in the house.

He opened the cabinets. Found the bowls. Found the spoons. Found some unsweetened corn cereal. He put cereal in the bowl. Poured milk on it. Set the bowl on the table.

Liana tried to stand. She groaned and slumped back on the couch. The transfusion hadn't replaced the lost blood. It had been just enough to keep her alive. Her body was working double time to catch up.

Carver brought the cereal to her. She couldn't use her arm very well, so he sat on the coffee table across from her and scooped cereal onto the spoon. "Here comes the airplane." He held it out to her.

She rolled her eyes then leaned forward and ate it.

"I don't need you spoon feeding me. Just hold the bowl."

He held the bowl and let her use the spoon with her good arm. She devoured it in a hurry.

"Want more?" he asked.

"Toast, please."

"Butter and jam?"

"I don't care. I'm just so hungry."

Ritter walked downstairs. He wore long sleeve pajamas and a nightrobe like some guy from the nineteenth century. "I have bacon and eggs. You'll need a lot of iron in your diet."

"Yes, please." Liana groaned and leaned back.

Sandra hurried downstairs in a robe that looked considerably more modern. "You poor dear. How are you feeling?"

Liana managed a smile. "All roses, doctor."

"I'm a nurse, not a doctor." Sandra put a finger to Liana's neck. She went to a closet and pulled out a digital blood pressure reader. Put it on Liana's finger. She produced a digital thermometer and put it in Liana's mouth.

Ritter turned on the gas stove. Heated a cast iron skillet. Before long, bacon was crackling, and pancakes were cooking on a griddle. He threw pork sausage in the skillet after the bacon was done.

Carver helped Liana to the table. Eased her into a chair. Her eyes were watering by the time she sat down. She wasn't on pain killers, but she was taking the pain like a champ. The bullet had gone into her right shoulder. Luckily, she was left-handed.

Ritter watched Liana take a bite of sausage. He turned to Carver. "What are you planning next?" He waved off the question. "Better yet, I don't want to know."

Carver was already halfway through a stack of pancakes. He washed them down with orange juice while keeping an eye on the view out of the picture window in the front of the house. It was a habitual thing.

"Frankly, I'm surprised these people haven't paid you a visit already." Carver watched Liana struggle to cut her pancakes. He took a table knife and did it for her then turned back to Ritter. "Did you convince them you don't know anything?"

"I must have." Ritter gave his wife a look and something unsaid passed between them. "Sandra wanted to move. But during the investigation, Holly and I played dumb. Like we couldn't believe all this happened under our noses. I think we convinced them that the mayor was able to keep us in the dark and Rhodes was the only one who started to figure out what was really going on."

Sandra laughed. "That's not far from the truth. Plus, those bastards from Breakstone kidnapped and threatened you."

"I hope they continue to believe you don't know anything." Carver helped Liana cut another pancake and asked her a simple question. "Do you want to stick around here or come with me?"

Liana blinked. "Is that a trick question? I'll die if I stay here. I don't even know who to trust anymore."

"I need to know more about Lucas. How he met Paola. Everything."

"I already told you what I know." She shook her head. "We really didn't keep in touch. I was shocked when I found out who she was."

If that was the case, she wasn't all that valuable to Carver after all.

A look of horror crossed Liana's face. "My God, I don't even know if I can trust my own agency. I'm afraid to report in or ask for help."

Carver couldn't reassure her. The NSA wasn't exactly known for being trustworthy. Like most federal agencies, it was driven by politics. It was powerful and protected by whichever party controlled the government at the time.

Liana was just another replaceable cog in the machine. A pawn someone figured they could sacrifice once it had been used.

She looked at Carver. "I'm coming with you. I want to find out exactly how they found Lucas. Paola is the only one who knows for sure."

"Doubtful." Carver cut another pancake for her even though she'd stopped eating. "Even the men who tried to kill you don't know why they're doing what they're doing. The powers that be probably figured you'd be more driven to find Paola, given what happened to Lucas."

Carver wondered if there was more to Liana's relationship with Lucas. Were they just coworkers? Friends? Lovers? It didn't really matter.

Ritter pushed his plate away and leaned back. "There's something else you don't know."

Carver turned to him and waited for him to continue.

Ritter cleared his throat and looked down at the table. "There were a lot of bodies at the factory. A lot of anonymous cartel men the FBI had trouble identifying. We weren't privy to the list. They figured we were just trash local police."

Carver kept waiting for the payoff.

"Turns out one of those dead men was Christiano Herrada. Son of Pedro Herrada."

"The son of the Herrada cartel was at the paint factory?" Liana frowned. "Why would they put him in this backwoods town?"

"I tried looking into how many kids this Pedro guy has," Ritter said. "There are a lot of them from various women."

"Was he particularly attached to this kid?" Carver asked.

"Rumor had it that there was a hefty bounty placed on the heads of the people involved, including the women who were sex slaves. There was a two-million-dollar reward for you, Carver."

Liana's eyes widened. "That's a huge bounty for someone who's not even a head of state."

Carver knew from experience that she was right. "Apparently, Christiano was someone special to him. Maybe a firstborn son?"

"I'm sure it was compounded by the fact that you killed all his men and took his money too." Ritter smiled. "In any case, you have some very determined people looking for you."

"That's old news." Carver pieced together a few bits of the puzzle. "The same people are looking to collect the other bounties too. If they're well-informed then they might suspect Paola is the key to finding me and the women."

"I also think the FBI had a list of the trafficking victims. They found a laptop that Paola had been using. Apparently, she kept track of the women that were kidnapped for Jasper's pleasure." Ritter shuddered. "It's possible the list fell into the wrong hands."

"Not just possible, but highly likely." Carver slid that puzzle piece in with the others. He was starting to understand why the shadow agency, Enigma, had dipped its hands into this fray. They didn't care about Paola or the women. They cared about drawing out Carver.

They were helping the bounty hunters. They hoped that since Carver cared enough to rescue them from the cartel in the first place, that putting them in danger might draw him out again. They probably thought he'd kept in touch with them.

He hadn't. They could have died down to the last woman and he wouldn't have known. All except for one. Paola was the only reason he was here. Enigma's plan was working but only because of one person. One person he should have let go a long time ago.

Carver bit into a piece of bacon and thought about her dark eyes. Her soft skin. Her smile. It was so hard to draw out that smile because of everything she'd been through. He felt like an idiot for caring, but here he was, being stupid.

Maybe he was looking at things the wrong way. He was trying to find Paola to protect her. Maybe it would be better if he pulled this thing out by the roots. Paid Pedro Herrada a visit. Gave him a farewell gift. Maybe a bullet through the head or a knife in the heart.

Unfortunately, Pedro was somewhere in Brazil. Carver would have to find him first. The man might be protected better than the U.S. President, but Carver would eventually find a way through the chinks in his armor.

By the time he did, Paola would almost certainly be dead. That left him no choice. Carver had to find Paola first. Put her somewhere safe. Then he could concentrate on the root of the problem.

Liana watched him closely. "What are you thinking?"

"Next steps."

"And those are?"

He shook his head. "I'll keep them to myself. Just in case any of you are captured and tortured for information."

Sandra laughed nervously then stopped and stared at Carver. "Oh, you're serious."

Carver nodded. "I don't think you're safe here. Maybe you've got time to liquidate your assets and go, but that might just alert the wrong people that you're about to run."

"Christ, Carver." Ritter sighed. "Why do you have to scare us like that?"

"Not trying to scare you. Just making sure you understand the position you're in. Holly did the right thing and ran. Maybe they don't think you know anything. Maybe you have nothing to fear. On the other hand, maybe the cartel will decide to eliminate anyone involved and send someone to stage a murder suicide."

"He's not wrong," Liana said. "The NSA is watching your accounts. If you'd asked me yesterday, I would have said you have nothing to fear. But if you try to take the money and run now, they'll assume something changed. They'll want to know why you're running."

"And they'll pounce," Carver said. "So, maybe it's best if you stay here and play dumb."

Sandra was pale. "Abraham, maybe we should pack light and leave. We can find another way to get our savings."

"Leon can probably help," Carver said. "He could convert your savings to crypto and send it to you. But you'll want to be long gone before then."

"I'll think about it." Ritter said. "I think we'll be fine staying."

Liana grimaced. "Your choice."

"Got a pen?" Carver said.

Sandra pushed back her chair. Got him a pen and paper. Carver wrote an email address on it. It was one of many anonymous email addresses Leon used.

He handed the paper to Sandra. "I'd go somewhere with public Wi-Fi and create a new email address if I were you. Then send an email to this address and tell Leon that Carver sent you. Maybe summarize who you are. Ask if he can help. He might still have the resources even though he's a wanted man himself."

"Never thought I'd be associating with outlaws." Ritter sighed. "Damn it, Carver, I'm scared now."

"You should be scared," Liana said. "And we should go now before someone decides to check this place on a hunch."

"They wouldn't connect us to this place," Carver said. "As long as Ritter never mentioned meeting and helping me."

"I didn't," Ritter said. "I told them I only caught a glimpse of you once after your arrest."

"You didn't mention sniping a Breakstone armored truck with a Barrett fifty caliber?"
Ritter grinned. "Nope."

"Good." Carver finished his pancakes. He took his plate and dinnerware to the sink.
Went to Liana and looked at her plate. "Finished?"

She nodded. "I'm starting to feel better."

"Don't rush it, dear." Sandra patted her hand. "You need to be very careful not to tear
your stitches."

"Thank you for everything." Liana used her good hand to push herself to her feet. Her
face paled, but she kept the pain from her face.

"Maybe you should disappear too," Carver told her. "Coming with me isn't going to
be any safer."

She turned to him. "I have nowhere to go. I want to come with you."

He trusted her about as much as he trusted anyone who'd just been betrayed by the
people they thought they could trust. She was feeling vulnerable now, but that would pass.
Then she'd get angry. Think about revenge. She'd eventually accept her fate and decide
how best to move on.

Carver had been through the same emotions himself after being framed for crimes he
hadn't committed. After his dishonorable discharge, he'd had trouble adapting to civilian
life. Then he'd realized it was much better than taking orders and fallen into a happy
existence.

Maybe Liana would find her own happy existence. Maybe she'd be killed the moment
she showed her face. In any case, she was tangled up in this mess now, so it seemed best to
let her finish it.

Plus, she wasn't exactly helpless. Even with an injured shoulder, she could still watch
Carver's back. And sometimes, having a wingman was like having eyes in the back of your
head.

Provided this wasn't part of an elaborate scheme to embed herself with Carver. This
was the NSA, after all. They might be willing to sacrifice a few men if it meant their agent
could earn his trust.

But what was the endgame? If Liana was still their loyal agent, then they could have
surrounded the house and taken Carver last night. The only reason to let him keep
running was because they wanted something else. Someone else. Probably Paola.

But why?

He didn't have an answer. Probably because there was no answer. Probably because
Liana wasn't playing the long game. But it was a good idea to play it safe anyway.

Liana was watching him carefully. "You don't trust me."

"Nope. But don't take it personally. I don't trust many people."

"I promise I'm not going to betray you."

Carver raised an eyebrow. "At least not unless it benefits you."

"I'm not that kind of person."

"You're an NSA agent. They only hire those kinds of people." Carver waved off whatever she was going to say next. "You can come with me."

Liana shook her head slowly. "Thanks, I think."

Carver nodded at the Ritters. "Thanks for the help, and good luck."

Abe Ritter shook his head. "Short and to the point as always."

"Yep." Carver headed for the door.

"Hold on." Sandra fetched a small duffel bag. Gave it to Carver. "Gauze and tape so you can put fresh dressing on her wounds. You'll want to change them at least once a day until the seeping stops."

Carver took the bag. "Thanks." He went to the car. Put the bag in the back seat.

Liana gritted her teeth as she walked down the stairs in front of the house. She didn't complain or ask for help. She opened the passenger door herself. Turned her back to the car and dropped into the seat. Rotated her legs and got situated.

She tried to reach across with her left hand to close the door. Couldn't reach it. Carver walked around and closed it for her. He dropped into his seat and started the engine. Turned the car around and got going.

He turned off the country road and onto a two-lane highway. Aimed the car south toward Morganville. He would take a northern backroad to avoid Morganville completely. Less chance of being spotted that way.

Carver was about a half mile down the road when he saw a black Sprinter van coming from the other direction. "Put your seat back and stay out of sight."

Liana did what he said. Carver put his sun visor down to block his face. Slumped in his seat to look shorter. The van whizzed past. It was probably going over ninety.

Carver raised his foot off the gas pedal but didn't hit the brakes. He watched the van climb the hill behind them and vanish on the other side.

"That's not good." Liana raised her seat. Looked back. "Could they be going somewhere else?"

Carver shook his head. "Doubtful. There's only one place they could be going."

The van was going to the Ritters'.

CHAPTER 18

Carver pulled off on the shoulder of the road.

He waited for an old blue pickup to pass by then turned around and went after the van. He slowed at the top of the hill and looked at the highway. It stretched like a ribbon through the forest before winding its way up a mountain.

The van was already on the country road leading to the cabins. It would arrive at Ritter's in moments. And he didn't have a way to call ahead and warn them.

"There's probably six operators in that van." Liana put a hand on Carver's wrist. "There's nothing you can do."

She was probably right. The van was like the one Carver had stolen. It was armored. Anything short of explosives wouldn't do much to it. The operators were also wearing body armor.

They weren't going to kill the Ritters. Not right away, at least. Their objectives were most likely to question them. Would they do it on site so they could stage their deaths more easily? Or would they take them somewhere and make them disappear?

Either way, the Ritters didn't have much time left in this world.

Liana fished Carver's burner phone out of the cup holder. She called a number. "Abraham Ritter. Morganville, Georgia." She listened. Ended the call. Made another call.

Ritter's voice answered. "Who's this?"

"They're coming for you. Leave right now. You've got maybe five minutes. Take the boat across the lake now." Liana ended the call.

"Did you just call information?" Carver asked.

She nodded. "I noticed the Ritters have a landline phone. Most old folks still do."

Carver should have thought of that. "I don't know if they'll make it out."

"They should have time to use the boat," Liana said. "There are more houses on the north side of the lake. Maybe they can get help from someone."

"Maybe." Carver looked at the maps app. The lake was north of them and on the left side. Ritter lived on the first road to the left right before the lake. There was another road just after the lake. There were houses along that side of the lake.

If Ritter crossed the lake, he'd be going toward one of those houses.

Carver made a U-turn. Gunned the car north. He passed the road to the Ritters'. Crossed a small bridge over the lake. Took the next left on the other side. Followed the road until the map app showed he was directly across the lake from the Ritters' house.

There was a big new lake house on this side. It had a modern design. Like someone stacked cubes haphazardly on top of one another and called it a day. There were huge windows on all sides. Everything inside was visible.

It was a terrible design, tactically speaking. At night, the people inside would be clearly visible with the lights on. Anyone outside would be invisible in the dark. Just thinking about it made him want to punch the designer.

"Wait here." Carver got out. Walked to the house. It was dark inside. Looked vacant. It might be a rental or a second home that was rarely used except on weekends. He looked around the corner. Saw Ritter and his wife crossing the lake in the flat-bottomed fishing boat.

The motor wasn't made for speed. It was made for trolling around the lake at a leisurely pace. They must have left the house the instant Liana warned them because they were more than halfway across.

It was quiet this far from the city. Quiet except for the boat motor. The puttering was audible even from Carver's location. It would be audible all around the lake because sound carries over water.

Carver looked at Ritter's house through the monocular. He saw the van whip into the driveway. Saw six operators pour out of it. They ran toward the house and vanished on the other side.

They wore the same gray and black urban camouflage as before. They had the same tactical gear too. Body armor. Helmets with NV goggles. Carver knew what it was like to be in full gear. Weapons, ammunition, body armor, armored helmet. It was all extra weight.

True, it protected the wearer, but it also hindered them. Not just with the added weight but with a reduction in sight, hearing, and sensation. Despite that, it was still better to have it than to run into a house on a wing and a prayer.

That reduction in hearing was helping Ritter right now. The operators were probably hearing chatter through their headsets and the rattle in their helmets right about now. They were probably staging at the front door. Preparing to knock it off its hinges.

If just one of them hadn't been wearing a helmet and an earbud, they'd hear the boat motor. They'd run around the house to investigate. They'd see the targets escaping and react. But apparently, they were all helmeted and on comms and that made them deaf to the environment.

Carver couldn't see them because Ritter's house was in the way. But he knew protocol. He had a good idea what they were up to. Right before they rammed the door down, there would be a pause. A moment of silence.

In that silence they might hear the drone of the boat engine. They might hear it and disregard it as background noise. Maybe they'd think it was someone mowing their lawn. Maybe Ritter would get lucky and no one on the assault team would think their targets were escaping across the lake right now.

Maybe.

The French doors on Ritter's back deck had big windows in them. Carver knelt and angled the monocular so he could see the front door through those windows. The front door rocked inward. The assault team rushed in, operators clearing all the angles.

Two of them rushed down the hallway while the others cleared the front rooms. Ritter was almost across the lake. Just another fifty yards to go to the dock behind the big cube house. Ritter glanced back at his house.

Sandra was huddled low in the boat. As low as she could go, given how shallow the boat was. Ritter was hunched over. Making his profile as small as possible.

One of the operators looked out the French door window. He opened the door. Ran to the back deck. Pointed at the boat. He raised his rifle. Aimed through the aimpoint.

He had a short-barreled CQB M4. It was good for clearing a house, but he'd be hard-pressed to hit anything at almost two-hundred yards. It would be a hard target even with a regular M4 and a scope.

Shooting the Ritters didn't seem to be their intention anyway. They wanted them alive. Wanted them for questioning. The operator lowered his rifle and ran back into the house. Seconds later, the squad piled into the van. Wheels screeched on the driveway as it backed out to the gravel road.

Ritter nearly rammed his boat into the dock. He looped a rope to a post and helped his wife out. They hurried toward the house, faces tight with concern.

"No one is home," Sandra said. "What are we going to do?"

Carver edged around the corner. He hadn't seen a weapon on Ritter, but he didn't want to startle the man and get shot by accident. "Get into the car."

Ritter gasped and put a hand over his chest. "You nearly gave me a heart attack."

"Oh, thank God!" Sandra pulled Ritter by the hand. "I thought you'd left us to die."

Carver slid into the car. Ritter and Sandra climbed into the back.

Liana looked back at them. "Are you okay?"

"For now." Sandra shivered. "If you hadn't called, we'd be dead right now."

"Not dead." Carver shifted the car into drive and gunned it back toward the highway. "After everything that happened yesterday, they decided to pull out all the stops. Question anyone who might possibly have information."

"Oh my God." Sandra gripped Ritter's arm. "What are we going to do? Where are we going to go?"

"We'll be fine, dear." Ritter patted her hand. "I'll figure it out."

"Let's start by dumping your phones," Carver said. "Get burners and contact Leon like I told you."

Ritter had a small duffel bag with him. He opened it to show bundles of cash. "I already have an emergency stash. I thought we might need it after everything that happened the last time you were in town."

"Don't go to any relatives. Don't go anywhere linked to you. Contact Leon and find out if he can help you secure your funds. If you try to do it yourself, they'll find you." Carver hit the highway and turned north.

North wasn't the direction he wanted to go, but it was the best play for now. He could risk going south and passing the van. Maybe they could hide the Ritters in the trunk. But there was a chance the men in the van would stop and search the car.

The car crested a hill. Carver kept an eye on the rearview mirror. He didn't see the van yet. That was good. That meant the driver wouldn't see this car. There wasn't any other traffic on the road, so they'd stick out.

He drove down the other side of the hill. The road was flat for a distance. By the time they reached the next rise, they'd be out of sight of the van. They'd also be miles off course for Marietta.

There was also another problem. Liana had called a landline with his burner phone. They would probably check the phone. See the number of the last call. They could use the number to track the phone.

He picked up the phone. Turned on the screen. Glanced at the call log. He didn't see the call to Ritter's house.

Liana took the phone. Opened the web browser. Showed him a plain web page with a blank field on it. "I used an anonymizer. It's a company asset."

"NSA?"

She nodded. "One of many. It's untraceable. Just enter a number."

"I almost didn't answer," Ritter said. "But then I figured it might be Carver."

"You were almost right." Carver checked the map. Plugged in a new route. It would add another forty minutes to the drive, but that was better than the alternative.

Ritter leaned forward. "Can we stop in Blue Ridge? I want to get a couple of burner phones."

"You turned off your old phones?" Carver said.

"Yes, but I don't want to lose everything that's on them."

"Don't login to any of your accounts on the new phones," Liana said. "They have access to software that can pinpoint location through wi-fi. You'll need to go completely off the radar."

"Wonderful." Ritter leaned back. "I'm not a heavy phone user but you have to get a new app for everything these days. My banking app is on there."

"Put it in airplane mode and do a factory reset," Liana said. "That will erase everything."

Ritter turned his phone on. Followed her instructions. He did the same for Sandra's phone. Carver kept to the winding backcountry roads and wended his way southwest. It was pretty country. Mountainous.

The two-lane highway had hairpin curves and no guardrails to catch you if you made a mistake. He liked it. Wished he could stop and smell the roses. Set up a tent on the mountainside. Cook over an open campfire. Open a beer. Lean back and enjoy the vista.

When they reached Blue Ridge, Carver stopped at a shopping center. He turned around. "Give me your phones."

"What are you going to do with them?" Ritter handed them to Carver. "Toss them in the trash?"

Carver shook his head. "Not exactly." He pointed to a cell phone repair store. "Grab a couple of phones from there."

"Can't we just remove our SIM chips?" Ritter said. "Swap them out with prepaid SIMs?"

"Your phones have hardware IDs in them too," Liana said. "Swapping the SIM cards isn't enough."

"Okay." Ritter got out. Walked stiffly around the car and opened the door for his wife. He helped her out.

Sandra put a hand on Carver's arm when he got out of the car. "Thank you for your help. I know you didn't have to, but you did anyway."

Carver didn't have a response. He pointed to a gas station. "I'm going to get gas. I'll meet you back here."

"You're not going to leave us yet?" Ritter asked.

"Not yet. Probably closer to Atlanta."

Ritter nodded. "Thanks."

Carver dropped back into the car. He shifted into drive and drove to the gas pumps.

"I'm going to the bathroom." Liana tried to open the door and winced. "This is going to be a disaster."

"Nothing you can't handle one-handed." Carver walked around and opened the door for her. They walked into the building. He got in line while she went to the bathroom. When it was his turn, he gave the attendant forty bucks in cash. Went back outside and started pumping gas.

While that was going, he looked around. Looked for a way to confuse their trail. Didn't see any good candidates. At least not here.

Liana exited the store. Walked to the car. Her face was a little pale. A little pained. Carver knew from experience that it wasn't easy getting your pants down one-handed with a gunshot wound in the shoulder.

She didn't complain. She got in the car and managed to shut the door herself. Carver drove back to the cell phone store. Sandra and Ritter were already waiting on them. They got in. Carver got back on the road.

A couple of hours later they reached Interstate 75. Carver pulled into a truck stop. He turned on the Ritters' phones and stopped next to a truck with northern plates. He didn't know if that meant it was headed north but figured the odds were good.

He made sure no one was looking, then zip tied the phones to the trailer's undercarriage. He slid back into the car and drove to a parking place with a clear view of the truck. Watched and waited in case someone had seen him.

The truck driver came outside moments later. A woman in cutoff jeans and a revealing shirt that were far too skimpy for the cold weather approached him. She smiled. Rubbed his arm. Pointed to his truck.

He gave her a wistful look. Said something and shrugged. She touched his crotch. Whispered in his ear. He shook his head. Pointed to the truck again. She rolled her eyes and walked away.

"I guess it's never too cold outside to be turning tricks," Liana said.

Ritter laughed.

The truck driver climbed in his truck and stared at the prostitute for a while before starting the engine and driving away.

"If they track the phone, they'll follow that truck?" Ritter said.

Carver nodded. "The phone batteries will hopefully die somewhere further north. Muddy the trail as much as possible."

"Creative." Liana popped four ibuprofen pills and chased them down with water. "You're an analyst's worst nightmare."

"Good." Carver got back on the road. The maps app showed him several motels in the area. He figured this location was as good a place as any to say goodbye to the Ritters. He looked at Ritter in the rearview mirror. "I'm going to find a motel for you. A place that takes cash and doesn't require ID."

Ritter nodded. "Thank you, Carver."

Carver found a place about five miles off the interstate. There were restaurants within walking distance. The Ritters would be able to make do without a car for the time being.

Sandra hugged Carver. "Thanks for coming back for us." She wiped tears off her cheeks. "I just feel so lost. What are we going to do now?"

"We'll manage, honey." Ritter put an arm around his wife's shoulder. "Leon replied to me. He said he's got a person who can liquidate everything and put it into crypto accounts."

"Good." Carver dropped back into the car. Checked the map. He was feeling a little lost himself. Marietta was next on the menu, but where in Marietta?

Liana seemed to sense his concern. "Marietta has the highest concentration of Brazilians in Atlanta. My people already looked to see if Paola has relatives in the U.S. but came up empty."

In other words, they had no starting point. No idea where to go next.

For all Carver knew, Paola might already be dead.

--- ✦ ---

CHAPTER 19

Carver was dead in the water.

He imagined what Rhodes would do. She'd put herself in the shoes of the person she wanted to find. Ask herself what they would do. When people were on the run, they felt desperate and alone.

They searched for things that gave them comfort. The familiar. Even when their lives were in danger, they needed something to make them feel grounded. Paola had probably come to Marietta because there were a lot of Brazilians in the area.

That meant she was probably somewhere frequented by Brazilians. Places with Brazilian food. Brazilian culture. Miami had a place called Little Brazil. There was a Little Haiti and Little Havana too. A lot of cultural pockets. Did Marietta have something like that?

Carver said what he was thinking. "Paola was in Miami because other Brazilians live there. The Brazilian population is much smaller here. Concentrated into a smaller area. We need to find where Brazilians congregate."

Liana nodded "Foreigners tend to gravitate toward other people who share their culture. It's instinctual. It makes them feel more at home."

"Makes sense, but it doesn't tell me where to go." He steered onto the road. Pointed the car towards Marietta. He gave it some thought and came up with a few ideas to narrow down the geography. "Search for Brazilian restaurants in the area."

Liana was already tapping on her new burner phone. "I searched for Brazilian grocery stores, bakeries, and butcher shops. I came up with a couple of shopping centers that have all three in one place."

"Why not restaurants?"

"Because most of them are just Americanized versions of Brazilian restaurants. They're big chains that aren't popular with real Brazilians." She tried to type on the phone with her right hand and winced. "I really wish I hadn't taken a bullet in the shoulder."

"Better than the chest."

"True." She tilted her head slightly and stared at the phone screen. "There's a hair and nail salon in this one shopping center. It's next to a Brazilian bakery." She scrolled the map. "There's another shopping center with similar shops a couple of miles away. I say we start with one of them."

"Show her picture around? Ask if anyone's seen her?"

Liana nodded. "Not you, though. People will take one look at you and assume the worst."

"I don't look trustworthy?"

"Ordinary people will view you as a big, scary guy who's stalking a woman." She patted his arm. "They won't know you're just a cuddly teddy bear."

Carver nodded. "You're Brazilian, injured and female. They'll feel more sympathetic and inclined to help."

"Exactly."

Another thought occurred to him. "Any chance other people have already been asking around about her? Other federal agents?"

"I don't think they have a clue where she is, but I could be wrong. Getting shot opened my eyes to a lot of unpleasant possibilities." Liana closed her eyes and took a breath. "This constant pain is so annoying."

"Ibuprofen not doing the trick?"

She shook her head. "Barely. I don't want to take any more than eight hundred milligrams at once, though."

Carver followed the GPS route to the nearest shopping center. It was small. Maybe ten shops total. The building formed a U shape around the parking lot. There was a salon, a liquor store, a bakery, and other miscellaneous shops.

He parked as far away from the building as he could so people wouldn't see him and Liana together. "I'm going to get something from the bakery. Want anything?"

"I'm good for now." Liana reached across her body with her good arm and opened the door. She pushed it open with her foot. Got out. "I'll check out the salon first."

Carver slid out of his side. There was a bakery van in front of the car. He stayed behind it. "You really think Paola fled from Miami to here and then went and got her hair done?"

"She's a Brazilian woman. Keeping her hair done is life."

Carver looked at Liana's tight hair bun. "You don't seem too concerned with it."

Her mouth dropped open slightly. "What do you mean by that?"

"Nothing. Just an observation."

She pressed her lips together. "My hair looks good when it's down."

"So, let it down. Act casual." He looked at her clothing. She was still wearing the sweatpants and shirt Sandra had put on her after tending to her wound. "We probably should have gotten you fresh clothing first."

Liana looked down at herself. Nodded. "You're right. No self-respecting Brazilian woman would walk around like this. I'm definitely not on top of my game right now."

"On the other hand, you're injured. People might understand."

She gave it some thought. "True. They'll just think I'm an injured slob." Liana straightened. "I'm going to the salon. Wish me luck."

Carver saw a woman walking out of the salon. She wore an apron, the kind that kept clients' hair from getting on her clothing. Her shoulders were bare, thanks to a sleeveless dress. Well, almost bare. There was a thick bandage on her left shoulder.

She stood outside, a haunted look on her face. She was trembling. Staring in horror as if seeing something that wasn't there. She leaned against the outside wall and closed her eyes. Carver had seen that look before.

He'd seen it on the faces of people who'd witnessed something so horrible their minds couldn't process it. They couldn't stop seeing it over and over again, like a nightmare playing on loop in their heads.

It was most commonly referred to as post-traumatic stress syndrome. PTSD. And this woman had it written all over her face. It almost certainly had something to do with that bandage on her shoulder.

Liana had noticed her too. "I think I see a person of interest."

"Me too."

"I can't even put my finger on why I think she knows something."

"It's a combination of things," Carver said. "Might be completely disconnected from Paola. Maybe she got robbed at gunpoint. But I doubt it."

Liana pursed her lips. "Do you think she's one of the sex trafficking victims from Morganville?"

Carver shook his head. "I don't recognize her."

"Okay. I'll go talk with her first. Find out if there's a connection." Liana walked toward the salon.

Carver waited for a moment, then walked out from behind the other side of the van and went to the bakery. He went inside and ordered a coffee and coxinha, all while watching Liana through the window.

The other woman seemed startled when Liana first spoke to her. Like she'd been lost in another world. Carver couldn't make out what they were saying by reading lips. Probably because they were talking in Portuguese.

The other woman seemed to loosen up after a minute. She nodded a few times and motioned Liana into the salon. He figured Liana hadn't gone straight to questioning the woman about Paola. She'd probably asked to get her hair done.

If there was one thing Carver knew about hair salons, it was that people talked a lot when they were getting their hair done. It was a prime place for gossip. Probably more so with women than men in his experience.

He took his coffee and food and sat outside at a table. The bakery was a busy place. The liquor store next door was even busier. The salon windows were tinted so he couldn't see inside. He focused on everyone else in the vicinity.

Nothing about these people raised any alarms. They all looked like ordinary people going about their lives. Working, picking up supplies, enjoying baked goods. The usual stuff.

He had a picture of Paola on his phone. He couldn't just go around asking if anyone had seen her. Not unless he had a good cover story. They might believe he was a brother or relative. But it would be a hard sell.

Carver wished he had a picture of the two of them together. He could pose as a boyfriend or husband. But he hadn't let Paola take pictures of them. He hadn't wanted to risk his picture getting out there even though she didn't use social media.

On the other hand, Carver had been prepared to find her by himself. He'd planned to use the boyfriend angle even though he had no proof the two of them were together. He'd also been prepared to use other means at his disposal. Some of them not so gentle.

Carver came up with an idea that was better than sitting around doing nothing. He went into the bakery. Went to the counter. The woman behind the counter walked up and smiled. Said something in Portuguese.

The language barrier was another factor he'd have to overcome. He smiled. "My wife came here and ordered coxinha earlier. I'm supposed to pick it up for her."

The woman stared blankly at him. Carver used the translator app on his phone. Showed the translation to the woman.

She read it. Nodded. Replied in Portuguese. "Name?"

"Paola." Carver showed her a picture to go along with the name.

The woman stared at the pic. There was no hint of recognition in her eyes. She shook her head. Said something else. Carver gave her the phone with the translator app open. She typed in a reply and gave it back to him.

He read it. *I'm sorry. I don't have an order for a Paola. Are you sure she came here?*

Carver frowned. Scratched the back of his head and looked confused. He typed another message and showed her the translation. *Sorry, I must be mistaken.*

He smiled, waved, and left. The man in the liquor store spoke heavily accented English. Carver went through the same routine. Said his wife came by to special order some alcohol and showed the man the picture. The man hadn't seen her either.

Carver worked his way through the other shops like that. No one questioned that she was his wife or seemed suspicious of him. People tended to let their guards down when they thought a man was doing an errand for his wife. They wanted to be helpful.

He worked his way around to the butcher shop. A young guy was cutting meat behind the counter. He greeted Carver in Portuguese. "Todo bem?" It translated to "Everything good?"

Carver nodded. "You speak English?"

The man nodded. "Yeah. Sorry, I thought you were Brazilian."

Carver didn't think he looked particularly Brazilian, but he wasn't going to complain. "My wife came in and ordered something for me to pick up. Name is Paola."

"We have two orders for two different Paolas." The butcher glanced at paper bags sitting in a refrigerated case. "What's the last name?"

"This is her." Carver showed him a picture.

"Oh, I think I remember her." He frowned. "You sure she placed an order recently? I think I saw her like a week ago or something. She was getting some bacon-wrapped chicken."

Carver feigned confusion. "I could have sworn she said she was coming here."

"Yeah, she came here. Then she said she was going to the salon and would come pick up the chicken afterward." The butcher looked up like he was thinking. Then he tilted his head slightly. "That's strange."

"What is?"

The butcher shook his head. Stared at Carver. "Okay, what's going on here?"

"What do you mean?"

"You have proof she's your wife?"

Carver was suddenly very interested. "Why would you ask that?"

The butcher raised his hands. "I'm not saying anything else. I don't want trouble."

Carver sighed. "Okay, here's the honest truth. She's a friend of mine and she went missing. I think she might be in trouble with a cartel."

The butcher stared at him, probably partly from surprise at the sudden admission. Probably partly because he didn't want to get mixed up with the cartel either.

"Anything you can tell me might save her life. Please."

Something finally shook loose in the other man's head. He blew out a breath. "There was another guy asking about her last week. He spoke flawless Portuguese, but he looked

American. He had a similar story to yours. Said she was his girlfriend and sent him to pick up an order."

"Describe him."

"He's light skinned, black hair and blue eyes. Like those real piercing blue eyes, you know? He also seemed real full of himself."

"Did he give a name?"

"No. And I didn't like his vibe, so I didn't tell him anything."

"I have a better vibe?" Carver asked.

The butcher shrugged. "I mean, you look kind of scary, but you come across like every other Brazilian husband who's running an errand for his wife, you know?"

Carver didn't know. He didn't have any idea what that meant.

The butcher kept talking. "I just hope you're not lying. I saw that other guy stake out the shopping center. He went to the bakery and just sat there. Then a couple of days ago he stopped showing up."

"Do you know the people who work at the salon?" Carver said.

"Not really, but I see them around. I say hello sometimes." He frowned. "Why?"

"I just noticed one of them had a shoulder injury."

The butcher seemed to think it over. "Yeah, I remember seeing the girl with the big bandage." His eyes flared. "You think that guy did it? He figured out your girl went to the salon, didn't he?"

"Maybe so." Carver didn't like where this was going. "Thanks for your help."

"Wait." The butcher walked around the corner, a cleaver in his hand. "You swear you're not after this girl?"

"I am after her, but only because she's a friend. It sounds like this other guy you described is after her for the cartel. I have to find her before he does."

The butcher's hand tightened around the handle of the cleaver. He looked worried. "I don't know what to believe."

"You don't have to believe me. But you have helped me." Carver turned and left. He wanted to go tell Liana what he'd discovered but didn't want to ruin whatever angle she was working. He went to the bakery and got another cup of coffee. Picked up a newspaper. Sat down and started reading.

He wasn't idly reading. He was looking for stories that stuck out. Stories that might link to Paola. He skimmed over the first few pages. Didn't see anything noteworthy. Just stories about local politicians, street crime, and so forth.

The local section focused more on this general area. There was a story about a festival scheduled for Saturday. A story about a dog someone saved from traffic. A story about another accident at a bad intersection.

There was one story that stood out. A story about a woman whose home was broken into. Money and valuables were stolen and then the home invader raped her.

The woman said she was almost certain the perpetrator was sent by someone in the neighborhood who didn't like her. She said she'd notified the homeowner about multiple HOA violations and gotten into a big argument with the other woman.

The woman's name was Aliyah Butler. It was a name that caught Carver's attention even though he was skimming the article. He went back to the beginning and read it more slowly. He read the description the victim gave the police.

The rapist wore a ski mask, but he had piercing blue eyes. Carver put that together with the name Aliyah Butler. He could finally put a face to the name.

She was one of the sex trafficking victims.

CHAPTER 20

Carver slid more puzzle pieces together.

Piercing blue eyes weren't common. They also weren't easy to fake with colored contact lenses. Which meant that the rapist was almost certainly the same guy who was after Paola. But why would he take time to rob and rape the HOA president?

Was he staking out Butler's home in the hopes Paola might go there? Did he decide to kill some time by violating one of the neighbors? There was a picture of the victim in the article. She certainly was not easy on the eyes.

She was short and dumpy but wearing a tight outfit that exposed her midriff. Her makeup was plastered on thick. Her jewelry was gaudy. She stood out and not in a good way. Why would the guy stalking Paola go out of his way to rape this woman?

Carver realized he was asking the wrong question. Rapists were sick and demented. What they did had nothing to do with attraction. It was about power. About sexual gratification from inflicting pain and taking away someone's bodily autonomy.

If this guy was following Paola, it stood to reason that he wouldn't have gone after this other woman unless she somehow got in the way. That seemed to be the most likely explanation.

He continued reading the story.

The police had tried to question Butler, but she wasn't home. They'd found evidence of a home intrusion and even a possible kitchen fire. It looked like the homeowner had packed and left in a hurry, which made the cops even more suspicious.

It made Carver suspicious too, but not for the same reasons. It made him think that Butler knew she was in danger and left town as fast as she could. It made her a person of great interest to him. But now she was on the run.

He skimmed the rest of the newspaper. Didn't see anything noteworthy. He turned on his phone. Searched for more local news. One story stood out in a sea of headlines. *Woman Falls to Death from Hotel Balcony.*

It was not only unusual, but it reminded him of Miami. There was no connection, but people falling from balconies wasn't something that happened every day, not even in big cities. He read the story.

The woman, identified as Angie Milton, was found dead in the alley by a hotel employee. Judging from her injuries, she'd fallen from one of the higher floors. They traced it to a balcony near the top floor.

The occupant stated that he'd come back from the hotel bar and found his balcony door open. Police confirmed his story. They also found hair on the floor that matched the victim's.

There was no record of which room the woman had been staying in. A hotel employee remembered seeing the woman with a dark-haired male with very noticeable blue eyes.

Carver stared at the description of the man for a moment. He hadn't expected to find any connection, but this certainly seemed like one. It wasn't a particularly useful connection, but it pointed to an obvious pattern in this man's behavior.

The bartender at the hotel bar also remembered seeing the same man with the woman. She remembered him because he kept flirting with her when his girlfriend went to the bathroom. He'd paid in cash, so there was no credit card record.

The hotel was still working on finding which room they'd stayed in since no one remembered the man's name. Carver didn't think the man would have killed his girlfriend if he'd signed into the hotel under a real name.

This was a person who felt he was so far above the law that he openly showed contempt for it. Even so, it seemed strange that he would toss his girlfriend off a balcony. Something must have triggered him.

Just like something had triggered him with the HOA president.

He sounded narcissistic. Angie had probably done something to infuriate him. Maybe she'd questioned his authority. Maybe she'd told him he was ugly. It was impossible to know for sure. Either way, it pointed to one vital fact.

This man was dangerous. He wouldn't hesitate to kill or to demonstrate his power over other people. If anything, it seemed to get him off. He didn't seem like the usual cartel thug. He sounded like a freelance killer.

If he was, he wasn't very disciplined. He'd committed two high-profile crimes within hours of each other. He'd left a very visible trail. Most professional killers weren't flashy like that. They focused solely on the target. Collateral damage was usually minimal, unless the job called for carnage.

Whatever the case, if he had a list of the sex trafficking victims, it meant he had connections in high places. He had access to privileged information. It meant Paola was in imminent danger.

Liana stepped out of the hair salon. Her hair was down. It was straight and glossy black. Her face looked different too, but he couldn't pinpoint why. He left the bakery. Headed for the car.

She saw him. Waved him over. Carver changed direction. Met her outside the salon. "Your hair looks good."

Liana stroked her hair. "Of course it does. Brazilians don't play around when it comes to hair."

"What did you find out?"

"She's not talking to me. She just said she had an accident."

"You asked her directly?"

Liana shook her head. "No. I worked my way around the question. Unfortunately, she's very tight-lipped about it."

"I think I know why. What's her name?"

"Nilva."

"Thanks." Carver opened the door. Went inside. The woman with the bandage was standing next to an empty barber chair. She stared blankly at the mirror. The fear in her eyes was easily visible.

He walked over to her. "Nilva."

She gasped. Looked at him and shrank back.

Liana joined him. She looped her arm through his. Spoke in Portuguese.

Nilva put a hand over her chest. Nodded. Replied.

Other women in the salon were looking at them, eyes filled with curiosity. They wanted the scoop.

"Ask her to join us out front," Carver said. "Tell her I know what happened and we're here to help."

Liana leaned forward and whispered to Nilva. The other woman trembled but followed them outside.

Carver led them away from the window so they couldn't be seen. "Ask her if a guy with piercing blue eyes did this to her."

Liana relayed the message. Listened to the reply. "Yes. He has light skin, black hair, very blue eyes. He's very handsome and athletic looking."

Carver showed Nilva his picture of Paola. Nilva's eyes widened. She spoke rapid Portuguese to Liana.

Liana listened and translated for Carver. "This man was looking for the woman in the picture. Somehow, he found out she came to the salon and saw Nilva. He followed her home. After Nilva's husband came home, this man came inside and tied them up at gunpoint. He stabbed her in the shoulder when she wouldn't talk."

Carver already knew the answer, but he asked anyway. "Did he rape her?"

Nilva froze when Liana relayed the question. She looked down. Tears welled in her eyes. Several seconds passed before she nodded. She started shaking like it was freezing outside. She wasn't shaking with sobs. She was angry.

The rapist made her feel powerless. He tortured her. Threatened her. Took everything from her.

Liana put a hand on Nilva's good shoulder. Said something else. Nilva looked at her. Nodded.

"He threatened to kill her if she talked," Carver said. "Ask her what she told him. I don't think it matters now, but we might as well know."

"Why doesn't it matter?"

"I'll tell you in the car."

Liana asked Nilva. Got an answer. She spoke to her in a soothing voice. Rubbed the other woman's arm. That didn't seem to help too much.

Carver wasn't the soothing type. He didn't think it was possible to make another person feel better with nice words. At least not when it came to something like this. "Tell her that we're after the man who did this, and when we find him, we'll kill him."

Liana looked at him. Frowned. "Really?"

"Yes, really."

She sighed. Told Nilva.

Nilva's eyes lit with ferocity. She gripped Carver's hand. Spoke directly to him. The anger in her voice made it clear that she approved. That she wanted this man's head delivered to her in a box.

Liana translated. "She prays that God helps you deliver swift justice and says you are his avenging angel. She wants us to let her know when it's done so she and her husband can feel safe again."

Carver nodded. "I will."

Nilva kissed Carver's hand. Dried her face with her hands. She took a pen from her apron and wrote her phone number on a slip of paper and gave it to him. Then she went back inside the salon without another word.

Carver walked back to the car. Liana walked alongside him, a curious look on her face. He opened the car door for her. Not because he was a gentleman but because he wanted her shoulder to heal.

He was going to need someone watching his six. Someone who could shoot a gun. Unfortunately, she probably needed a good two to three weeks to heal from an injury like that. She was going to have to shoot with an injured shoulder.

Carver dropped into his seat. He turned on the car and got the heater going. He told Liana about his conversation with the butcher. About the news stories he'd read. She connected the dots on her own.

"So, this guy brought his girlfriend with him on a business trip. He got a room at a fancy hotel under a fake ID. He tracked down Paola by threatening this woman and her husband, but he still let them live even after seeing his face."

"That tracks so far," Carver said.

"He threatened to kill Nilva and her husband if they said a word then raped her." Liana shook her head. "He went on to rape this HOA woman and then tossed his girlfriend off the balcony of the hotel all within the same night."

"Yep." Carver added in another detail. "The girlfriend showed signs of sexual abuse before her death."

"Oh, God." Liana grimaced. "What kind of psycho are we dealing with?"

"I'm still trying to figure that out." Carver plugged in the name of the subdivision where Butler lived. He didn't have an exact address, but this was close enough. He guided the car out of the parking lot and followed the GPS directions.

"I'm not a behavioral analyst, but he's definitely a psychopath."

"So, he believes he's always right and has no conscience." Carver also wasn't a behavioral analyst, but he'd known sociopaths and psychopaths all his life. In fact, he'd worked alongside them in the military. He was probably one himself.

"From what little we know of him, yes. He's a textbook psychopath." Liana stared out the side window. "He's not unlike some of our assets. Makes me wonder if he's a freelancer for the agency."

"It doesn't really matter. Most of this ties back to Enigma, so he's either directly or indirectly working for them." Carver shrugged. "Probably."

"I hate not being able to call the office for information." She blew out a breath. "I could probably identify him in twenty-four hours. There are some off-the-books assets I could use, but I'd have to be very careful about it."

"You might still be in good standing with the agency, but this guy's identity would be a well-hidden secret." Carver turned at an intersection and checked to see how much further he had to go. The GPS said it was three miles and eighteen minutes away.

He had traffic to thank for that. It was mid-afternoon. Rush hour, apparently. He'd spent as much time as possible away from big cities. Traffic was certainly a major reason why. The other reason was because nothing good ever happened to him in big cities.

Liana didn't seem to mind the traffic. She stared at the road, lost in her thoughts. She seemed to sense him looking at her and turned her gaze on him for a moment. Then she returned to looking at the road without comment.

The subdivision came into view about fifteen minutes later. A tall brick wall surrounded it like it was a little kingdom. A gate provided the only way in or out. The turn lane on the right-hand side of the road was completely blocked thanks to traffic waiting on the light and traffic turning into the subdivision.

Every so often, the subdivision gate would open, and two cars would slip through, but it wasn't doing much to free up the blockade. Carver got in line. As luck would have it, no one else turned into the subdivision ahead of him.

He reached the gate and pulled into the visitor's lane. There was a keypad and a display with the directory. He scrolled down the names until he found the name Fani Wilson. That was the name of the HOA president from the news story.

Carver dialed the three-digit number. A woman answered on the second ring.

"Hello, this is Fani Wilson, President of Eternal Gardens. How can I help you?"

"I'm here to talk to you about the events of last night," Carver said. "We still have a few questions."

Suspicion filled her voice. "You're the police?"

"No, we're reporters."

"Oh!" Her voice brightened. "Come on in. Follow the road to the last intersection, turn right, and you can't miss my house at the end." There was a buzz. The call ended and the gate opened.

"You're good at that," Liana said. "What exactly did you do in your former life?"

"Worked in the service industry." Carver drove through the gate.

"No, seriously."

Carver didn't answer. He slowed at the first intersection. Saw police tape at a house at the end of the road on the left. That was almost certainly Butler's place. He'd come back after they spoke with Fani.

There was a slim chance she knew anything useful, like where Butler had gone, but there was a chance her attacker might have let slip some useful bit of information.

Carver kept going straight. Found Fani's house easily. She was right when she said he couldn't miss it. Not with the gold mailbox and a giant sign out front proclaiming her title. There were no similar signs in any of the other yards he'd seen.

"Talk about a violation of HOA rules." Liana huffed. "The rules are for thee and not for me."

Carver parked. Walked to the front door. It opened before he reached it. The short, chubby woman from the pictures in the news story greeted them with a bright smile. She looked at the car with confusion. "Oh, you're not with the TV station?"

"We're an independent news organization with a large social media presence," Liana said. "We reach more people every day than the TV news does in an entire week.

"Oh, really?" The disappointment morphed into enthusiasm. "How large is it?"

"It's called Syndicated News National. We have roughly twenty-five million followers across multiple platforms."

Fani looked it up on her phone. Her eyes brightened and her mouth dropped open. "That's amazing! Come on in!"

They went inside. The house looked clean but rundown. Like it hadn't been renovated since the year it was built.

Fani led them to the den and motioned them toward the couch. "Do you want me to tell the story from the beginning?"

Liana took out her phone. "I'm going to record with this. Is that okay?"

"Absolutely."

She trained the camera on Fani. "Tell us what happened, Ms. Wilson."

"I was upstairs watching television and I thought I heard a noise. I came downstairs and saw this man in a ski mask coming out of the garage." She shivered. "He took me at gunpoint. Took me upstairs and threatened physical harm if I didn't do what he said."

Liana feigned concern. "That sounds terrifying. What exactly did he say to you?"

Fani looked away briefly. "He just said to give him my jewelry and money. So, I did. It was terrifying." She shivered. "Then he pinned me down. Ripped off my panties. He pulled down his pants and made me—"

"We don't need graphic details," Liana said. "Just the basics."

"Oh yes, of course." Fani smiled brightly. "Let's just say he had his way with me."

"Was he wearing protection?" Liana asked. "Did the police swab for DNA evidence?"

"He wasn't wearing protection and he finished inside me." She shivered. "It was like he was on some kind of power trip and wasn't afraid of anything."

"Did he threaten to do something to you if you went to the police?"

"Yes. And even stranger, after he finished, he said if I was lucky, I might have his kid."

Liana's eyes widened. "He was actually hopeful that he got you pregnant?"

"Yes!" Fani shivered again. "I never saw his face, but he had a great body. Amazing blue eyes." She shuddered. "But there was no humanity in those beautiful eyes of his. He's a monster."

"Did you get checked for diseases?" Liana said.

"I took a morning after pill to make sure I'm not pregnant, and I was tested. I have to wait a couple of weeks to get the rest of the tests to make sure I didn't contract HIV or something worse."

"He didn't say anything else?"

She shook her head. "No. Just a lot of crude stuff during sex. He kept asking questions like, do you like that dick? Is it the best you ever had? I'll bet you love this, don't you?"

"Disgusting," Liana said. "Sounds like a real animal."

"What was really weird though was he had this super fake British accent. It was so over the top I almost started laughing at one point."

"He faked a British accent?"

Fani nodded. "I'm no expert on accents, but this one was so fake it was laughable. I guess he was just trying to disguise his voice."

"Sounds like a very disturbed individual." Liana shuddered. "Did you notice anything else?"

Fani frowned. "There's something kind of strange. He saw the parking tickets I'd written this week in my office and took them all. He said it was to give my victims a reprieve." She huffed. "Some people just don't follow the rules, you know?"

"All too well," Liana said.

"It didn't matter to me because my ticket pad makes copies in triplicate, so the copies were still there." Fani quirked her lips. "But when I went to get the copies, I noticed one was missing."

Liana raised an eyebrow. "How did you know one was missing?"

"Because I'd written it just a few hours earlier." Fani smirked. "That got me to thinking. He must have taken that copy. Which means he took all the other tickets from my office to cover up that he was really only interested in the one."

"What was the ticket for?" Liana asked.

"It was for an improperly parked car just down the road from Aliyah Butler's house." Fani's forehead wrinkled. "That was when I knew the car belonged to that man and that he was sent by that bitch!"

That perked Carver's ears. "What information is on the ticket?"

"The usual," Fani said. "Make, model, color, and license plate number."

That was the important information Carver had hoped to find. With something like that, he might actually be able to track where the car was going. "Do you still have a copy of the ticket?" Carver asked.

She shook her head. "No. Like I said, the only other copy was in the ticket pad, and he must have taken it."

"Do you remember what the car looked like?"

She frowned. Looked up, like she was trying to recall it. "I can't picture it. I think everything else that happened to me last night is messing with my head."

And just like that, they'd hit another dead end.

CHAPTER 21

Carver needed that car's description.

The license plate would have been even better, but he'd take anything he could get at this point. This guy was chasing Paola. Carver was dead in the water without actionable intel.

Liana frowned. "You don't have anything to go on? No license plate? No description?"

"Of course, I do, girl." Fani laughed and clapped her hands once like she'd won a prize. "I always enter the information into the computer right away. Otherwise, it doesn't get done."

"Do you usually keep a paper copy?" Liana asked.

"Always. I have to keep them for audits." Fani laughed again. "That man asked me if I'd entered the information in the computer. I told him I hadn't because I didn't want him erasing everything. He thought he was helping people avoid justice, but he underestimated me."

"Smart move," Liana said. "May we see this information?"

"Of course. Spread it far and wide. Maybe someone will catch this asshole."

"Aren't you concerned he'll come back for you?" Liana asked.

"I don't think he will. He'll be running scared now." Fani pushed up from her chair. Led them upstairs to an office. She sat down in an office chair and moved the mouse on the desk. The monitor blinked on. She opened a spreadsheet. Scrolled down to a section with yesterday's date on it.

The description and license plate were there.

"Oh, I almost forgot." She took out her phone. "I also took pictures of the car. I always take pictures so I can prove they were violating the rules if they try to contest the ticket."

"And you think this man is somehow connected to one of the people in this subdivision?" Liana said.

"Yes." Fani's lips curled with contempt. "The timing is just too perfect to be coincidence." She scrolled through images of other people's front yards. Pictures that had apparently been taken just a short time ago.

"Looks like the neighbors are constantly violating the rules," Liana said.

Fani sighed. "It's a full-time job keeping up with the slobs. I want this place to be a jewel in the center of the city."

"You're doing a great job." Liana gave her a thumbs up. "It must be extremely difficult and demanding."

"Thank you so much." Fani beamed. "It's a thankless job, but I am driven to keep our community clean and perfect." She stared at something on her phone. "Ah, here we go." She turned it around and showed them a picture of the car.

It was a black Honda CRV. An older model. The same kind of car that always seemed to be driving slowly in the passing lane when Carver was in a hurry to get somewhere.

"Can you send me those images?" Liana gave Fani the burner phone's number.

"Absolutely."

"Did you take pictures of the violations for this other woman's house? We want to take a deep look at this woman. Find out if we can connect her to the crime perpetrated against you."

"That would be amazing!" Fani's eyes lit with almost demonic pleasure. "I'd love to see her burn."

"We'll do what we can to help." Liana winked. "The juicier the story, the better."

"Here you go." Fani texted several images to Liana. "She was always getting visits from strange men. She told me they were her brother and boyfriend, but I didn't believe her. I think she was trying to run a brothel from her home."

"A brothel?" Liana's eyebrows rose. "Did you document the men coming to her home?"

"I wanted to, but I wasn't able. I just saw that four or five visitors a day were ringing her number from the main gate. Most people barely have one or two a day." Fani tutted. "Something was up. Maybe the man who assaulted me was her pimp."

"We'll get right on this and let you know what we find." Liana turned off recording. "In the meantime, if you think of anything else, please let me know."

"When do you think my story will be live?" Fani asked.

"It will have to go through editing and production, so hopefully within a week or so."

"Can you post my social media links with the story? I make custom candles, and this might help get out the word."

"I'd love to. Just text them to me." Liana stood. "Thank you so much for your time, Ms. Wilson."

"Absolutely!" Fani giggled and clapped her hands with excitement.

They left and got into the car. Liana showed Carver the pictures of Butler's house. There were clear images of the cars in the driveway. License plates and everything. Fani was nothing if not thorough.

"She said they can't park in the driveway or leave the garage door open." Liana shook her head. "God, what a little dictator."

Carver followed the cul-de-sac around and drove toward the gates. He turned right onto Butler's road and parked in the driveway. There was police tape over the front door and the garage.

One of the cars from the pictures was still in the driveway, a gray minivan. The white SUV was gone as was the silver Honda. The pictures showed a pair of men getting out of the SUV.

It looked like Fani had staked out the house. She'd probably been watching it for a while before confronting Butler and company.

Liana frowned and stared intently at one picture. She showed it to Carver. A blonde woman stood at the front door as the two men approached it. There was another woman behind her. A woman with black hair. The face was hard to make out.

Liana magnified the image. "Is that Paola?"

"It's a woman with black hair." Carver stared at the shape, form and height. "Matches Paola's outline."

"I'd bet it's her."

"I think you're right. The man followed her here. He parked on the road and watched. Probably got out at some point when it was dark and went to the house for a closer look. That was when Fani gave him the ticket."

"He saw the ticket had his license plate and description on it and went to her house to get rid of the ticket." Liana went silent for a moment. "Fani discovered him. He also found out the ticket book made two copies, so he needed to get all the copies. He decided to exert his power over her while he was at it. Live out his sick rapist breeder fantasy. A guy like that needs to be castrated or put down like an animal."

Carver got out of the car. He opened the door for Liana.

"Thanks." She pushed herself up without too much effort, but pain flashed briefly across her face. "You don't strike me as the kind of guy who routinely holds doors open for women."

Carver didn't have a response for that, so he walked to the front door. Tested the handle. It was locked. He went to the fence. Unlatched the gate and swung it open.

The back door was locked, but the door jamb had been broken. Probably when the police rammed it open. He pushed it open. Stepped through the police tape barricade. He briefly looked over the kitchen.

The cabinets around the gas stove were blackened. Like a sudden flash of intense heat had hit them and just as suddenly dissipated.

Liana sniffed the air. "This area was filled with gas. Something lit the gas and caused these burns."

The microwave door hung slightly open. Carver opened it all the way. Forks, spoons, and aluminum foil were piled inside. The safety latch was broken. He grinned. "Paola tried to blow him up."

"Seriously?" Liana looked it over. "She turned on the gas, turned on the microwave, and left the house."

"She knew he was here." Carver walked into the dining room, but it looked dusty and unused.

He went into the foyer. A staircase led to the second floor. He stepped into the den. A sectional couch curved around the room. The upstairs balcony overlooked the stairs. He went to the window and pushed the curtain aside.

A thin wire ran from the window and down to the baseboard. Carver followed the wire to the other end. Found a pinhole camera attached to the window casing.

"A wired camera?" Liana said.

"Looks like it. Makes it so you can't detect it with a wireless camera app."

"Smart." Liana looked at the TV screen. It was broken. Like something had struck it. She looked around. Pushed the coffee table aside with her foot. There was a tablet computer beneath it.

She picked it up. Examined it. The screen wasn't broken. The corner was chipped. She turned it on. "Someone threw this at the television. It bounced off and slid under the coffee table."

Carver wondered if it had been done in self-defense. The television was nowhere near the door or an entrance so if the tablet had been thrown at an intruder, they would have been standing in front of the television.

He looked over her shoulder at the tablet. "What's on it?"

"Just a bunch of games." Liana tapped on the icons. One was poker. Another was a puzzle game. About halfway through, she tapped on an icon that pulled up images instead. Not images. Video feeds.

"It's a hidden app for the cameras." Carver grunted. "I guess she followed my advice after all."

"What advice was that?"

"Always use cameras or motion sensor alarms to guard your position if possible. Never let your guard down. Those kinds of things."

"If it were anyone but you saying that I'd call them paranoid."

Carver raised an eyebrow. "Taking precautions isn't paranoia."

Liana tapped the menu in the app. There were several saved video clips from the night before. She opened one and played it from the moment a man hopped off the brick wall in the backyard and walked toward the house.

The man was looking right at the camera. There was no light in the back yard, but the camera had decent night vision. Enough to give a clear look at the man's face when he got closer. There was no color to the image because of the night vision, but it was good enough.

"That's our sexual predator slash assassin." Liana took a picture. "Looks like your girl is smart. She's a survivor."

"Yeah. She did good."

"You sound like a proud father." Liana laughed.

"I'm just glad she's okay." Carver did feel a bit proud. Paola was staying ahead of the game, just barely.

Liana looked at the tablet from the edge. "There are smudges on the glass. I don't see any fingerprints. Just dirt.

"Dirt?" Carver took the tablet and inspected it. There were faint dirt smudges. "Someone with dirty gloves. Probably the intruder. He might have seen something on the tablet that made him angry enough to throw it on the television."

"Probably his own stupid face." Liana froze the image of the man at the back window.

"We have a face," Carver said. "Now we just need a way to track these license plate numbers."

"I have the resources, but I'm afraid to try to use them." Liana tapped a fingernail on the tablet. "I could make an encrypted call with the burner, but every call is traced. Even if I reached one of my techs, they wouldn't be able to transmit results without notifying my boss."

"Once they find out it's you, all kinds of flags will be raised. Anything you ask for will be transmitted to a third party."

"Third party?"

Carver nodded. "The same shadow organization controlling the operators who almost killed you. They have several names, but I call them Enigma."

Liana didn't look surprised. "There are always conspiracy theories making the rounds. The existence of a powerful shadow organization is one of the most popular. I think the reason for that is because it truly exists."

"Oh, it exists all right. You're living proof."

She made a face. "Maybe. Or they could just be rogue operators working for a rogue at the agency."

"It's possible."

Liana pressed her lips together. "I just find it hard to believe a massive conspiracy at the highest levels of government is possible." She laughed mirthlessly. "Have you met any politicians? Most of them aren't very bright. They're either bored rich people or they're idiots who can't get a real job."

"That's not something I'd expect to hear from a G-man."

Liana laughed. "Joining the agency wasn't exactly part of my life plans."

"Were you in the military?"

"I was."

"Which branch?"

"I can't talk about it."

Carver stared blankly at her. "In case you hadn't noticed, you're on the run."

"I know, but I think it can all be worked out." Her gaze went distant. "I don't think I'm out in the cold. I just need to see this through and then go back in."

"And act like nothing happened?"

"Maybe." She shook her head. "I'm still working through things in my head."

Carver wasn't sure if he believed her or not. Had everything at her home been an elaborate show so she could gain his trust? Getting a hole blown through her shoulder was a hell of a way to do it.

Not only that, but he'd eliminated one of their operators. It didn't seem like the cost of admission was worth it.

He put himself in their shoes, whoever they were. Why would they want Carver? What value did he offer? He couldn't think of anything. They considered him a threat. A thorn in their side.

In that case, elimination was the best tactic. Embedding an agent with him gave them ample opportunity to eliminate him. Liana probably could have ended him during the drive. He hadn't let his guard down, but all it took was a single gunshot in close quarters to do the trick.

Maybe she was an unknowing implant. They knew Carver had protected Paola. They knew there was some connection there. Maybe they wanted to see how he'd react if Liana's life was in danger.

Would he rescue a complete stranger? Would he rescue a potential enemy combatant?

That answer was apparently yes. His reaction had been instinct. Liana had been an unknown at first. Then he'd discovered her identity and considered her a threat. Then the assault team had shown up and cast things into doubt.

Carver had saved himself. Been ready to leave. He'd heard the order to terminate her, reacted unfavorably to that order, and saved her. And now they were here.

Liana watched him closely. "You still don't trust me."

"I don't trust many people."

"Understandable." She pressed her lips together. "I'm not on your side, okay? I want to help you because of Paola. Not for any other reason."

"So, at the end of the day, you're an agency woman. You'll go back to them."

She nodded. "Yes. But I want to see this through. I don't think I can do that from the inside. I need to be out here with you."

"Because of Lucas and whatever your relationship is to him."

"He was a fellow agent. I was close to him."

"As in you were friends? Or something more?"

Liana sighed. "Lucas and I had a moment. But it was short. He was a man obsessed with revenge against the Herrada Cartel. I don't need that kind of person in my romantic life. Plus, the agency wouldn't approve of it."

"They normally don't. It's a big no-no."

She laughed. "A big no-no? You don't look like the kind of guy who says that."

"What's your primary motivation for sticking with me?"

"I just told you that. Lucas is a part of it, but now that my eyes are open and I know more about Paola and you, I just want her to be safe. And I want this rapist tortured for a long time before putting him out of his misery."

"That's not something I'd expect to hear from a federal agent."

"I said the quiet part out loud, okay? Death is too good for some people. I know as a federal agent I shouldn't advocate for that, but I'm a special agent, not some run of the mill cop. I have a little leeway and I don't care what you think."

"In this particular case, I approve," Carver said.

"I don't need your approval."

"I didn't say you did."

Carver wanted to believe her. He needed someone he could trust. Someone who would have his back. If she was with Enigma, she'd be willing to do anything. He'd learned that lesson in San Francisco. He didn't feel like learning it again.

He'd seen intelligence agents do all kinds of crazy things to gain the trust of others. What if everything he'd found in her house had been part of the setup? What if the fake IDs and the NSA ID were planted?

Maybe that was one step too close to paranoia.

Those IDs had been too well hidden to be planted for his benefit. They would have been placed somewhere slightly more obvious to ensure that he found them. She was an NSA agent. Having fake IDs was sometimes part of the job.

The questions he needed to ask were more elementary. Even if he trusted her, was she useful to him? Should he keep her around or leave her somewhere?

The answers seemed obvious. She couldn't use agency assets to help them. She had an injured shoulder and couldn't help him much in a firefight. But she had good instincts and the intelligence to go along with it.

If he abandoned her, he might be leaving her to die. She might see no other choice except to go back to the agency and find out what fate awaited her there. Even if the NSA was welcoming, Enigma would almost certainly interrogate her.

It would almost certainly be the last time she was seen alive.

Carver shook off the questions for the time being and studied the tablet. He scrolled through the other video clips. They were all from the same night. There was no audio. The cameras didn't have that capability.

He watched all the video clips at double speed. They were motion activated, so most of them featured the man. Two clips captured by the cameras in the front windows didn't seem to have been triggered by anything. At least by nothing Carver could see.

The other video clips from the front cameras featured the two men arriving in the SUV and the confrontation with Fani. The last couple of clips seemed to show nothing. There were no insects or anything else that might have triggered the camera.

He was about to chalk them up to errors but something in the last clip caught his attention. He slowed it down to normal speed. Watched closely.

"What are you looking at?" Liana stared at the screen. "Nothing's there."

Carver kept watching. Then he saw it. The slight movement that had triggered the camera. It was a shadow just outside of night vision range. It was hard to make out, but it looked like it was near the silver Honda.

He tapped the settings icon and lightened the image as much as possible. The shadow stood out in a little more contrast, but not enough to see details. It was almost certainly the man from before.

Carver went to the previous video and found the shadow on it. He set the brightness to max and watched it. The shadow crouched next to the Honda. It appeared to be doing something to the undercarriage.

The video ended. The next video started when the shadow was moving away from the car. It wasn't much to go on, but it was enough for Carver to know what had happened. The man had put something on the car.

It was being tracked.

CHAPTER 22

Decker watched the red blip.

It had stopped north of Chattanooga for the night. He went to the location and found the silver Honda parked at a cheap motel. It would be easy enough to eliminate Butler now and take Paola, but he was curious about where they were going.

And he liked to play with his prey.

Paola thought she'd outsmarted him. She might even think she'd killed him. Decker was almost giddy at the thought of showing her just how wrong she was. He imagined the surprised expression on her face when he showed up at her doorstep. He laughed until his ribs hurt.

"Thought you outplayed me, didn't you?" He couldn't stop grinning. "Stupid bitch." He was going to savor this cat and mouse game.

Decker kept a close watch on the front window of the motel. He waited to see if Paola had more cameras. To see if she had any other tricks up her sleeve. She was probably keeping a close eye on the news.

He'd also kept tabs on the news. Fani had gone to the police. She hadn't been able to describe him because of his ski mask, but it was still infuriating that she hadn't taken his threat seriously.

At his earliest convenience, he was going to pay her another visit. He would let her see his face this time. Explain to her that she'd signed her own death warrant. Then he would choke the life out of that fat little bitch while he had his way with her.

There really wasn't anything quite as exhilarating as dominating someone while watching the life drain out of their eyes. That was real power. His only regret was that once they were dead, they couldn't appreciate the lesson they'd learned.

He planned to simply kill Aliyah Butler. The thought of sex with Jasper Whittaker's leftovers was disgusting. She was already so low in life that she wasn't worth his attention.

But that would have to wait. There were other reasons he hadn't simply stormed in and claimed his victory. He wanted more. There was a slight chance Paola would lead him to other women on his list.

Being patient had its rewards. He was nothing if not patient.

Decker was falling asleep out of boredom when something jerked him out of his drowsiness. Almost two hours had passed since he'd parked, and nothing had happened. Now a white SUV was pulling into the motel parking lot.

A short woman got out. Walked to the door. She raised a fist, but the door opened before she could knock. Decker couldn't see who answered. The woman went inside. She looked familiar. Not because he'd met her, but because she was one of the few targets he had a picture of.

He opened the dossier file on his phone. Scrolled down the pictures. Found the woman who'd gone inside. She was short. Caucasian. Blond hair and brown eyes. Name was Lacy Hood. That was interesting because she was also officially listed as dead.

Decker hadn't crossed her off the list, though. He'd known better. She'd probably gone into witness protection and assumed a new identity. She didn't have to be a witness in a court case to get that protection.

This proved beyond a shadow of a doubt that Paola was in contact with the women on the list. But why had she brought this woman out of hiding? It was almost certainly because Paola was looking for a safe place to lie low.

What better place to hide than with someone under the protection of WITSEC?

The motel was outside Chattanooga and half a mile off the highway. It was surrounded by forests and mountainous terrain. There were two dim streetlamps lighting the gravel parking lot. That made it easy for him to approach the motel unseen.

He kept to the edge of the motel parking lot. Reached the building. Stayed close to the wall and went to Paola's window. He took out a small suction cup. Put it on the window. Plugged in the earphones. Put them on.

It was an old-school device, but it worked well in low tech situations like this. The clarity of the conversation was a little muddled but intelligible. The strong Brazilian accent of the speaker told him it was Paola.

She was describing what had happened in Marietta. Telling them that her trap hadn't worked. Otherwise, the news would have reported a gas explosion and a burned corpse. She said that Aliyah needed a safe place to stay for now.

The other woman answered. "She can stay with me however long she needs. I have a totally new identity. There's no way he'll find me."

Want to bet? Decker thought. He grinned.

Lacy kept talking. "Do you still have the money?"

Aliyah answered. "Yes. Leon helped me put it in a secure account."

"He did the same for me. I don't know what I would have done if Paola hadn't introduced me to him."

"He is a good person," Paola said. "He wants to do the right thing. Punish the bad people. But now he has people looking for him too."

"No good deed goes unpunished." Aliyah sighed. "Paola, why don't you stay with us?"

"I can't. I need to contact Leon. Tell him someone is looking for you and the others. The encrypted app I used to contact him was on my phone and it was destroyed in Morganville."

Lacy spoke. "How do you plan to find him?"

Aliyah said something before she could answer. "What we really need is that Carver guy. He could handle this stalker no problem."

"I wish," Paola said. "I could only contact him with the same app." She went silent for a moment before continuing. "I also had a backup email address Carver gave me in case I lost the phone, but I don't remember the password for it."

"Because it was on the phone?" Aliyah said.

"Yes. I'm so stupid."

Aliyah laughed. "Don't be too hard on yourself. I can barely remember the PIN for my phone, and I used it all the time. Well, before tossing it off that bridge during the drive up here. We need to get burner phones tomorrow."

Lacy spoke. "I'll talk to my WITSEC handler. Maybe we can get you a new identity too."

Aliyah groaned. "God, just when I'd met a nice guy, too. His friend liked Paola, but she wasn't interested."

"Not interested?" Lacy laughed. "Come on, girl. You need to blow off some steam."

Aliyah made an exaggerated grunt. "She had a boyfriend in Miami, but he was killed."

"He was no boyfriend," Paola said. "He was using me."

The other women gasped.

Decker already knew this part. Paola was talking about Lucas. There was a slight crack where the curtain didn't cover the window entirely. He looked up and down the parking lot to ensure no one was out here with him, then angled for a view inside.

He saw the woman sitting on the bed. Aliyah and Lacy were staring in open-mouthed surprise at Paola.

"Hold up, girl." Aliyah's forehead pinched. "You told me he was your boyfriend."

"I did not know what to tell you. It all happened very fast." Paola shook her head and looked down. "We were supposed to meet for a date, then I saw him being chased by two men."

Lacy's mouth dropped open. "Say what? Who were they?"

"At the time I didn't know." Paola's forehead pinched. "Lucas kept running. I walked away very calmly until I was away from the park where we were supposed to meet. Then I ran to my apartment and took my go-bag."

"Holy crap." Aliyah looked stunned. "You didn't tell me any of this."

"Because it's horrible." Paola slumped. "Later, I received a text from Lucas. It said if I received his message then he was probably dead. He was an agent with the National Security Agency. He was using me to get to the cartel."

"The NSA?" Lacy looked confused. "I thought the DEA dealt with drug cartels."

"Apparently, the cartel is into a lot more than drugs." Paola sighed. "I knew something was off about Lucas, but I went against my instincts because it felt good to have someone in my life again."

"Aw, you poor girl." Lacy hugged her.

Aliyah looked confused. "Why did Lucas think he could use you, of all people, to get to the cartel?"

Paola looked down. "He was just crazy, I think."

"Didn't you have access to their computer records?" Aliyah said.

Paola paused. She stared blankly for a moment. "I did download some files I shouldn't have had access to. There was a shared cloud folder. I think someone accidentally uploaded the file to the wrong folder. I copied it and later noticed the original file had been deleted from the folder."

"What was in the file?" Lacy asked.

"It was a map of the United States. There were different colored dots from one side to the other. There were symbols next to the dots."

"Whoa." Aliyah looked stunned. "Cartel operations?"

"I don't know. There was no key explaining what the dots were." Paola stared blankly at the wall for a moment. "I kept the file for myself. I thought maybe I could use it to escape the cartel. Then Carver came along and killed everyone, so I thought I was free."

"Did anyone else know about this file?" Aliyah asked.

Paola nodded. "A month before Carver came to town, I sent the file to someone I trusted to see if they could decipher it."

Lacy's eyebrows rose. "Who?"

"It was someone my father knew. Someone who helped him launder money for the cartel." Paola bit her lower lip. "He said he would look into it, but I never heard back from him."

"Which means someone knew he got that file. Someone probably killed him." Aliyah grimaced. "And they know you have it."

"Maybe." Paola shrugged. "It's possible the NSA or some other government agency intercepted the email. Maybe Lucas knew I had this file and thought he could get it from me."

"Maybe he should have just asked." Aliyah rolled her eyes. "Men."

Lacy laughed. "Yeah, men."

Decker could hardly believe his ears. Paola had dirt on the cartel. That explained why they wanted her alive. That explained why her bounty was so high. It also explained why Lucas thought she was valuable to him.

The cartel, of course, hadn't told Decker anything about this map file. This was a real game changer. Paola had something of great value to the cartel. Once he had her, he could find out where she'd stored this file.

Armed with that information, he could negotiate a higher fee from the cartel. Paola's bounty was already a million dollars. Maybe he could stretch that into ten times the amount. He just had to be careful not to overplay his hand.

Pedro Herrada wasn't the kind and forgiving sort.

The women kept talking, but their conversation wandered into gossip. They talked about men and having families, and all the boring crap women loved to talk about. It didn't sound like they were going to talk business again anytime soon.

Decker didn't have any more GPS trackers or he would have put one Lacy's car. Aliyah was going home with her in the morning. Their bounties were just a fraction of Paola's, but he didn't want to lose them.

Paola didn't say where she was going next. She did say at one point that she planned to contact Leon and disappear again, but first she needed a new phone and a way to contact him. Decker was certain that she was talking about Leon Fry, the former CEO of Breakstone.

The government had seized the company assets after Morganville and Leon had gone off the radar. Which meant he could certainly help Paola disappear. That was a smart move on her part. Staying off the cartel's radar was good for her health.

Unfortunately for her, she wasn't going to have a chance to disappear. Decker was going to follow Paola's every move. Spy on her for as long as it took to find out where she was keeping the map file.

He suspected it was in a cloud account connected to her cell phone. She hadn't replaced her lost phone yet. Once she did, she'd install the apps that connected to her cloud account. That was when he would strike.

He knew all kinds of unpleasant ways to make people talk. But he was hopeful she would unknowingly give him the information he needed without all the fuss. Then he would bend her to his will. Make her understand just how stupid she was for thinking she could kill or outsmart him.

Once he'd broken her psychologically, he'd deliver her and the map file to the cartel. He would walk away a rich man. A powerful man. A man who could retire and do whatever he liked.

Decker fantasized about negotiating the finder's fee with the cartel. About multiplying the million-dollar bounty times ten, fifteen, or even twenty. Hell, twenty million was chump change for the cartel. They'd almost certainly be willing to pay that much for the safe return of the map file.

He would start at twenty million. Negotiate from there. If he was lucky, he might end up with fifteen million or more. Maybe they'd take the first offer. Then he could retire and do whatever the hell he wanted.

Decker watched the women as they started to get ready for bed. They thought they were home free. Completely safe from him. He imagined the shock and terror on their faces when he showed up to claim their bounties.

It was going to be glorious.

CHAPTER 23

Carver wanted to hit the road running.

The problem was, he didn't know which way to go. Where had Paola decided to go after leaving Aliyah Butler's house? She could be anywhere, completely unaware of the danger following close behind. The man had put a tracker on her car.

He was probably watching her right now. Planning his next move. Would he kill her the moment he had the chance? Would he violate her first? Toy with her? Use her to get to the other women?

Carver was standing in the same spot Paola had been hours before. Right in the middle of Butler's den. He'd missed her by just a few hours. Those few hours might cost her everything.

"You look disturbed, Carver." Liana snapped her fingers to get his attention. "What are you thinking?"

"The killer put a tracker on Paola's car." He showed her the video. "He's right behind her and I have no idea where to go."

"Contact that Leon person you told me about."

"Already did." Carver didn't expect to hear back from him anytime soon. He calmed his mind and thought about what Paola might do next. If she was following the protocols he'd taught her, she would hole up in a motel somewhere. Preferably a place that didn't require an ID.

She'd lost her phone so couldn't contact him or Leon. She hadn't sent anything to the secure email accounts he'd set up in case of a situation like this. There had to be a good reason she hadn't done that yet.

Maybe she didn't remember her login information. Maybe she didn't remember their email addresses. All that information had been on her phone. She should have memorized them. They were simple. Easy to remember.

Despite losing her phone, she'd still contacted Aliyah Butler. Maybe she'd contacted Butler before losing her phone. Maybe she had a way to contact her without her phone. It was impossible to know without direct confirmation.

When Carver and Paola were still together, still living near the beach, she'd constantly worried about the women Jasper Whittaker had violated and abused. She worried the cartel would come for them one day.

Carver had told her it was best not to think about it. Best to leave it alone. But Paola hadn't been able to do that. She'd worried herself sick about it. Then she'd contacted a few of them.

Before long, keeping those women safe had become a personal mission for her. She'd created a survivors' group. Carver hadn't approved but he'd given her advice. Told her how to keep the group anonymous and under the radar.

Some of the women had been glad Paola reached out. They were glad to know she cared. Others hadn't been so receptive. They hated Paola and viewed her as complicit in Jasper's crimes. That hadn't stopped Paola from trying to help them too.

Some understood Paola was as much of a victim as they were. Others understood it but could never overcome the hatred. It was understandable after what Jasper had done to them. He'd used them like toys. Raped them. Beaten them. Killed some of them.

Carver had slit Jasper's throat. Watched him bleed out in his own bed. The women trusted Carver, but not Paola. But he hadn't taken it upon himself to help them beyond that. That wasn't his job. He just wanted to enjoy life. To be left alone.

He'd told Paola to let it go. He'd told her that maintaining contact with these women was an unnecessary vulnerability. He'd told her it would eventually get her killed. That eventuality had finally come knocking on her door.

And now it might be too late.

There was another side to that equation. Paola's vulnerability might be turned to Carver's advantage. Paola was on a mission. She'd returned to Morganville to save the women living in the mansion.

Then she'd come to Marietta to see Butler. The timeline suggested that she'd been living with Butler for a while. During that time, she'd probably contacted the other women via email and warned them about the imminent danger.

Once she realized her living situation with Butler was compromised, the two women had fled somewhere else, unwittingly leading the killer to their new location. That certainly wasn't good, but it wasn't bad either.

The killer was after all the women. He was probably smart enough to let Paola lead him to them. Which meant Paola was probably still free. Still alive.

If she did as Carver instructed her, she'd go to a motel and avoid meeting the other women in person. Judging from her actions so far, he felt certain she wouldn't follow protocol. She'd probably meet with one of the other women on the list.

In fact, it was almost a certainty Paola would do that. Not because she wasn't following protocol, but because she felt safer staying with someone she trusted. That was why she'd gone to stay with Butler.

It was why she would eventually meet with one of the other women and ask for sanctuary. It wasn't logical to Carver, but logic didn't always play into situations like this. People acted irrationally when they wanted to feel safe.

Which meant that though Paola was making the killer's mission easier, she was also making Carver's task of finding her easier too. He just had to divine who was next on the list.

Carver remembered some of the names and some of the faces of Jasper's victims. He hadn't wanted to know their names, but Paola had made sure he did. She'd thought it would make Carver more willing to help them.

It hadn't.

Several names stuck out in Carver's mind. Names Paola had mentioned multiple times. Among them was Aliyah Butler—the woman Paola had been with in Marietta. The woman who was on the run with Paola now.

Another was Mary Ross. She was from San Francisco, but Paola told him that Mary decided to leave California and move to Boston. He remembered Tina Compton, a girl who was just fifteen years old when Jasper abused her. She was from Los Angeles.

Paola had told Carver that Tina wanted to become an actress, so she'd gone back to Hollywood. Presumably, she was still out west. Very far from Marietta.

Carver reviewed all the names in his head. Thought about where they lived. One of those names and locations hit him immediately. There was a blond woman, Lacy Hood, from Tennessee. She was one of the women with mixed feelings about Paola.

She hadn't hated Paola. Hadn't forgiven her either. She was a fence straddler. Which meant in an emergency situation like this, she would probably help Paola. Give her a place to stay. If true, the killer would now have three women in his sight.

Carver remembered something else. Something important.

Lacy had organized a meetup with the other women. She'd wanted to have an annual meetup to make sure everyone was doing okay, and everyone felt supported. She'd wanted to hold it in Chattanooga. Paola had said it was almost two hours from where Lacy lived.

He closed his eyes and envisioned the conversation. They'd been at a bar on the beach drinking beer. Her body was tanned from the sun. Salty from the ocean water. He remembered tasting it on her lips.

The memory rekindled something inside of him. Feelings he didn't want to feel any-more. Feelings that made his current task even more urgent. He saw her at the beach bar with him, her eyes bright with life. With an inner light.

More than anything in the world, he didn't want that light to die.

Stop feeling and think!

He pushed away the emotions and remembered the conversation.

Paola smiled and looked at the beach. "I love it here. I wish Lacy would have the others come to the beach, not some hotel in Chattanooga."

Carver sipped his beer. "Guess you're more of a beach person than a mountains person."

"Beach or the mountains?" She smiled. "Beach every time." Paola stared at her beer. "I'm surprised she invited me. She wanted me to come to her home in Cook to help her prepare."

Carver frowned. Had she said the city name was Cook? Or was it something else? He took out his phone. Searched for Chattanooga, Tennessee. Centered the map on the city. He searched for Cook. It automatically corrected it to Cookeville.

"That's it." He snapped his fingers. "She must be going there." He headed for the front door.

"Huh?" Liana followed him outside. "Going where?"

"Cookeville, Tennessee." Carver opened the passenger door for her.

She dropped into the car seat. "Did you pick that name out of a hat or do you know for sure?"

Carver closed her door. Slid into the driver's seat. He told Liana about his conversation with Paola. "Paola went to Morganville to warn the women there. She went to Marietta to warn Aliyah Butler. It would make sense that she's going to the next closest person."

"Why not just call these people and warn them?"

"She probably already contacted them. Now she's probably looking for a safe place for her and Aliyah Butler to lay low. But there is no safe place with a tracker on her car."

Liana blew out a breath. "What if you're wrong? What if we drive up there and find out she went in another direction?"

"I don't think I'm wrong." Carver put the city name into the GPS. He didn't have a home address, but this would do for now. "Based on the actions that took her to Morganville and Marietta, I think it's reasonable to assume she's linking up with another of Jasper's victims."

A blue line appeared on the map. Carver reversed out of the driveway. Left the subdi-vision. Let the blue line guide him. A few minutes later, he reached the interstate. Traffic was light, so he accelerated to eighty-five miles per hour and hoped he didn't encounter a zealous traffic cop.

It was a three-and-a-half-hour drive. That was three hours and thirty minutes for the killer to do whatever he wanted. The three women would feel safe at Lacy's. They'd have no idea the killer knew exactly where they were.

"I can't find Lacy Hood in the phone directory," Liana said. "I can't even find anyone with that last name in the entire area. Are you sure she lives there?"

"Paola told me she was in witness protection."

"Great." Liana grimaced. "No way to know what name she's using then."

"I'm afraid not." Carver recounted other memories where Paola talked about the women. He didn't remember her ever mentioning Lacy's new alias.

Liana stared out the side window. "How are we supposed to find her when we reach town? What if she doesn't live in town?"

"Good question." Carver didn't have any bright ideas. He didn't have any dim ideas either. If the town was small enough, a person could ask around at the local diner or grocery store and have favorable odds of finding someone who knew who you were looking for.

Problem was, he didn't know much about Lacy except her physical description. She had blond hair, was five foot four inches, slim build, pale skin. That description could be just about anybody in these parts.

Finding her was going to be ninety percent luck.

Liana was fiddling with her burner phone. "What does Lacy look like?"

Carver described her. "What good does that do?"

"I'm using a third-party search tool to comb social media accounts in that general area." She scrolled down a list. "The problem is she might have dyed her hair or otherwise changed her appearance."

Carver glanced at the website she was using. It was called Social Seeker. He'd seen it before. Techs with Scion used it to comb through social media in combination with facial recognition software. It was an anonymous site on the dark web. Difficult to access unless you knew what you were doing.

Liana seemed to sense his unspoken question. "I'm using a modified Tor browser to access a dark web backdoor."

"It bypasses the cellphone service provider's firewall?" Carver had used Tor on desktop computers to access the dark web. Using it via a cellular connection had been problematic in the past. Some providers blocked it.

"Yep." She scrolled through results. "The agency has non-indexed websites with software in case a field agent needs something in a pinch."

"That doesn't seem very secure."

"The sites are monitored by software that records where every request is coming from. If it's not within a geofenced location, the request is denied."

Carver looked at the time left on the GPS and went a little faster. "How large are these geofenced locations?"

"Not very large. I used a VPN to make it look like my IP address is in one of those locations. That granted me access to the software. Access to the apps doesn't require logins but they do record devices and locations. The VPN will make sure that information doesn't show our real location."

"Doesn't the NSA have ways of tracing even through VPNs?"

"Yes, but it takes longer." Liana tapped on her phone. She flicked her finger up the screen. Stared at something. Showed it to Carver. "What do you think?"

He looked at the picture of a blonde woman talking to a tall, dark-haired male. Nodded. "That's her. I'm surprised she has social media. WITSEC normally tells them to avoid it at all costs."

"This isn't her account. I used the image filter to find pictures of all people matching her description in the area."

"I don't remember Social Seeker having that capability."

"It doesn't. I'm using an image search tool with it." She showed him three pictures of Lacy. "These were all at community events. Someone else took the pictures and posted them to their own social media or group page. The caption under this image tells us everything we need."

Carver glanced at the caption. It read: *Brenda Johnson talks with Mayor Bragg.* He grunted. "Seems like she's keeping a high profile for someone who's supposed to be in hiding."

"Some people are too extroverted to hide in the shadows." Liana drilled into the post with the images. She kept reading and scrolling.

The car was cruising at ninety miles per hour. Carver knew it was risky, but he didn't want to slow down. The killer might already have Paola and the other women. They might already be dead.

"Yes!" Liana pumped her fist and hissed in pain. "Damn it. I keep forgetting about my shoulder."

"What did you find?"

"Lacy held a school fundraiser at her house." Liana showed him the picture of a stately old house. "It's near downtown."

Carver plugged the address into the GPS. It didn't change the arrival time much, but now he knew exactly where he was going. "Good work."

"I finally feel useful." Liana kept looking through images. "I wish I had access to facial recognition. That would be a game-changer."

"That requires too much horsepower for a phone to handle."

"Yeah. There's a website I could upload images to, but they would all be flagged for later review." She stared at the phone screen. "If I put Paola's picture on here and asked facial recognition to locate her on security cameras and so forth, it would put her on the agency's radar."

"What are the odds of it finding her?"

"It would depend on the camera coverage of the area she's in and whether or not those cameras are sending images to our network."

Carver thought it over. "I say we do it."

"Really?" Liana looked confused. "I thought you wanted Paola off the radar."

"I do. Just not with Paola's picture." He reached into the backseat and grabbed the tablet they'd found in Butler's house. Turned on the screen. Played back one of the videos and paused it at the perfect spot. "I want you to upload that mugshot."

She laughed. "Devious."

"I have my moments." Carver saw a patrol car on the side of the road ahead. He slowed to eighty, figuring with a speed limit of seventy, the cop wouldn't care.

They whizzed past. The cop car stayed in place, lights off. Carver kept watching it in the rearview mirror until they crested the next hill and lost sight of it. He pulled off an exit to get gas and to take a restroom break.

Liana picked up some snacks. Carver was the only one with cash, so he paid. It was one of those big, fancy gas stations with restaurants and everything inside. There were cameras everywhere.

He tried to keep his gaze averted but it was just about impossible to avoid being on camera. "Do these cameras send images to the agency network?"

"It's doubtful. We usually have to request video from geographical locations that we want to search." She managed to open the car door and get inside by herself despite the pain flashing across her face. "There's simply too much data to process if everyone uploaded video feeds."

"They make it look simple on the crime shows. Like they could just find anyone if they passed by a camera."

"Project Raven was designed to do exactly that. The software would have constantly monitored every social media account, every public and private security camera, and cell phones to map the paths of almost every person in the nation." Liana opened a bag of potato chips. "They had massive server farms set up, but the Senate National Security Committee shut it down."

Carver raised an eyebrow. "Or did they?"

"The software algorithm had serious issues and it was costing billions to develop, so even if the committee hadn't shut it down, there's no reason to think they actually got it up and running."

"It always costs the government billions somehow." Carver shook his head. "I wonder where that money is really going."

"Most projects have multiple funnels," Liana said in a matter-of-fact voice. "There's the project funnel, kickback funnels for various politicians, and then corporate funnels. So, for a project slated to cost a hundred million, only about ten million of that would be for the actual project. The rest would be divided among politicians, political action committees, and corporate interests."

Carver frowned. "And you know this how?"

"There have been multiple instances where we were working with other agencies to bring down criminal enterprises only to have the task force disbanded because it was a government-funded criminal enterprise." She sighed. "You don't even want to know how much money those task forces waste."

"I always knew there was corruption. Guess I didn't know just how much there was."

Liana tapped her phone screen. "Okay, I uploaded several images to the facial recognition servers. This ought to be interesting."

Carver looked at the images. They weren't in color, but they were good enough for facial recognition. They were images of the killer who was after Paola and the other women. Liana had limited the search area to the interstate and highway corridor leading to Cookeville, Tennessee.

That would narrow the search considerably. If the killer came into view of any cameras along that path, then he would show up in the search. The NSA might have him in their crosshairs soon. Then Carver would know for sure they were travelling in the right direction.

Because if he'd guessed wrong and Paola wasn't coming this way, then she and Butler would be completely at the killer's mercy.

CHAPTER 24

Decker tested the edge of his knife.

He imagined it slicing through clothing like butter. Laying Paola bare and vulnerable before him. The terror in her eyes energizing him. Engorging him. He blew out a breath to calm himself.

It wasn't time for that, yet. He had to be patient.

The lights were out in the motel room where the women were staying. They'd gone to sleep an hour ago. He'd waited to make sure they weren't going anywhere before crossing the road to get some food at the twenty-four-hour diner.

He dribbled syrup on his waffle. It was late for dinner, but he was starving. The waitress topped off his cup with the motor oil they called coffee. It was thick and smelled burnt.

Decker decided not to drink any more since he needed to get some sleep. He wanted to be fresh when the women left in the morning.

Lacy and Aliyah were going to Lacy's house. Paola was going somewhere else. She hadn't said where. The others hadn't asked. That was smart. They couldn't give up the locations of the other women if they didn't know where they were.

Unfortunately for them, they hadn't accounted for someone like Decker. The only question in his mind was would he keep the tracker on Paola's car and follow the other women to Lacy's place, or vice versa?

Paola was the grand prize. She was the goose that laid the golden eggs. The one who seemed to know where all the other women were. If she continued to lead him to the other women, then he was happy to let her do that.

Maybe she wasn't planning on visiting anyone else. Maybe this was her last stop before vanishing. She probably had cash. She could probably buy another car and get rid of the Honda. If that happened, Decker might lose her forever.

Choices, choices. What was the best course of action?

Lacy had never mentioned her address during the conversation with the others. She'd mentioned being in witness protection but hadn't said what her new name was. Paola hadn't mentioned how she'd contacted her.

Decker could continue to follow Paola. If she didn't meet with any other women and went back on the run, then he could capture her and find out what she knew the hard way. If he could renegotiate her bounty, then finding the other women became a moot point.

He finished off his waffle. Paid the bill in cash. Went outside and walked to the gas station next door. He wanted bottled water and snacks for the road in case it was a long drive.

The gas station was old and small. The man behind the counter was equally old and small. He watched Decker with an eagle eye. As if he expected Decker to steal something.

That irked him, but he decided to let it go. He pulled his ballcap a little lower and looked for the bottled water. There was beer in a small glass refrigerator. No water.

He finally found packs of water on a nearby shelf. It wasn't even refrigerated. Decker turned to the old man. "Is this all you have?"

"Yep." The old man shrugged. "I can't afford to run one of those fancy gas station stores."

Decker sighed and picked up a six pack of water. It didn't even have a brand name on it. "What is this crap? You should carry Barrington Springs. It's the cleanest bottled water there is."

"I got tap water." The old man seemed amused. "Certified clean by the local water treatment center."

Decker slapped cash on the counter. "I'll just take this."

The old man gave him change. Decker wanted to throw it back in his face. Tell him to invest it in real bottled water. Instead, he left. Crossed the road to the motel. Went into his room and sat on the bed.

He put the water on the dresser and considered his next move. After serious consideration, he decided which car was most important to track and made peace with his decision.

Decker set an alarm on the tracking app to let him know the moment it started moving again. He settled down on the rickety motel bed. It wasn't the worst he'd ever slept on, but it wasn't great either.

He closed his eyes and imagined the fun he would soon be having. He imagined the frightened looks on the faces of the women when they saw him coming for them. Imagined them screaming and running.

He could almost see the hopelessness sweeping across their faces when they realized there was nowhere to run to. They would plead and beg for their lives. They would tell him everything he wanted to know if he promised not to kill them.

Then he would relish the despair on their faces when they realized their time on this world was over.

AN ALERT PINGED on a computer six hundred and thirty-two miles away.

An analyst studying a flagged file saw the alert appear at the top of the queue. It was nothing new. In fact, it happened all the time. The computer algorithms weren't smart. They just did what they were programmed to do.

If a file met certain criteria, then it coded the flagged file accordingly. The majority of files were low level. Code Blue. This one was Code Orange, one level below the highest level, Code Red. The file she was studying now was Code Yellow.

It was a dumb filing system. She'd suggested using numbers instead of colors. It had been explained to her that a former President liked the colors better than numbers. He'd long since been out of office, but miles of red tape and bureaucracy stood in the way of even the simplest changes.

She opened the orange file. Looked at the images. They were gray. Like they'd been taken with an infrared camera. Probably home security given the domestic fence in the background. The image had been submitted remotely from an IP address in McClean, Virginia.

It was close to Langley. Close to the CIA. But it wasn't one of their IP addresses. It just happened to be nearby in one of the geofenced locations that allowed someone to access the facial recognition upload site.

The software had already returned results for the search. The face belonged to Mike Decker, an FBI field agent. Any federal agents were automatically flagged Orange. The politicians liked to get a jump on misbehaving agents before negative blowback affected their political careers.

The agent studied the file. Studied the results. The submission had restricted the search for Decker to a narrow corridor stretching from Chattanooga, Tennessee up to Cookeville, Tennessee. There were two hits. One from a gas station in Chattanooga.

Decker had apparently gone inside to purchase bottled water. The security footage showed him coming from a diner next door. When he left, he hadn't gone to a car. It looked like he'd gone to a motel across the road.

Why was someone looking for this guy?

She studied the submitted images. There was no locational information in the metadata. The description fields had no useful information in them. The agent who'd submitted this hadn't followed protocol.

The site didn't require a login because it was geofenced and anonymous. It was a way for agents to quietly send and upload information without breaking cover. They were supposed to enter their name or ID number for requests. This agent had done neither.

One thing was certain. This was above her paygrade. She wasn't about to upload the results to the site. Not without getting clearance to do so. Normally, she would send an email with an orange flag to her section chief.

This request was so strange that she decided to walk it over personally. She flagged the file and emailed it. Then she left her cubicle and walked to the elevator. She took it up one floor. Walked down the hallway. Took a left. Stopped at the first door on the right.

The office was small, but it had a nice view of the parking lot. More importantly, it had a door and privacy. Her cubicle had none of those things. She knocked on the open door. "Mr. Walker, do you have a moment?"

Ronald Walker looked up from his computer. He looked at her blankly. "Who are you?"

"Georgina Morales, level one analyst."

"I don't have you on my calendar."

"Sir, it's about a flagged file I just emailed you. I don't know what to do with it."

He sighed. "I appreciate your following protocol, but I really don't have time to review every single questionable file that comes across your desk. If everyone with a questionable file darkened my doorway, then I'd never get anything done."

Georgina could see the reflection of his computer monitor in the window behind him. He was looking at nude images on his computer. Probably surveillance from a private residence. Might even be someone famous. There were rumors that the upper brass liked to pass around things like that.

"Sir, I just want to make sure I'm cleared to release search results to a field agent who didn't—"

He waved her away. "You're cleared. I'll reply to the email right now." He typed on his screen. Looked up. "Done. Goodbye."

She had a few things she wanted to say about his dismissive behavior, but that would only cause trouble. "Thank you." She returned downstairs. Found the approved request on her computer.

She sent the results to the site. Returned to the file she'd been studying. She hadn't been working on it long when her phone rang. She answered. "Analyst three one eight four one."

"Georgina, this is Ronald Walker." He cleared his throat uneasily. "I was just informed that I might have been too hasty in approving release of that record. I am revoking the release."

"Sir, I already uploaded it."

"Delete it and archive the request as denied."

"Sir, I don't have deletion rights to that site. Once I approve a file for release, it uploads, and I can't access it. We'd need a tech to do that."

"Then do that," he snapped. "I'm holding you responsible if that file is downloaded."

"But sir, you—"

"Do it!" He ended the call.

Georgina wiped her sweaty palms on her pants. Her heart was racing. Partly from anger. Partly from fear. She dialed the IT department.

A bored sounding man answered. "This is support."

"I authorized an upload to our remote facial recognition site and my boss changed his mind and told me to delete it. Can you do that?"

"No."

She waited for him to continue, but he didn't. "Who can?"

"Um." He went silent. "Let me escalate. Please hold."

The phone went silent. She waited, clenching her hands to keep them from trembling. Angry thoughts bouncing around in her mind. If her asshole boss hadn't been so busy looking at surveillance porn, she wouldn't have this problem right now.

Someone finally picked up. "Support."

"Yes, I need your help deleting a file from the field agent portal."

"Field agent portal?"

"Yes, the website where they upload facial recognition requests." Her voice was shaking. "My boss approved a file's release then he changed his mind."

"Oh." He went silent. Keys clicked in the background. "What's your authorization code?"

"What do you mean?"

"I need an authorization code to delete any files from this site. Your manager should have given you one."

"He didn't."

The IT guy cleared his throat. "Request one from him. Call me back."

"This is urgent! He said he'd fire me if someone downloads that file before it's deleted."

"Too late for that then." Keys clicked loudly. "Two downloads so far."

"Are you kidding me? I just released it a few minutes ago!"

"Sorry. I'll lock the file for now so no one else can download it."

Georgina slammed the phone down on the receiver. She took a long, deep breath. Called Walker. The call went to voicemail. She repressed a shriek of anger and went to the elevator. Took it to the second floor. Went to his office. He wasn't inside.

She walked around his desk. The computer screen hadn't even been locked. It was protocol to lock it every single time you left it alone. She took out her phone. Snapped pictures of the screen.

On it were lurid images of a man and woman in the throes of hardcore sex with a sex swing. The man looked familiar. He wasn't remotely attractive, but the woman was gorgeous. Odds were it was a politician.

She moved the image and looked at the folder. She saw the name on the files and shook her head. It was the House minority leader. The notes attached to it said all versions of this were to be found and deleted from the internet before it got out.

The minority leader was in the same political party as the President, so that made sense. She took more pictures then walked down the hallway. She found Walker coming out of the office at the end of the hallway.

That was the head manager's office. Walker was with Carlton Jones, the senior manager. Both men looked like they'd just been slapped in the faces. Walker saw Georgina and hurried over to her. He grabbed her arm and led her down the hallway to his office.

"Is it done?"

"I need an authorization code."

"What?" Walker walked around to his computer. He dropped into the chair. He looked as stressed as Georgina felt. He tapped on the computer keyboard. "Which one is it?"

"Sir, I don't know."

"I'm not talking to you." He tapped a single finger on the keyboard. "This must be it." He typed for a moment. Scribbled numbers and letters on a sticky note pad. He handed it to her. "Get it done."

She hurried out and to the elevator before he asked any questions. She hit the button and waited.

A tall man appeared at her side. "Analyst Morales?"

She flinched. Looked up at him. She didn't recognize him. "Yes?"

"I need you to come with me."

"Who are you?" She looked at his security badge. It didn't have a name.

"I just need you to come with me."

"Sorry, but I have an urgent request to deal with."

He took her arm. "I'm afraid this can't wait."

She froze, unsure what to do. Cold sweat prickled her scalp. "I'll call security if you don't release me."

"I'm afraid they don't have the authority to intervene."

Georgina tried to calm herself, but her hands were trembling. "Sir, I have to get this authorization number to IT so they can delete some files."

"We both know it's too late for that." He put a hand on her shoulder. Guided her into the elevator. Took her to the top floor.

He walked her to a conference room. Three people sat inside. One was Hector Gonzales, Director of Homeland Security. One was Latonya Pierre, the deputy director. She didn't recognize the third person.

The man pulled out a chair. "Sit down."

Georgina sat down. She looked at the mystery woman across from her. The badge was black. It granted unfettered access to everything. Not even Gonzales or Pierre had black badges.

She remained silent. It was better to let them talk.

The mystery woman opened a slim, black laptop. "Analyst Morales, you may call me Jane. It has come to our attention that you handled a file pertaining to FBI agent, Mike Decker. I want you to tell me everything that happened from the moment it came across your desk."

Georgina told them everything. "I only did what I was told. I'm trying to get it deleted."

"That's no longer necessary," Jane said. "We will take it from here."

"But the file was already downloaded twice." Georgina looked at the faces around the room. "Am I going to lose my job?"

"No, of course not." Jane leaned forward and put her hand over Georgina's. "Just remember that your work here is classified. You can't speak about it with anyone, not even fellow analysts unless explicitly authorized."

"I never talk about work. I love my job."

"Good, good." Jane patted her hand and sat back. "You may return to your desk."

"Thank you." Georgina looked at the other people in the room. They hadn't said a word. If anything, they looked like they were waiting for permission to speak. Who in the world was this Jane person?

The man who'd brought her there was waiting outside the door like a guard dog. He glanced at her but didn't say anything. She hurried to the elevator. Took it down to the first floor. Went back to her desk.

She sat down and breathed a sigh of relief. Logged into her computer. The email and files related to Decker were gone from her computer. There were no traces it had ever been there. And that filled her with immense relief.

She had a feeling that this Decker fellow was in a world of trouble. He'd caught the attention of some very powerful people. Georgina didn't want to know a thing about it. She wanted to get back to her job and forget this ever happened.

Because they were probably about to rain hell down on this Decker guy.

CHAPTER 25

A Gulfstream C-37A roared down the runway.

It lifted off from Andrews Air Force base just an hour after the order had been given. It wasn't the fastest personnel jet they had or the largest, but it could carry twelve people and could land on small airfields in remote locations.

Only eight people were on this flight because their cargo took up the last few rows of seats. The men on the flight had grown accustomed to such luxury though it hadn't been the norm in their previous lives.

Some of them conversed quietly. Others caught some shuteye. One of them studied the mission briefing. He looked at the pictures inside. Studied the dossier on Mike Decker. Studied the dossier on Liana Cardoso.

The images of Decker were confirmed. It was suspected that Cardoso had been the one to submit them anonymously. There were no other field agents in the area that would have done this. Cardoso had good reason to be careful.

She hadn't been disavowed, but she was listed as missing, possible rogue. She'd interfered in a previous operation that had been intended to bring in a dangerous fugitive. Her interference resulted in multiple casualties.

He knew firsthand that wasn't entirely true. Cardoso had been useful to his employers and then she hadn't. She'd probably done something to make them question her loyalty. Or maybe she'd just pissed someone off.

Either way, he'd been given the go-ahead to terminate her. Things hadn't gone to plan. This time, he'd make sure they did.

It was suspected that Cardoso had either been taken captive or was now in league with the same man who'd taken out two operators. There was a physical description of the man but no name to go along with it.

The facial recognition search results for Mike Decker had been downloaded by agency officials twice. It had been left as a honeypot for whoever submitted it. Moments later, it had been downloaded a third time. The IP address was from a VPN. They hadn't been able to trace it, but the briefing suggested Cardoso had received it.

Aside from the information on Decker, the file was thin. At least they had a probable location on Decker. There was no location on Cardoso, but it was suspected that she'd travel to the same location as Decker.

The jet landed on a small airfield a little over two hours after takeoff. The jet taxied to a stop outside a hangar. The men formed a line from the back of the jet to the tarmac. Those in the back passed the duffel bags of equipment to the next in line.

Within minutes, all the equipment was on the ground. They picked up their respective bags and hustled to a waiting Sikorsky UH-60 Black Hawk helicopter. It was modified with a faring over the tail rotor to keep sound from traveling groundward.

Baffles redirected the main rotor soundwaves skyward. The helicopter was still loud but redirecting the air vibrations made it much quieter when heard from the ground. It was about as close to a stealth helicopter as they'd gotten.

The Black Hawk lifted off and angled toward Highway 111 outside of Chattanooga. It was two hours until sunrise. That gave them an hour and a half of darkness to complete their mission.

The squad leader briefed his team on the way there. He told them who was needed alive. Who could be brought in alive or dead. What to do in case unknown targets presented themselves. Collateral damage was authorized within reason since this was a priority one mission.

Due to the early morning hour and remote location, he thought there would be minimal non-targets present. And if a person matching the description of the dangerous fugitive was present, they were to take him alive at all costs.

CARVER HIT THE BRAKES.

"Stop!" Liana said for the second time.

He pulled to the side of the road. "What's wrong?"

She showed him her phone. Showed him a video of the man who was tracking Paola. "I can't believe it worked. They posted the file just ten minutes ago."

Carver pulled to the shoulder of the road. They were halfway between Cookeville and Chattanooga. In the home stretch. "What's in the file?"

She gasped. Showed him a dossier. "The man's name is Mike Decker. He's an FBI agent."

Carver studied it. The color picture showed the striking blue eyes Fani and Nilva described. That was the man who'd assaulted them. No question about it. "Not exactly a model agent, is he?"

"No. He's dirty as hell." Liana's lips curled in disgust. "If he was working in an official capacity, he could have pulled his badge anytime. Instead, he tortured and raped women."

Carver handed the phone back. "Where is he?"

"Looking now." She pulled up the map and entered coordinates. "You've got to be kidding me."

Carver looked at the dot on the map. It was nearly an hour back the other way. They'd passed right by it. Well, almost. It was a quarter of a mile off the highway.

Liana answered his next question before he asked it. "The timestamp on the last sighting was two hours ago."

It was almost zero four thirty. Sunrise was at zero six thirty-five. He wheeled the car around. Gunned it down the highway. The speed limit was fifty-five. It wasn't even a suggestion to him at this point.

He forced the car up to ninety miles per hour. It wasn't built for speed. The wheels were out of alignment, so the entire car vibrated like it was going to fly apart.

There were few cars on the highway. A white SUV went past in the opposite direction. Two more cars went past after that. He kept an eye out for Paola's silver Honda. Didn't see anything even close to it.

It took forty minutes to reach the turnoff. He slowed at the traffic light and turned right. The lit sign of a gas station came into view on the left a moment later. A neon diner sign flickered beyond it.

The motel was surrounded by trees. Its sign either wasn't working or it wasn't on. A single streetlamp flickered in the parking lot. A silver Honda was the only car parked there. It had to be Paola's.

There were two cars parked at the diner. A white sedan and an old pickup truck. The early morning breakfast crowd, maybe. There was an old truck parked at the gas station. No cars fueling at the pumps. The car probably belonged to the attendant.

Carver didn't want to whip straight into the motel parking lot. If Decker was inside, he didn't want to let him know someone was coming. He drove past the motel. Past the diner. The crumbling foundation of a house long gone was next door.

The yard had gone wild with weeds and bushes. The driveway had weeds growing up through it. He parked on it anyway. Got out. Opened the trunk and chose his custom M4 carbine over the snub-nosed M4 he'd appropriated in Morganville.

He attached suppressors to the M4 and his Glock. Put the Glock in his magnetic shoulder holster since it wouldn't fit in a normal one with the suppressor attached.

Liana stood next to him. "Can I get a weapon?"

Carver glanced at her injured shoulder. "It'll have to be a handgun."

"Yeah."

He had a long barrel .357 magnum. It was something he'd picked up in El Fuerte even though it wasn't a gun he'd use if he had a choice. He didn't think Liana would like it either, so he chose the Glock G43x.

It was small and compact. Not great for shooting long distance but it would be easier to handle than the .357. He checked the chamber. It was clear. He slid a magazine into it. Loaded the chamber.

He put two more magazines into her front left pocket so she could reach them.

"Good thing I'm left-handed." She practiced removing the magazine and putting it back in since it required two hands to do it efficiently. She winced in pain. Nodded. "Okay, I can do it."

Carver strapped on his M4. "Don't shoot me in the back."

"Maybe just once in the shoulder?"

He nodded. "Just wait until Paola's safe."

She smirked. "Deal."

Carver took out his NV goggles and put them on. He tested the other pair he'd taken from the truck in Morganville. They didn't work. The battery pack wasn't in the hard case, and it wasn't attached to the goggles, rendering them useless.

That would make things inconvenient. The only other device with night vision was the monocular. He gave it to Liana even though it would be hard for her to use in a pinch.

They hurried across the dark highway. Entered the woods on the other side. Carver pulled down his goggles. Looked around. Didn't see anything or anyone. They crept along the outer edge of the trees.

He stopped and examined the motel. No movement. He motioned forward. Liana put a hand on his back since he could see where they were going. Carver hooked left at the end of the tree line.

He went to the back of the motel. Saw a single light on in a back window. It lined up about where the silver Honda was parked. His heart beat a little faster. He wondered what he was going to find.

Paola's car was the only one in the parking lot. That could mean Decker had taken her in his car. It could also mean Decker was parked across the street and was watching from the diner. Carver took the monocular from Liana and scanned the diner with it.

He saw a man sitting in a booth. The man was staring out of the window at the motel. The man wore a ballcap low over his face. It was hard to tell from this angle if it was Decker or not. Decker had been wearing a hat in the surveillance video from the gas station.

The odds were good this guy wasn't Decker. But it was better to proceed as if it might be. Just in case. He tucked the monocular away. Used the night vision goggles to study the area behind the motel.

The back wall was maybe twenty yards from the tree line. There was patchy grass and hard packed dirt. He started moving again. Liana kept her left hand on his back. He kept his pace steady. Kept his wits about him.

Carver dreaded what the motel room might hold. But he couldn't let his fear control him. If he found the worst-case scenario, then he would deal with it. He would hunt Decker down. Kill him inside FBI headquarters if he had to.

And he would make him suffer.

They reached the window. Carver steeled himself. He looked through the window. Saw the bathroom on the other side. It was a small window, but he could fit through it if he needed to. It was locked so he'd need to break it to get in.

The front door was the better option.

"Do you hear that?" Liana gripped his shirt. "Strange sound."

Carver realized he'd been so focused on what he might find that he'd shut out his other senses. He listened. Heard a faint sound. It wasn't a car engine. It sounded like a ceiling fan on high.

He heard a short burst of noise, like a turbine whining and then it was gone like an animal shriek in the night. Maybe it had been a semitruck. Maybe it had been a gas generator. It was hard to tell.

He heard it again. This time it lasted a moment longer. Suddenly, he knew what it was. He knew why it sounded familiar even if there wasn't much sound. He knew for certain that they were out of time.

Carver made a split-second decision. It was probably a dumb decision. Probably the dumbest he'd made in a long time. He smashed the window with the butt of his M4. Raked out the shards with the butt until the frame was clean.

"What are you doing?" Liana hissed.

Carver didn't have time to explain. "Wait here." He leaned the M4 against the building. The window was about chest high and just big enough for him to slide through. He pulled himself up. Slid through headfirst. He landed on his hands.

He pulled his legs through. Went down on his hands and knees and looked around the corner. There were snack wrappers on the bed. Empty wine bottles on the dresser. No Paola. No Aliyah. No Decker.

There was no clothing. No blood. No signs of struggle. That didn't mean anything. Decker could have come in with a gun and made them all get in his car. He could have fit Paola and Aliyah in his trunk. Bound and gagged them.

Carver pulled himself back through the window. He rolled onto the ground. Grabbed his rifle. Took Liana's left hand. "We've got to go now."

She didn't ask questions. She followed him along the backside of the motel and to the woods on the opposite side. The faint fan blade sound seemed to come from the west. The same direction they'd approached the motel from.

He couldn't be sure he knew what was causing the sound, but he felt reasonably certain about it. He cut to the right on the other side of the motel. Kept going across the road toward the gas station. They went behind it and into the darkness there.

There was a wide strip of pavement behind the gas station and the diner. There was a dumpster located behind the diner. Beyond the asphalt was more forest. Carver took Liana around the rear of the diner and to the west side. They stopped there.

"Can you explain what's going on?" she asked.

"That sound was from a stealth chopper."

She laughed. "There's no such thing."

"It's a chopper outfitted with baffles and farings to redirect the sound waves upward so people on the ground only hear the slight whump of the rotors. When it lands, you can hear the turbines.

"That's what those sounds were?"

He nodded. "Someone pulled out all the stops. Someone who got the same file we did."

"So, my plan worked. Kind of."

"Yeah. Except we're too late. Paola isn't here. Decker isn't here."

Liana hissed. "You think he got them?"

"Maybe Paola decided to switch cars like I told her to do in an emergency. Maybe that's why her car is here. But I doubt it."

"Yeah. I don't see anywhere to get a car around here unless she knows how to hotwire one."

"I taught her a few things, but cars these days are much harder to hotwire." Carver put on the NV goggles. He saw reflections in the woods across the street. Saw figures moving among the trees.

He tried to count them, but it was hard to make them out. It looked like eight or nine bodies. They were making a beeline for the motel. He didn't know if they were the same guys who raided Liana's house, but they were armed to the teeth and going in hot.

Liana's plan had worked all right. She'd stirred up the hornet's nest. And the hornets were more than ready to sting.

CHAPTER 26

Carver didn't know where to go next.

If Decker had Paola, they could be anywhere. If Paola had left with Aliyah, maybe they'd gone to Cookeville. That was the only logical place to go next. Unless he could gather more information.

The operators encroaching on the motel were about to find out what he'd just discovered. That the motel room was empty. Then they'd radio HQ, tell them the situation. HQ would pour all their resources into scouring the area for more information.

The most logical source of that info would come from the security cameras at the gas station. The same cameras that had captured Decker's location. Which meant Carver had to get to that information before HQ did.

Carver checked the time. It was zero five thirty. The diner and gas station were both open for business. He leaned his rifle against the side of the building. Took Liana's hand. Started walking.

"Where are we going? Don't we need to get the hell out of here?"

"Not yet." He told her his idea.

She pulled on his hand to make him stop walking. "This is extremely risky. There's a kill squad right across the street!"

"You can wait here. I'll be back."

"No." She sighed. "I'll go with you."

They walked around the gas station. Went into the store. An old guy probably well into his eighties sat on a stool behind the counter. He was watching the news on a small television. He frowned. Looked at the empty gas station bay.

"You folks staying at the motel?"

Carver shook his head. He opened his mouth to talk but Liana beat him to the punch.

"Sir, our friend was staying at the motel, but she's gone missing. She said something about a strange man who kept bothering her. He's a little over six feet tall, dark hair, blue eyes—"

"Oh, I remember that fella." The old man made a sour face. "He came in here looking for some kind of fancy bottled water. I told him this ain't that kind of store. He looked real angry for a second and then he just smiled like it was nothing." The old man shook his head. "Something about him just wasn't right."

"We're really worried he might have done something to our friend. Her car is still at the motel, but she's gone and she's not answering her phone."

The old man ran a hand through his beard. "Well, I don't pay much attention to anything except when someone pulls up to the gas pump, but I do remember seeing three cars over there earlier." He looked out the window. Squinted into the darkness. "I only see one car over there now."

"Do any of your security cameras face the motel?"

He waved to a bank of old LCD monitors on the wall to his left. A handwritten sign said, *Smile! You're on Candid Camera!* Two cameras were inside, one behind the counter looking out and another in the back corner of the store.

Another camera watched the gas pumps. It was angled down, so only a part of the motel parking lot was visible. But it might be just enough to catch a glimpse of any cars there.

"Well, this one might have something." He pulled a small laptop from under the counter and set it on top. Clicked the mouse a few times. He turned it around. "I reckon that's about the best shot you'll get."

The image showed outside at dusk. The motel parking lot was barely visible. Carver could see the rear bumpers and tires on three cars parked across the street. One was silver. One was white. The last one was black.

The black car was parked near the end of the motel. The other two cars were parked right next to each other. But he couldn't tell what kind of car the white one was. He couldn't make out the license plate or any other identifying feature.

Liana snapped her fingers. "We passed four cars on the way here. A white Lexus, a white Ford, a black Toyota, and a red Nissan."

Carver nodded. "Yep."

"What if Lacy came to the motel and they drove off in her car?"

"And Decker is following them."

"That helped?" the old man said.

"It helped a lot." Liana beamed at him. "Thank you so much."

"My pleasure, young lady."

Carver looked outside. He saw two silhouettes crossing the road. They were just stepping into the light of the gas station. "Is there a back exit?"

"What?" The old man looked confused.

Carver saw a door on the other side of the store. He hurried toward it. Went through. Entered a small stockroom. There were boxes piled on one side. A large freezer door. An exit door.

He pushed through it. Liana was right on his heels. They stepped out behind the store. Hustled in the direction of the diner. He caught a glimpse of two operators standing outside the gas station. One was pointing up, probably at the cameras.

He and Liana continued along the back of the restaurant.

A woman stepped out of the back door and tossed a full garbage bag into the dumpster. She jumped and shouted in alarm when she saw them. "Lord, you like to have scared me to death!"

Carver didn't respond. He kept going.

"Sorry," Liana said. "We're just out for a stroll."

"Next to the dumpster?" The woman stared in disbelief.

Carver went around the corner of the restaurant. He crossed through a wedge of trees between it and the derelict house next door. He found the car. Opened the passenger door for Liana. He started the car and kept the headlights off.

There wasn't much he could do about the reverse and brake lights. He backed onto the road. Unfortunately, he had to go back past the motel and gas station. Leaving the headlights off would look suspicious, so he turned them on and started driving.

The headlights struck several operators standing around Paola's car. They had the doors and trunk open and were looking through it. The motel room door was also open. A dumpy middle-aged man in a bathrobe was standing outside staring at them. Probably the manager.

A pair of operators were inside the gas station. Another was inside the restaurant. One of the operators next to Paola's car stared at Carver's car as it passed by. He tapped the shoulder of his companion.

His companion looked at them. Tried to wave them down. Carver pretended not to notice and kept going. Once he was a couple hundred yards away, he gunned the engine. Got back onto the highway. Headed north for Cookeville.

Liana breathed a sigh of relief. "Whew. I was worried they might try to force us to stop."

Carver wasn't breathing any sighs of relief just yet. Paola was about an hour ahead of them now. Maybe more. She and Aliyah, and possibly Lacy were headed to Cookeville with the devil chasing right behind them.

He took the car up to ninety. That was well past its comfortable limit. The wheels were vibrating so badly that he worried one might fly off at any moment. But he didn't slow down.

"Carver, I'm sorry. I wish I'd received the locational data sooner."

"Not your fault." Carver glanced at the GPS. Things weren't as bad as they could have been. Paola and the women were still alive. Carver had an address for Lacy. They were about an hour and a half away. Probably less if he could maintain this speed.

Paola and the others were probably already at Lacy's house. They'd probably reached it moments ago. Decker was probably reconnoitering the place. Deciding what he was going to do and how he'd do it.

Sunrise was in another thirty-five minutes. Maybe Decker would find somewhere to get breakfast. Maybe even get some sleep now that he knew where to find his targets. He'd probably wait until night to go inside.

On the other hand, he might be impatient and ready to go now. He might force his way into the house right after the women arrived. People were especially vulnerable when they arrived at home. They felt safe. They weren't paying attention to their surroundings.

Carver had used that to his advantage more times than he could count. He'd followed someone home. Caught them completely unaware right outside their house or followed them right inside their house.

Decker might do the same. He would probably secure the women somewhere in the house. In a basement if one was available. Then he'd make breakfast there. Get some sleep in the comfort of Lacy's bed.

The possibilities weren't endless but there were a lot of ways this could go down. Carver thought back to the woman who'd been thrown off the hotel balcony. He thought about Fani Wilson. About the hair stylist Decker had tortured and raped.

Decker did what he wanted when he wanted. He was a man used to having his way with women. He was careful, but he had an impulsive side. When the opportunity presented itself, he couldn't resist rape. He probably viewed it as sexual domination.

Fani was ample evidence of that. Same with the hair stylist. Decker was probably fantasizing about what he'd do to the three women when he caught them. He'd probably be so worked up about it that he'd want to go in immediately.

"Stop obsessing over it." Liana touched his leg. "Decker is a man who likes to play with his food. We've got time."

"I'm not obsessing over it."

"Now you're lying to yourself."

Carver nodded. "Yep."

"We have time, Carver." She squeezed his leg. "We'll get there in time."

The headlights painted a car on the side of the road. A white SUV. He slowed. Pulled to the side of the road behind the SUV. It was a Lexus.

"Shit." Liana stared at it. "The white Ford I saw was a truck. I doubt Lacy drives a truck."

"Wait here." Carver got out. Jogged to the SUV. The right rear tire was flat. He looked it over with his tactical flashlight. Found a screw embedded in the top of the sidewall. A car jack was under the car, but it wasn't fully extended.

It looked like it had been put there and maybe used but for some reason the tire hadn't been changed. Paola knew how to change a tire. She could have done it easily. But Decker might have pulled over behind them. Pretended he was there to help.

He could have taken them without a fight. Put them in his car. He could have fit two women in the trunk and another in the back seat, provided he was equipped to secure that many people. A person like Decker probably had a bag full of plastic cuffs and rope.

Carver examined the ground. The loose gravel on the asphalt was disturbed near the tire from whoever attempted to jack up the car. There were no drag marks. No indications of a struggle.

There were indentations in the grass from someone standing there. The grass was bent as if another vehicle had pulled up behind the Lexus, but no tread marks. He wasn't exactly an expert tracker. Someone with more experience might be able to piece together exactly what had happened here.

Carver looked inside the SUV. Tested the doors. They were locked. There was a travel mug in the cupholder. A tissue box. A grocery bag with trash in it.

There were other odds and ends that typically accumulated in cars. There were no bags inside. No purses. No indication that the occupants had been forced to leave without taking their belongings.

The back seats were folded down. A section of the trunk had been lifted to access the spare tire. Carver looked through the back window and saw a small, empty space for a donut spare. It looked like they'd tried to change the tire but didn't have a spare.

Decker might have pulled up. Pretended to help them. When he saw there was no spare, he offered them a ride into town. Lacy probably figured she could return for the car the next day. Maybe she'd called roadside assistance, and they couldn't get to her tonight.

Carver went back to his car. Dropped into the seat.

"Well?" Liana asked.

Carver gave her his assessment. "They got a flat. Looks legitimate. They pulled over to change the tire and didn't have a spare. Decker probably pulled over and gave them a ride."

"Oh, God." Liana grimaced. "What do you think he'll do?"

"He thinks he's a smooth operator," Carver said. "He'll probably try to charm them. Take them to Lacy's place. She might invite him inside. He might enjoy playing the part of knight in shining armor for a while before springing the surprise on them."

"Judging from what little we know about him he sounds like a classic narcissist." She looked at the dossier on him. "I mean, look at him." She showed Carver a picture of the man. He had the confident smile of a man who knew he was good looking. Someone who felt like he could get any woman he wanted.

Carver figured rearranging that face with his fists would be a punishment worse than death for someone like that. He'd enjoy disfiguring Decker but leaving him alive even in that state would be a mistake.

Decker was obviously a serial rapist. Demonstrating his power over someone got him off. He was one of the worst examples of a federal agent. A job in the federal government attracted him because he enjoyed power and prestige.

He looked down on civilians. He looked down on local law enforcement. He felt like he had the ultimate power of the land backing him up and it gave him leeway to do whatever he wanted. Not all federal agents were like that, but in Carver's experience, a lot of them were.

Decker just happened to be a worst-case scenario.

Carver forced himself to stop thinking about what Decker might do. He switched modes. Started thinking about what he was going to do. How he was going to approach whatever situation he found when he got to Lacy's house.

He felt ninety percent certain that he'd find Decker and the women at Lacy's house. The uncertainty lay in what kind of situation they'd be in. Would Decker be toying around with them, or would they be tied up?

It didn't matter. Carver would take the same approach. He'd reconnoiter the house. Find out where Decker was. Ascertain what weapons he had on him. Find a way into the house. Neutralize Decker but keep him alive if at all possible.

Carver had a lot of questions for the guy, and he knew exactly how to squeeze the answers from him. He'd threaten to smash Decker's pretty face unless he told him everything. And if he cooperated, Carver would promise to let him go.

How Carver would let him go would be the kicker. He might let him go over the side of a cliff if one was nearby. Or let him go in the path of a semitruck. The options were endless.

"I just remembered that Paola knows what he looks like," Liana said. "She saw his face in the camera footage."

"It was black and white. Maybe she wouldn't know it was the same guy right away."

"I don't know. Even with the ballcap on, I could tell it was the same guy in the gas station security footage." Liana patted his arm. "I don't think he could fool Paola."

"You're probably right." Carver allowed himself to feel a little bit better about it. He pushed the ignition button. The car engine hummed on. He shifted into drive. Pulled onto the road.

Something caught his eye. It wasn't much. Just a glint of something ahead. This time it wasn't a car. It was something too high to be anything landbound. Instinct kicked in.

He turned off the headlights. Hit the brakes. Tires screeched. The car shuddered to a stop. He slammed the shifter into reverse. Backed up behind the Lexus. Slammed the car into park.

"What the hell?" Liana was looking out the front window. She wasn't talking about his driving. She was looking at the same thing he was.

Carver turned off the car. He opened his door. Jumped out. Liana didn't ask questions. She was already opening her door.

Brilliant lights struck Carver in the face. Whining turbines roared. A helicopter rotor thundered.

A UH-60 Black Hawk landed in the middle of the road and operators poured out of it.

— • —

CHAPTER 27

TWO HOURS EARLIER

Decker was so close to the women he could taste them.

He still hadn't made up his mind who he was going to follow. He was leaning toward tracking Lacy's car and following Paola. That way he could take her when he wanted and come back for the others later.

His plan was simple. Follow the money. Paola was as good as money to him. Claiming the bounties on the other women was just icing on the cake.

Decker lay down in the creaky bed and dozed lightly. The sound of a car door closing woke him. He was up in an instant and at the window.

The three women were putting bags in Lacy's car. Pulling things from Paola's car and putting them into the Lexus SUV. Decker didn't understand why. Everything in their conversation pointed to Paola going her own way.

What had changed? Were they onto him?

He shook his head. No, they weren't acting with urgency. They were talking and casually loading the Lexus. They didn't look worried. He put his listening device against his window. Listened to the faint conversation outside.

They were too far away for him to hear anything. He checked the time. It was just after five in the morning. Why were they doing this? What had changed? He didn't know. Maybe they'd changed their minds about what to do. Women were like that. They were fickle and prone to flip-flopping.

Whatever the case, this simplified things. Now he didn't have to worry about deciding whether to follow Paola or the other two women. He just had one car to follow. This car was going to lead him straight to Lacy's house.

That would be the best place to abduct the women. As long as Lacy didn't have a husband or kids, it would be easy. If she didn't live alone, that was fine too. The more the merrier. Spouses and kids were great leverage for interrogation.

If Lacy had a husband and kids, then he might be tempted to have fun with her, even if she was leftover gutter trash from Jasper Whittaker. There was something about making the husband and kids watch their mom get ravished by a real man that sent blood rushing into his groin.

The Lexus's headlights came on. Decker blinked out of his fantasy and watched the vehicle turn around and get on the road. He took a leak. Grabbed his bottled water and his duffel bag. Hopped into his car.

He left his headlights off and pulled to the edge of the parking lot. He saw the Lexus's taillights heading back toward the highway. He counted to ten then pulled onto the road. It was pitch black outside so he turned on his headlights.

He kept the taillights in sight. Watched them turn north onto the two-lane highway. He turned onto the highway about twenty seconds later. Another white pickup truck passed by and got between him and the Lexus.

That was good. It gave him cover. He followed a few car lengths behind the pickup. The driver apparently wasn't in a hurry to get anywhere and was doing just fifty in a fifty-five zone. The Lexus wasn't going much faster, but it was gaining distance with every mile.

He slammed his hand on the steering wheel. "Idiot drivers." He felt a strong urge to fire a few shots at the other driver when he passed him.

The Lexus's taillights disappeared over a hill. There was room to pass the pickup before the hill, but another car was coming. By the time it passed by in the other direction, it was too late to pass before the hill.

Decker was impatient but he wasn't stupid. Passing on a blind hill was a dumb move. Dying in a head-on collision in the middle of nowhere wasn't on his bingo card.

The pickup crested the hill. Decker reached the top a few seconds later. He saw the Lexus's taillights just ahead. They were much closer now. In fact, the pickup was gaining on them. Decker slowed to give the pickup more space.

The Lexus pulled onto the shoulder of the road. It was leaning to the right. Its hazard lights came on. The pickup's brake lights brightened. It slowed and pulled behind the Lexus. Decker slowed down too. He wondered what was going on.

The lean of the vehicle and the wobble as it pulled onto the shoulder of the road was indicative of a flat tire. He slowed down as he passed by the pickup truck. It was one of those redneck specials with a raised suspension and big tires.

The interior light of the pickup was on. Two young men were inside. One hopped out and walked to the Lexus. Decker was tempted to stop and pretend to help as well but he didn't feel like getting his hands dirty.

Those good old boys could change the tire for the ladies just fine. They'd be back on the road in twenty minutes easy. He drove to the top of the next hill and pulled to the side of the road. It was a good vantage point.

He took out his binoculars. The truck's headlights lit the Lexus and the people around it. The women stood outside the vehicle. Lacy was talking to one of the men as he pulled a jack from the back of the SUV. She touched his arm. Smiled. She was flirting with the guy in typical slut fashion.

It turned him off to the idea of ravishing her in front of her family, if she even had a family. His taste in women was highly selective. Sometimes he didn't mind slumming it when a tantalizing situation presented itself. But watching her talk to that man just made Decker want to cut her throat and toss the body in the garbage where it belonged.

One of the men jacked up the back of the Lexus. The other pulled a small donut spare from the back. He talked with his buddy. Put the spare tire on the ground. Pushed down on it. It looked flat too.

The other guy talked to Lacy. Pointed a thumb at his truck. It was a crew cab, so there was plenty of room for passengers.

Lacy talked to Paola and Aliyah. They nodded. Gathered their things from the Lexus.

One of the rednecks tossed the spare tire into the bed of the pickup. He went to the Lexus and lowered the jack, so the tire was touching the ground again. Then he went back to the truck and climbed in.

Lacy and the women climbed into the back seats of the pickup. Decker was surprised that Lacy didn't try to sit up front with the redneck she'd been flirting with. She was a filthy whore. Pure trash. Why even pretend to be otherwise?

Decker desperately hoped she had a family. He would force the men from the pickup into the house along with the women. Then he'd tie up Lacy's husband and kids. Tell them what a horrible slut she was.

He'd make her and that redneck perform in front of everyone. He'd make him violate her in every way possible. Then he'd kill them both. At that point, he'd probably have to kill the husband and kids too.

Staging it as a murder-suicide was probably the easiest way to go. Make it look like the husband found Lacy in bed with the two men from the pickup. Make it look like the husband shot them both. Killed the kids. Killed himself.

Decker laughed out loud. He shivered with pleasure. The idea of such a crazy scene flushed him with power. It was so perfect he could hardly stand it. He wished he could tell Angie about the things he did, but she'd never understand.

He flinched as he remembered she was dead now. Splattered like a bug in an alley. Maybe he could find a girlfriend that he could tell everything to. A woman who'd understand why he was the way he was.

A woman who understood that he deserved to have fun when he needed it. A woman who would remain faithful to him and treat him like a king. That was almost impossible in the modern world, but maybe he'd get lucky.

Modern women were encouraged to be as slutty as they wanted. They were encouraged to demand everything from men and give nothing in return. He was fully supportive of women's rights. He wanted a woman with a good job. A woman who could stand on her own.

A woman who would understand his worth. Who would understand just how lucky she was to land someone like him.

Most women were intimidated by men like Decker. Mainly because there weren't many men who were on par with him. He literally had it all. Good looks. Money. A great job. True power.

He was about to have even more once he landed this big fish.

Decker blinked out of his fantasy and realized the pickup was back on the road. It was coming toward the hill. He got back in his car. Shifted into gear. Pulled onto the road. He drove at a leisurely 45 miles per hour. Put his ballcap on and pulled it down low.

The pickup driver wasn't driving like an old man anymore. He was going a little over the speed limit this time. He drove up on Decker's bumper for half a mile, the headlights blindingly bright in the rearview mirror.

Decker clenched the steering wheel. Resisted the urge to unload his handgun on the driver. "Just pass already, you damned moron."

The pickup engine roared. It sped past, the oversized tires humming loudly on the asphalt. Decker glanced over. Saw the shoulder of the front passenger. He saw black hair in the rear window.

It was Paola's hair. She was facing away from him. He hadn't met her yet, but she'd impressed him back at Butler's house. She'd tried to kill him. Not many women could pull that off.

Hell, he could probably count the number of strong women he knew on one hand. It was too damned bad that she was his key to financial security. Otherwise, he'd make her his own.

"It is what it is," Decker muttered to himself. He watched the pickup pull in front of him. Saw the heads of the three women in the back window. He made a finger gun and mimicked shooting Butler and Hood in the heads.

Hood was in the middle. Butler was on the left and Paola on the right. Paola and Hood were facing Butler. Hood was talking. The pickup truck gained distance and before long, Decker couldn't see the women anymore.

He let them get about twenty car lengths ahead, and then matched their speed. He yawned long and hard. Damn, he was tired. Whatever he decided to do, he was going to get some shuteye shortly thereafter.

Hopefully, Hood had a basement. That would be the easiest place to keep everyone until he was ready for showtime. As much as he wanted to let Paola lead him to other women on the list, he was just going to have to interrogate her for the information instead.

About thirty minutes later, they entered the small town of Cookeville. The highway led to a traffic light in the middle of downtown. It continued past a stately red brick building that was City Hall.

It was six thirty-five in the morning. The sun was coming up. There was more traffic on the road. Decker kept a couple of cars between his car and the truck. The truck turned right on the next road. The car in front of Decker went the same way, so he followed.

The truck turned onto Broad Street. It turned left onto North Maple. Pulled into a driveway on the left. There was a house with a huge front yard facing Broad Street. The sides of the house were surrounded by trees.

Decker slowed in front of the driveway but didn't want to stop. The yard was bordered by thick bushes and trees, hiding the side of the house from sight. He glimpsed a detached garage and a brick wall.

The house had wood siding. He wasn't sure what color it was. Light pink or salmon maybe. It didn't really matter. He knew where Hood lived now. He knew where the women would be.

There was nowhere to park on the side of the street, so he took another left at the end of the block. This road was wider. It had plenty of space for parking. He pulled to the right side of the street. Hopped out of the car.

There was no house across the street. Apparently, Hood's yard stretched for an entire block. Her front yard bordered Broad Street and her back yard touched whatever street he'd parked on.

Decker ran across the street and through the trees on the other side. The yard was huge. The house looked renovated. Hood had obviously put a lot of her cartel money into buying this place.

The sun was coming up so he couldn't rely on hiding in the darkness. His plan didn't really call for stealth anyway. He was going to corral everyone into the house immediately. The men from the pickup and the women.

Everyone would be tired. Paola and the others hadn't gotten much sleep. The pickup boys had probably woken up early for their own reasons too. None of them would be alert. None of them would be ready for what was coming next.

Decker had half a mind to pretend to be a local on a walk, but Hood probably knew everyone in a small town like this. It was risky even with the ball cap pulled low to shield his face.

She probably knew all her neighbors. Plus, Paola knew what he looked like from the surveillance footage. Even though she'd seen him in grayscale, he was a hard man to mistake for anyone else.

This would be a good old-fashioned bum rush. Plain and simple. No one would have a chance to react. The rednecks were probably helping the women take their luggage inside. Everyone would be caught off guard.

The pickup truck engine rumbled. It backed out of the driveway before Decker was even halfway across the yard. The growling engine faded into the distance as it drove away.

So much for his humiliation plan. So much for rednecks violating Butler while her husband and kids watched. That was disappointing but it wasn't a showstopper. He could think of plenty of other ways to have fun.

There was a brick wall around part of the back yard. Decker used it for cover. Edged along the side. Came to the back door. There were lights on inside. He looked through the back door window. Saw the kitchen.

No one was in the kitchen. He tested the handle. It was locked. His entire bum rush idea was going nowhere. The backdoor was made of fiberglass. He could probably kick it in unless the door jamb was reinforced.

Doing that was a last resort. He'd have to slow his roll for a moment and assess the situation. Or he could just knock on the door. This was a small town. Hood would almost certainly open it without thinking.

Then all Decker had to do was force his way inside. That seemed to be the easiest method. His handgun was tucked into the back of his jeans. He wouldn't need it right away. Usually, shoving his way inside while occupants were off guard worked like a charm.

He knocked on the door. No one answered. He knocked again, louder this time. He decided to ask if he could borrow some eggs. Didn't neighbors ask to borrow sugar and eggs all the time?

Decker imagined confusion on her face when he asked for eggs and then shoved his way into her house. He imagined the confusion turning to shock and terror. It was enough to make him laugh.

No one had answered the door yet, so he knocked one more time. An elderly lady shuffled into view. She saw him through the window and frowned. Walked to the door. Didn't open it.

"I told that man at the newspaper that I don't want to renew my subscription." She had a commanding genteel southern accent. "Go back and tell him I get all my news from the internets."

"I'm not with the newspaper. I'm here to see Lacy. I wanted to borrow some eggs."

"Eggs?" She looked confused. "Who is Lacy? There's no one here by that name, young man."

"Isn't this Lacy Hood's house? She just arrived with two other women?"

"Son, I don't know any Lacy Hood or two other women. I live here by myself. But I do have some eggs you can have if you need them. Does it matter if they're brown eggs? I have mine delivered from Little Timmy Stephens' farm." She laughed. "Well, I guess he's not so little anymore. I used to teach him in third grade, you know. He was knee high to a grasshopper and now he's six feet five!"

Decker listened in confusion. Was this woman toying with him? Was she so senile she didn't even know that three women had just entered her house? Where in the hell were Paola, Hood, and Butler?

"Son, are you all right?" The woman was unlocking the door. "You look a bit ill."

Decker shook his head. "I'm sorry. My wife just texted me and said she found the eggs. I'm sorry to have bothered you."

"Oh, it's no bother at all, young man." The woman opened her door. "Are you new in town? I'm Esther Crumbley. I used to teach at the old school. It's gone now. They're building that monstrosity across the road to combine all the schools since there aren't enough children in town to justify three different buildings."

This woman was going to talk him to death. "Thank you, Esther." Decker gave her a full dose of his best smile. He winked. "I'll be sure to come back, and we can talk all about the schools."

She smiled. "You do that now, you hear?"

Decker hurried away down the driveway.

Esther called out after him. "Nice to meet you, young man."

Decker reached the sidewalk and raced around the corner of Broad and North Maple. He looked up and down the sidewalk. It was clear now what had happened.

The women didn't trust men. Not even the men who tried to change their flat tire and gave them a ride into town. They distrusted men so much that asked to be dropped off here. Then they must have cut across the yard and gone to Hood's real house.

And now he had to find them all over again.

CHAPTER 28

Carver dashed into the forest.

Liana was right behind him. She grunted in pain but didn't cry out. Men shouted from behind them. The whumping of helicopter rotors was clearly audible now, probably because the chopper was still on the ground.

The duffel bag of weapons hung heavy on Carver's back. He'd snatched it out of the trunk on the way around the car. There was no way in hell he was leaving his tools behind. Especially not when facing an enemy like this.

Shouting echoed from behind. The sound of turbines faded as the Black Hawk rose into the air. Its lights were off. It was easier to scan the forest with thermal imaging than using a spotlight.

No doubt someone was watching them right at this very moment. The thick tree canopy would shield them a little but not enough to completely hide their heat signatures. There wasn't much they could do about that right now.

The terrain was rocky and mountainous. Carver's night vision goggles helped him navigate but Liana was stuck using his monocular. She was slowing him down. He was going to have to buy them time. He just had to figure out how.

Laying down suppressing fire might work but the helicopter would keep tracking them. Or would it? Where had the helicopter come from? How far had it traveled to get here? Had the troops onboard been local or transported from somewhere else?

Carver stopped running and looked up. He saw the chopper hovering two hundred feet overhead.

"What are you doing?" Liana panted.

He took the monocular from her. Lifted the NV goggles off his face and used the monocular. Zoomed in on the chopper. He got a good look at it and handed the monocular back to Liana. "Keep going."

She put the monocular to her eye and started picking her way up the rocky slope. Carver looked back and spotted enemy contacts fifty yards back. They were walking fast, not running. The chopper had their targets in sight so there was no need to risk breaking legs.

Running through terrain like this even in daylight came with a high risk of stepping on rocks or roots the wrong way and twisting an ankle. They were in no rush. Their quarry was tagged and being tracked from the sky.

But there was something they weren't considering.

A specialized chopper like that would have come from an air base. Arnold Air Force Base was the closest. He only knew that because he'd seen it when searching the map earlier. If the chopper and the operators onboard were stationed there, then it would have flown maybe seventy miles to the motel.

It had landed, disgorged the troops, and probably remained running so it could take off quickly again. It was a specialized chopper made for stealth and troop transport. Not for long-range operations.

Black Hawks with extended fuel tanks had a range of nearly twelve hundred nautical miles. The extra fuel tanks were attached to the Black Hawk's wings. It enabled the chopper to deliver troops far inside enemy territory.

This Black Hawk didn't have wings. It didn't have extended fuel tanks. It didn't have side weapons either. It was strictly made for silently carrying troops short distances and dropping them on a target.

This chopper had baffles beneath the main rotor and a faring over the tail rotor to redirect sound skyward. Those modifications added significant weight. Added weight resulted in greater fuel usage. Greater fuel usage reduced range.

Carver had been in a similar chopper a few times before. Once he'd been on a mission in mountainous terrain. The mechanic had warned his team that the standard range of three hundred miles would be reduced to about two hundred and thirty miles, give or take due to wind shear and other atmospheric conditions.

The math was simple even with no exact figures to use. The chopper had flown seventy or eighty miles to the motel. It had hovered there for several minutes. Carver had been nearly thirty minutes down the road and spent several minutes inspecting the Lexus before the chopper appeared.

It meant the chopper had been using a lot of fuel during the last forty-five minutes. If Carver's estimations were correct, it might have at most twenty or thirty minutes of fuel left. It needed enough fuel to return to base, so he could safely cut that time in half.

In ten or fifteen minutes that chopper was going to have to leave. It would return to base to refuel while the operators continued the pursuit.

Since the operators weren't running after them and were instead relying on the chopper to track the targets, then Carver and Liana might be able to run out the clock. He would know for sure that the clock was running out if their pursuers started running after them.

Seasoned military operators didn't run unless they had to. It was important to conserve energy. To reduce the risk of injury from environmental causes. Once the chopper told them it had to go refuel, they'd have no choice but to pick up the pace.

From what Carver had seen, these operators were travelling light. They had rifles, sidearms, and body armor. If it was the same body armor they'd worn in Morganville, it weighed no more than five to ten pounds.

The ballistic helmets added maybe two to three pounds. The M4 rifles fully loaded added eight pounds plus extra magazines. Add in the other equipment and these boys were carrying somewhere around twenty to thirty pounds of extra weight.

That was nothing compared to training with hundred-pound packs in the desert. That didn't mean these guys were in peak shape, but they didn't have to be. Not when Carver had significant handicaps.

Carver had an injured partner without binocular night vision. He was also carrying nearly a hundred pounds in his duffel bag. He'd reconfigured the straps for a back carry, but that didn't make it any easier.

This was going to require trickery, not speed to stay alive. He didn't know how they were going to outsmart a chopper and eight armed men, but he'd have to figure it out soon. He'd have to time it perfectly, too.

It wouldn't be the first time he'd evaded aerial-assisted ground pursuit. If he wasn't successful, it would almost certainly be his last.

The terrain angled sharply uphill just ahead. There were more trees, more exposed roots, more rocks. Leaves and pine straw also made footing treacherous. With Liana in tow, it was even more daunting.

But that was fine. Just fine.

Carver had a clock running in his head. A countdown to do or die. The question was, could they make it to the finish line in time?

Liana stopped. "Carver, I don't know if I can make it up there. We should go around."

"Going around is a one-way ticket to a hole in the ground." Carver kept walking. "This way is our ticket out of here."

"How in the hell is that our ticket out? Are you expecting a chopper of our own to pick us up?"

"Trust me." Carver took her hand and pulled her after him. "First, we need a little distraction." A firefight was a losing proposition. That was why he hadn't found a fortified position and tried to defend it.

They could flank him easily. It also seemed they didn't have orders to kill him on sight or they would have opened fire a long time ago. They also didn't stand much of a chance of hitting him through all the trees.

Carver likewise would have a difficult time hitting anyone. But that didn't matter. He just needed to delay the operators' approach by a minute or two. "Keep going." He pointed Liana uphill.

"What are you—"

"Keep going," he said in a commanding voice.

Liana gave him a look of concern, then kept going, the monocular pressed to her left eye.

Carver unslung the duffel bag. He pulled out the snub-nosed M4 and clicked a magazine into it. He loaded the chamber. Slung the duffel bag back on. He removed the suppressor. Maximum noise was necessary here.

He took cover behind a boulder. Aimed at the heat signatures behind him. Fired in single shot mode, spacing the shots about a second apart. The operators took cover, vanishing behind trees and boulders.

Carver fired several more rounds. Then he turned and hurried up the slope after Liana. She wasn't very far ahead. He passed her. Gripped her forearm and pulled her up a steep section. She got her footing and pressed on.

The operators were still behind cover. Their respect for his ability to hit them from this distance and through the trees was misplaced, but it was exactly what he needed. He kept going. Kept helping Liana up the difficult parts.

She groaned in pain but soldiered on. A moment later, so did the operators behind them. Carver took a few more potshots. They took cover again. This time, they didn't stay put for long. They were onto his scheme.

He fired until he emptied the magazine. Tossed the M4. He didn't like it that much and it was better to shed the extra weight.

The operators came out from cover again. This time they were jogging. A couple of them slipped and fell. One of them slid back down the steep slope.

That was good. Real good. Their newfound speed could only mean one thing. He looked up. The chopper was heading away, the thermal signature from the turbine exhaust ports clearly visible.

It kept going. Carver kept climbing. Kept an eye on the chopper to make sure it was really gone. Liana pulled herself to the crest of the slope. The downhill wasn't as steep, but it looked more heavily forested.

The chopper's heat signature faded into the distance. The operators were struggling up the slope. A new countdown had begun.

Liana was slipping and sliding in leaves on the downslope. Carver caught her arm to keep her from falling. He helped her down about twenty feet from the summit. Then he pulled her downhill at an angle.

They had ten minutes to make this work. Ten minutes to put as many trees between them and the pursuers as possible. Going downhill was no easier than going up. Tripping and breaking a leg was even easier due to the extra speed.

There were a lot of boulders. A lot of trees. A lot of cover. That was good. This was going to work. They reached the bottom of the steepest part of the slope within eight minutes. Took cover behind a rocky outcropping.

Carver stopped Liana. He looked up at the slope. It was almost impossible to see the crest from this angle. There were simply too many trees between them and it. That was perfect. He pulled Liana along behind him. This time, they stayed in the small hollow between the hills.

They followed the edge of a stream where the terrain was easier to navigate. They kept walking. Carver kept looking back. Kept checking to see if the crest of the hill they'd come down was visible from here.

After a solid ten minute of walking, he caught sight of the crest. No heat signatures were standing sentinel there. Hopefully that meant they'd continued straight. Even if they realized what was happening, it was now too late.

"We're doubling back," Liana said. "The road is about eight minutes ahead."

"Yep. Good guess."

"It's not a hard guess. I know that we're going back in the opposite direction."

"I'm talking about the time estimate."

"Oh." She stumbled over something. Remained upright. "I tend to keep a mental clock going in situations like this."

"Me too. Less risky than constantly looking at a watch."

"Agreed." She went silent.

They walked at a somewhat leisurely pace as the number of tree roots increased. If the operators realized what was happening and doubled back, they'd face the same terrain. Running through a forest at day or night was no easy task, despite what the movies showed.

The bank of the road came into view moments later. Liana put a hand on his arm. She pointed to her eyes. Pointed toward the road. Carver was already scanning the area, but he appreciated her tactical awareness.

He nodded. Kept scanning. Saw nothing. They crept up the bank to the road. It wasn't very steep, but it was enough to take cover behind. Carver looked up and down the road. No heat signatures.

He left his duffel bag in the bank and crawled up to the car. Looked beneath it. Caught a hint of red up the slope in the tree line on the other side of the road. They'd left someone behind to watch just in case he doubled back. Whoever it was didn't seem to be closely watching the car.

They'd probably gone prone on the other side of the road and watched for a while. Then they'd grown complacent. They also had a downward facing angle on the car. They couldn't see him looking from beneath it.

He scooted back down the bank. "Watcher on the hill. I'll take care of it."

Liana nodded.

Carver opened his duffel bag. Took out his M4 with the scope. He put on the silencer. Clicked a magazine into the well. Loaded the chamber. He crouch-walked along the bottom of the bank. Crawled up next to the front passenger wheel of the Lexus.

He slowly crawled around the front of the vehicle. Turned on the thermal imaging in the scope. Lifted his NV goggles. Looked through the scope. He caught the profile of the watcher. They were in a prone position, but the location of their hands indicated they weren't weapons ready.

The other operators might have radioed him and asked him if he saw anything. He would have reported negative. He would have assumed that anyone coming this way wouldn't expect a watcher in the trees.

Carver wasn't just anyone. Otherwise, he'd have been captured at gunpoint by now. These people weren't trying to kill him but taking him captive was no better. They might be people simply following orders, but that didn't earn them any lenience.

He aimed at the target. There was no wind right now and the distance was maybe a hundred yards. He'd practiced a lot with this scope. Calibrated it multiple times. Knew how to adjust for most variables.

The suppressor was another variable he could account for. He aimed a little higher. Pulled the trigger. The suppressor coughed. The thermal outline of the watcher went from prone to flat and limp.

Carver gave it a moment to make sure the target was down. He scanned the tree line for more watchers. Saw none. He hurried back to the car. Liana saw him coming and emerged at the top of the bank, the duffel bag in tow.

There was another problem Carver was already aware of. A problem he'd noted the moment he got close to his car. It meant they might not be going anywhere, at least not in the car.

The tires were flat.

CHAPTER 29

Carver slid his duffel bag into the back seat of the car.

He examined the tires. Someone had knifed the sidewalls on the driver's side tires. The passenger side tires looked okay. Maybe they hadn't knifed the passenger side tires so the car would look okay if viewed from the eastern approach.

It was a smart move. They'd anticipated the quarry doubling back. The watcher was the first part of the trap. The flat tires ensured they couldn't hop in the car and speed away. By the time they reached the driver's side and saw the flat tires, the watcher could have taken them at gunpoint.

Liana knelt next to the front tire. "Do you have a spare?"

"Yep." Carver popped the trunk. He took out the jack. Put it underneath. Jacked up the front.

"What about the back tire?"

"The front tires are more important. It's hard to steer with a flat front."

"It's going to be hard driving with a flat." Liana shook her head. "The rim will eventually eat through the rubber and the tire will fall off."

Carver spun the wrench and quickly removed the five lug nuts. He got the spare tire. It wasn't fully inflated, and it had a little dry rot around the edges. It would have to do.

Liana ran to the Lexus. She smashed open the front window with the butt of her gun. Opened the rear hatch. Looked inside where the spare tire normally was. "Damn, I was hoping they had a can of flat fixer."

Carver was already putting on the spare. He was counting down the seconds in his head. If the operators doubled back, they could be here any minute.

Liana stared at the flat tire. She ran back to the Lexus. She lowered the jack under the Lexus. Grunting and groaning, she tugged it out one-handed. Went to the other side of the Lexus. Pushed the jack beneath it.

She began awkwardly turning the jack handle. Keeping it steady with a foot until the scissor jack made contact with the bottom of the car.

Carver finished tightening the lug nuts. Lowered the jack. Pulled it out and took it to the trunk. "Let's go."

"Wait." Liana waved him over. "Your car is a Toyota Camry. It uses the same bolt pattern as a Lexus. The SUV tire is a little bigger, but I think it'll work."

Carver studied the rear tire on the Lexus. He studied the flat tire on the Toyota. Then he checked the time. "Move." He hurried over. Spun off the lug nuts. Yanked off the tire. He grabbed the jack from the trunk and put it under the jack point at the back of the car.

He pointed to the forest. "Keep an eye on the trees. Someone might have realized their watcher isn't talking to them anymore."

"Roger." She took cover at the front of the car and scanned the forest with the monocular.

Carver removed the rear flat tire in thirty seconds. He put on the Lexus tire. It fit into the wheel well just fine. He tightened the lug nuts.

"Movement!" Liana hissed. "Seventy yards and closing."

Carver tightened the last bolt.

"Sixty yards."

Carver lowered the jack as fast as he could.

"Fifty."

He yanked it from beneath the car. Opened the back door. Shoved his duffel bag onto the floorboard. "Get in."

Liana slid into the back seat. Carver got into the front. The interior lights were off, but the approaching operators didn't need lights to see their thermal signatures.

He started the car. Thankfully, they hadn't disabled the engine. He gunned the accelerator. Headed north.

"They didn't even shoot at us," Liana said.

"They must have orders to bring us in alive."

"They want you alive. Me, not so much." She leaned back in the rear seat and sighed. "I'm so tired I'm ready to pass out."

"Go ahead. You've got time."

She put a hand on his shoulder. Squeezed it. "Thanks for getting me through that."

"You got yourself through it just fine."

"Don't bullshit me, Carver." She groaned. "My shoulder is on fire. Every time I tried to use that arm it just locked up."

"Hardly surprising. Take a pain pill and get some sleep."

"I don't want to be foggy. I want to be ready in case another chopper drops out of the sky."

Carver didn't reply. He kept the car pointed north. Toward Cookeville. Liana laid down in the back seat and buckled herself in. That was a smart move. No telling what might happen next.

Sudden braking or a frontal impact would slam her into the back of the seats if she wasn't strapped down. At the very least it would seriously aggravate her shoulder injury. At the worst, well, it wouldn't matter much at that point.

He estimated the time the chopper would take to return to base. To refuel. To get back to the operators. It would take thirty minutes minimum. Cookeville was another forty-five minutes away. That gave the chopper a hypothetical fifteen minutes to close the gap.

The car was shaking even worse when he hit ninety this time. The spare tire was in bad shape, but it was holding for now. There was also a slight scraping sound from the back. The Lexus wheel was slightly wider than the original, so it was probably rubbing the wheel well.

The steering wheel wobbled back and forth despite his efforts to keep it steady. He slowed down to eighty. All the speed in the world wouldn't do him any good if the front tire popped. He also couldn't afford to go any slower.

Slow and steady would lose this race.

It occurred to him that he hadn't accounted properly for the time the chopper might return. The chopper had begun its journey to base moments before Carver and Liana doubled back. It had taken them a full fourteen minutes to make the return journey.

Another four minutes for him to snipe the sentry. Another five minutes to swap out the tires. That was twenty-four minutes total, give or take. They were now ten minutes into the second leg of this journey.

The chopper was almost certainly headed back to the operators by now. They would load their dead companion on board. Strap down the body. Climb in and lift off. The Black Hawk would close the distance in no time.

He entered the small town of Spencer. Slowed down to fifty-five miles per hour in case the local police had a speed trap. There wasn't much to see of the town from the highway. Just a few scattered buildings here and there.

The horizon was turning pink. There were a few more cars on the road. That would be good. The chopper couldn't hide in the night sky. It would be clearly visible. That didn't mean the operators would act any differently, though.

Roaches usually scattered in the light. But these guys were acting on orders from on high. They could do what they wanted, and no one would be able to question them because no one would know who they were.

He glanced back at Liana. She was out of it. Drooling from the side of her mouth. There was a spot of blood on her shirt. She'd probably reopened the wound. It wasn't bleeding too badly, though and there wasn't anything he could do about it anyway.

Carver checked the map. The next town was Sparta. It was twenty minutes or so from Cookeville. The name of the town was fitting because he might have to stop there and make a last stand.

It didn't seem likely that he could press on to Cookeville before the chopper caught up. Just reaching Sparta would be cutting it close. He did some math. Studied the street view of Sparta while keeping one eye on the road.

The name of a building stood out to him. He looked at it in street view. It was perfect. He plugged it into the GPS. Fifteen minutes away. That was doable. The steering wheel shuddered as if it disagreed.

The spare tire felt like it was going to explode at any moment. Maybe it was fine. Maybe the dry rot he'd noticed hadn't sunk past the surface. Or maybe the tire was about to shred to pieces. Maybe he'd drive into town with a bare rim throwing sparks off the asphalt.

It wouldn't be the first time Carver had driven the wheels off a car. There weren't too many firsts left for him when it came to things like this. He'd been shot at in cars, rammed, had the tires blown out, and had even jumped a car over a small stream once.

Cars didn't handle jumps well. They handled them about as well as big potholes. Most cars were front-heavy because of the engine. Even if you got them airborne, they would nose headfirst into the ground seconds later.

That was what had happened to Carver. He hadn't had much of a choice at the time. It was a bad decision, but it was a better decision than not trying at all. The car's radiator had cracked on impact.

The front shocks had bottomed out and one of the tires had burst. That was from a jump of no more than fifteen feet.

The seatbelt had nearly dislocated Carver's shoulder. The airbag had deployed and smacked him square in the face. His pursuers had stopped their car. Hopped out and unloaded everything they had into his car.

Carver had been able to get out and take cover with the engine block between him and the pursuers. If he'd been knocked unconscious, that would have been the end of his story.

He looked in the rearview mirror and saw a dot on the horizon. The chopper was back. He checked the GPS. Five minutes to the destination. This was going to be close. Real close. He hadn't expected them to be this close already.

They were a full ten or fifteen minutes ahead of schedule.

The dot was getting bigger by the second. They probably had him zeroed in. Probably had a scope on him right this moment. The terrain was flatter here. No hills to conceal him. But what it lacked in hills it made up for with trees.

Carver glanced back with the monocular. He zoomed in and realized this wasn't the same chopper that chased them in the forest. It didn't have the tail rotor faring or the baffles. They'd scrambled another chopper to pick up the operators.

That was why they were ahead of schedule. That was why they were practically breathing down his neck at this point. If not for the rattling front end of his car, he'd probably hear the whump of the rotor blades already.

He reached the turnoff. Slowed down. Took a right at the traffic light. Trees concealed the chopper from him. They would have seen where he turned but now, he was invisible to them as well.

The building he'd scoped out was on the right. It was a self-serve carwash. He pulled into a stall. It was nice and deep. There were trees on the back side of the property so the chopper wouldn't see the car from the sky.

Liana moaned. Sat up. "Are we there yet?"

"No." Carver turned off the car and got out. He could hear the rotor blades clearly. He edged to the back corner of the stall and looked up. The chopper was higher now, hovering over the intersection where he'd turned.

He ducked back into the stall. Looked toward the highway. Morning traffic was light. Hardly surprising in a town like this. There was a motel nearby. A few pedestrians on the sidewalks.

There weren't enough people for him to blend into a crowd but that was to be expected in a town this size. He put on a hoodie. Covered his head.

Liana climbed out of the back seat. Her face was pale. She was trying to hide the pain, but it was evident on her face.

Carver dug through his duffel and found a ball cap. He gave it to her. He couldn't take the duffel bag with him. Not now. It would be too obvious even if he slung it on his back. He took the Glock and put it in his shoulder holster.

"What now?" Liana said.

"We find new wheels."

"Okay." She winced.

Carver looked her over. "Maybe it's better if you stay behind and sleep in the car. We should be safe for now."

"No, I can help."

He shook his head. "You need sleep. I'm going to find another car."

"Are you going to steal one?"

"No." He dug a wad of cash out of the duffel bag. "I'm going to find a cash lot."

She slumped. "Okay. I'll be here."

He put a hand on her shoulder. "Good work with the Lexus tire. We wouldn't have made it otherwise."

She tilted her head slightly. "Is that a helicopter I hear?"

"Yeah, they scrambled another one. One without the sound dampening. That's how they caught up to us so fast."

"So, this is what it feels like to be hunted like an animal." Liana rubbed the back of her neck. "I guess it's payback for all the manhunts I've coordinated."

Carver didn't have a response to that, so he just nodded. He already knew where he was going next, thanks to the maps app. It was a fifteen-minute walk. A walk that was sure to be scrutinized by the operators in the Black Hawk.

There wasn't much tree cover between here and his destination. Just concrete and asphalt. He watched the helicopter from the cover of the car wash for a moment. It was hovering far overhead.

He saw the glint of binoculars. The glint of rifle scopes. They were looking in all directions.

"Maybe you should wait it out," Liana said.

"Maybe." He waited and watched. The chopper didn't seem to be going anywhere. This one had a pair of reserve fuel tanks mounted on the wings. It could hover there for just about as long as it wanted.

A pickup truck pulled into the neighboring stall. It was covered in mud. Judging from the oversized tires and the lift kit, it wasn't a work truck.

Carver walked around back and went into the stall. The driver was just dropping out of the truck. Carver smiled and waved. "Hey! My car broke down and I was wondering if I could pay you to give me a lift somewhere."

The driver blinked as if just now realizing someone else was there with him. He was a young guy. Probably mid-twenties. "Uh, sure. Are you from around here?"

"No, just passing through." Carver took a twenty from his pocket. "I just need to go to the gas station down the road. Pick up some oil."

The driver took the twenty and smiled. "Yeah, man. Hop in."

Carver considered getting his stuff and Liana into the pickup, but that would just draw attention. Make the young guy think something fishy was going on. It was better to go by himself. Keep suspicion low.

Carver opened the door and pulled himself up and in. The driver climbed in and backed out of the stall.

"Where's your car?"

"In the next stall." Carver laughed. "I thought I could squeeze another hundred thousand miles out of her, but she burns oil like it's gasoline."

The driver looked at the Toyota. "Those are good cars. Heck, you can go three hundred thousand miles in them, or so I heard. Pretty much drive the wheels off of them before you need another one."

"I think I about drove the wheels off of her today." Carver shook his head. "Oh well."

The young guy drove down the road toward the gas station there. He looked up at the Black Hawk. "Is that a UH Sixty? What the hell is a military chopper doing here?"

"Did you serve?"

"Yep. Marines. In and out in four, though." The young guy shrugged. "Just not the same as it used to be. Too much PC crap these days. I couldn't take it anymore."

Carver saw the gas station on the right and pointed it out. "That's it."

"Cool." The young guy pulled over and parked. "If you're getting oil, don't you need a ride back?"

Carver patted his stomach. "I've got to take care of some business first. My breakfast isn't sitting right with me."

The young guy laughed. "Hey, I know how that is."

"I'll just walk back. Thanks for the ride."

"Sure thing." The pickup guy pulled out of the parking lot and turned south toward the car wash.

Carver waited for the pickup truck to get a good distance away then walked next door to the used car dealership. It wasn't much of a misdirection, but any little bit helped just in case.

He went inside before a salesman came outside. He wanted a roof over his head while the chopper was circling.

A middled-aged man sat at a desk inside. He was staring at a computer monitor. He flinched when the door opened. Cleared his throat. "Hey! How can I help you?"

Carver had noticed a Toyota outside, but he wanted something a little bigger this time. "How much for the minivan?" He was already looking up the make and model online.

"That's a really good vehicle. Fully serviced, new tires, fresh oil change. And it's—"

"You have a dollar amount in there somewhere?"

"Ten thousand, sir. We also offer financing."

"I'll give you four grand in cash."

"That's quite a lowball offer."

Carver showed him the prices on a car sales website. "Yeah. I don't see a single one from that model year selling for over five grand."

"How about five thousand then?"

"Four thousand, take it or leave it."

"Well, you drive a hard bargain, but I'll take it."

"It runs, right?" Carver lowered his hoodie and gave the man a good hard look. "I need something that runs well or I'm going to be upset."

The dealer gulped. "I can assure you that it's one of the best running vehicles on the lot. My wife has used it several times recently."

Carver let his stony gaze linger on the man for a moment before nodding. "Okay."

"Let's get the paperwork filled out and we'll have you on your way." The dealer cleared his throat. "There's a small fee—"

"Just sign the title over. I'll take care of it when I get home. I've got a long drive and I'm ready to go now."

"But sir—"

Carver stepped closer. "Just sign over the title."

"Yes, sir." The dealer went into an office at the back. He returned with a title. Showed Carver the back where he'd signed it so it could be transferred.

"Thanks." Carver handed him the cash.

The dealer counted it quickly. Nodded. "Everything is in order." He handed Carver the keys. "Thank you for your business."

Carver went outside. Got in the minivan. It reeked of synthetic pine odor thanks to the deodorizer hanging on the rearview mirror. He put the key in the ignition. Twisted it. The engine hummed to life. It didn't sputter or make strange sounds. That was a good sign.

He pulled onto the road. The chopper was no longer hovering. It was on the move. Unfortunately, it wasn't going away. It seemed to be moving somewhere purposefully.

Right over the car wash where Liana was hiding.

CHAPTER 30

Carver watched the Black Hawk.

He zoomed in with his monocular. One of the operators sitting on the side of the chopper was pointing down at the car wash. Carver couldn't tell if it was an urgent gesture or if the guy was simply telling the pilot to check it out.

Whatever the case, the chopper was heading that way and dropping lower. The few pedestrians walking the streets were taking notice of the strange activity. It wasn't every day that a military chopper hovered over a small town like it was looking for something or someone.

That kind of activity was bound to make people nervous. To make civilians think maybe something bad had happened or was about to happen. Someone was almost certainly calling the local police. Asking them what in the hell was going on.

Carver zoomed in on the Toyota in the car wash. He saw Liana's head poking up in the back seat. She was probably feeling like a trapped animal. There was no way out without being seen.

The guy with the pickup was still there washing off his muddy truck. He was wearing headphones. Probably listening to music and oblivious to the chopper. Even without headphones he could probably filter out the noise. Just an added "benefit" of having been in the military.

Another car was parked one stall down from the Toyota. They'd stopped soaping down a compact car to step outside and gawk at the Black Hawk thundering overhead. It was midmorning now. The people of Sparta were up and about.

And they had an intruder in their midst.

Carver drove down the street. He kept his speed moderate. Kept it casual. He didn't want to draw the attention of the chopper crew by going too fast. He wanted to be just another meaningless blip on the road. After a tense few minutes, he reached the car wash.

A police car with flashing lights was parked about two blocks down. A cop stood outside, one arm braced on the open door, a radio mic in his other hand. He was probably asking someone what to do about the chopper tearing apart the morning calm in his little town.

Carver saw the real threat farther down the road. It wasn't another chopper. It was a line of black Sprinter vans turning off the highway. They'd really sent the cavalry this time. The Black Hawk would provide aerial support and the operators in the vans would search the ground.

He turned into the car wash. Parked in the stall next to the Toyota. There was an overhang in the back, so he ducked around that side. Liana was already out of the car. Already trying to lug Carver's bag out of the trunk.

"A minivan?" She smiled weakly. "Are we starting a family?"

"I thought I'd surprise you." Carver hefted the duffel bag. He grabbed other odds and ends from the trunk. Carried around the back of the stall and stuffed it into the minivan. He went to the Toyota again.

Liana was spraying it down with glass cleaner. Spraying it all over the faux leather seats, the steering wheel, the dashboard.

"That's good enough." Carver motioned her over. "We've got incoming."

"More incoming besides the chopper?"

"Yeah. Ground troops."

She hurried after him. The side sliding door was open, so she hopped in the back seat. Carver got in the driver's seat. He hoped the chopper hadn't noticed that he'd only been in the stall for four minutes.

He backed out. Turned around in the parking lot. Pulled onto the road and headed east, away from the Sprinter vans. He took the next road north. Watched the chopper in the side and rearview mirrors.

It was holding position over the car wash. He couldn't see the car wash anymore, but he imagined one of the vans pulling into the place and seeing the Toyota. He imagined men pouring out of the van and surrounding the car.

They'd realize it was empty. They'd run to the neighboring stalls. Talk to the guy with the pickup. Ask him if he'd seen the people in the Toyota.

Things could go one of two ways. The pickup guy didn't seem like the type to blindly trust the government. At least not from the way he'd been talking to Carver. But he also might not want any trouble and tell them what they wanted to know.

He'd say he'd seen the car. Talked to the big guy who owned it. Taken him down the road to the gas station to get some oil. They might ask why the big guy didn't want a ride back. He would tell them the big guy had tummy troubles and might be unloading his guts in the gas station bathroom.

The operators would hurry to the gas station. No one inside would have seen Carver enter. Then they'd know that hadn't been his primary destination. That it was a misdirection. They'd go to the businesses nearby.

One of those businesses would be the used car dealership. They'd ask the salesman if he'd seen a big guy in a hoodie. The salesman would say, "Yes, as a matter of fact, I just sold him a brown Chrysler minivan with new tires and a fresh oil change."

The chopper would immediately redeploy in a search pattern based on the last time Carver had been seen. One of the operators in the chopper would probably remember seeing a brown minivan enter the carwash.

They would know that Carver had returned to pick up Liana and his belongings from the Toyota. They would know that he couldn't have gone far yet.

The local cops would be fed a bullshit story. They'd be told that a pair of fugitives had come through here. An APB would be put out on the minivan.

Carver and Liana would be in custody by lunchtime.

But the chopper hovered in place. Maybe the pickup guy had decided not to tell them anything.

Maybe.

Carver kept driving. Kept glancing back at the chopper. It hovered in place for five minutes. Then it began to move. It went north toward the dealership.

The operators had probably told the pickup guy that Carver was a dangerous fugitive. That he'd killed women and children. The pickup guy had probably stared at them, wondering if that was the truth.

He'd eventually decided it was the truth. Or he'd decided he didn't want any trouble. Carver looked like the kind of guy who went around murdering women and children for fun.

The pickup guy had told the operators what they wanted to know. They were on their way to the gas station and shortly thereafter, the dealership.

Carver gritted his teeth. He should have asked for a ride to a place two streets over. Maybe to a random house. Not a gas station right next door to the dealership where he planned to purchase a car.

When it came right down to it, he'd done what he could in the time allotted. If he'd been dropped off two streets over, that would have taken another five or ten minutes to reach the dealership.

By then, the vans would have reached the carwash and Liana would be in custody. The brown minivan had served its purpose. It had bought them maybe fifteen or twenty minutes. At four thousand dollars, that was about two hundred and fifty bucks a minute.

There were two routes to Cookeville. One took thirty-four minutes. The other took twenty-four. He was already on the longer route, state route 84. Reaching Highway 111 required cutting the long way across town or taking some back country roads.

It was too risky changing course now. He'd just have to keep going and hope he got a good enough head start on the chopper before they found out about the minivan.

He also had one other advantage. The people after him didn't necessarily know that he was going to Cookeville. They might not know where he was going and send the chopper to search in a radius.

If that was the case, he might be home free all the way to Cookeville.

"What's the sitrep?" Liana asked from the back seat.

"Tenuous." Carver accelerated now that they were outside of the city limits. The terrain was hilly, sparsely forested due to open farmland along the roadside. It would be hard to hide near the highway.

In fact, it would be hard to hide within a mile of the highway since there were so many open fields. He had little choice but to keep the car pointed north and keep the speed well above the legal limit.

Eight minutes later, he reached the city limits of a small town. He blinked and the town was already behind him. The GPS told him to turn left on Cherry Creek Road. He did as instructed and left the highway behind.

There was just as much open farmland along this route as there had been on the highway. It seemed hillier here but that might just be his imagination. Even so, he kept looking for possible places to take cover if the chopper came after them.

He rolled down his window. The wind whistled past, but it wasn't enough to cover up the whump of a distant chopper. The sound was faint. Like it was far behind them. Carver pulled off the road and into a thicket of trees.

It wasn't much, but it was enough to shield the van from aerial view.

"Are they close?" Liana said.

Carver didn't answer. He got out. Scanned the sky with the monocular. He saw the chopper, a dot on the horizon. It had gained altitude and was a little southwest of their position. He zoomed in as far as the monocular could manage.

That was just enough to see an operator scanning his direction with a monocular of his own. The chopper was tilted forward, moving almost due north if Carver was eyeballing it correctly. It was miles away, but they could cross that distance in minutes.

The minivan was confined to the roads. It couldn't go anywhere fast enough to outrun a UH-60. Carver wished he'd bought a Dodge Challenger instead. Then again, there were so many twists and turns in the road that high speed would just be a recipe for disaster.

He had to think of a better way to get away from the chopper. A way that still got him to Cookeville.

One way was to abandon the minivan somewhere it couldn't be seen from the road or the air. Then he and Liana could hoof it cross-country the rest of the way. Unfortunately, that would require nearly a full day of walking.

Liana wasn't in any kind of condition to make that walk, especially not when they'd have to climb hills and hop fences along the way. Some farmers or ranchers might not take kindly to trespassers.

There was another way, but it was risky. Real risky. And he'd only have one, maybe two shots at it. At this point, the risk seemed worth it. Because trying to outrace a Black Hawk across mostly open terrain was a losing proposition.

Liana stood next to him. "What are you thinking?"

Carver unzipped his duffel bag. He had an assortment of rifles inside. Things he'd collected on his travels. Some of them he'd acquired from individuals he'd unalived at some point. Some he'd purchased on the used gun market.

Unfortunately, he didn't have the one rifle that would make this much easier. A Barret fifty caliber with a high-powered scope would have clinched the decision. But something like that was just too heavy to carry around in a duffel bag that was already weighed down by other guns.

It was too long. Too bulky. Just too much to keep on hand. He'd have to put it in a separate carry case. Running through the forest with a duffel bag and a sniper rifle case would have been a no-go.

Carver had a nice M4 with a scope. He had a few handguns and even a bullpup that fired .556 ammo. But none of those were going to take down a Black Hawk. Not unless he unloaded a hundred rounds into the engine.

A Black Hawk was moderately maneuverable. It was somewhere in between a Little Bird and a Chinook when it came to agility. Loaded down with operators and equipment, it became less wieldy, but still quick enough to get out of the way of a madman firing little .556 rounds at it.

Carver pulled out another bullpup rifle. This was one he hadn't seen much in the wild. At least not until he'd uncovered the cartel's arsenal in El Fuerte. He'd taken it more out of curiosity than anything else.

He'd played with it a few times. Calibrated the scope. Tested the range. Rated it as powerful but lacking in long-range accuracy. It wouldn't be his first choice for what he needed to do, but it was all he had.

It was a GM-6 Lynx. A bullpup fifty cal. A bizarre configuration for such a powerful rifle. But the best part about it was the weight. It was considerably lighter than a full-length Barret fifty caliber and it was much shorter.

It traded long-range accuracy for portability. But the power should theoretically be about the same. A fifty-caliber bullet to a Black Hawk engine was a fifty-caliber bullet to a Black Hawk engine.

It would be enough to take it out of commission. The trick was going to be hitting the engine before the chopper got close enough to drop troops on him. It was too distant for him to hit now.

The scope was powerful enough to see the engines clearly, but the shorter barrel reduced the accuracy considerably at such a distance.

"That is one strange-looking rifle." Liana ran a finger along the barrel. "A bullpup fifty-cal?"

"Yep." Carver watched the chopper. Gauged its flight path. It seemed to be splitting the distance between the two northern routes. Or maybe it was flying directly over the other highway. It was hard to tell from this angle.

There was only one way to do this, and it was going to be tricky. He shoved a magazine into the mag well. Loaded the chamber. He picked out a large tree standing in a distant pasture. There was no livestock around. No humans either.

He put on hearing protection. Gave a pair of earmuffs to Liana. She put them on. He braced the rifle against a tree trunk since it didn't have a bipod for a prone setup.

Carver aimed at a point on the trunk right where a large branch had been pruned at some point. He put it dead center in the scope. He tested the wind. There was a slight breeze. He adjusted for it. Took a deep breath. Released it. Pulled the trigger.

The gun bucked hard. The report barked and echoed into the distance, clearly audible even with hearing protection. A big shell ejected from the side and a fresh round was chambered. Carver saw a puff of bark where the bullet hit the tree.

He checked it with his monocular. He'd missed dead center by about two inches. That wasn't too bad considering the tree was easily two hundred yards away. He adjusted the scope. Tested the wind. Adjusted accordingly. Fired.

The slug hit dead center this time. It left a big hole where it hit. It might have even gone clear through the tree. Now all he had to do was repeat the process on a rapid, airborne target. Easier said than done.

If he missed, it was game over.

CHAPTER 31

Carver had to take down a Black Hawk with a rifle.

He fired one more round from the Lynx. It punched into the same spot on the tree. Dead center. His calibrations were spot on. At least for a stationary ground target.

Liana removed her hearing protection. "Nice shooting. Do you plan to shoot the pilot?"

"An engine. Easier to hit." He pulled out the magazine. Cleared the chamber. Reloaded the magazine to full. He put the duffel bag on the back floorboard in front of the third-row seats. He put the Lynx on the floorboard behind the passenger seat and put the magazine in the center console.

Liana climbed into the passenger seat. "You're going to bait them, aren't you?"

"It's the only way." Carver buckled up. "Strap in. Be ready to get out if things go sideways."

"Yes, sir." She mock saluted with her left hand.

He handed her the monocular. "Keep an eye on our friends."

She took aim with the monocular. "Ready."

Carver pulled back onto the road. He gunned the engine. Got the minivan up to seventy. The road wasn't too curvy or hilly, so he was able to maintain speed. "Anything yet?"

"Nothing."

He kept driving. Followed a curve around a hill. Dipped down into a hollow. Rolled up the other side to a taller hill. For several seconds, they were naked and exposed on the high point. Then they dove back down into another hollow.

"Nothing?" he said.

"Nothing."

Maybe the men in the helicopter didn't know what they were looking for. Maybe they hadn't gone to the dealership and found out about the van. It looked like they might make it to Cookeville without a fifty-cal intervention.

The road continued through the hollow for a decent stretch, keeping them out of sight of the chopper. It was looking more and more like they might make it.

"Maybe they don't see us," Liana said. "Or maybe they're just stupid."

"It's not over until it's over." Carver wasn't letting down his guard just yet. "Keep watching."

They went up a rise and back to flat terrain.

"Oh, crap." Liana had her eye to the monocular. "They're coming straight at us. They must have seen us before we went into that dip."

Carver rolled down his window. Looked out and back. The Black Hawk was nose down and coming on hard. It was maybe two miles away and doing probably a hundred and fifty knots. It would reach them in seconds.

"It's not over until it's over," Carver said.

Liana was already focused on the next goal. "There's a good spot." She pointed to a dirt road leading toward a pasture. It passed through a thicket of bushes and trees.

Carver slowed and took the turn. He went into the trees. Hit the brakes. Hopped out and opened the sliding side door. Liana tossed him the magazine. He caught it one-handed. It was big and heavy. He snapped it into the well.

The thunder of the chopper was getting closer by the second. Carver ran to the edge of the trees. He loaded the chamber. Braced the barrel against a tree. Aimed at the right turbine.

There were two engines on a UH-60. A single engine failure wouldn't normally result in a crash. One engine was enough to maintain altitude and land safely. Carver wasn't sure if that was true.

He just remembered what a pilot once told him when they were flying low under enemy fire. The pilot also said there was a chance of losing control and crashing. But that he could safely land in an emergency.

The chopper was a little over two hundred yards distant. He zeroed in on the engine. It was a big target even if it wasn't fully exposed. An air intake jutted from the side. Just next to it was the turbine engine.

The chopper crossed into range. It was already slowing down. Preparing to do a quick landing near the trees, if Carver was guessing right. He took a breath. Released it.

Pulled the trigger.

A hole appeared in the fuselage. It was right in front of the air intake. It should have punched right through the engine. But there was no smoke. No sounds of distress from the chopper.

The pilot, however, was taking evasive action, pulling hard left and angling the chopper so the engine wasn't an easy target. That irritated Carver. He didn't understand why the engine wasn't fatally damaged. Why the chopper was still flying at full power.

He fired three more rounds into the bottom of the chopper. The rounds punched right through, nice and clean. If anyone was sitting there, they probably punched through them too. He aimed at the bottom right about where the pilot was sitting.

Smoke boiled from the exhaust on the right side. The chopper whined loudly. Something popped. Flames burst from the exhaust. Black smoke boiled from the damaged turbine. The chopper angled back the way it had come.

The pilot was trying to keep it airborne. At least until he could get out of Carver's line of fire. He probably thought Carver would start sniping at them on the ground. That wasn't a bad idea, but it wasn't a good idea either.

There were several operators on the chopper. He'd only been able to see the ones sitting on the sides. There were probably more sitting in the middle seats. He estimated at least eight. Maybe seven if they hadn't replaced their dead comrade.

The chopper went down next to some trees in a distant field. It landed hard, but safely. Carver took a good long look and saw he was right. There were seven operators inside. One of them was screaming and bleeding. Another was slumped over.

The others were scrambling out, giving medical attention to the bleeding one. They wore the same urban camouflage they'd worn in Morganville. They didn't wear flag patches or anything to show their military affiliation.

Given everything Carver had observed he felt even more certain that these guys weren't black ops. They were one level deeper. Dark ops. Night ops. Blind ops. There were a lot of names for them, but they all meant basically the same thing. They were even more illegal than black ops.

Illegal, of course, was a relative term when it came to governmental entities. They followed the law on the surface and did whatever the hell they wanted under cover of darkness. And yet, here they were operating in broad daylight.

"Jesus Christ." Liana stood next to him, the monocular to her eye. "Who in the hell are these people? How many operators do they have?"

"Get in the van." Carver followed his own order and went to the van. He removed the magazine from the Lynx. Cleared the chamber. Loaded the loose round into the magazine. He put the magazine in the rifle and put the rifle on the floorboard.

It wasn't ideal leaving an unsecured rifle on the floor, but neither was it ideal being chased by dark ops forces in a Black Hawk helicopter.

He strapped in.

Liana was already in her seat, face pale with pain. She buckled in. Managed a pained grin. "Great shot, by the way."

"I shot at it four times. I thought the first shot missed the engine."

"Well, you hit something."

"It was sloppy." Carver backed down the dirt road. The tires hit asphalt. The back window burst. Metal shrieked. Daylight shone through two more holes in the sliding door.

Carver gunned the engine. Someone was sniping from the chopper's position. "Maybe I should have gunned them down."

"They're pissed." Liana ducked in her seat. Made herself as small as possible.

"Cant' blame them. Nothing like watching fifty-caliber rounds punch through your squad mates to piss a person off."

They careened around a curve. No more holes appeared in the minivan. No more bullets tried to take off their heads. They were out of line of sight.

"Seven holes." Liana frowned. "Four bullets should have left eight holes."

"The eighth one is where the back window used to be," Carver said.

"Oh yeah, you're right." She released a long sigh. "I should have realized that, but I'm so damned tired."

"Imagine how those operators feel." Carver studied the GPS. "We've got fifteen minutes."

Liana looked through the monocular. "Nothing in the sky. They obviously have vast resources if they can send a stealth chopper and then scramble another one within minutes."

"They probably have unlimited support, but a limited pool of operators." Carver noticed the check oil light had just blinked on and hoped a bullet hadn't put a hole in the engine. "If it's anything like my old outfit, you can't just bring in anyone. They have to be thoroughly vetted. Make sure they have what it takes to go completely offline."

"Offline?"

"Erased."

"You were one of those guys?"

Carver nodded.

"You're tight-lipped about it."

"Not exactly something I want to discuss with an NSA field agent."

"A rogue field agent." She sighed. "Maybe. I don't even know if I can go back. Now I'm an accomplice to killing whoever these guys are."

"I doubt your boss even knows they exist. I doubt your boss even knows where you are right now or that you're a fugitive."

She raised an eyebrow. "My boss isn't exactly a big man in the company, but he'd almost certainly know about off the books operatives."

"These aren't your typical black ops operators." Carver shrugged. "But what do I know? I was just an operator, not someone giving orders."

"I'm just scared, you know?" She stared at the road ahead. "What if I go back in and they throw me in jail?"

"What's the alternative?"

"Running." She shook her head. "I don't want to live like that."

"You're not just some field agent." Carver glanced at her to see how that statement impacted her. "Not unless it's standard protocol to give field agents half a dozen different false IDs."

"That box you found is a standard go box. I take it everywhere with me in case an operation goes south."

"Yeah, but you're in the States. You can just call the agency to bail you out."

"Sometimes, yes, but that box is standard protocol for deep cover agents." Liana shrugged. "I don't know what else to tell you."

Carver didn't know if that was true. She didn't really have a reason to lie about it. She didn't really have a reason to tell the truth, either. He just decided to take her word for it. At least for the time being.

She'd had plenty of chances to prove she wasn't on his side. Plenty of chances to grab a gun and take him down. She hadn't tried to do any of those things. If she was just playing along, she was doing a damned good job of it.

He wasn't exactly the trusting sort and for good reason. Maybe he'd never entirely believe her. But for now, she seemed to be on his side. If push came to shove and she had to choose him or her job, he knew which one she'd pick.

There were bigger fish to fry on the near horizon. First and foremost was reaching Lacy Hood's house without drawing undue attention. All this chopper business had put him hours behind Decker.

The women might already be dead by now. He'd tried not to think about what he might find. Decker had all the time in the world to do anything he wanted to them. The only hope was that Paola had somehow eluded him.

He decided that driving straight to Hood's home was the best strategy. He wouldn't waste any time or take any major precautions. As it was, he might be hours too late.

The check engine light came on about a mile outside of town. The temperature gauge had been creeping up slowly but surely and the oil light had been on for miles now. Something had either happened to the engine or the salesman at the used car place had sold him a lemon.

Somehow, the minivan made it to Lacy Hood's address. It was a nice two-story white house right at the corner of Hudgens Street and Whitson Avenue. It sat on two acres of land not far from downtown. The driveway was in the back next to a detached garage.

A red Honda SUV was parked behind the garage. A black Chevy pickup sat next to it. The Lexus had probably been towed by now and was sitting in a tire shop somewhere.

They were probably wondering why the rear wheel was completely missing. They could find it on his Toyota in Sparta if they wanted it back.

The garage door was open. There was a classic Ford Mustang parked inside. Everything looked peaceful. Idyllic, even. And there was no sign of Decker's car.

That didn't mean anything. He might have come and gone. The women might have been raped, tortured, and murdered. The only peace in this house might be the peace of death. It was possible Decker had taken Paola with him since she was more valuable alive than dead.

Liana looked at her phone. Back at the house. "This is definitely the place."

Carver wondered if this was the moment she'd been waiting for. If Liana had gone through all of this just so she could lay hands on Paola and Carver. If Paola was inside and everything was okay, then maybe she'd wait until everyone was nice and comfortable before calling in the troops.

Maybe he was teetering into paranoia. Maybe everything would be fine. A few hours from now, they might all be eating dinner and laughing about shooting down a military aircraft.

Liana watched him quietly. Almost as if she knew what was going on in his head. She pursed her lips. "Well, are we going to sit out here all day? Are you scared Paola's dead body is inside the house?"

"Decker had hours to do whatever he wanted." Carver opened the car door. Stepped out. He strapped on his Glock. Fastened the suppressor.

Liana got out and held the compact Glock in her left hand. She watched Carver closely.

He walked toward the house. Walked down the driveway to the back yard. There was a screened in porch. The door wasn't latched, so he went through.

He steeled himself and looked through the back windows. Heavy curtains blocked the view. He tested the door. It was locked. He considered breaking in, but opted for a less violent approach just in case everyone inside was alive and well.

Carver knocked on the door. He heard a little voice shouting. "Mommy, someone's knocking!"

He heard footsteps. The curtain moved aside in the window on his right. A woman looked from him to Liana. Her brow furrowed. The curtain closed.

Carver heard the woman shouting. "Honey, someone's at the back door."

Someone else shouted back "What?"

"I said, someone's at the back door!"

"Who is it?"

"I don't know!" the woman shouted back. "That's why I'm calling you!"

The man shouted a reply. "All right, all right, I'm coming!"

A moment later, the lock on the door clicked. The door swung inward. A heavyset man with a thick beard stared at them in confusion. His face was red. Like he'd hurried to get there. "Can I help you with something?"

Carver looked at the man's presumed wife and kid behind him. The woman didn't match Lacy's description at all. "Is this Lacy Hood's house?"

The man frowned. "I don't know who that is."

"He means Brenda Johnson," Liana said, using Hood's WITSEC name.

"Still don't know who that is." The man glanced back. "Do you, honey?"

His wife shook her head. "I'm sorry. I think you have the wrong house."

"Hang on. I have pictures from social media." Liana showed them the picture of Lacy and the mayor. Showed them the post about her holding a fundraiser at the address of their house.

"We've never had a fundraiser here." The man stared at the image.

His wife stepped closer and looked at it. "We didn't host that. It was a neighborhood potluck to raise money for the school."

The man stared at the image. "That's the mayor but I don't know the woman he's shaking hands with. And I can tell you for sure she doesn't live here, or I'd be in a heap of trouble with my wife."

His wife laughed. "That's true. I'm sorry, I don't recognize her either."

Carver nodded. "Sorry to bother you. Thanks for your help."

He and Liana walked back to the minivan. He climbed inside and stared at the road ahead.

"I don't understand," Liana said. "Maybe it's a fake social media post to throw people off?"

"Maybe," Carver said. One thing was certain.

He had no idea where Paola and the others were.

CHAPTER 32

Carver didn't know where to go next.

He put the key in the ignition and turned it. The engine sputtered. The dashboard warning lights lit up like a Christmas tree. He tried again.

Again, nothing.

The minivan was dead. He got out and opened the hood. Looked at the engine. It looked okay. He looked underneath it. Saw a small puddle of oil. He slid underneath and saw the problem.

There was a hole in the oil filter. A bullet must have deflected and hit it perfectly. The odds of that were off the chart, but here they were and there it was. At least that meant the used car guy hadn't sold him a dud.

In the end, it didn't matter. He needed a new ride. An anonymous ride. The minivan had gotten them where they needed to go. At least, where he'd thought they needed to go. Now it was a known vehicle.

There was no doubt in his mind that the people after him would utilize all their resources to hunt him down. They probably didn't know where he was going, but they could guess.

Liana stood next to him. "What's wrong with it?"

"Hole in the oil filter." Carver pushed to his feet. He opened the map app and looked at it. "I don't want to leave it here. If the people after us find it here, they'll go straight to this house and ask questions. Find out that we were here asking about Brenda Johnson and Lacy Hood. Then they'll canvas the neighborhood to find us."

"True."

Carver found an auto supply store on the map. It was about a fifteen-minute walk. "I'll get oil and a filter. You can wait here."

"Get a car cover too. We can still drive the minivan and put the cover over it."

Carver raised an eyebrow. "Good idea."

"Do you have enough money to buy another car?"

Carver had access to a bank account Leon had given him some time ago, but he didn't want to share that information with her. "I have a few bucks laying around."

"As much as I want a nap, I'll come with you. I don't feel safe staying with the car."

"Fine by me." Carver started walking. He didn't like leaving his guns behind, but he also didn't want to haul the duffel bag along with him. A big guy like him with a bag like that would stand out. People would remember him for sure.

He still had the Glock in his shoulder holster. That was good enough for now.

Liana stared at the social media pictures she'd pulled up. "The person who posted these images is Sharon Watson. Maybe we can find her and talk to her."

"Does Brenda Johnson exist on social media?"

"No. Like I said, WITSEC highly discourages any social media presence."

"But they could easily have an account with fake name and photos."

"They can. But if they post a real image, then someone with a program like mine might find them."

Carver mulled it over. "Where does Sharon Watson live?"

"I don't see an address, but we could probably find one in a phone book." Liana opened a website and ran a search. "There are three of them in town."

"We'll start there next."

She pursed her lips. "I have another slightly dumb idea."

"Let's hear it."

"What if we bought spray paint and painted the minivan?"

Carver laughed. "Not a bad idea, but it'll take time. We'll have to tape up the windows and key holes."

"We could get it done in an hour. It's cheaper than buying another car." She chuckled. "It'll look like crap, but it might be enough to throw off our pursuers."

Carver reached an intersection and turned left on the sidewalk. They were ten minutes from the destination. "We'll also have to patch the bullet holes and put something over the broken rear window."

"Duct tape and trash bags will work in a pinch. We won't even stand out."

"True," Carver said. "We probably wouldn't have the only minivan with a bad paint job and duct tape on it. Just need to find a nice private spot to take care of repairs."

"Shouldn't be a problem in a small town like this." Liana pointed to the forested areas on the outskirts of town. "We can go somewhere around there."

There was something else on Carver's mind. "Tell me again why you were in Morganville."

"I was keeping an eye out for Paola or for you. I was given a few details about what happened in Morganville, but I wasn't specifically told why they wanted you."

"How well did you know the members of the goon squad that nearly killed you?"

"I only knew they existed. I didn't know anything else about them. I was just put in charge of the police department with Maberly playing the part of chief." She narrowed her eyes. "Why? Still don't trust me?"

"I'm just trying to understand why it's worth all this manpower just to track me and Paola down."

"I couldn't tell you. The top brass tend to look at the grunts as expendable no matter how specialized they might be."

"Big mistake." Carver shook his head. "You don't find people like Rhodes or Jericho every day. You don't throw good assets like that away unless you're stupid."

"I don't know who those people are."

"Former squad mates." Carver saw a police car driving toward them. He didn't want the driver to see him and Liana. He had an innate distrust for authority, but in this case, there was more to it. Local law enforcement was often utilized as eyes and ears for searches.

By now, there would almost certainly be a description of him in circulation. Maybe even a picture despite his best efforts to avoid cameras.

"LEO incoming," Liana said.

"I noticed."

There was nowhere to go. The next street was half a block away. There were houses and yards to their left and the same across the street.

Liana took his right hand with her left. She turned him toward the red brick house on his left and gestured toward it. "I want you to smile and nod and look enthusiastic, okay? Like I'm talking about how wonderful this plain little brick house is."

Carver smiled and nodded. Kept his back angled toward the police car as it approached. It seemed to slow a little as it approached, but he couldn't be sure. He listened to the tires pass behind him from right to left.

He saw it continue onward out of the corner of his eye but didn't turn to look straight at it. Liana kept talking about flower gardens and renovations until the patrol car was well down the road. Then she let go of his hand and started walking again.

Carver walked alongside her. "You seem to have experience avoiding police."

"I was something of a troubled youth."

"Not surprising," Carver said.

She sighed. "I was worried my bad decisions would keep me from landing a job as a field agent. I was shocked to discover it was a pro being a former con, not a con."

"Field agents have to get their hands dirty." Carver shrugged. "It's best if you have experience beforehand even if you went to jail for it."

"My life skills included stealing cars and larceny."

"Good life skills to have if you want to become a fed."

Liana laughed. "I set myself up for that one."

They walked two more blocks and turned right. The car parts store was a single-story metal building, not one of the fancier national chain places. Not that Carver had anything against fancy auto parts stores. This one just happened to be the closest.

A few vehicles were parked out front. One of them was a tow truck with a blue sedan secured on the back. Carver stopped and stared at it.

"What's wrong?" Liana asked.

"Nothing's wrong. I just know what we have to do next."

She followed his gaze. Snapped her fingers. "The Lexus."

He nodded. "The Lexus. I thought about it when we were at that house. It was just a passing thought about why it wasn't in the driveway."

"Lacy Hood's car might lead us to Lacy Hood and the others."

"Yep." He walked down the bank of the highway to the parts store. He went inside and told the young guy behind the counter the make, model, and year of the minivan. The parts guy brought him the right filter and a few quarts of oil. Carver purchased it with cash.

The parts guy put the items in a plastic bag. Carver took it and went back outside where Liana was waiting.

"I made some calls," she said. "I found the Lexus."

"Where?"

She pointed to a tire store on the map. "I told the guy I was with the insurance company. Told him I needed to look at the wheels because one was missing. I told him I wanted to make sure it still had the OEM wheels."

"He bought the story?"

"Of course. This is routine for him. He said to stop by and take a look." She bit her lower lip. "It's a thirty-minute walk, though. Be better if we repair the van and drive it."

"Did you ask if Brenda had been by to look at the car?"

She nodded. "Lacy, aka Brenda, called and asked for a tow. The tow truck driver called and told her about the missing wheel when he picked up the car."

"They must have her address on file, then, right? Maybe a credit card under the Brenda Johnson alias."

"Possibly. I think I can talk them into letting me see that information." Liana looked at the dirty sweatpants she was still wearing. "Provided I can look professional."

Carver looked at his own attire. It was dirty and worn. "Let's fix the van and go clothes shopping. There's another problem, though. If Decker is still looking for the women, he might have the same idea we do."

"That's a good point." She grimaced. "I have an idea." She made another call while they walked back to the minivan. "Hey, Dustin, this is Patty with Brenda's car insurance company again. I forgot to ask if my colleague, Joe, might have already contacted you. He might have already stopped by." She listened to a response. Nodded. "He has dark hair and very noticeable blue eyes."

Liana nodded and listened for a moment. "Okay, thanks so much. If he does stop by, could you give me a call? I'd prefer not to duplicate our work if possible." She laughed. "I know, right? Thanks again."

"Masterful," Carver said. She was good at improvising. Good at playing a role. She'd even changed her accent to make it sound more southern. "Your southern accent could use some work, though."

"Thank you, thank you." She mock bowed and winced. "Ugh, I'm so tired of this shoulder pain."

They turned onto the street where they'd left the minivan. Carver grabbed Liana and pulled her back behind a tree.

She grunted in pain. "What the hell?"

Carver looked around the tree. Saw the patrol car that had passed them earlier. A police officer was walking around the minivan. Talking on his radio. He went to the back of the van and spoke into his radio again. Probably reading off the license plate numbers.

Liana peered around him. "Well, shit."

"Yep." Carver checked the map app again. "Plan B."

"And that is?"

He pointed to a second-hand clothing store. There were a lot of them in town. That wasn't unusual for small towns. Dollar stores were prevalent too. "We'll get clothing and go to the motel down the street to clean up and change."

She released a sigh. Nodded. "Okay."

"I need to get my stuff from the van first."

"Is that wise?" She watched the officer. "This place will be crawling with local LEOs in no time."

"It might not. They might have orders to keep their hands off the van and leave it to the feds."

"You think?"

He nodded. "They'll tell him to leave it alone but keep an eye on it."

"You think he'll follow orders?"

"I think he'll go to the same house we did and ask if they saw us." Carver held up a hand. "Wait here."

"Don't do anything stupid."

"No promises." There was a strip of trees and a house at the corner. He walked down the driveway. There was no backyard fence, so he continued through the yard and into the neighboring home's backyard.

The trees bordered the road where the minivan was parked. He could see the vehicle through the trees. The officer was standing there looking at the white house Carver and Liana had visited. He was probably asking himself if he should talk to the people inside or leave it up to the feds running the show.

Most cops were good people doing a difficult job. They took their orders seriously. Did what they needed to do and went above and beyond the call of duty if necessary. But feds usually rubbed the locals the wrong way.

The feds looked down on local law enforcement. They got bossy. Made sure the locals knew who was in charge and who had the power. They didn't understand that the locals were their most valuable assets because they knew the town and the people.

Carver couldn't hear the radio chatter. He didn't know if the cop was talking to a fed or dispatch. The look on the man's face said a lot without words. The cop didn't like what he was hearing.

He replied with one word and started walking toward the house. This guy didn't like taking orders from the feds. He was probably feeling protective about the people he considered under his protection too.

Carver let him get a distance away, then crept through the woods and to the van. He unlocked the sliding door and got his duffel bag and other items. Then he locked the door and went back through the woods.

Liana slow clapped when he appeared. "You're crazy."

"I like my tools."

"You mean your guns?"

Carver usually considered guns nothing more than tools. But in the case of the Lynx fifty-cal, he was starting to form an emotional attachment. He slung the bag over his back. Headed for the second-hand clothing store.

They reached it after a twenty-minute walk. A few people looked curiously at the duffel bag when he walked in. A few people looked concerned.

A salesclerk stopped him. "Sir, do you mind leaving that up here?"

Carver didn't want to draw too much attention, so he left it up front next to the clerk. "Thanks." He picked out some appropriate clothing for nighttime activities while Liana did the same.

She also picked up a skirt and white blouse that looked appropriate for an office setting. Carver paid for the items. Unbeknownst to Liana, he still had plenty of pocket cash thanks to her go box.

Carver reclaimed his duffel bag, and they took the short walk to the motel. The manager insisted on an ID until Carver gave him a three-hundred-dollar deposit. That quieted him down real fast.

They went to the room and Liana made a beeline for the bathroom.

While Liana was showering, Carver laid down and took a nap. He woke up to the whine of a hair dryer. Liana was dressed in her new skirt and blouse and was drying her wet hair.

Carver chose a fresh set of cargo pants, a black t-shirt, and underwear and went into the bathroom. He cleaned off all the grit and grime. Judging from the color of the water, he'd accumulated quite a bit during their jaunt into the forest.

His old clothing was torn and filthy, so he bundled it up and shoved it into the garbage.

Liana was looking out of the window. Carver already knew what she was looking at. He'd heard it when he was still in the shower. He went to the window and looked anyway.

A helicopter hovered in the distance.

CHAPTER 33

Carver examined the helicopter with his monocular.

It wasn't a Black Hawk this time. It was a small, black chopper. Its crew complement was a pilot, copilot, and operators in side-mounted seats.

"A killer egg," Liana muttered. "Never thought I'd be on the wrong end of one of those things."

It wasn't really a killer egg, but Carver didn't correct her. The chopper was an MH-6 Little Bird. It was unarmed and designed to deliver troops to places where a Black Hawk couldn't easily land. It was designed for urban settings. For maximum maneuverability.

The real killer egg was the AH-6, the armed version of the MH-6. It was called a killer egg because it packed an extremely hard punch for something so small. The M134 miniguns were especially popular on the AH-6. It could spit enough lead to take down an entire squad in seconds.

The crew were wearing black and gray urban camouflage. Same as the men from the Black Hawk. They might be the same guys from earlier. What was left of them, anyway. Or they might be fresh meat.

Carver couldn't guess how many people they had to throw at him. He wondered if these guys were specialists or grunts. Pilots were a rare commodity. They didn't want to just throw them away if they were smart.

Either way, the town was now being watched from the sky. Carver reconsidered his wardrobe choices. He pulled another set of clothing from the bag. Stripped off his cargo pants and black shirt.

Liana raised an eyebrow. "Going out in your underwear?"

Carver pulled on a pair of jeans, a green flannel shirt, and pulled on a ballcap. He stuffed cash into his pocket. Strapped the shoulder holster over the shirt. Holstered the Glock. Pulled on a light jacket to cover it.

Liana tried to slide the compact Glock into the waistline of her skirt. It didn't fit well. "I want a shoulder holster. This looks ridiculous."

Carver dug a concealed carry holster from his duffel bag. It looked like a small satchel with a long flap on the top. He gave it to her. "Slide this into the waist of your skirt. The flap will catch on the hem of the skirt." He demonstrated by sliding it into his jeans. Showed her how to pull up on the flap for quick access to the gun inside.

"Wow, I really like that." She slid it under the skirt. Used the blouse to cover the flap. She practiced a quick draw. It took her a couple of tries to get it out fast. She grinned. "This is amazing."

"You can keep it."

"Really?" She beamed at him. "You really know how to treat a girl right, Carver."

He opened the motel door. "Let's go."

"Wait." She touched his arm.

He looked back at her. "Yeah?"

"Look, I get why you're standoffish, but I'm on your side."

"You're on your side, whatever that may be and it's fine." Carver shrugged. "You do what you have to do, and I'll do what I have to do."

"I don't like the way that sounds."

"You don't have to. Right now, our goals coincide. Later, they might not." He opened the door and stepped out. "It's best if we keep our distance so we can do what we need to do later."

"That sounds ominous." Liana closed the door behind her and locked it with the key. "Carver, I won't betray you."

He was already walking. "It's not really betrayal if you're looking out for your own best interests. Best case scenario for you is you get to go back to work without repercussions, right?"

"I think so." She bit her lower lip. "I mean, it's what I enjoy doing. But I also don't like being used. I don't like feeling expendable."

"You're working for the federal government. Almost everything is political. Someone somewhere sees you as an unnamed asset. As something they can use to advance their career or something they can use to persecute political opponents."

"We do good things too." She laughed wryly. "We look out for the American people. We keep them safe. We and the other federal agencies are a shield over the nation."

"They're supposed to be for the greater good, but they're often a tool used to keep people in power." Carver shrugged. "There are always tradeoffs. I think I'd rather have more risk than perceived safety. Fewer feds looking over my shoulder, not more."

"And yet, you were in the military. You were in special forces."

Carver didn't say anything. He was curious to see if she knew more about him than she let on. But she didn't say anything about Scion or dark ops. She just looked at him like he should defend his position.

He didn't think it was worth the trouble. Not if they might try to kill each other in the near future.

Carver checked the GPS. It was going to take thirty minutes to reach the tire shop. A town like this didn't seem to have a taxi service or buses. He didn't want to use a rideshare because he'd need an app and a credit card.

On the other hand, there was a used car dealership just ahead. Buying two used cars in a day was the last thing Carver wanted to do. But he really didn't have a choice.

Other pedestrians stopped to look at the chopper hovering over their town. They were pointing. Talking amongst themselves.

Carver glanced at the chopper. It was a distance away, apparently slowly scanning the streets. Probably searching in a grid pattern. At the next intersection he saw another chopper in the distance doing the same thing.

He pointed it out. "Limitless resources being used against American citizens."

"Maybe they think you're a domestic terrorist."

"What do you think?"

"I don't know what to think. You haven't told me anything. Just vague hints."

"I just wanted to be left alone. Then my former commander wanted to see me. I went to see her. Found out she was dead." He figured she already knew some of this story so there was no harm in telling her his side. "A local cop and a pair of Breakstone mercs tried to frame me for her killing. In the end, it didn't work out too well for them."

"What really happened? Who killed all those cartel members and Breakstone operators?"

"What do you know about Breakstone?"

"The dossier said the former owner was a key proponent of privatizing special operations. That Congress wanted private special forces they could use domestically and abroad, something the U.S. military can't do due to Posse Comitatus."

"That's about right."

She continued. "But one of the Breakstone partners, a guy named Leon Fry, was embezzling money and making side deals that ruined the company. His other two partners, Chad Dorsey and Tony Menendez got killed fighting the cartel in Morganville."

"Looks like Breakstone and the cartel killed each other."

"Except the evidence was all wrong. The cartel members were killed with their own weapons." Liana watched him closely. "They were killed with seven-six-two rounds, not five-five-six."

"Weird. Maybe Breakstone used Kalashnikovs instead of M4s."

"Yeah, right." She rolled her eyes. "I know you had something to do with it, but there's no official mention of you."

"I was just an innocent bystander."

She laughed. "We both know that's not true. But I find it hard to believe one man could kill that many cartel members, not to mention all those Breakstone mercs."

Carver figured he'd said enough. "Let's just say that I got mixed up in something thanks to my former commander. I left town and went to the beach to enjoy a nice, quiet existence with Paola at my side. She wanted more and left me after a few months. Went to find her own path to happiness."

"Do you love her?"

Carver stopped walking for a moment. His left eye twitched three times. Then he started walking again. "I don't want her dead. I want her to enjoy a nice long life."

"You love her. Maybe not romantically, but you care for her."

"It's a problem." He kept walking.

"Aw, that's cute. The big bad military boy has a soft spot."

"It's a weakness and now you know it." He gave her a direct look. "Also know that if anything happens to Paola, there will be consequences."

Liana gulped. "I would never, Carver."

"And yet, you were working for people clearly looking for her and me."

"But I didn't know." Liana gripped his forearm. "I know now."

"If you say so." Carver stopped at the used car dealership. It was a small place with a lime green cinderblock building in the middle of the lot.

A man emerged from the building and hurried toward them, a grin on his face. "Hello, hello! I'm Sherwin Michael Williams, no relationship to the paint company, or I wouldn't be here." He belly laughed.

Carver didn't know what he was talking about. Paint wasn't something he thought much about. He walked down the row of cars. Most of them didn't have prices listed. That was annoying. He turned to Sherwin. "I need something cheap I can buy with cash."

"Sir, we have some great deals today. All of the cars on my lot have been serviced and are in tip-top running condition."

"What's the lowest priced vehicle on the lot?"

"First, let's start with what you want to do with your vehicle. You need utility? Gas mileage? Something sporty?"

Carver worked his jaw back and forth. He looked down at the man. "Give me prices, or we're walking."

"I see what you are." Sherwin nodded. "An all-business kind of man. Very well, I'll tell you the prices."

Liana patted the hood of an old beige car. "How many miles on this ninety-three Cadillac Deville?"

"Over two-hundred thousand."

She looked through the windshield. "Seats look like they're okay. The windows are tinted super dark. Are they legal?"

"They are legally tinted, yes."

"Can you get the key and show us it runs?"

"Yes, but you do realize it's a classic, right? This is not some cheap clunker."

"This car was traded in two years ago by Jerome Smith for four-hundred dollars. We will give you six hundred dollars to take it off your hands. At this point, we'll be doing you a favor."

His mouth dropped open. "Do you know Jerome?"

"No."

"Then how did you know that?"

She pointed toward the hovering chopper. "I have my resources." Then she put a finger to her lips. "We're undercover."

"Oh, my." Sherwin looked from the chopper to her and back to the chopper. He straightened up. "Can you tell me what's going on?"

"No, Sherwin, I can't. And we really need to get this car. Otherwise, we'll be riding around in black SUVs and looking conspicuous while we hunt down a dangerous fugitive." Her eyes widened and she put a hand over her mouth. "I shouldn't have said that."

"Say no more." Sherwin beamed. "If you have the money, I'll get the keys and title."

"Please do."

He ran inside. Carver stared at Liana. "You're dangerously good at that."

"I know." She smiled. "I have access to a VIN lookup tool. It told me everything."

"How convenient."

Her smile faded. "I get it, Carver. The feds know all. They see all. They're watching everyone. But it is nice having that power at my fingertips."

"It all depends on the hands that wield it." Carver walked around the Cadillac. He liked it. It was a classic. Probably had that old leather smell to it. Probably rode like it was on clouds. It wouldn't be great for high-speed handling, but it checked all the other boxes, including having a trunk big enough to put three bodies in. Maybe four if he broke all their limbs.

Sherwin returned with the keys. He handed them to Liana. "Go ahead. Test it out."

She did. She drove it around the parking lot. Lowered and raised the automatic windows. Looked at the engine. Looked in the trunk. The engine looked clean despite the high miles.

"They don't make them like this anymore." Sherwin closed the hood and patted it. "So, it's a deal?"

"Yep." Carver handed him the cash. Took the title. The back was signed.

"Honestly, I'll kind of miss this car. It's been here so long that it became something of a landmark." Sherwin sighed. "Well, good luck with the search. I do hope the citizens of Cookeville aren't in any imminent danger."

Liana gave him a serious look. "That remains to be seen. Remain vigilant, citizen."

Sherwin looked mildly confused but nodded. "Yes, agent. I will."

Carver dropped into the driver's seat. He considered going to the motel for his bag, but decided they'd wasted enough time and needed to get to the tire shop.

They got there in two minutes. Traffic was almost nonexistent. The lack of traffic lights helped too. The caddy handled nice and soft, just like he thought it would. The seats had that old-leather smell, and the suspension was like riding on clouds.

He pulled into the parking lot on the side of the building. Looked around for Decker's black car. It wasn't there. Maybe Decker hadn't thought of this idea or maybe he didn't know where the Lexus was. He might be driving to each tire shop and looking inside.

Liana got out. "I'll be right back."

Carver wanted to go inside with her but figured it would look suspicious for him to tag along. He decided to trust her and let her do her thing. He leaned the seat back a little and relaxed.

The weather was cool, not cold, so he lowered the window to let in the breeze. The buzz of the distant helicopters almost lured him to sleep. The ambient sound reminded him of being on base or in the field. It didn't help that he'd only had a light nap in the last twenty-four hours.

Carver was ready to sleep, but he decided to remain vigilant instead. Just in case Decker came by. If he caught Decker, he'd eliminate the threat to Paola, at least for the time being. Then he could lure away the dark ops posse and lead them on a merry chase around the country.

Fifteen minutes ticked past. No Decker. No Liana. He was about to get out of the car and go look for her. Letting her go in alone had been a mistake. What if she'd decided giving up Carver was the only way to get back in the good graces of the agency?

What if she also now knew where Lacy Hood lived and was relaying that information to her people?

What in the hell had he been thinking? He got out of the car and hurried toward the building. She might have slipped out of the back. Gone away to report to her federal overlords.

Instead, he found her inside talking to a young clerk behind the counter. He had a goofy smile on his face. He was blushing and nodding vigorously at whatever she was saying. He handed her a printout.

Liana touched his hand. Smiled warmly at him. Said something else that made him blush a little harder. Then she turned and walked toward Carver and the door. There was a brief hesitation in her step when she saw him but then she walked right past without reacting.

The clerk seemed to shake out of his dream state and looked at Carver. "Sir, there's a brief wait. Please take a number and I'll be right with you."

There were three other people sitting around with sour looks on their faces. Probably waiting their turn. Probably angry because the clerk had spent the last fifteen minutes flirting with an attractive woman.

Carver went outside. Liana was already sitting inside the car.

He dropped into the driver's seat.

Liana turned toward him. "You panicked, didn't you? Thought I was up to something."

"It crossed my mind."

She sighed. Handed him the slip of paper. "I wish I had something more to give you, but they don't have her address or a credit card on file. She's paying cash."

He looked at the work order for the Lexus. There was nothing except the name Brenda Johnson on it.

Liana watched him closely. "He said the work will be done tomorrow around lunch. They ordered a new wheel, and it won't arrive until late morning."

"Then we need to be here tomorrow morning waiting for Lacy to show up."

"Yeah."

He could tell by the tone of her voice that she was feeling demoralized because he hadn't trusted her. Or she might be acting. She'd done what she said she was going to do. She'd probably been in there so long because there were other people waiting.

"I know you'll never trust me. I wish I could say something to make you feel otherwise."

"I don't trust many people. It's nothing personal." He handed the work order back to her. "Thanks. This gives us a time and a date to be here. I guess until then we can rest and relax."

"I'd like that." She gingerly touched her shoulder. "I think my stitches have come loose."

"I can fix that. We'll get some supplies."

"I appreciate that, Doctor Carver."

Carver pulled out of the parking lot. He drove to a nearby pharmacy. Picked up supplies. He walked next door to the pizza place and got a large meat lovers pie to go. He drove back to the motel.

Liana looked tired and pale, but she ate four slices of pizza. "This is so good. I can't remember the last time I pigged out on pizza."

Carver pulled a chair next to the bed after she finished. "Let me see the shoulder."

She took off her shirt. Lowered the bra strap, wincing when it grazed the wound.

Carver leaned close and examined the wound. A few stitches had ripped loose. Hardly surprising given everything they'd been through.

He wiped local anesthesia on the wound. Reworked the broken stitches. Rubbed antibacterial ointment on the area and dressed the wound with gauze and tape.

Liana winced a few times but handled it like a champ. She looked at his handiwork when he was done. "Not bad. A little more practice and you'll have it down pat."

Carver didn't like the way the bandage crinkled when she moved. "Hang on." He carefully peeled it off and resituated it. Smoothed it out.

He looked up. Met Liana's gaze.

She leaned forward and kissed him on the lips. "Thank you."

Carver liked the kiss more than he wanted to admit. But he didn't trust the kiss. Not one little bit. "You're welcome."

She yawned. Rubbed her eyes. "I know it's early, but I'm going to sleep. It feels like we've been awake and on the run for a week."

"Good idea." Carver set the chair next to the table. He went to the other bed and lay down on it, hands clasped behind his head. He stared at the ceiling. He was tired. Dead tired. But there was too much going on in his head.

He didn't want to sleep. He wanted to spend the night searching for Lacy's Hood's house or hunting down Decker. But it was best to get a solid four to six hours so he'd be well-rested for a worst-case scenario.

Tomorrow he would be waiting when Lacy picked up her car. She would take him to her house where the other women were hopefully alive and well. He would finally see Paola again.

If Decker hadn't gotten to them first.

CHAPTER 34

Decker smashed his fist through a window.

The house was old. It had single-pane windows. Breaking one was hardly a challenge. Even so, he had a cloth wrapped around his fist to muffle the sound and to protect his hand from being shredded by glass shards.

This window was on a back door leading into a garage. He picked the shards out of the frame. Reached his hand through the window. Unlocked the door from the inside. Opened the door and stepped into the garage.

He'd spent most of the day driving around and casing houses in the vicinity of the pink house. About midday, the calm had been interrupted by military helicopters. It had been a strange sight to see them hovering around town.

Decker had sent an inquiry to the Bureau and to the cartel. Neither knew the reason for there to be MH-6 Little Birds with military personnel flying around the town. He'd hoped his mysterious benefactors might chime in and clarify the situation.

They hadn't.

The official word around town was that a military prisoner had escaped, and they were looking for him. That sounded like a cover story if Decker had ever heard one. He suspected they were almost certainly sent there on orders by his mysterious benefactors.

He had a feeling the choppers and personnel were their backup plan if Decker didn't find Paola and the others. He could be wrong, of course. But he had a gut feeling he wasn't.

The choppers had left a few hours later. Apparently, they hadn't found who they were looking for. Decker had continued reconnoitering the neighborhood around the pink house. He'd watched people leaving and coming from the houses.

He'd narrowed down his list of houses where Lacy Hood might be living, and the garage of the house he was currently standing in was on that list.

There were no cars in the garage. It smelled musty. It looked dusty and unused aside from faint tire tracks in the dust and a black spot where oil had dripped onto the concrete. It had been a while since car tires last made those tracks.

He went to the door leading into the house. The door had a window with a clear view of the kitchen. As expected, it was a vintage kitchen complete with orange vinyl flooring. It had a matching orange General Electric oven and stove combination that was probably almost eighty years old.

He tested the doorknob. It was unlocked. That wasn't promising. If the women were here, they would almost certainly have locked all the doors at night. It was still dark outside. The clock was ticking into the wee hours of the morning.

Decker raised the night vision goggles off his face and rubbed his eyes. Image intensification was invaluable, but it sometimes gave him a headache. He pinched the bridge of his nose. Gave his eyes a moment of rest. Lowered the goggles.

He entered the kitchen. The floor creaked under his weight. He winced and moved more slowly. That didn't help much. Something ticked in the hallway. There was a click and the central air kicked on.

It roared like the ancient system it probably was. The creaking floorboards were no longer an issue, that much was certain. He continued down the hallway. The house was small and single story, so it didn't take long to clear the rooms.

There were three bedrooms and two bathrooms. The bedrooms were furnished but didn't look lived in. The last bedroom had miscellaneous items on the dressers and nightstands that told him it was the only room in use at this house.

It probably belonged to someone old. Someone who'd bought this house new. Someone who was probably in an old folks home right now. Or maybe they were away visiting family.

Decker opened all the doors in the house. He didn't find any stairs leading to a basement. This was yet another wrong house. Paola and the other women weren't here. But he was getting close. He had to be.

After losing the women at the pink house, he'd jogged around the neighborhood. Jogged up and down the streets looking for women lugging suitcases after them. There was no way they could have gotten far without him seeing them.

He knew for certain they hadn't gone east. They would have passed through his line of sight if they had. Once the pickup truck had gone, they'd crossed through the front yard and gone west. They were hiding somewhere within the three blocks west of the pink house.

Since Paola knew what he looked like, he couldn't simply walk around knocking on doors. He'd waited until it was dark so he could see people inside their homes without them seeing him. The four homes on the same block with the pink house were occupied by families.

They were good-sized homes. Each one was probably twenty-five hundred square feet or more. That was enough space to have a family and hide three women, but that didn't seem like the kind of living situation Hood would enjoy.

She either had a family of her own or she lived alone. He was starting to lean more and more toward her being a solitary creature. That made him a little sad because he couldn't stop fantasizing about violating her in front of her husband and kids.

This house was the last house on this side of the block facing Broad Street. There were more buildings on this side, but they were businesses. One was a barbecue restaurant, and the other was a technology repair shop.

Decker left the house. He closed the back door. The broken glass probably wouldn't be noticed for a while if the homeowner was old. Since nothing had been stolen, they might think it was an accident.

He hopped the fence in the back yard. The home behind this one had a pool. A flood light with a motion sensor clicked on, momentarily blinding the NV goggles. He lifted them off his eyes and scurried into darkness. Crouched next to the hedge near the back windows.

A moment later, the floodlight clicked off. He pulled the goggles back down. Crouched low so the hedges blocked him from triggering the motion sensor again.

Everyone was asleep now so he couldn't just look through windows to see who was inside. His plan was reduced to breaking and entering. This house posed slightly more of a challenge since the back door didn't have a window.

Decker had lockpicking tools. He could probably unlock the bottom lock in four minutes. The deadbolt was probably also engaged so that would take him another four to five minutes.

Going through all of that might be a complete waste of time. There was an easier way to tell if his quarry might be inside the house. He opened the side gate. Walked around to the front yard.

This house didn't have a garage. An SUV and a pickup truck were parked in the driveway. Considering Hood drove a white Lexus, it seemed unlikely that she'd have two Fords parked in her driveway.

If there was only one car, then things would be different. One car meant that either one person lived here or that it potentially belonged to Hood's husband. Two vehicles was a complete set, husband and wife. It would be extremely unlikely that they also had a Lexus.

Decker was playing the odds based on the number of cars outside. It was far easier and less risky than playing the odds of breaking into a home just to see the occupants. There was too much that could go wrong.

He'd already reconnoitered the houses earlier, but people hadn't returned home from work yet. A glance at the cars or lack of cars in the driveway during the day wouldn't have told him the entire story.

There were two houses with closed garages. Two houses that were potential locations for the women. Decker took off the night vision goggles and gave his eyes a moment or two to rest. Once eyes adjusted to the darkness, he walked to the first house with the closed garage door and walked around it.

It was a detached garage with windows on the side. He looked through the windows, but it was too dark to see anything. He put on the NV goggles. A shelf against the window blocked his line of sight.

He continued around the garage. The windows on the opposite side weren't blocked. There was a single car in the two-car garage. A mid-sized Toyota SUV. If this was Hood's place, then that was either her backup car or her husband's.

Decker studied the front of the house. He studied the front yard. The hedges. Everything was well manicured. Taken care of. Was Hood the kind of person who kept her place maintained, or was she so mentally damaged that she let her house fall into disrepair?

Her late model Lexus answered that question. It looked new. It was white and clean. At least from what he could tell under the streetlights around the motel. Someone who kept their car clean usually kept their house clean. He had no evidence to back up that assertion, but it felt right.

That made up his mind. He examined the side of the house. There were motion-triggered floodlamps on the front and the side fascia boards. He approached from their blind spots. Got close to the house so he could walk beneath them.

Decker went to the side gate. It was latched from the inside. He slid his knife up through the crack and unlatched it. The back yard was well manicured. There was a nice wooden deck with furniture on it.

The grass was perfectly mown. A gravel bed with small bushes in it bordered the lawn and the fence. Whoever lived here clearly loved their plants. It was enough to make Decker shudder. Why anyone would invest so much time in something so worthless was beyond him.

He walked up the deck stairs. Examined the French doors blocking his way inside. They were fiberglass with double-paned windows. Almost certainly tempered glass. The same kind of glass used for car windows.

Picking the locks would take too long and Decker was impatient to get on with this. It felt like he'd been wandering this neighborhood for hours. Thankfully, tempered glass wasn't all that difficult to break.

He pulled a small tool from his lockpicking case. It was a moderately weighty piece of metal with a sharp tip. Thieves used it to break car windows with a tap so they could get at the goodies people left in their seats.

Decker tapped it against the window. The tempered glass crumbled like sand. He tapped it against the inner pane. It crumbled the same way, making almost no sound as the pieces fell onto the carpet inside.

He cleared the glass out of the way and stepped through. Listened carefully in case there was a dog inside. A barking dog would put a quick end to his investigation. He didn't hear anything.

The den and the hallway were carpeted so he didn't bother creeping. If anyone woke up, he'd put a gun in their face to keep them quiet.

The first two bedrooms were empty. The last bedroom had occupants. Two old people snoring away beneath the covers. Decker clenched his fists. This search was going nowhere. Where in the hell had Paola and the other women gone?

Maybe he was completely wrong. Maybe they were in one of those houses he'd skipped because they had too many cars in the driveway or because he'd seen a family already occupying the house.

Unless this house had a basement, Paola and the others weren't here. Decker wasn't going to leave until he was absolutely certain. He backed out of the room and looked through the rest of the house.

There was a basement door in the kitchen. It creaked when he opened it. Wooden stairs led down into darkness. He eased his weight onto one and walked halfway down. There were shelves down below.

There were jars of preserves and other odds and ends on the shelves. No women. This house was another dead end. He went back up to the kitchen. A light was on in the hallway. He heard the soft tread of feet on carpet.

A man with a shotgun appeared in the hallway. Decker almost put a bullet in his head, but that would raise too many alarms in a small town like this. He ducked through the broken French door window and hurried down the deck stairs.

"Who's there?" an elderly voice called out. "Show yourself!"

Decker didn't understand why people said things like that during a possible home invasion. They were just giving away their position to someone who might have a gun. As much as he wanted to teach the old man a lesson, he was more concerned about finding his prey.

He went to the last house on the block. Stared at the closed garage. The garage door had no windows. He walked around it. No windows on the sides or the back. Was this the correct house or yet another dead end?

Decker was almost too tired to bother. But if the old man in the last house noticed the broken windows, he'd almost certainly call the cops right away. A patrol car would be here in minutes, provided someone was still awake to take the call.

A town this size probably had someone on duty twenty-four hours. Assuming they did was safer than assuming they didn't. That was fine. He could be in and out of this house in less time than it took the local hillbilly cops to arrive.

Flashing lights interrupted his thoughts. "What the hell?" He hid behind the garage. Watched as a patrol car squealed into the driveway of the house he'd just left. It was one house down from this one and too close for comfort.

The front flood lights came on. The old man appeared in the doorway, the shotgun dangling from one hand. The patrol officer hurried up, a handgun at the ready. Apparently, he was itching for some action.

That changed Decker's plans. Breaking into this house wasn't happening. At least not tonight. He'd have to come back tomorrow. Just the thought of more delays and time in this backwoods town was enough to make his teeth ache.

He was tempted to put down the cop and the old man. He could stage it. Make it look like the old man shot the cop by accident. Make it look like the old man thought the cop was the robber.

Decker grinned. That would be too perfect. He pictured it in his head. Worked out the logistics. It would be easy. But it would also make a lot of noise. Lights were already coming on in the house next to him.

People heard the sirens. They heard the screeching tires. They were waking up. Looking out windows. Wondering what the commotion was all about. Decker hustled to the safety of nearby bushes. He watched as four people emerged from the house he'd almost broken into.

A mother, father, and two boys stood on the front porch. The father said something and walked next door. Probably told the family to stay put while he investigated. At least that answered the question of who lived in the house.

It certainly wasn't Paola and the other two targets. Not unless they were cowering in a basement. Decker clenched his fists and shook with rage. Where in the hell had they gone? How could they have vanished in such a short period of time?

Only one thing made sense. They'd had someone waiting to pick them up. Someone parked on the road in front of the house. They could have hopped in a car and been gone before Decker realized it.

Since he'd assumed they'd gone into the pink house, he'd gone straight to the back door. He hadn't looked in the front yard. His interaction with the old woman in the house had taken nearly five minutes. That was plenty of time for the women to vanish.

Did Paola know he was following them? Was that why she'd left her car behind? Was that why they'd given the men in the pickup truck the wrong address to deliver them to? Decker couldn't fathom how Paola would know he was following them.

Sure, she'd been smart to place security cameras around Butler's house, but was she smart enough to know her car had a tracker on it? He didn't think so. Women didn't think like that. They didn't think tactically.

This was just blind luck. Blind luck that they'd gotten a flat tire. Blind luck that some men in a pickup had been there to pick them up. Blind luck that they'd given those men the wrong address and gone somewhere else.

Decker started walking. Another cop had arrived, and more people were coming out of their homes. He needed to get out of here before someone noticed the stranger in their midst. Strangers never fared well in small towns like this.

If anyone spotted him walking alone this close to a crime scene, they'd assume he was the perp. It didn't take much deductive reasoning to conclude that. He walked back a few streets. Found a nice quiet one undisturbed by cops and cut east toward his car.

He couldn't stop thinking about Paola. How he'd let her slip through his fingers when all he had to do was take her and the others by force at the motel. He'd gotten greedy. Wanted more when his plate was already full.

It wasn't his fault though. Not really. Following Paola to the other women had been the right call. Decker had done everything by the book. He'd wanted the horse to lead him to water. Instead, the horse had bucked him off and jumped the fence.

On the bright side, the horse was still in a field nearby. Decker felt certain that Hood lived somewhere in this town. That she was somewhere close. All he had to do was stick around and watch long enough and she would show her face.

It was impossible to remain hidden in a town this small. She would need groceries. She'd want to go to a restaurant. She and the others would eventually venture out and Decker would spot them.

They had to eventually—Decker paused mid-thought. Of course. Why hadn't he thought about it before? The solution was braindead simple. He jogged back to his car. It had been a full day. He might be too late.

Even if he was too late, it didn't matter. This was a small town. It shouldn't take him any time to track down the one place Hood would have to go soon. He didn't need to find her. She'd come to him.

He reached his car. Slid inside. Opened the maps app on his phone. There were four tire shops in town. Two of them doubled as mechanic shops. There was another mechanic shop that didn't sell tires. He discounted that one.

The Lexus might still be on the side of the road, but he doubted it. It had almost certainly been towed into town. It was almost certainly sitting at a tire shop right this very moment. All he had to do was figure out which one.

Find the Lexus, find the women.

There was another reason Lacy Hood was so hard to find. She wasn't listed in the phone book. He hadn't found a social media presence of her at all. That meant she was being protected. There was only one agency he could think of that had a hand in that.

He texted a data analyst who'd helped him with sensitive information before. He kept it as cryptic as possible. *Lacy Hood. Morganville. Possible WITSEC. Standard finder's fee.*

The analyst was probably asleep, but she'd be on it first thing in the morning. By the time he finished breakfast, she'd have found Hood's alias.

And then nothing could stop him from finding her.

CHAPTER 35

Decker had everything he needed to find his quarry.

Well, almost everything. He'd just finished breakfast. The analyst had sent him the WITSEC data on Lacy Hood. He read her text and couldn't believe what he saw.

Lacy Hood alias Brenda Hood. No other information available.

That was it? No more information? How was that even possible?

Decker clenched his fists and repressed his anger. He typed out a reply. *Home address? Phone number?*

The analyst responded a moment later. *There was no other information in the file. Maybe erased? Maybe she took the new ID and went off the radar. I searched the geographical area you gave me. No results. Social Security number has not been used to apply for any kind of credit.*

He fired back another question. *What about the license plate on the Lexus?*

The wait for an answer was longer this time, but it was no more helpful than the last. *The car was registered by WITSEC. It isn't linked to the alias or a home address. I'm pursuing other leads. I also sent an information request to Homeland Security. Maybe they'll give us something.*

Hood was a cagey little bitch. Most people in witness protection didn't have the kind of money needed to truly disappear. They had to get jobs. They had to get mortgages and credit cards and car loans.

Hood had cartel money. Enough money to take a new identity and vanish. She could buy most things with cash. She could purchase property with the help of lawyers and shell corporations.

He had her alias. No home address. No phone number. That meant he was back to hunting for the Lexus. At least having the fake name would make it marginally easier.

Decker checked the time. It was eight in the morning. Right about the time most tire shops opened for business. He wished he'd thought of looking for the Lexus yesterday. Now it might be too late.

Fixing a single flat tire was usually a fifteen-minute job. The Lexus might have already been in and out of the shop. If that was the case, he had a backup plan.

There were several tire shops, but he filtered out the places selling used tires and a couple of car dealerships that came up in the search. He ended up with a much shorter list. If none of these panned out, he'd add back in the places he hadn't checked.

He started at the southern end of town. A big box store with a tire shop. They had multiple repair bays. No sign of a Lexus in any of them. He walked around the parking lot. Didn't see the Lexus.

Decker went inside and talked to a teenager behind the counter. "My wife told me she had her Lexus RX 350 towed here to get a flat fixed. I was just seeing if it was done yet."

"Oh, I can check that for you." The teenager tapped on his computer keyboard. "Name?"

"Brenda Johnson."

The kid tapped on the keyboard. Frowned. "I don't see her name listed. You said it was a Lexus?"

"Yeah. It's white."

"I don't see that in our repair logs. Are you sure she had it towed here?"

"Ugh, women. She probably had it towed somewhere else and just gave me the wrong name. I'll call her."

The kid laughed. "Yeah, women."

Decker left the shop and went to his car. He entered the address of the next closest tire shop into the maps app and drove there. He gave them the same performance. Got the same results. No records of a Brenda Johnson or a Lexus.

By the time he reached the fourth shop, he was beginning to wonder if the Lexus had even been towed to town or if it was still sitting on the side of the road. He was pulling into the parking lot when he caught sight of a white Lexus SUV inside one of the two repair bays.

It was Hood's car. No doubt about it.

There was a diner across the road from the tire shop. He noticed a parking spot with a tree positioned right in the middle. Decker pulled into that spot, so he had a clear line of sight to the repair bays on one side of the tree.

Thanks to the tree, anyone working in the front office across the road wouldn't be able to see that someone was sitting in the car watching with a monocular.

Most civilians weren't situationally aware enough to notice such things. Most could hardly list any details in their environment. Decker had learned the hard way that it was better to be safe than sorry.

Even civilians with their blinders on had a slight chance of noticing him. They might get suspicious. Call the local police. Then Decker would have a new headache to deal with.

He took out his monocular and zoomed in on the Lexus. Two wheels had been removed. A man placed one of the tires in a machine that spun the tire around to make sure it was balanced.

Decker only remembered one flat tire. Had something happened to the other one? Or had it been removed for another reason? The question was answered a moment later when the repairman opened a box and pulled out a new rim.

He put it on a tire mounting device and began fitting a new tire onto it. Apparently, something had happened to the other rim. It must have been damaged when Hood pulled off the road.

Decker checked the time. It was ten thirty. The car probably wouldn't be ready for another thirty minutes to an hour if they were replacing two tires, but he wasn't going anywhere. Someone would eventually show up to get the Lexus and he would be waiting.

Time ticked past at a snail's pace. Decker tried not to get too comfortable. He didn't want to doze off. He got out of the car. Stretched. Went into the diner and got himself a large cup of coffee to go.

The coffee wasn't strong or good. He didn't frequent diners. He didn't like greasy, oily, food. He didn't like cheap food. Diners were for poor people, not for people with money. But sometimes, sacrifices had to be made.

Doing what he had to do to stay awake was well worth the sacrifice. He'd nearly lost his prey when he underestimated them before. He wouldn't make that same mistake twice.

Decker had to give Hood credit where credit was due. She was a sneaky little paranoid bitch. She didn't trust anyone except apparently her fellow former sex slave and Paola. He was going to take great pleasure in killing her.

He was going to make her suffer as much as possible for all the trouble she'd put him through. He imagined all the possible scenarios. All the possible ways to make her cry and beg and plead for her life.

Decker was almost a hundred percent certain she wasn't married. Someone that distrusting and paranoid couldn't have a loving relationship. She'd probably been used by Jasper Whittaker so many times that she didn't even want to have sex anymore.

She was disgusting. A used sex toy. Making her have sex before she died would be deliciously torturous. Decker just didn't want to do it himself. He wanted a proxy to do it for him. Since it was highly doubtful there was a man around the house, it looked like he might have to do it another way.

He could violate her with ordinary household objects. He could tie her down and force things into every orifice while she screamed and writhed and cried. Decker would get in her face and mock her mercilessly.

"That's what you get, bitch. If you'd made it easier for me, I would have made it easier for you." Decker laughed at the delicious imagery. God, he was going to enjoy this. He might even record it so he could watch it over and over again.

A beige Cadillac turned into the tire shop parking lot and parked. It was a vintage model. Old and ugly as sin. He'd never understood the allure of driving cars that handled like bathtubs on wheels.

A woman with dark hair got out of the passenger side. She went into the front office. Decker shifted to the passenger side of his car so he could see her better through the monocular.

She was hot. Tall and athletic, but curvy where it counted. Full lips. Big eyes. Typical Latina build. Her only lacking quality were the small breasts. But those could be fixed for a price.

Decker wondered what someone like her was doing riding around in an old Caddie like that. Was it her dad's car? Did she have a sugar daddy? Women like that usually did. They didn't want to work. They wanted daddy to pay for their hair and nails.

The Latina spoke to the clerk. Walked back out to the Cadillac. She walked confidently. Like a woman who wasn't afraid of anything and knew what she wanted. She looked around as she walked. Like she was noticing everything. Like no detail was too small to miss.

He knew women like that. Most of them were FBI agents. Was this woman a cop? Or was he just reading too much into this? That Cadillac certainly wasn't an unmarked police car. Her skirt and blouse didn't look like something a cop would wear.

Decker shook his head. She was just a typical Latina queen. That kind of woman always looked around like she owned the place. Like she was daring anyone to tell her otherwise.

He licked his lips at the thought of what he'd like to do to her. If he wasn't tied up waiting for Hood to show and claim her car, he'd almost certainly follow this woman home and show her what a good time really was.

The car she was in didn't move. It sat in the parking lot. She'd probably come to check on her car and found out it wasn't ready yet. Now she was waiting for it.

There were only two repair bays. One had the Lexus. The other was servicing a mid-sized Kia. That was probably her car. It looked like they were mounting the tire on it, and it would be ready shortly.

Decker looked at the progress on the Lexus. The guy was removing the first tire from the balancing machine. It had taken fifteen minutes from the time he'd started balancing it until mounting.

It would probably take a similar amount of time for the other wheel to get the same treatment. By that time, the Latina would be gone. He really didn't like the idea of missing out on her.

He zoomed in on the car with the monocular. The windows were so darkly tinted that he couldn't see inside. He couldn't even see silhouettes. Was she really dating a guy with an ancient Cadillac?

She walked like a queen. Like someone with confidence. There was no way that car belonged to a boyfriend or husband. It had to be her dad. She looked like she was in her twenties, but Latina women always leaned on their dads for help.

He wrote down the license plate number. Tracking her down would be easy. He unlocked his phone and texted the information to the home office. Requested an address for the car registration.

There was another text waiting for him. A text from an unknown number.

Hello Decker. I'm your guardian angel just letting you know we have an asset in your vicinity. She is deep undercover so I can't divulge more information. She is tracking the same bounties you are. You will still get your full cut even if she reaches them first.

Decker's face burned with anger. "Are you kidding me?" He started to reply to the text when another one arrived.

Don't be angry. You can have Lacy Hood and Aliyah Butler to do with as you please. Amos Carver and Paola Barros are ours.

It wasn't the money that concerned Decker. It was the cartel's reaction to someone else getting Paola that he was worried about. He sent back a reply.

The cartel won't be happy with me if I let someone else take Paola Barros.

Amos Carver was an entirely different subject. There was a cartel bounty out for him. They had a name and a description, but no pictures of the guy. He was a ghost. A dangerous ghost. Decker could handle him, no problem, but he needed to know what the guy looked like first.

It was interesting that his guardian angel mentioned Carver in the same sentence as Paola. It meant the two might be together. Which meant Decker could possibly get a twofer if he was smart about it.

A thrill of excitement ran through him. He could easily ask twenty million for Carver. The cartel would gladly hand it over. It was a cheap price to pay for someone who'd cost them millions of dollars in lost cash and destroyed their operation.

First Decker had to figure out who this undercover agent was. He had to figure out how close they were to finding Carver and Paola. They must be really close if he was being notified. Which meant the military choppers he'd seen yesterday were connected.

For them to say it was an undercover agent meant that the agent was embedded somewhere useful. They could be with Paola and the other women, or they could be with Carver. It made sense either way, because the mystery agency wanted both.

Decker opened the briefs about Paola and Carver on his phone. There was a connection between the two. A romantic connection, probably. Something had happened and the two weren't together anymore.

There weren't many details about it, but the few that had been gathered came from Paola, not from Carver. Someone had been talking to her. That someone was probably Lucas. He might have been working for the federal government, but that didn't mean he wasn't a double agent for the mystery agency.

Since Lucas was dead, it also meant he wasn't the undercover agent they mentioned. It meant they had a mystery asset on the inside. It seemed to be much easier to embed someone with Paola than with this Carver guy, but maybe they'd somehow done it.

He read through the briefings twice to make sure he didn't miss anything. They were short. Barely five pages each. Most of the information was conjecture. The scraps of firsthand information, however, were enough to see what was happening.

Paola had left Carver. The two had gone separate ways. But that didn't mean Carver wasn't protective of her. The mystery agency was using Paola as bait to catch a big fish. And their undercover agent was helping.

It seemed everyone wanted these two. They were a complete set. Decker didn't have to guess as to why. Paola was the bait. Men like Carver usually knew when to cut bait. But every man had a weakness.

Paola was the bait Carver couldn't cut. Even more importantly, she was leverage. Decker didn't have enough information to know why they'd want leverage on this Carver guy. He must have some valuable intel because it seemed a lot easier to just kill him.

Decker put away the phone. Stared at the tire shop across the road. The Lexus was being driven to the parking lot on the side of the building. It was ready to go. He hoped he didn't have to wait much longer before someone came and picked it up.

Another thirty plus minutes ticked past. Decker was on his second cup of foul-tasting coffee. He was getting antsy. Getting frustrated. Some people took forever to pick up their cars. What if Lacy didn't come for several hours?

His bladder let him know it was full, but he couldn't go inside the diner to pee. Lacy might come by and be gone in the space of two minutes. He was too close to finishing this to take that risk.

Decker got out of the car. He dumped the rest of the coffee into the grass. He got back into the car. Peed in the to-go cup. Got out and dumped it in the same spot he'd dumped the coffee. He caught a glimpse of movement across the street.

A female figure about Lacy Hood's size had stepped out of the back door of a white compact car. A hoodie concealed her head and face, but strands of blond hair had escaped and fluttered in the breeze.

The driver of the white car backed up and left. Probably a rideshare, but Decker wrote down the license plate number just in case. He sent it to the Bureau for identification. A response had already come back for the Cadillac's plate.

It belonged to a local used car dealership. Which meant the Latina probably worked for the dealership and was picking up a car that had been getting work done on it. Someone else from the dealership had given her a ride here to pick it up.

But that didn't matter right now. What mattered was that someone who might be Lacy Hood was entering the tire shop. This was it. The mouse had finally revealed herself. In this case it wouldn't be a cat following her. It would be a lion, stalking its prey.

The Latina got out of the Cadillac. She walked toward the tire shop, hurrying as if trying to catch up with the woman in the hoodie. Decker zoomed in on them with his monocular. Another figure suddenly blocked his view.

He lowered the monocular. Saw the two women talking. Saw a big guy standing next to them, right in the way of his line of sight. The driver's door to the Cadillac hung open, meaning the big guy had been driving it.

Why in the hell were the Latina and her driver talking to the woman. Did they know her? It was a small town, so everyone probably knew everyone else. The woman they were talking to turned so he could see her face.

"Son of a bitch." Decker wanted to punch something and break it.

The woman wasn't Lacy Hood. She wasn't Paola Barros or Aliyah Butler. She was a nobody. A random woman who had nothing to do with this. There were several vehicles parked on the side of the building. One of them might be hers.

Decker watched them talk. The blonde looked confused then shocked. Her mouth dropped open. She put a hand on the big guy's arm. Started laughing and talking like she was extremely excited.

He kept watching them because there was nothing else to do.

The Latina spoke with the blonde then motioned toward the building. The blonde nodded and they all went inside. The blonde talked to the tire shop employee behind the counter. She paid cash.

He gave her a key. She walked outside. Said something to the Latina and the big guy. Then she climbed into the Lexus.

Decker straightened in his seat. He became laser focused on the Latina and the man with her. He examined them with his monocular. It didn't take a rocket scientist to realize who they were. Not with all this new information.

Hood was beyond paranoid. She'd sent someone else to pick up her vehicle. These two people were waiting on the Lexus to be picked up because they also didn't know where Hood lived, and by extension where Paola was hiding.

The reaction the woman had to the big guy was telling. He looked menacing but she'd been happy to see him. She must be another one of Whittaker's former sex slaves. And the big guy?

That was Carver.

CHAPTER 36

Carver felt like he was being watched.

He kept scanning the sky for choppers. Kept watching the streets for windowless black Sprinter vans. The skies were clear. The streets were empty of suspicious vehicles. At least as far as he could tell through the motel window.

Enigma had pulled out all the stops to find him and Liana. They'd chased them every mile of the way between that motel and Cookeville. Then they'd been so blatant as to use military choppers for an aerial search of the town.

He hadn't been back to see if the minivan was still parked where he'd left it. He imagined the local cop had reported it and the family in that white house had been questioned.

They knew Carver was in town. They knew Carver was looking for Paola. So, why had they stopped searching? Had they found him? Were they waiting for him to lead them to Paola? Or was he in the clear for now?

There were no answers, only questions. And until he knew what he was dealing with, it was best to be vigilant. It was best to be ready for any situation. Because being surprised by something was a quick way to end up dead.

This might not even be the work of Enigma. Maybe it was the cartel. Maybe it was another dark ops organization. There really was no way to be sure. In the end, it really didn't matter who it was. What mattered was what they were doing.

Liana stepped out of the bathroom. Her hair was wet. She had a towel wrapped around her. She'd removed the gauze and tape from her wound. It looked like the stitches Carver had made were holding up okay.

Carver turned back to the window. He kept watching the cars drive by. Kept waiting for a black van to screech into the parking lot and disgorge operators in urban fatigues. He was so close to finally finding Paola. If anything could go wrong, it would go wrong now.

Liana cleared her throat. "Help a girl out?"

He turned around. She'd put on panties and a bra. He walked over and inspected her wound. It was dry. He put fresh antibiotic ointment on it and fresh gauze and tape over that. Then he went back to the window.

"Are you being paranoid?"

"Yep."

"Good." Clothing rustled as she dressed. The hair dryer turned on a moment later. She joined him at the window ten minutes later wearing a navy-blue business skirt and white button-up shirt. She turned in a circle for him. "Do I look like I mean business?"

"You look like an undercover FBI agent."

She laughed. "Exactly the look I'm going for. Just in case I have to pretend to be an insurance adjustor again."

"I'm pretty sure most adjustors don't dress that professionally." Carver shrugged. "At least not in this day and age."

"You're probably right, but this is how I usually dress. It just feels right even if the clothing is second hand."

Carver got his duffel bag. He went outside and stowed it in the Cadillac's rear floorboard. He'd checked all the magazines to ensure they were loaded. He had five-five-six, fifty caliber, and nine-millimeter all loaded up.

His long range M4 had a magazine in the well. The Glock in his shoulder holster did too. The chambers were loaded and ready to fire. He didn't want to have even a split second of hesitation if something went down.

That was partly because he knew there were probably still people in this town actively hunting him. It was also partly because he still didn't know if he could fully trust Liana. She was locked and loaded too.

All it would take was for her to draw on him the moment he was distracted. He was torn between what his gut felt, and his brain told him. Could he trust her? His gut said yes. His brain said no. One of them was right.

He'd find out soon enough which one.

Liana gave him a sideways look. She seemed to know what he was thinking but didn't say anything. She knew telling him she could be trusted wouldn't matter. Only her actions over time could prove that.

He knew just about how long that period of time would be. It would be just moments after they reached Paola and the others. That would be when the men in vans and choppers descended on them.

Liana wouldn't have to draw her gun or try to take him prisoner. She could play innocent until the very end.

It pissed him off that he couldn't trust her because he actually liked her. She was smart and capable, and she understood tactics. She noticed the same things he did and pointed out things he'd missed.

It was nice being on equal tactical footing with someone. Someone who had some inkling about what it meant to be on your toes and had an eye for detail. That was why she was an NSA field agent. It was why she would probably continue to be an NSA field agent after this was over.

She might even get a big promotion for bringing in Carver and Paola. Not necessarily because the NSA wanted them but because Enigma did.

Carver started the Caddy. He backed it up. Wheeled it onto the road. He drove down the street to a nearby diner. They went inside and had breakfast. Carver was feeling extra hungry, so he ordered extra bacon.

Liana ordered pancakes and sausage. "I wish they had French toast. I haven't had it in ages."

"You can get it when you go back to Washington."

She looked at him almost wistfully. "Yeah, I guess I can. If they don't execute me first."

"They won't if they're smart. You're smart and capable. Better than most feds I've met."

A smile warmed her face. "That's quite a compliment coming from someone like you."

"It doesn't mean I like who you work for. Or even agree with it." He sipped his coffee. "You're wasted on them."

"What else would I do?"

He shrugged. "I have no idea."

Liana laughed. "Well, guess I'm stuck being a nasty old fed."

"Guess so."

The food arrived. They ate quickly and in silence even though they had plenty of time before the Lexus would be ready for Lacy Hood to pick up. Carver got a tall cup of coffee to go. He had a feeling he'd need it.

He watched the other diner patrons closely. Kept an eye on activity outside. Kept looking around for anything suspicious. Nothing stuck out. Everything seemed to be status quo.

Liana was keeping an eye out too. But he couldn't depend on her. He couldn't trust her a hundred percent. It might be better if he left her here or dropped her in the middle of nowhere. But she knew where he'd be, so he might as well keep her close.

They left and got back in the car. He drove to the tire shop. Backed into a parking space on the side of the building but with a clear view of the repair bays and the entrance. If Lacy showed up to get the Lexus, he'd see her.

"I'll go check to make sure the repairs are on schedule." Liana got out and went inside the tire shop office.

Carver looked at the nearby streets. He lowered the window a crack so he could hear the distant approach of a helicopter. He highly doubted they'd come for him now. If Liana was working with them, they'd let him lead her to Paola.

Then the trap would be sprung.

Part of handling a trap was knowing it was there. That didn't always mean it was best to avoid it. Sometimes it was best to spring the trap and be ready to surprise the people who set it. This was not one of those times.

The trap would include overwhelming force, of that he could be certain. Lacy's house would be surrounded and there would be no choice but to surrender. But if he was wrong and Liana could be trusted, then nothing would happen.

There was no value in embedding an agent except to lead to the capture of two people Enigma wanted to lay hands on. They wanted Carver because he'd caused them trouble and they wanted Paola because she meant something to him.

He couldn't think of any other reason they'd want her, but they obviously did want her if Liana was their agent. Otherwise, they would have simply taken Carver while he slept.

Time ticked on and Carver kept wracking his brain for solutions. How would he handle the trap if one existed? Why would they want Paola? What value did she offer them besides leverage on him?

Then he zeroed in on the crux of the matter.

Carver was an irritant. Someone they wanted out of the way. Someone they wanted dead and buried. Paola had done nothing to them. She had no valuable information. She was leverage against Carver, but for what?

Carver had no information they wanted. He had no intrinsic value to them. Almost no intrinsic value. There was one thing Carver could help them with if he was so inclined. It was one thing Enigma wanted desperately.

To capture Leon Fry.

Leon had been proactively acting against Enigma. Assassinating their agents. Stealing their information and putting it out there for all to see. His goal was to break their hold on politicians and destroy their power and influence.

Carver didn't know if Leon was really making a dent in their operations, but he was certainly someone they wanted dead even more than himself. Carver and Paola were in contact with Leon. They could possibly provide information that would lead to his capture.

Paola was leverage against Carver. Carver had actionable intel that could lead to Leon. That was why they wanted Paola. She was perceived as being the key to getting information from Carver.

Liana returned from the office. She got back in the car. "They said it'll be finished soon. That means Lacy should be along soon to get it."

Carver kept his face emotionless. Sipped his coffee. Reevaluated his revelations. Everything lined up perfectly. There was no question in his mind that Enigma needed Carver and Paola alive because they wanted to capture Leon.

Once the trio of troublemakers was dealt with, Enigma would have free reign. And the person who might bring this plan to fruition was sitting right next to him. He took a long, deep breath. Feigned a yawn.

"Don't you just love stakeouts?" Liana said.

"Love them." Carver looked over at her. "Why do you think Enigma wants me so badly?"

She frowned. "That question came out of left field."

Carver watched her closely. Said nothing.

Liana raised an eyebrow. "I don't know, Carver. I assume you've been a thorn in their side, and they want you dead."

Carver figured she had just enough information to reach that conclusion. He hadn't given her details about Leon or anything else. It was also clear that he wasn't going to trick her into betraying knowledge she shouldn't have.

Either because she didn't have it or because she was an expert at compartmentalizing data. She was also a pro at playing a part. Maybe her actions didn't matter that much. Maybe it was the actions of Enigma's operators he should be looking at.

Either they had been ready to eliminate her, or they had pretended they were ready to eliminate her. Maybe they'd wanted Carver to intervene. To save her. Or maybe they'd wanted him to see her escape death, so he'd accept her as a fellow fugitive.

In either case, they'd sacrificed a man that night and they'd sacrificed others since then. Which meant if Liana was their inside man, then the men they were sending after them were sacrificial lambs who knew nothing about their true aims.

Carver had seen people sacrificed in the name of the greater good. Some people went willingly. Some people went to their deaths not knowing they were being set up to fail. Those orders always came from the top. From people with no real skin in the game.

Was that the case here? Had Enigma knowingly sent people to die just so Liana could gain Carver's trust?

On the other hand, he might just be completely overthinking everything. Occam's Razor theorized that the simplest answer was most likely the right one. Maybe those men really had planned to kill Liana.

Maybe Liana meant nothing to them. Maybe she was as much a pawn as he was. And maybe he was just a madman full of conspiracy theories.

"You've been staring blankly out of the window for almost two minutes, Carver." Liana put a hand on his arm. "Don't overthink things."

Movement caught his eye. Something across the road at the diner. He thought he saw someone moving around next to a tree in the diner parking lot. He didn't get a good look at them, but it looked like they were dumping out a cup of coffee.

A moment later, a white car pulled into the tire shop's parking lot. It stopped and a small, feminine figure in a hoodie got out of the back seat. A lock of blond hair escaped the hood.

Liana jumped out of the car in a flash. She hurried after the person, catching them before they went into the tire shop. Carver got out. Followed her. The white car backed out past him. It turned onto the road and drove away.

He saw the face hiding beneath the hood. It wasn't Lacy. Wasn't Aliyah or Paola wearing a blond wig. It was a stranger with a familiar face.

She did a doubletake when she saw Carver. She grinned with delight. "Carver?"

He realized why she looked familiar. She was one of the women held captive by the cartel. One of Jasper Whittaker's sex slaves. Carver didn't remember her name, but he remembered her lunging at Paola shortly after being freed from a cargo container.

He remembered her trying to claw out Paola's eyes at one point. She and some of the other women hated Paola. They knew she worked directly for Jasper. They knew she sent requests for blondes or brunettes, Asians, Caucasians, or Latinas depending on Jasper's appetite that day.

They knew some women never came back because Jasper killed them for his own sexual pleasure. They blamed Paola as much as they blamed Jasper. At least they had at first. Later they'd come to accept that she was as much a prisoner as they'd been.

Being given millions in cartel cash also went a long way toward forgiveness.

The woman's name finally came to Carver. "Jill Borden."

"Yes!" She took his hand. Kissed it. "You're still my hero."

Liana looked confused. "Wait, so you're another one of the cartel's victims?"

"I am. Lacy sent me to get her car."

Carver had only one thought on his mind. "Is Paola with her?"

Jill's eyes darkened for a moment. Her smile faded. "Yes. Paola warned us that the cartel found her. She says they have a list with our names on it and put kill bounties on our heads."

"Why are you here then?" Liana said. "Why is she gathering you and the others? If someone is after you, then coming together only makes it easier."

"We found out that two women are already dead. Tina and Mary were killed in their homes."

"Where did they live?" Liana asked.

"Mary was in San Francisco and Tina was in Los Angeles." Jill shook her head. "There are others we haven't been able to contact through our emergency channels, so we decided it was better to get together and figure out a new plan. Lacy wants to see if witness protection can help."

Carver didn't want to wait around a moment longer. Especially not when a black van or military chopper could swoop in at any time. "Where is Paola? Tell me how to get there."

"I can take you." Jill touched his hand. "Let me get the car and you can follow me."

"Okay. Do it. Carver was itching to get out of here. He was itching to finally see Paola. But he could sense danger. He could feel it in his bones. And even if it wasn't imminent, he knew when and where it would come.

If Liana was going to betray him, it would be just minutes from now.

CHAPTER 37

Decker had Carver in his sights.

He sent a picture of the blonde for analysis. He wanted to know who she was and why she was picking up Hood's Lexus. Was she a neighbor doing a favor or was she something more? Maybe someone working for WITSEC?

The woman climbed into the Lexus moments later. The Latina got in with her. Carver didn't seem to like that arrangement. He put a hand on the Latina's arm. Talked to her. She shook her head a few times and that was that.

Carver got into the Cadillac and waited while the women in the Lexus talked about something.

Decker's phone buzzed. There was a hit on the blonde. She was Jill Borden, one of Whittaker's victims. He laughed. Congratulated himself. This was turning out to be a real bonanza.

Paola's idea to congregate these women all in one place just made it way too easy for him. The only bump in the road now was Carver. It would be difficult to take him alive, but still doable.

There was a larger bump in the road. More like a pothole. His guardian angel. He or she thought their people would pinch the bounties before him. Somehow, Decker had to prevent them from doing that without pissing them off.

To do that, he'd have to spring a trap before they did with their undercover agent. He wasn't sure how to pull that off.

His phone buzzed again. There was a video attachment to the text. Several images as well. He looked at the text first.

You owe me a drink, Decker. I hit the jackpot. My source at Homeland Security got me an address for Lacy Hood aka Brenda Johnson. My facial recognition search for Paola Barros also found the following videos and images.

Take a look at them. You won't believe what you see.

Decker didn't care about that right then. He was already plugging Hood's address into the GPS. Already pulling onto the highway before the Lexus and Cadillac got going. It was a ten-minute drive.

Ironically, the house was on White Cemetery Road almost right across from the cemetery it was named after. The house was on a large plot of land. There were metal barns, garages, and a big residence.

His search area hadn't even been close.

Hood's house was close to town but far enough away to be secluded. Decker gave it an eight out of ten stars for location and defensibility. At least from the front of the house. If he drove down the long driveway, they'd spot him immediately.

That wasn't the plan.

There was a road that bordered Hood's land. There were trees on that side. Outbuildings. Plenty of places to approach the main residence undetected. He was going to capture the grand prize and set up his own defenses instead.

Then he could take Carver without a struggle. He'd take him calmly, coolly, and without incident. Because Carver's grand prize was Paola, and he wouldn't do anything to jeopardize her. If he did, then Decker would put him down like a dog and never look back.

The cartel wanted him alive or dead. Preferably alive, but sometimes things just didn't work out.

Decker opened the images the analyst had sent him. He glanced at them as he drove. It took him a moment to realize their significance. He played the video and realized the images had been captured from it.

Seeing the images animated. Seeing Paola's smiling face, her laughter, made him understand all too well why the cartel wanted her so badly. Why his guardian angel wanted her so badly. And the best part?

Carver had no clue about it.

CARVER HONKED THE HORN.

Jill finally shifted the Lexus into drive. She turned left onto the road and drove north. Carver pulled out after her. She seemed to be in no hurry to get to the destination and it was enough to incite road rage.

She finally gathered some speed. Turned onto the highway and drove west.

Carver didn't like that Liana was riding with Jill. She'd told him it was just in case they got separated. Just in case something happened between the tire shop and Lacy's house. He didn't buy it.

It sounded like a way for her to spring the trap without Carver being next to her. He'd notice if she tried to send a covert text while sitting in the seat next to him. Jill wouldn't have a clue. Jill was probably talking Liana's ears off, oblivious that a signal had been sent to unleash the hounds.

He could have dragged Liana to the car. Forced her to ride with him. But that would have made a big scene. It might have caused someone in the tire shop to call the police. Jill might have freaked out too.

Carver had seen no choice but to let it play out. At least to a certain point. He already had a plan in mind. The moment they reached the house, he planned to grab Paola and go. He'd leave the others to fend for themselves.

Enigma didn't particularly care about the other women. They might just leave them alone rather than dealing with the hassle of killing them and covering up the murders. And if Liana was on their side, she'd be in the clear despite failing their ultimate objective.

Carver would have to ditch the Cadillac fast. He'd have to find new wheels as soon as possible because the moment they knew he'd fled with Paola choppers would be covering the escape routes.

He revised the plan slightly. He would take Paola into a back room like he wanted to talk with her or be alone with her. Then they'd jump out of a window. That way Liana wouldn't know they were gone.

It also meant he'd have to park the Cadillac somewhere she couldn't see from the house. He wouldn't know where that spot was until they reached the house. It meant he could only preplan so much.

They passed by a cemetery on the left and a house on the right. Jill turned onto the next driveway. Carver drove up to the driveway and saw it was probably a hundred yards long. He quickly pulled up the location on the maps app.

He turned on satellite view and examined the options. There was lots of open space around the house. Lots of outbuildings. Metal garages. A large wooden barn next to a thicket of trees.

The driveway led to a wide concrete pad. There was a metal garage to the east side of the house and one directly behind it on the north side. There didn't seem to be a fence around the property, but it was hard to tell from the image.

Carver pulled down the driveway. The Lexus was already parked out front. The women weren't in the car, so they'd probably gone inside. They were probably wondering why he wasn't hot on their heels.

The driveway forked to the left and ended in front of the house. He went straight instead. That took him to the concrete pad and the metal garage on the back side. Two pickup trucks were parked inside the metal garage.

There was plenty of space inside, so he parked to the right of them. The pickups looked almost new. They were both full-sized Toyota trucks. Both were unlocked. He checked the cupholders and the sun visors for keys. Found nothing.

He checked the glove box and center console. Nothing. He pushed the sunglass holder in front of the rearview mirror. There was a fob inside. He pulled it out and pushed the start button on the dash.

The truck rumbled to life. He pushed it again to turn it off. Pocketed the key fob. This was it. This was his escape route. He just had to pull it off before the enemy cavalry arrived. He removed his duffel bag from the Cadillac. Opened the back door of the crew cab and put the duffel bag on the back floorboard.

He wanted to be able to start the truck and go before Liana realized what was happening.

Carver hurried to the house and tried the back door. It was locked. He jogged around to the front door. Went inside. The house looked and smelled newly renovated. The den and kitchen were one giant room.

A large couch was in the middle of the den. It faced the front door. Lacy was sitting on it. Jill sat to her right. Aliyah was next to Jill, and Paola was sandwiched between Jill and Liana. They weren't talking or smiling. They were all tense, faces filled with apprehension.

It wasn't because Carver had taken so long to come inside. It was because of the person standing behind them. The person holding an HK416 with a nice fat suppressor on the end.

Decker grinned. "Surprise!"

A MESSAGE ARRIVED.

Car is here.

The person holding the phone had been waiting for this message for a long time. It was hard to believe the day was finally here. The car was here, and everything was coming together splendidly.

Resources were already in place. They were miles out from the target. Positioned to approach from every direction. Not to pick up a car, of course. There was no car. Car was just short for something else. It was short for a name.

Carver.

He and Paola Barros were together in one place. Just as planned, they'd drawn each other together. They'd proven the strength of their connection. Carver would almost certainly do anything for her, and she would do anything for him.

Together, they would be the key to finding Leon Fry, the man who'd been throwing wrenches into their plans left and right. The man who was responsible for billions of dollars in damages, delays, and loss of personnel.

And that would be just the start.

Carver had proven himself dangerous. He'd proven himself capable. He'd proven that he could be very valuable as an operator. But he had to have the right motivation.

And Paola was the one to provide it.

CHAPTER 38

Carver hadn't expected this.

He hadn't expected to find Decker inside waiting. Several possibilities ran through his mind. Had he already located the women and taken them hostage, then sent Jill to pick up the Lexus in the hopes that Carver would be right behind her?

That was a possibility, but first he would have had to know Carver was hot on Paola's heels. He would have had to know that Carver was using the Lexus as a lead. The man was an FBI agent, so anything was possible.

Whatever the cause, it didn't matter. What mattered was that Decker's rifle was pointed right at Paola. He wasn't waving it around the room or pointing it at Carver. He had it aimed right where he needed it to be to make Carver compliant.

That was what irked Carver the most. There was one human in the world he didn't want to die. One human whose death would cause him more pain than he wanted to admit. And he couldn't even understand why.

It was his weakness. His fatal flaw. All he had to do was turn around and leave. Leave this place behind and go live his life. Let These women die. Let Paola die.

Decker's grin grew wider. "Don't be ashamed, buddy. We all have our weaknesses."

Carver wondered if Decker was the only thing he needed to worry about. If Liana was still working for her masters, she would have sent a message the moment she reached this location. A small army would be on the way right about now.

"What do you want?" Carver asked.

"You and Paola." Decker tossed a pair of handcuffs toward Carver. They landed on the floor in front of him. "Put those on. Then I will lead you and Paola outside and we'll go."

"And the other women?" Paola said.

"They'll be fine. You and Carver are the real money." Decker nodded at the handcuffs. "Put them on now."

"You're a real piece of trash," Liana said. "How can you call yourself an FBI agent?"

"You must be the secret agent I was told about." Decker tapped the suppressor on Liana's head. "My guardian angel told me all about you, so you don't have to keep playing the part."

Liana winced when the suppressor struck her. "I'm not playing a part, you sick bastard."

Carver stared at Decker. "You know there's an undercover agent?"

Decker laughed. "Man, I don't blame you for not realizing it. She is a hot piece of tail. If we had more time, I'd definitely have my way with her."

"Just like you did with Fani Wilson and Nilva?" Liana turned her head to glare at him. "Just like you did with Angie before you threw her off the hotel balcony?"

"You're a spitfire, girl." Decker tapped her on the forehead with the suppressor again. "I'd love to beat that fire out of you." He turned back to Carver. "Thanks to your little side piece here, we don't have much time before the shit hits the fan. I suggest you get those cuffs on right away or I'm going to start executing bitches."

"Fine." Carver didn't see many ways out of this, but he agreed with Decker that getting away from the house within the next few minutes was crucial to his survival. At least with Decker he had a chance. If vanloads of operators surrounded the house, his odds dropped to zero.

Liana shook her head. "Carver, don't believe this basic little bitch. I'm not undercover. I'm really on your side. Decker's a narcissistic psychopath with a tiny dick."

The next part happened fast. But not so fast that Carver didn't see it coming. Decker's lips curled up in rage. He flipped his rifle, so the butt was facing down, and the barrel was facing up. His finger left the trigger and wrapped around the stock as he raised the butt to slam it down on Liana's head.

He wanted to shut her up. Put her in her place. That was just the kind of guy he was. Shooting her was easy. Beating her and torturing her to death was more his style. Especially when a woman dared to call him names.

Carver already had his hand wrapped around his Glock by the time Decker was raising the rifle butt. Carver raised and aimed just as the rifle was slamming down on Liana's head. Except Liana's head wasn't there anymore.

Liana was watching Decker. She'd wanted to elicit this reaction. She'd expected it. She rolled forward off the couch and onto the floor as the rifle butt crashed down and missed.

Carver didn't want to fire right away. Paola's head was right in front of Decker's center mass. The rifle was in the way of his head. But he had no choice. He aimed high and pulled the trigger. The bullet pinged off metal. Probably the rifle barrel.

Decker was slightly off balance after missing his strike on Liana. It wasn't enough to make him stumble, but it was enough to keep him from bringing the rifle to bear on Carver or Paola.

Paola's eyes widened when she saw Liana dive off the couch. She wasn't looking behind her. She couldn't see what Carver saw, but she didn't need to see it to realize now was the time to act.

She dove forward off the couch toward Carver. Crawled on her hands and knees and ducked behind the kitchen cabinets to the left. They wouldn't provide much cover unless there were pots and pans inside.

Decker's rifle would shred right through cabinets like they were paper. But he didn't seem to be too concerned with tracking her. He saw the gun in Carver's hand and was responding to the most immediate danger.

The other women were still on the couch. Still right in Carver's line of fire. Decker must have disarmed Liana because she would have already been shooting Decker if she had her gun.

"Get down!" he shouted.

Lacy dove to the floor. Aliyah followed suit. Jill was still on the couch. Still frozen with fear. She didn't matter. She wasn't in his line of sight.

Carver aimed at Decker's center mass and fired. But the women's delay had given Decker time to recover. He fired. There was nowhere for Carver to go. No cover to hide behind. He dove sideways and fired.

Every one of his shots missed. There was no way for him to hit Decker, but that wasn't the point. He just needed to buy some time. Enough time for him and Paola to get out of the house.

He rolled onto his back and fired three more times. Decker ducked behind the couch. Carver fired into it. Decker shouted in pain.

Carver stood. Kept the gun trained on the couch. He'd fired the last shot in his magazine, but he didn't want Decker to know that. He grabbed a magazine from his back pocket while simultaneously ejecting the empty one.

Decker popped up from behind the couch as Carver was swinging the new magazine into the well.

"You're too much trouble." Decker's finger twitched on the trigger.

There was a scream. "No!"

A shot rang out. Paola was suddenly in front of Carver. Blood sprayed. Sharp pain seared Carver's right arm. He saw Paola go down. Heard another shot ring out. His magazine was already in the well.

He loaded the chamber as a bullet whizzed past and thumped into the wall behind him. Something blinded him. Something hot and wet. He fired until the magazine was empty. Heard Decker cry out in pain. Heard a rifle thud on the floor.

Carver wiped his eyes. His fingers were covered in blood. He looked down. Paola was face down on the floor, still as death. There was an exit wound near her upper shoulder. A pool of blood forming on the floor.

There was a snapping like a magazine being ejected. Decker was reloading.

Carver charged forward. Leaped over the couch like an Olympic hurdler. Found Decker trying to put in a fresh magazine. He yanked the rifle from the other man. Saw a wound in Decker's leg. Carver kicked him right in the bullet hole.

Decker shouted. Carver gripped the man by his shirt and felt a bulletproof vest beneath it. He used that to hoist the other man off the ground. Adrenalin and rage surged through Carver. Paola's blood dripped into his mouth. He spat it in Decker's face.

"There's no saving you now." Carver hurled Decker into the wall. Slammed him so hard Decker's head punched through the drywall. He shoved the other man against the wall. Elbowed him in the jaw.

Bones cracked and broke beneath the onslaught. Decker screamed.

Carver spun Decker around and hurled him into the kitchen oven. Glass shattered. The stainless-steel bent. He yanked a stainless-steel pan off the counter and smacked it into Decker's face over and over until it was just a bloody pulp.

Decker wasn't screaming in pain anymore. He was groaning and drooling blood all over the floor. And that was a good thing as far as Carver was concerned. Because it meant he could still feel the pain.

Carver gripped Decker's crotch with one hand and the top of the Kevlar vest with the other. He yanked him off the floor. Held him over his head like he was doing a clean and press at the gym.

He swung Decker down right over a metal stool. Decker's spine struck the back of the stool. There was a loud crack. It wasn't from the chair. Air wheezed out of Decker's lungs. He slipped to the ground limp and dead.

Carver looked at Paola. Liana and Aliyah had lifted her off the floor and shoved a towel against her wound. Paola grimaced in pain and that was good. Damned good.

She was alive.

Carver stormed over to her. Cradled her in his arms. "Everyone out back now. We've got to go."

"Why?" Jill stood over Decker. "He's dead! We should stay here and help Paola. Maybe call the ambulance."

Liana gripped Carver's arm. "I swear to you by all that's holy, I am not here to spy on you or help anyone capture you. But if Decker's handler told him they have an agent, then I believe them."

Aliyah snatched something from Jill. It was a phone. She turned on the screen. Turned it to Jill. "Unlock it!"

"What? Why?"

"I said to unlock it!"

Jill averted her face from the phone. "I'm not—"

Liana gripped the other woman by the neck and made her face the phone. The screen unlocked. Liana took it and opened the most recent text. It said, *Car is here.* The number was blocked. There were no other texts, but it was clearly a code of some kind.

"I should have known," Lacy said. "Jill tried to act like she didn't still hate Paola, but I could see it in her eyes." She faced Jill. "Do you hate her so much that you'd put us all in danger?"

"You can all go to hell!" Jill backed up from them, face red with anger and hatred. "Yes, I hate that bitch! She sat by and watched Jasper rape us over and over again! She watched that fat bastard kill women and did nothing!" She lunged for Paola who was still in Carver's arms.

Liana swept Jill's leg out from under her in one smooth motion. Jill's head hit the floor. Liana stared down at her. "If you try to get up, I'll break your leg. Stay there like a good dog."

Jill began to sob. "No, please. I was doing it for us. Paola deserves to feel all the pain and agony we did. She deserves to suffer!"

Aliyah looked at her with disgust. "Paola was a victim like the rest of us. The cartel killed her father. She was forced to work for them. And then she helped us escape. Set up a rescue network so we could help each other."

"You're the one who gave us up, aren't you?" Lacy's mouth fell open. "You're the reason Lucas and the cartel found Paola in Miami and started all of this!"

"I want that bitch to pay!" Still sobbing, Jill tried to sit up.

Aliyah kicked her in the head. Jill went down hard. Her head lolled.

Lacy picked up Decker's rifle. She aimed it at Jill, apparently not realizing there was no magazine in it. She pulled the trigger. Naturally, nothing happened.

"Look, we don't have time for this." Carver motioned toward the door. We've got to go, now!"

Lacy grabbed a Glock off the floor. It must have been Decker's sidearm. She aimed it at Jill and pulled the trigger. Two shots missed, putting holes in the wooden floor. The third shot hit Jill in the stomach. The fourth in the chest.

Paola cried out. "Lacy, no!"

"She betrayed us!" Lacy threw the pistol at Jill and missed by a mile.

Liana grabbed her by the shoulder. "We've got to go now!"

Aliyah grabbed Lacy. "Honey, let's go."

Eyes filled with tears, Lacy nodded and turned to follow them.

Liana ran to the back door and flung it open. Carver hurried past her and outside. He nodded at the truck since Paola was cradled in his arms. "Open it."

Aliyah ran past him and opened the back door of the crew cab pickup. He put Paola inside. The towel was stanching the blood for now, but he didn't think it was enough to hold it for long. Her face was pale, but she managed to sit upright while he buckled her in.

Aliyah climbed into the other side and sat next to Paola. Lacy hopped in next to her.

Liana was close behind them. Her head tilted. "You hear that?"

Carver scanned the horizon. He didn't hear choppers. Didn't see any. But he did hear the growl of loud engines in the distance. They were coming.

He climbed into the driver's seat. Shifted into drive. He went through the back yard, such as it was. There was a barbed wire fence that hadn't showed up in the map overhead image, but he plowed right over it with the big pickup. He bounced through ruts and grass and reached a small road on the other side.

Liana was looking at the map app on her phone. "Keep going straight. Due north."

He reached a crossroads. There was no traffic, so he kept going north. The road went up a hill. It wasn't very high, but it was a good vantage point to see Lacy's house. He stopped the truck. Got out and looked through his monocular.

Low-flying stealth choppers were approaching from the tree lines to the east and west. Three black vans filed down the driveway and fanned out to surround the house. One chopper hovered over the house.

Operators slid down ropes and landed on the roof. The other chopper landed behind the house and disgorged troops. Within seconds, the house was surrounded by operators in black and gray fatigues.

"Urban camo? Really?" Liana laughed. "Is that the only camouflage they have?"

"Guess so." Carver got back in the truck. Turned to look at Paola. The bleeding had stopped. He wasn't sure how since the bullet had punched through right under her clavicle. It must have been a much cleaner hit than he'd thought. "How are you feeling?"

"It hurts, but somehow I'm alive." Paola touched his hand. "Thank you, Carver."

"Why are you thanking me? You're the one who took a bullet for me."

The other women laughed.

Carver didn't laugh. "Let me see the wound."

Paola lifted the towel to show a small wound. "It went right through me."

"Because Decker, for some reason, was using armor piercing rounds," Liana said. "I guess he thought Carver might be wearing body armor."

"I don't understand," Paola said. "Armor piercing sounds like it would do more damage."

Liana shook her head and pointed to her own injured shoulder. "A regular round did this. It pancaked on impact and made a bigger hole. The armor piercing round is designed to punch through body armor then ricochet off the body armor on the other side of the torso and bounce around through your insides. Without body armor, it goes right through the human body, causing much less damage than a standard round."

"So, it's good?" Paola asked.

Liana laughed. "Being shot is never good."

Paola smiled. "Now we both have shoulder injuries."

Liana smiled back. "Twinsies."

Carver started driving north. He didn't know where they were going, but anywhere besides here was good.

"You saved us again." Aliyah put a hand on his shoulder. "Thank you, Carver."

"I wanted to message you, but my phone was destroyed," Paola said. "I tried to use that backup email you told me about, but I couldn't remember the login."

Carver grunted. "I figured."

She shook her head. "How in the world did you find me?"

Carver gave her the short version of the story. "I found out the cartel knew where you were. In retrospect, it looks like Jill told them your location. I found out that your cell phone had hit a tower in Morganville before going offline."

"That's where Carver met me," Liana said. "That's a fun story."

Carver ignored the interruption. "A little detective work and luck kept me going in the right direction. And here we are."

"Master of understatement." Lacy laughed. "This dude wiped out—"

"Let's not get into that," Carver said. "The less you say, the better off we all are."

"God, you're insufferable sometimes." Liana huffed. "He hasn't trusted me at all this entire time. He thought I might betray him to the feds."

"Who are you, exactly?" Paola asked.

"She's with the National Security Agency." Carver met Paola's gaze in the rearview mirror. "I had doubts about how we ended up together."

"They were really going to kill me," Liana said. "You really saved me. It wasn't just for show."

"Do you believe her now?" Paola said.

Carver shrugged and kept driving.

"Jackass." Liana shook her head. "I don't know how you put up with him."

"I haven't put up with him for a long time," Paola said in a soft voice.

"Do you think Jill is the one who set everything in motion?" Carver said.

Paola nodded. "I was living in Miami. I was happy and things were good. Then I met this man named Lucas. I could tell he had sadness inside of him. Like something bad had happened to him and it made me trust him."

Carver nodded. "Standard tactic."

"He's just saying that because he's jealous," Liana said.

Paola continued. "We started dating. Then one night I was waiting for him in the park. I saw him being chased by men with tattoos that identified them as cartel members. I was so shocked I didn't know what to do at first. Then I ran home, got my emergency bag, and ran."

"Good," Carver said.

"Later, I received a text from him. It told me that if I received his message then he was probably dead. It told me that he was with the NSA, and he'd hoped to use me to take down the cartel." Paola shook her head. "I felt so betrayed."

"Lucas was obsessed with the Herrada Cartel," Liana said. "I know because we worked together from time to time. He was a good guy, but he had tunnel vision bad. He didn't care what he had to do or who he had to hurt if it meant getting revenge on the people who killed his family."

"That's so sad." Aliyah sighed. "But it's no excuse to put other people in harm's way. He almost got all of us killed, and I'm not just talking about the people in this car. I'm talking about Jasper's other victims."

"Somehow, Lucas found out from Jill where Paola was living." Liana shook her head. "I just can't figure out how or why she chose him."

"Maybe she didn't," Carver said. "She probably told someone else. Lucas probably had certain names and information flagged in the NSA database. Thanks to the Patriot Act, all that information is shared across different federal agencies."

"True," Liana said. "And when he found out, that mystery organization found out. And since Lucas was probably being watched by the cartel, they figured out something was up soon thereafter."

"That mystery organization is referred to by several names," Carver said. "Corporate and Headquarters are a couple, but the one most used seems to be Enigma."

"Has a ring to it," Liana said. "And it describes them perfectly." Liana pulled out a phone that wasn't her burner phone. "Maybe this will have some answers."

Carver looked at the device. "Is that Decker's phone?"

"It is, indeed." She pulled out a plastic bag with a thumb in it. "And this is the finger that opens it."

"Good work."

"Oh, God." Aliyah looked sick. "You chopped off his thumb?"

Paola smiled. "Carver collected many fingers in Morganville."

"Out of necessity." Carver checked the map and took a right onto a road leading north. "Did you put Decker's phone in airplane mode and remove the SIM chip?"

"Of course." Liana tutted. "I'm not about to give our pursuers an easy way to track us."

Carver saw no signs of pursuit. No helicopters. No black vans. Maybe, just maybe, they were finally in the clear.

And this nightmare was over.

CHAPTER 39

Operators stormed Lacy Hood's house.

They cleared the rooms. Searched it from top to bottom. They checked all the outbuildings and environs. All they found were two people.

One was a woman, mid-twenties, blond hair, slim build, blue eyes. She was bleeding from multiple gunshot wounds but was still alive. The other was a man. His face was disfigured. His bones were broken in multiple places.

Somehow, he was still breathing.

The squad leader radioed it in. The response came immediately.

"Get them both medical attention. We need answers."

The squad leader did what he was told. He medevacked both people via helicopter. Sent them to the nearest major hospital with a trauma ward in Nashville. Then he rounded up his men and they headed out, leaving behind surveillance equipment in case the targets returned.

His commander wasn't happy. In fact, she was furious. Thankfully, she didn't blame him or the men. She blamed someone named Decker. If Decker was the badly injured male they'd found in the house, he'd better hope he died, or the commander would make him wish he had.

DECKER OPENED HIS EYES.

Everything was blurry. He felt lightheaded. Numb. He didn't know where he was. He turned his head, but something restricted movement. He tried to touch his face, but his arm seemed to be tied down.

He tried the other arm. It was also fastened down. He blinked several times. The view became clearer.

"Good. You're awake." The voice was distorted. Like it was coming through a voice disguiser.

"Where am I?" Decker could hardly talk. His jaw ached and felt stiff.

"The hospital. We found you near death. Where are Carver and Paola?"

"I had them." Decker's speech was slurred. It sounded like he had a speech impediment because he could hardly move his jaw. "I had them for you."

"We already had them. All we needed was for you to stay out of the way." The figure moved closer, but the room was dim, and the face remained shrouded in shadow. "But you decided to go in anyway. You got greedy."

"No. I helped. I helped!"

"Where did the targets go? What vehicle were they in? Did you overhear anything?"

Decker remembered Carver's enraged face. He remembered Carver lunging at him. It was the first time Decker had been that terrified in his entire life. Because suddenly, he knew that he'd ended up in a fistfight with someone he couldn't beat.

How had he not killed Carver? He'd shot him with the rifle.

The voice broke through his thoughts. "I asked you a question."

"I don't know. I was holding them for you. I promise."

The figure leaned down close but remained to Decker's side. He couldn't turn his head to see the face. The person got right next to his ear. They weren't using the voice disguiser this time.

They just whispered in his ear. "Normally I would kill you. But I think you've discovered a fate worse than death, especially for someone of your variety."

Decker detected a faint accent, but he couldn't place it. He couldn't tell if the voice was male or female. "What do you mean?"

"I'll let the doctor explain." There was a slight rush of air, and the person was gone.

Moments later, the lights in the room brightened. A middle-aged man looked down at him. "Mike, I'm Dr. Forsyth. I just want you to know that even though things weren't looking good, you're going to be just fine."

"What's wrong with me?" Decker hated how his voice sounded. He sounded like the retarded kid from high school. Decker had tormented that idiot every chance he got.

"Let's do some tests first." The doctor walked to the end of the bed. He did something to Decker's foot. "Do you feel that?"

"What did you do?"

The doctor showed him a sharp metallic object. "I'm poking your foot. Do you feel it?" He did it again to both feet.

"No. Nothing."

The doctor worked his way up Decker's legs. "Anything?"

"No." Panic rose in Decker's chest. His heart pounded so hard it felt like it was choking him. "What's wrong with me?" Now he sounded like a retard when he shouted and cried. What the hell was wrong with him?

"Mike, I have some bad news. You're paralyzed from the waist down. You are also suffering partial paralysis of the arms, but I think that might clear up given which bones in your spinal column were shattered."

"Shattered?" Decker's chest heaved. He sobbed uncontrollably, sounding more and more like someone with mental deficiencies because he couldn't move his damned jaw. "Why can't I talk?"

The doctor winced. Pulled out a mirror. Turned it toward Decker. Decker's face looked like it had been run through a meat grinder. Most of his teeth were missing. His jaw had wires in it. His eyes were almost swollen shut.

He looked like a monster.

Decker couldn't hold back anymore. He couldn't keep it in no matter how hard he tried. The tears. The terror. The disgust at his own face.

He screamed and screamed and screamed until his throat went hoarse. He understood what that person had meant by sparing his life as punishment. She had left him in a state worse than death.

"Nurse, please sedate him. I don't want him tearing out any stitches."

A woman came in. She looked at him and recoiled in disgust. "Jesus. That's hard to look at." She jabbed a needle into Decker's arm. He could see the needle but there was almost no sensation when it slid in.

The doctor stood next to her. "You really need to work on your bedside manner, Doris."

"Sorry." She winced. "I've just never seen someone come in with such a horror show for a face. He fell out of the ugly tree, hit every branch on the way down, and got pounded by the ugly monster at the bottom."

The doctor chuckled. Glanced at Decker. "Sorry, Mike."

Decker was too drowsy to respond. The sedation kicked in. As consciousness faded, he began to wish that Carver had just killed him.

CHAPTER 40

Carver stopped in a small town for medical supplies.

Paola was going to be fine, but he wanted to make sure her wound didn't become infected. He also thought a few stitches might be a good idea. Speaking of which, Liana had torn her wound back open during the tussle at Lacy's house.

He gathered everything he needed. Went back outside to the truck. Handed the supplies to Liana. She looked pale and in pain, but she was holding it together okay. Paola and the others were dozing.

The GPS showed fifteen miles to the destination, a lake house Lacy had purchased through a proxy. She'd used her cartel money wisely, buying safe houses through shell companies that were in no way connected to her.

Liana was reading texts on Decker's phone. "Man, this guy did a lot of freelance work for criminals. And he uses FBI resources to help him."

"How did he find Lacy's house?" Carver asked.

"I'm only about a quarter of the way through the texts. This idiot kept everything." She grimaced. "And you wouldn't believe how many license plates and other personal information he used FBI resources to look up just so he could hook up with women."

"He found out where they lived?"

She nodded. "Let me rephrase that. If he couldn't charm a woman into bed with him, he'd rape them."

Carver wasn't surprised. He'd worked with men like that. Men who enjoyed dark ops because it freed them from consequences for their crimes against humanity. "Skip to the end. I need to know if this place we're going to is compromised."

Liana scrolled down. It took a few seconds for her to reach the end. She read the texts from earlier in the day. "Someone in Homeland Security found the house WITSEC purchased for Lacy. That was how he found out where she lived."

"Information sharing between federal agencies is easy thanks to the Patriot Act." Carver's unit, Scion, had been formed in the wake of the Patriot Act.

Unbeknownst to him until recently, it had paved the way for a vast network of dark ops cells, each one ignorant of the other, much like terrorist cells. They were set up to operate independently. To quash any perceived threats to U.S. security.

Leon had explained it to him before. Told him that Enigma might have originally been one of those cells but now it was controlling the others. He'd tried to convince Carver to help him eradicate them, but that was a no-go.

Carver wanted peace. Not a continuation of his days in the military.

Liana gasped.

Carver glanced at her. "What is it?"

She looked back at the women slumbering in the back seat. Back at the phone. "Just something unexpected."

"Snuff video?"

"Thankfully, no, but I wouldn't be surprised if he'd made some of those." She shuddered. "I haven't even gone through his videos or pictures yet. I'm almost afraid to."

"He's dead now."

"I know. And I think maybe death was too easy for him considering what I know about him now. This man deserves to suffer."

Carver pulled down a dirt road. He followed it through the forest, the truck's headlights piercing the darkness. He was tired. Ready to sleep for a whole night and day. But first he needed to patch up Liana and Paola.

Then he needed to set a perimeter. He wouldn't rest easy until he'd fortified their position.

They reached the cabin. Calling it a cabin was like calling a house a shed. This place was new construction. It was two stories high. Big and modern. The outer walls were mostly windows, offering a view of the forest from inside, but displaying the occupants like animals in a cage.

Carver hated it.

With the lights on inside at night, anyone could see everything happening in the den and kitchen area. It looked like the room above that area had big windows too. It was probably the master suite.

He hoped there were curtains. Otherwise, he'd have to make a trip into town and get some blackout curtains or black paper.

Liana chuckled. "This house is your worst nightmare, isn't it?"

"Why would anyone want the inside of their house visible and open for anyone to see?" He shook his head.

Lacy yawned and leaned forward in the back seat. "It's not like that. The windows have a privacy tint. You can't see in during the night or day even if the lights are on inside."

"Oh." Carver was somewhat mollified. "Glad you considered that."

"Paola wrote down all the tips and tricks you gave her." Lacy smiled. "I made sure my safehouses would be Carver approved."

Paola touched Carver's shoulder. "Following your advice kept us alive even when I couldn't contact you."

Carver cleared his throat. "Good."

Lacy got out and punched in a code on a keypad next to the garage. The door opened and Carver parked inside. She entered another code on the keypad next to the door to unlock it.

Paola took Carver's hand, and they walked inside. He led her to a stool at the kitchen bar and examined her wound. He applied local anesthesia and started stitching.

She smiled at him as he worked. "You're very cute when you're concentrating on something you're not good at."

"It's a defense mechanism." Carver shrugged. "If I look cute, the patient won't realize that I'm screwing up."

She laughed but her smile quickly faded. "You came for me even though you had no idea where I was."

"I promised I'd help you if you ever needed it."

"Why?"

Carver didn't answer.

"Carver, tell me why."

He kept silent and continued stitching the wound.

"This is why we can never work." Her accent was still strong, but her English was better than it had been the last time they'd been together.

He nodded. "I know."

"Then why did you come for me?"

Carver cut the thread and studied his handiwork. "I couldn't not come for you."

"That makes no sense."

He didn't want to put it into words. It felt strange to admit to anything. Especially to admit to this weakness that infected him when it came to her.

She squeezed his hand. "Tell me."

Carver took a deep breath. Everything in his gut told him not to admit what he was feeling. But her dark eyes compelled him to say something. "You are my weakness."

Tears pooled in her eyes. "And you are mine."

He brushed her tears away with his thumbs. "It's dangerous."

"If I was anyone else, would you have come for me?"

"I don't do hypotheticals."

"He would even though he'd never admit it." Liana had come up behind Carver while they were talking. "I mean, he saved me even though he thought I was an enemy."

"I didn't see any sense in letting you die."

"That's what you told me when you saved me." Paola smiled. She took his hand and kissed it. "Why is it so hard for you to admit to feeling something?"

"It's just the way I am." He motioned Liana to the stool next to Paola's. "Your turn."

Liana offered a tight smile. "In a minute. I've been debating whether to show you something. Something I found on Decker's phone."

"Why?"

"Because it's personal."

He frowned. "I'm confused."

"Me too," Paola said. "He has something about Carver on his phone?"

"Sort of." Liana turned the phone toward Carver. A video was playing. In the video was a large gathering of people at a large table. They were eating, drinking, laughing.

There were children running around. A birthday cake. Party hats. A man with gray peppering his black hair and beard sat at the head of the table. He was talking to a similarly aged man in the chair to his right.

There were younger adults next to them, most of them talking and laughing amongst themselves. They were drinking wine and dining on steak and lobster. It was quite a setup.

Judging from the music playing in the background and the skin tone, the people were Latino. They were at a birthday party, probably for one of the kids running around. He wasn't sure exactly what he was looking for.

A young woman came up behind one of the women at the table and hugged her from behind. The other woman turned around and exclaimed something. The language sounded Portuguese. Then the two women turned and faced the camera.

Carver blinked. He paused the video. Stared at it for a long moment.

"There are pictures too." Liana stopped the video and pulled up the pictures. They were images of a large family posing for a picture. All but the people standing in the center had been cropped out.

Someone had labeled the picture with the names of the people. The graying man at the head of the table. The man sitting next to him. The young men and women sitting near them. The young woman who'd hugged the other woman from behind.

They were all smiling for the camera. They looked happy. Like everything was good with their lives.

The graying man at the head was Andre. The man to the right was Luis. The first young man was Pedro. To his right was Jessica. And to her right was the last person he'd expected to see in a picture like this.

Because these people shared the same last name. Herrada. These were members of the Herrada Cartel. Jessica Herrada was the now deceased mayor of El Fuerte. She'd been killed right in front of Carver.

Pedro was her brother who'd take over for the deceased Andre Herrada. Jessica had been handling their widespread business dealings in southern California and ruling El Fuerte with an iron fist.

"Carver, what's wrong?" Paola looked concerned.

Luis was Andre's brother. If what he'd been told was true, he'd embezzled money from the cartel and his own brother had him killed. It was that one face and name that reinforced why he didn't trust anyone. Why he couldn't believe anything people told him.

He handed the phone to Paola. She looked at the picture. She gasped and dropped the phone like it was burning hot. Tears filled her eyes.

"Carver, it's not what you think."

Carver picked up the phone and looked at the name and face. The face that matched the face of the woman right in front of him.

Paola Herrada.

CHAPTER 41

Carver handed the phone to Liana.

He picked up the thread and needle. "Take a seat."

"Nothing?" Liana looked stunned. "That's your response?"

Tears flowed freely down Paola's cheeks. "Carver, it's not what you think."

"Doesn't matter what I think." Carver wasn't surprised that she hid her family relations from him. "I never told you much about my family."

"Yes, but she's related to the Herrada family." Liana shook her head. "She's part of the cartel."

Carver just motioned toward the stool. "You going to sit down or not?"

Liana sat down. She took off her shirt and moved the bra strap out of the way of the bandage. A dark crimson spot stained it. She tugged the tape. Winced.

Carver pulled it off and examined the wound. It was a mess. The nylon thread had torn through the skin. "Too bad a real doctor isn't an option."

"Can I explain, Carver?" Paola touched his arm.

"You don't have to. You are who you are. If Jessica Herrada is your sister, then she's your sister." He paused. "Well, she was your sister."

"Not my sister. My cousin." She took the phone from Liana pointed to Luis. "That's my father. He was supposed to launder cartel money, but he embezzled it. Pedro killed him even against Andre's wishes. Pedro took over day-to-day operations. He decided I must have helped my father, so he punished me by making me work for the cartel."

Carver looked at her. "You don't have to explain yourself to me. I don't care about your past."

"But I do." She gripped his arm. "I want you to know I didn't betray you."

"I never said you did."

"But I could see it in your eyes." She shivered. "After everything you've done for me, you deserve the truth."

Carver rubbed local anesthesia on Liana's wound. "If it makes you feel better."

Liana rolled her eyes. "God, no wonder she left you."

"That's just the way he is." Paola smiled. "His emotions are locked in a vault. He doesn't want to care but I know deep down he does, or he wouldn't be here."

"His actions certainly speak louder than his words." Liana smirked. "Carver, you're a big softie."

"I'm just a teddy bear." Carver threaded the needle. "Now, hold still while I stab you repeatedly."

She laughed.

Paola sat down next to Liana. "I told Pedro I'd done nothing wrong. That I stayed distant from the cartel because I wanted nothing to do with it. He said it wasn't my choice. That the cartel was my birthright. Jessica agreed with him. They had big plans. Bigger than anything I could have imagined."

"I am curious about one thing," Carver said. "Do they have dealings with Enigma?"

"I don't know what that is."

"It's a shadow organization that seemed to have cells all over the country. They have their fingers in a lot of pies. They own a lot of politicians. They have the power of the government behind them. At least, covertly."

"My God." She pressed a hand to her cheek. "That's why they had helicopters and assault troops? I thought those were federal agents."

"They probably are federal agents. Just not the ones from the known three-letter agencies." Carver cut the old stitches from Liana's wound and pulled them gently out. "Anyway, keep going with your story."

Paola paused as if remembering where she'd left off. "Pedro sent Jessica to handle operations in southern California. He wanted me to do the same thing but in New York. I refused. He banished me to Morganville as punishment. Made me a secretary to that disgusting pig, Jasper Whittaker."

"Jessica was the mayor of El Fuerte. She was running a massive trafficking ring out of there, and not the kind you'd think." Carver told her a little about what he'd discovered in El Fuerte. "I wonder if they have something like that going on in New York."

"Possibly." Paola shrugged. "I don't know the details."

Carver cleaned Liana's wound and pierced the skin with the needle. He stopped talking and gave it his full concentration. He'd done plenty of work as a medic in the field but that didn't mean he was any good at it.

"Paola was right," Liana said. "You are kind of cute when you're concentrating on something you're not good at."

Carver didn't respond.

He finished. Rubbed antibiotic ointment around the wound. Put bandages back on. "Try not to rip them again, okay?"

"I'll do my best." She took out her phone. Opened the picture gallery. Showed him a picture of Decker's bloodied and pulped face. "I texted that image to Nilva, the woman from the salon. Now she knows she's safe."

Carver stared at the image for a moment. "Thanks."

Liana smiled. "My pleasure."

Carver stood and stretched. He was tight from bending over for so long. He was exhausted. He opened an app on his smartphone and looked at the perimeter around the cabin. An alarm would sound on his phone if something breached it. But he still liked to make sure the lines were green.

It was a simple setup. Battery-powered sensors spaced fifty feet apart would detect any movement and sound the alarm. They weren't picky about what caused the movement. Sometimes it was an animal. Sometimes a falling leaf.

Carver had used some variation of this ever since getting dishonorably discharged. He wasn't the trusting sort. If they could frame him for sex trafficking, then they could kill him in his sleep to keep him quiet.

Paola took his hand. "Carver, can we talk?"

"In the morning. I'm going to sleep." He went upstairs. Took a shower. Brushed his teeth. Fell into bed. He wasn't surprised when Paola slid into bed next to him moments later. She was freshly showered. She smelled great.

Carver pulled her close to him. He kissed her. Ran his hand down her body. She was naked. Soft. She smelled amazing. It reminded him of their time together. Made him long for those simple times.

But only for a moment.

And that was fine. Just fine. Because he was going to stretch this moment out as long as he could.

Paola pressed her lips to his. She bit his neck. His ear. She ran her fingernails down his back and whispered in his ear. "I missed this."

Carver gently stroked her cheek. "Me too."

Carver was the first one up in the morning. Sunlight filtered through the trees, lighting the kitchen and downstairs. It was a spectacular sight. Almost made him feel like he was camping outside.

It still didn't make him feel any better about being surrounded by giant windows. The interior might be shielded from the outside, but he felt exposed. That wasn't the only part of him that felt exposed and vulnerable.

Having Paola in bed with him again made him feel things he'd tucked away in that vault of his long ago. Now he had those mixed feelings tugging at his strings again. This time it was different.

This time it was stronger. This time he felt like maybe things could work.

Paola would always be running just like Carver. Maybe they could run together. Maybe this time he could give her more of what she wanted. Maybe not a family, but he could be a little more forthcoming with his feelings.

He shuddered. His parents had beaten his emotions out of him. Told him it was a sign of weakness. It was hard overcoming the biases they'd embedded deep inside him.

Carver made oatmeal and coffee. He took it to the back deck and ate while the world awakened around him. He'd just finished when Paola joined him. She held a banana in one hand and a coffee mug in the other.

She sat down across from him and smiled. Her eyes were red. It looked like she'd been crying.

"Something wrong?" Carver asked.

"Everything is amazing and terrible at the same time." Her lips quivered. She set the banana on the table.

Carver decided to get right to it. "I think I'm ready."

"For what?"

"For more. We can find a remote place, maybe close to a beach. We'll have to be careful, but I think we can avoid the cartel and Enigma and live out our lives how he want to."

Fresh tears rolled down her cheeks. She reached across the table and touched his hands. "Carver, I love you."

It was hard to say those words that had never been said to him. Not even by his parents. But Carver steeled himself and pushed them out one at a time. "I love you too."

Paola part laughed and part cried. "And that's what makes this the most difficult decision of my life."

He frowned. "Staying with me is a difficult decision?"

She shook her head. "It's an impossible decision. I love you, but we aren't meant for each other. You need to take your path, and I'll take mine."

"What path are you taking?" Carver said.

"I'm going to find the other women from Morganville. I'm going to make sure they're safe and relocated. There's no telling who else Jill betrayed, but I'm certain she divulged all our locations all to get revenge on me."

Paola held up the new burner phone Carver had set up for her. "I messaged Leon. He's willing to help."

Carver wasn't surprised. Leon was on a one-man crusade. "You realize that you'll be painting an even bigger target on your back, right?"

"Maybe. But it's worth doing." She gazed at him silently for a moment. "I'm right in assuming this is not something you want to do."

"I want peace and quiet. I want to enjoy life, not spend my years fighting other people's battles."

"And yet, here we are." She smiled gently. "I understand, Carver. That's why this is the right decision."

"Yeah."

"I'm excited for what's to come." Paola told him all about her upcoming plans.

Carver listened to her talk. He heard words but the substance drifted past without meaning. She wasn't going to stay with him. Carver had come back to her, but she had moved on.

And that was fine. Just fine. It was time to move on. This was closure.

Paola wiped the tears from her cheeks, but they kept flowing. "Carver, are you going to be okay?"

He turned the question back on her. "Are you going to be okay?"

She walked around the table. Sat in his lap. Kissed him long and hard. She hugged him and sobbed for several minutes. Then she stood up. Dried her face. "I will always carry a part of you with me."

Carver stood. Stared into her dark eyes. He brushed her soft lips with his thumb. Felt her cheek. Stroked her hair. He nodded. "I'll be okay."

"Good." She managed a smile. "Good."

Lacy came to the back porch. "Alan is here with our ride. Are you ready?"

Paola nodded. "Goodbye, Carver."

He leaned over and kissed her forehead. "Goodbye, Paola."

She walked past him. He followed her inside. Followed her to the front door. A white SUV was out front. A burly looking man sat behind the steering wheel. Carver didn't recognize him. He looked like he could win a fist fight. That was a good start.

Lacy took Carver's hand. "You can have the truck and cabin. They're so far off the books I don't think even Homeland Security knows about them." She held the keys and fobs out to him.

"Thanks." He took them.

"The keypad codes are here." She gave him a slip of paper. "Thanks again for everything. And if it makes it any easier, Paola is really torn up about leaving you. Hell, I wanted you to come along for more security, but she told us no. She said you wouldn't be onboard for everything we want to do."

Carver remained silent.

She continued. "We want to make sure all the other women are safe. We want to do something proactive to stop these human traffickers. We could really use someone like you. Is Paola right? Do you really not want to help?"

"It's not what I want to do with my life."

"I understand." She squeezed his hand. "Thanks again for everything you've done. For doing the right thing even when your life was on the line."

Carver watched Lacy get into the front of the SUV. The back window rolled down and Paola gazed at him. Her dark eyes were like bottomless pools of sadness. She waved one last time before the vehicle turned and drove down the dirt road.

"Ouch. That was painful to watch." Liana stood beside him. "Are you going to be okay?"

Carver turned to her. "What will you do now?"

"I have no idea." She sighed. "This opened my eyes to the cancer eating away at everything I hold dear. I wanted to be a part of the solution, not the problem. But there's no way I can make a difference if I go back."

"If you go back, they'll want to know why you were with me. Why you didn't try to escape. Why you didn't try to contact them."

"I know."

"The worst of it won't come from your boss or your boss's boss. It'll come from the people who are really in charge. From Enigma."

"I know."

Carver raised an eyebrow. "What don't you know?"

"What to do with my life."

"I could recommend you to Leon. He might give you a chance. Or he might think you're a member of the deep state trying to infiltrate his inner circle of one."

"I don't even know who the guy is." She shrugged. "But from what you told me he's a major thorn in the side of the powers that be. If I brought down someone like that then it would be a real career maker."

"Yep."

She pressed her lips together. "I like the idea of making a difference, but I'm not into killing people and blowing stuff up if that's what he's doing."

"No comment."

Liana threw her hands in the air. "This sucks. I don't know what to do with myself."

"You could have gone with Paola and the others."

"I don't want to do that either. And I know you don't want me around."

"I didn't say that." He nodded at the cabin. "I might stay here for a while. Enjoy the lake."

"You're not worried about Enigma finding you?"

"I'll just have to be ready for them if they do." He checked the time. "I need to go into town and get supplies."

"Like food?"

"Yeah, and other things. I want to beef up security here."

Liana looked out at the lake. "It is pretty here. But if I continue my absence, they'll assume I'm aiding and abetting a terrorist."

Carver shrugged. "Your choice. I'm going to town to pick up supplies."

"I'll come with you. I can decide later."

"Okay." Carver climbed into the truck.

Liana climbed in beside him. She shivered. "This is kind of exciting. I feel like my future is completely free and open. Well, aside from having no money to live on. And throwing my career in the trash. And my student and car loans."

"It's a good feeling," Carver said. "That's why I don't want to go around the country chasing bad guys." Carver started the truck and wheeled it around. "People can make their own choices even if that choice is to be led around on a leash. It's not my job to correct their mistakes."

"My job at the NSA was like babysitting an entire country."

"Just let it go. Fight your own battles and let others deal with their own."

"Good advice." Liana leaned her seat back. "Let's get some beer and burgers. I think we should celebrate having zero responsibilities."

"Sounds good to me." Carver headed down the dirt road and toward town. He was already missing Paola, but that was to be expected. She could make her own choices and he could make his.

A lake wasn't as good as a beach, but it would do for now.

It would do just fine.

BOOKS BY JOHN CORWIN-

Books by John Corwin
Want more? Never miss an update by joining my email list and following me on social media!
Join my Facebook group at https://www.facebook.com/groups/overworldconclave
Join my email list: www.johncorwin.net
Fan page: https://www.facebook.com/johncorwinauthor

PSYCHOLOGICAL THRILLERS
The Family Business
AMOS CARVER THRILLERS
Dead Before Dawn
Dead List
Dead and Buried
Dead Man Walking
Dead by the Dozen
Dead Run
Dead Weather Days
Dead to Rights
Dead But Not Forgotten
CHRONICLES OF CAIN
To Kill a Unicorn
Enter Oblivion
Throne of Lies
At The Forest of Madness
The Dead Never Die
Shadow of Cthulhu
Cabal of Chaos
Monster Squad

Gates of Yog-Sothoth

Shadow Over Tokyo

Into the Multiverse

THE OVERWORLD CHRONICLES

Sweet Blood of Mine

Dark Light of Mine

Fallen Angel of Mine

Dread Nemesis of Mine

Twisted Sister of Mine

Dearest Mother of Mine

Infernal Father of Mine

Sinister Seraphim of Mine

Wicked War of Mine

Dire Destiny of Ours

Aetherial Annihilation

Baleful Betrayal

Ominous Odyssey

Insidious Insurrection

Utopia Undone

Overworld Apocalypse

Apocryphan Rising

Soul Storm

Devil's Due

Overworld Ascension

Assignment Zero (An Elyssa Short Story)

OVERWORLD UNDERGROUND

Soul Seer

Demonicus

Infernal Blade

OVERWORLD ARCANUM

Conrad Edison and the Living Curse

Conrad Edison and the Anchored World

Conrad Edison and the Broken Relic

Conrad Edison and the Infernal Design

Conrad Edison and the First Power

STAND ALONE NOVELS

Mars Rising

Printed in Dunstable, United Kingdom